WOLF STOCKBURN

WOLF STOCKBURN
RAILROAD DETECTIVE

MAX O'HARA

PINNACLE BOOKS
Kensington Publishing Corp.
www.kensingtonbooks.com

PINNACLE BOOKS are published by

Kensington Publishing Corp.
119 West 40th Street
New York, NY 10018

All Kensington titles, imprints, and distributed lines are available at special quantity discounts for bulk purchases for sales promotions, premiums, fund-raising, educational, or institutional use. Special book excerpts or customized printings can also be created to fit specific needs. For details, write or phone the office of the Kensington sales manager: Kensington Publishing Corp., 119 West 40th Street, New York, NY 10018, attn: Sales Department; phone 1-800-221-2647.

PINNACLE BOOKS and the Pinnacle logo are Reg. U.S. Pat. & TM Off.

ISBN-13: 978-0-7860-4710-9
ISBN-10: 0-7860-4710-0

First Pinnacle paperback printing: April 2021

10 9 8 7 6 5 4 3 2 1

Printed in the United States of America

Electronic edition:

ISBN-13: 978-0-7860-4714-7 (e-book)
ISBN-10: 0-7860-4714-3 (e-book)

CHAPTER 1

If you were a bird flying overhead, your spirits would soar as in your keen raptor's mind you anticipate the carnage that would soon paint the sage and buffalo grass, the blood and viscera upon which you would soon be feasting.

Beneath you, the long, dark caterpillar of a train trundles over the gently rolling, fawn-colored land from the east. The caterpillar's stout head is the coal-black Baldwin locomotive trailing a plume of smoke from its diamond-shaped stack—a long, ragged guidon tearing and tattering as it thins out over the passenger, freight, and express cars abutted at the far end by the red caboose. The smoke that isn't blown away on the wind snakes its way into the passenger car windows, open against the broiling air rife with the smell of sweat, tobacco, babies' urine, and unwashed bodies.

You hear the constant, monotonous *chugga-chugga-chugga* of the straining engine with a hellish conflagration burning in its stout black belly, converting steam to motion as the large iron wheels grind and clatter over the seams of the quicksilver-bright iron rails. Occasionally, the whistle lifts its signature wail—mostly where farm and ranch trails cross the tracks but just as often when the engineer, bored and heady with his authority and the heft and power under his command, simply pulls the chain to hear himself roar.

A small dust plume appears on the prairie, maybe a mile away as you fly straight south of the tracks. Slightly ahead of the plume, a horse and rider take shape. The man rides low in the saddle, leaning so far forward that his chin is nearly resting on his horse's poll. The wind blows the flaps of his duster straight back behind him, whipping them violently; it bastes the front brim of his hat flat against his forehead.

The horse fairly flies across the prairie, its own head down, ears laid flat. The beast lunges forward with its front hooves, grabbing at the ground, hurling itself ahead with its back feet. Dust and gravel and small tufts of sod are torn out of the earth by the scissoring shod feet and flung behind with the dust.

Horse and rider are racing toward the train. Or, rather, toward the spot ahead of the train where the rider hopes to intersect it.

He's not the only one.

As you dip and bank and turn your head, loosing your ratcheting cry, the blood quickening through your predatorial heart, you see another rider, then another, and another, and another—all racing toward the train. They are spaced between forty and sixty yards apart in nearly a complete circle around the train. All are racing toward the same spot on the tracks ahead of the chugging locomotive, twenty or more horse-and-rider spokes converging on the hub of a wagon wheel, which is the railroad line.

A great roar assaults the air. You feel the concussion of the blast against your own delicate, feathered body and begin to bank away from the threatening sound before your innate curiosity brings you back. You see the black-stitched crimson ball of flames rising from the tracks maybe fifty yards ahead of the train at the point toward which the riders are converging.

The blast rips the tracks and ties out of the ballasted rail bed and flings them upward in a great cloud of churning dust and gravel. Almost immediately, the engineer pulls the chain to set the brakes, which grind and scream as they assault the wheels. The car couplings thunder as the locomotive is thrust back against the tender car and the tender car is thrust back against the freight car and the freight car is thrust back against the first passenger car, and on and on until the locomotive and all the cars screech to a stop on the tracks only a few feet from where the blasted rails lay twisted and charred around the large crater gouged by the dynamite.

As the last bits of gravel thump back onto the ground and the smoke from the blast is blown away on the wind, a pregnant silence settles over and around the train, like that which precedes a cyclone.

It's short-lived.

The growing thunder of galloping hooves replaces it.

A man sticks his head out of one of the open train windows and points toward the riders converging on the train in front of their own tawny dust clouds.

"It's them!" the man screams shrilly. "It's the Devil's Horde!"

Inside the passenger car, a woman screams.

Men shout. They curse.

A woman sobs.

A baby wails.

A great commotion begins inside the car and you can hear the rumbling with your keen hearing. Up where you are soaring on thermals, the wind rippling your sunshine-burnished feathers, you can distinguish the scrambling sounds inside the car from the thunder of the galloping riders.

Several guns are aimed out of the passenger car windows. In the locomotive, the engineer and the fireman have armed themselves, as well.

Guns bark and pop. Smoke puffs in the coach windows and from both sides of the locomotive.

The riders converge on the train. They whoop and yip like coyotes as they aim their own rifles and pistols and return fire on the locomotive and on the two passenger coaches. Some of the riders check their sweat-lathered mounts down to skidding halts and leap out of their saddles.

They drop to their knees and aim rifles from their shoulders, picking out targets on the train. They fire, whooping and yelling and pumping their rifles as the empty casings arc up and over their shoulders to flash in the sun before landing in the wild rye and bromegrass. Bullets blast out of the windows and the passengers scream.

Four riders leap from their saddles and run to the express car. Two duck under it, each carrying a burlap bag. The other two riders fire rifles at the express car's sliding door while shouts resound from within the car.

A man dressed in the blue wool coat and leather-billed cap of a conductor, a gold watch chain drooping against his vest, fires a pistol from the first passenger car's front vestibule. He triggers only two rounds before bullets punch into him from front and back, jerking him wildly. He drops to his knees and rolls gracelessly down the vestibule steps to the ground, where two of the attackers each trigger another round into him.

Four of the attackers run into both passenger coaches— two for each car, one entering by the front, the other by the back. Each is holding an empty burlap sack. They bellow commands and shoot their guns, and more passengers wail and scream and shout curses. In a little over a minute, the attackers emerge from the passenger cars, whooping and howling even more loudly.

Their bags have grown larger and heavier.

Another loud blast assaults you, pressing your feathers up taut against your slender body. The express car door has been blown open and into the roiling black smoke three of the attackers run, also carrying bags.

A passenger stumbles out onto the second passenger car's rear vestibule. He walks as though drunk. He is slender and he wears a gaudy checked suit. He is bald, and his rimless glasses hang by a single bow from one ear. He stumbles off the last vestibule step and falls to the ground. He scrambles to his feet, wails, "Don't kill me!" and runs straight out away from the train.

There is so much smoke, and the attackers are so distracted by their plunder, that they don't see the running man.

Laughing together, two attackers stumble out of the dining car, each holding a bag in which whiskey and wine bottles clank together. One sees the suited man fleeing to the north, running shamble-footed and almost falling with every third or fourth step.

"Hey, look there, Bryce!"

"Hah!" Bryce sets his bag on the ground then straightens, palming his pistol. "You wanna take him or should I?"

"Go ahead, but if you miss, you owe me ten dollars."

Bryce curses and, grinning, raises his pistol. "If I get him with my first shot, you owe *me twenty*!" He fires. The bullet furrows the prairie grass well ahead and to one side of the fleeing man.

The man howls, stumbles, and nearly falls before he gets his feet set beneath him again and continues running.

Bryce curses.

The other man mocks him and raises his revolver. He fires. That bullet also misses, blowing up bits of a prickly pear just off the running man's left heel.

Another attacker, hefting a bag he carried out of the express car, steps up in front of Bryce and the other man. He raises his short-barreled Winchester rifle, cocks, aims, and fires it one-handed at the running man. The bullet drills the running man in the back of the neck. His arms fly up as he falls forward to lie unmoving in the tall grass.

The man who shot the fleeing passenger turns to the other two attackers, showing his teeth like a vicious dog. "Now, will you two blanketheads get mounted and ride the hell out of here?"

They mutter and grumble and then both jog out to where their horses are milling, ground-reined about fifty feet out from the train, grazing or looking around at the carnage and switching their tails. More of the attackers leap down from the train and jog out to their horses. The train itself is quiet now though the express car is still smoldering after the explosion.

Four passengers lie on the ground outside the passenger cars, blown out of the windows when the attackers stormed onto the train. One stout old woman in a black sweater and dangling poke bonnet hangs out the window, half in and half out of a passenger car. A bullet hole pocks her forehead.

The train's engineer lies slumped over the side of the locomotive, arms and gloved hands drooping toward the ground. The iron housing of the locomotive around him is smeared with his brains and blood, the result of the bullet that smashed into the back of his head and exited through his left eye.

The fireman lies at the engineer's feet, writhing in unbearable pain from the bullets that invaded his body. He will be dead soon. Quietly, he prays for his soul, hoping that when he dies his beloved mother, dead these thirty years, will be awaiting him at the pearly gates, as she'd promised on her deathbed.

One of the train's two brakemen is running to the west between the tracks. He is sobbing and limping, for he carries a bullet in his right leg. He has several more bullets in his chest and belly but the adrenaline spawned by fear drives him forward, awkwardly hopping the ties.

From inside one of the passenger cars, you indifferently note the regular screams of a woman. "My baby!" she cries. "My baby! My baby! My baby!"

The attackers flee, retracing the spokes of the wheel away from the hub and toward all points along the horizon. One of them riding off to the west shoots the brakeman in the back twice without his horse even breaking stride.

The brakeman screams and falls. The rider continues riding past him, whooping victoriously and pulling his dust plume along behind him.

The others do the same.

They are gone as fast as they appeared.

Behind them, the express car smolders.

The young mother continues to scream with metronomic regularity: "My baby! My baby! My baby!"

You voice your own ratcheting cry of delight, lower a wing, and swoop downward.

If you hurry, you'll beat the buzzards.

CHAPTER 2

Wolf Stockburn rode his rangy, smoky gray stallion up to the stone well and swung his lean, long-legged frame down from his saddle. He spied movement in the corner of his left eye but did not turn his head in that direction. No stranger to ambush, he knew the best way to trigger a bushwhack was to let the bushwhacker know he . . . or they . . . had been spotted.

The stallion gave a low whicker of warning.

"Easy, Smoke," Wolf whispered, patting the big beast's wither reassuringly. "I saw it."

Calmly, he dropped the bucket into the well. It landed with a wooden thud and a splash that echoed up out of the stone-lined chasm. He winched the bucket up out of the well. Water slopped down the sides and made mud of the straw-flecked dust around the soles of his low-heeled black boots.

As was the case with most legendary men, Stockburn had been tagged with several nicknames over the years. One of them was the Gray Wolf. He'd come by the handle honestly, for there was something wolfish in Wolf Stockburn's demeanor. He sported roached hair coarse as wolf's fur and so gray that it was almost white and had been since his late twenties. His face was strangely, primitively handsome with deep-set gray eyes that sometimes appeared a faded blue. V-shaped, strong-jawed, his features were broad through the cheekbones, tapering down to a solid, spade-shaped chin. The predatorial nose was long. Contrasting sharply with the man's short gray hair and trimmed gray mustache and sideburns, his features were weathered and sun-bronzed.

Stockburn was a big man, over six feet tall, all gristle and bone, customarily clad in a finely tailored three-piece suit with a long black frock coat, white silk shirt with upraised collar, black foulard tie, gray-striped black vest, and black cotton trousers.

Owning the primitive senses of his Scottish warrior ancestors, Wolf's perceptions were keenly alert as he ladled up some water for himself. As he drank, he peered furtively up from beneath the severe ridge of his gray brows and the broad brim of his low-crowned black sombrero, directing his gaze in the direction of a small barn hunched on the yard's northwest edge.

When he had had his fill of the cold water, he stepped up in front of the stallion and set the bucket down so the horse could drink. He'd no sooner removed his hand from the bucket's rope handle than he spied movement again off the barn's far corner.

The horse had seen it, too. Smoke whinnied shrilly.

Lightning-quick, one of Stockburn's two single-action Colt Army .45 Peacemakers was out of its holster and clenched in his right hand. He swung hard right, raising and cocking the nickel-plated, ivory-gripped piece, and fired.

His bullet struck the barrel of the rifle aimed at him from around the corner of the barn. The clang of lead on steel reverberated shrilly. The rifleman screamed and staggered away from the barn as he dropped the rifle then lowered his right hand toward the holster on his right hip.

Again, Stockburn's .45 roared.

The bullet tore through the short, thick-waisted rifleman's hickory shirt, blowing dust and punching the man backward into a large cottonwood. The man's high-crowned black hat, trimmed with an eagle feather, bounded off his shoulder before tumbling to the ground. Glimpsing more furtive movement to his left, Stockburn whipped his tall cavalryman's body back that way, aiming the Peacemaker at the sprawling brush-roofed log shack sitting forty yards to the north.

Another rifle barrel bristled from behind the shack's partly open door.

Stockburn's Colt spoke two more times, flames lapping from the barrel.

As the thundering reports chased each other's echoes skyward, both bullets punched through the crude plank-board door. A man's muffled wail sounded from behind the door. There was a thump as the would-be shooter's rifle struck the shack's wooden floor. Then the door lurched open as the rifleman fell forward onto his face. He lay half in and half out of the shack, the bullet-scarred door propped open by his right shoulder.

Another gun thundered. This one had been triggered from inside the shack.

A man yowled.

A body flew out the large window to the right of the open door. The flying man wailed again as glass rained around him. His two long, black braids whipping around him like miniature wings, he landed with a grunt and a loud thud in the dirt fronting the shack. The double-barreled shotgun he'd been holding clattered onto the ground beside him. He writhed and groaned for a moment, gave another grunt, then relaxed with a final sigh.

Silence save for Smoke's uneasy whickering.

Boots thumped inside the shack.

The sounds grew louder until a comely female figure clad in men's rough trail garb appeared in the half-open doorway. "Damn!" she trilled, looking at the glass spilled around the dead man with the braids. "I just replaced that window last week!"

She turned her Indian-dark face with a patch over one eye toward Stockburn. Her good eye flashed wickedly. "Look what you made me do, Wolf!"

"I do apologize, Comanche." Stockburn scowled at the broken-out window. "A right fine window, too. Leastways, it was. Did you ship that all the way out here from Bismarck?"

"Where else?" asked the pretty half-breed Comanche in her late thirties, early forties—a lady didn't go around announcing her age—as she toed the broken glass with one of her high-topped, beaded moccasins. "Look at that!"

"I know, I know," Stockburn said. "Every time I ride out here—"

"You end up costing me money."

"Well"—Wolf shrugged, casting the woman a disarming grin—"I do appreciate you coring Santana for me. If he'd drilled me through that window it would have cost you twice."

The pretty, curvaceous woman scowled. "How so?"

Stockburn shrugged again. "This way you just have to pay for the window. If Santana had shot me, you'd have had to pay to have me buried. Or at least wear out a good horse riding to Thornton's Ford to send a telegram to my boss in Kansas City, have him send a wagon for me. Oh, the time and effort involved! This way, you can just drag Santana and his pards—I'm assuming those two are Mortimer Frieze and Spike Caine—off to the nearest ravine."

Comanche—born *Denomi* though she hadn't answered to anything but Comanche since she'd left her white foster parents in Texas many years ago—crossed her arms on her well-filled blouse and tapped a boot toe.

"Comanche!" Stockburn intoned. "You wouldn't just drag *me* off to the nearest ravine, would you?"

"Let's just say you're fortunate I don't have to make that decision." She paused, glaring at him with her one good, coal-black eye, then added for effect, "Yet."

A tittering rose west of the main shack. Comanche turned toward the sound of the commotion then drew her mouth corners down as she said, "I see your admirers have gathered."

"I wonder what woke them," Stockburn said ironically, having turned to the three brightly and scantily clad doxies standing on the stoop of the secondary shack sitting about fifty feet to the west of the main one, and back off the yard. It was sheathed in brush and shaded by cottonwoods. Between two cottonwoods hung a clothesline drooping with the weight of ladies' delicate, brightly colored clothes.

The sporting girls were milling and smoking, casting their own coquettish gazes toward the tall, handsome man with high-tapering cheeks and deep western tan.

In the bright sunlight reflecting off their skimpy clothes, and jet-black, copper-red, and gold-blonde hair, respectively, they resembled brightly colored birds in their soft pinks, greens, purples, and powder blues. One in particular—the green-eyed blonde—held Stockburn's gaze, broadened her smile, and gave her pink parasol an extra twirl.

"What . . . or *who*?" Comanche gave a husky chuckle. "They hear enough gunfire to be deaf to it by now. They heard the Wolf of the Rails was on his way here on his smoky-gray horse, and they've been waiting to feast their eyes on the manly likes of Wells Fargo and Company's senor detective for their Railroad Division."

Stockburn started to blush, a rarity for him, then frowned. "How'd they know?" He glanced at the two dead men again. "In fact, come to think of it—how'd Santana know I was headed this way?"

"One of their fellow riders of the long coulees saw you in Sioux Lance and rode out here to alert him and the others. A smelly devil named Bertram."

"Ah, Bertram. The wheelwright."

"That's the one."

Comanche had turned to stare at Miguel Santana, the big, thickly built man with two black braids, lying in the glass to her right. The one nearest Comanche was Mortimer Frieze. The first man Stockburn had shot over by the barn was Spike Caine. Or had been. All three were had-beens now.

This bunch, which included the older Hollis "Dad" Drago, had robbed a stagecoach near Pierre three days ago. Stockburn had heard about the robbery when he'd pulled into Fargo on the Northern Pacific, which he'd taken from his company's Northern District office in St. Paul, Minnesota. He'd had no idea he'd find the stage robbers here, but he wasn't surprised. When the outlaw gang made up of Santana, Frieze, Caine, and Dad Drago plied their nasty trade, they usually holed up somewhere in the belly of this vast territory, which was still mostly wild despite the coming of the iron rails and telegraph cables and rumors of imminent statehood.

Comanche's *ranch*, as it was called, though it hadn't been a working ranch in years but a general store, saloon, and brothel, was often a prime hideout for such desperadoes as Santana's lowly bunch.

"They were alerted by the outlaw telegraph, eh?" Stockburn turned to the doxies still fluttering on the stoop of the second shack. He grinned and pinched his hat brim. "Ladies . . ."

They batted their eyelids and flounced.

"Get your eyes off those girls, you rake," Comanche chided the detective good-naturedly. "The oldest is young enough to be your daughter. I, on the other hand . . ."

"Yes, you," Stockburn said, feasting his eyes again.

Comanche chuckled. He thought she might have even blushed though, like himself, he'd never known the half-breed beauty to blush.

She jerked her chin toward the shack. "Get in here. I'll buy you a drink."

"You know you've never had to ask me twice to drink

with you, Comanche." Stockburn returned the Colt Peace-maker to the black leather holster on his left hip. Its twin resided on his right hip. He closed his long black cutaway coat and strode forward, addressing his horse over his shoulder. "Stay, Smoke. I'll give you some oats after you've had your fill from the water bucket."

Stockburn rolled the dead man out of the doorway with his boot, then stepped through the door and to one side. He opened his coat with his left hand and closed his right hand over the Peacemaker's grips. "Where's Dad?"

"Out of commission." Comanche strode into the room's deep shadows, toward the bar at the far end. She shook her hair back from her face, adjusted the patch over her left eye, then set a labeled bottle of Old Kentucky onto the bar. She'd taken the elaborate mahogany bar with a complete backbar and mirror out of the Bismarck saloon one of her former husbands had owned. She'd scavenged the elaborate piece of hand-scrolled and deftly chiseled wood-work when the cork-headed sot had lost the saloon to the bank, before the bank had officially taken possession.

"He took a bullet to the chest," she said, regarding Dad Drago. "He's dying upstairs."

"He'll leave the world a better place."

"Getting so a fella can't ride over here no more, Comanche. Not less 'n he wants to risk getting shot just drinkin' your watered-down whiskey!" The speaker was one of three men sitting at a table near the room's far wall from which the head of a pronghorn antelope stared down in glassy-eyed contemplation.

He was a tall, long-faced, mean-eyed cuss whose right hand was draped over the walnut grips of the Schofield .44 holstered on his right thigh. He'd spoken to Comanche, but his colicky gaze was on Stockburn.

CHAPTER 3

The mean-eyed cuss was the foreman on one of the several sprawling ranches that had been established in the area after the coming of the Northern Pacific only a few years ago. The two men with Stink-Eye were punchers from the same operation.

Stockburn had seen all three before. Dakota Territory might have been sprawling, but its population was modest. While he couldn't remember the trio's names, he could remember that he didn't like any of the three but that he liked the foreman least of all.

Stink-Eye turned his glare on Comanche standing behind the bar then returned it to Stockburn and flared a nostril. His flat eyes raked the detective up and down, from the pointed toes of his black boots to the flat crown of his black felt sombrero. "So . . . there he is. The big man himself. The Gray Wolf."

Newspaper scribblers had started calling Stockburn that a few years ago, when tales of the legendary gray-headed detective's derring-do had started making their way beyond the wild western frontier.

"If I didn't water down my whiskey, you couldn't afford

it, Sorley," Comanche said with casual insolence. "George MacDonald doesn't pay you enough because you're not worth enough. You should be glad he pays you anything at all. Who else but that old English outlaw would hire as his foreman a stone-stupid army deserter and ex–cattle rustler like yourself?"

She'd said this smiling insouciantly across the room at Stockburn.

The other two men with Sorley—*Hugh* Sorley, Stockburn remembered—snickered. Sorley cowed them both with a look and returned his belligerent gaze to Stockburn. He and the other two were playing poker but Sorley, clad in deer hide chaps and a cracked leather vest, wasn't looking at the cards in his left hand. His right hand was still draped over the Schofield holstered over his belly. A long, slender cheroot smoldered in an ashtray near his left elbow. An unlabeled bottle sat on the table near a small pile of coins and greenbacks.

"He don't look like so damn much to me," Sorley snarled, his gaze still on the railroad detective.

"What you see is what you get, partner." The affable smile dwindled on the detective's face, and his gray eyes turned a shade grayer. "Now, kindly remove your hand from that old Schofield or I'll take it away from you and beat you with it."

Sorley's eyes, glued to Stockburn's, blazed.

The other two men smiled, cutting their own gazes quickly between the detective and the ranch foreman. They didn't say anything. Smoke from their cigarettes and Sorley's cheroot thickened around them, lit by the light from the window behind them.

Comanche said nothing. She stood behind the bar,

hands resting on the mahogany's edge. She, too, slid her gaze quickly between Stockburn and Sorley confronting each other like Brahma bulls in the same paddock.

The foreman glanced at the twin Peacemakers in Stockburn's holsters. The detective's hands hung straight down his sides. Neither hand was near either of his pretty pistols. Still, Sorley looked constricted. Hesitant. He was remembering the stories about Stockburn. He was faster than some, but some were faster. The thing about him, though, was that he never lost his edge. In fact, he could be as cold-blooded as anyone who'd ever ridden on either side of the law.

And he rarely missed.

Sorley might be faster. *Might* be. Still, his heart was thumping to beat the band. He had a feeling Stockburn's heart was beating at the same rate it had been when he'd first stepped through that door.

A single bead of sweat popped out on Sorley's left brow and dribbled down into that eye, burning it. The man winced at the sting, blinked. That seemed to be the deciding factor. That single sweat bead. Sorley removed his right hand from the Schofield's grips, brushed the sweat from his eye with the sleeve of his poplin shirt, and turned to the other two men at his table. "Well, you two gonna raise me that dime or you just gonna sit there with your thumbs up your behinds?"

As the poker players resumed their game, Stockburn walked the length of the room to the bar. The saloon was small, its walls garishly papered. It had once been the parlor of the slapdash ranch house that had been added onto several times from its original sod hut. Comanche rented rooms upstairs, mostly to muleskinners passing through while hauling freight from the railroad at Fargo to the farm and ranch supply towns in the belly of the territory along the Missouri River.

Comanche had bought the ranch when her husband, a former officer stationed at Fort Lincoln, had gone belly-up in Bismarck and she'd divorced him though she'd retained his name—Leopardi. The man was a second-generation American Italian. So, improbably she was Comanche Leopardi, though no one had ever called her anything but Comanche for years. She'd converted the ranch from a floundering ten-cow cattle operation to a locally famous—some would say *in*famous—general store, saloon, and hurdy-gurdy house. She held dances the second Saturday of every summer month in one of the barns, and folks within two hundred miles came for what usually turned into a weeklong shindig whose riotousness some had described with likely some degree of exaggeration as Custer's Last Stand without the Indians.

It was also said—also likely with some degree of exaggeration—that men had died here during those times, and that they'd been dropped into their graves with smiles on their faces.

"First one's on the house," Comanche said, splashing the liquor into a shot glass. "But you have to buy the next round."

Stockburn removed his sombrero, set it on the bar, and smoothed a short rooster tail at the top of his head. "I get taken every time I come here."

"Yet you still keep coming here."

"I'll take a cigar." Stockburn glanced at the glass humidor on the bar to his right. It had three sloping shelves. The more expensive cheroots were displayed on the top shelf in open boxes. Most of the boxes were ornately decorated and sported Spanish names. "From the top shelf."

"Big spender."

"Add it to my tab. I'll pay up before I go."

"Yes, you will. In more ways than one." She gave him a sly wink as she opened the humidor. "When will you go?" She chewed off the end of the cigar, spat it onto the floor behind the bar, then handed him the cheroot. She dragged a sulfur match across the mahogany then leaned forward to touch the flame to the end of the fat El Rio Sella. "Stay the night, perhaps? Just like old times?"

"I'd like to, Comanche." He gave her a regretful smile as he turned the cigar while she held the match to it. "Duty calls."

Aromatic smoke wafted around his bronzed face and gray-capped head.

"I figured it wasn't pleasure that brought you here."

"When does it ever?"

"You don't have to be so damned honest, Wolf."

Smoke jetted from his broad, copper-toned nostrils. "Have you heard of the Devil's Horde?"

Sorley and the other two punchers turned toward the bar, brows arched with interest.

Comanche said, "Who hasn't?"

"I'm on the scout for information about their whereabouts."

"One man alone? That's crazy. Even for you, Wolf." She waved out the match.

Stockburn removed the well-burning stogie from his mouth and picked up his shot glass. "I just need to find out where they hole up between jobs. Then I can send for U.S. marshals and soldiers from Fort Lincoln." He tossed back half the shot then took another couple of puffs from the sweet cigar.

"Still . . ." Comanche gave her head a slow, fateful shake.

"You haven't heard anything, Comanche? I figured you of all people out here would have by now."

Comanche shook her lovely, one-eyed head. "I know someone who would know, though."

"Who?"

"Drink up. You're gonna need a bracer."

Stockburn threw back the rest of his shot then set the glass back down on the bar.

Comanche refilled the glass and said, "Red Bascom."

Wolf gave a dry laugh. "He's in prison, Comanche. I put him there damn near ten years ago."

"He's out." Comanche threw back her own first shot then refilled her glass. "They paroled him just last year due to poor health. He has cancer."

"You were right." Stockburn tossed back the entire shot and gave the stogie another few pensive puffs before again regarding the gray coal at the end. "Good cigar."

"Fifty cents." Smiling, Comanche held out her hand, palm up.

Chuckling, Stockburn dug into his pants pocket for a coin then set the double eagle firmly in her palm.

Comanche widened her eyes. "That's a helluva tip. And you're not even going to spend the night?"

"No, but I'll take a bottle and a couple of these for the trail."

"Consider it done." Comanche dropped the coin in a can beneath the bar.

"Where might I find Bascom?"

"I don't know. Since he returned to the Territory, he's been quiet as a church mouse. I just hear rumors from muleskinners passing through on the freight road, the occasional traveling drummer or gambler." Comanche plucked the cigar out of Stockburn's hand, stuck it between her own full lips, and drew on it, making the coal glow. Blowing the smoke out over the detective's thick right shoulder, she said, "I know someone who might know, though."

Stockburn arched a curious brow at her.

"I'll tell you on one condition."

"Uh-oh."

"You spend the night."

Stockburn chuffed, said dryly, "You're a devilish delight."

"Yes, I am." She took another couple of puffs off the stogie then handed it back to Stockburn. Rolling her eyes toward the ceiling, she said, "Dad."

CHAPTER 4

"Be careful. He has a shotgun," Comanche said as Stockburn reached the top of the stairs.

The detective stopped and glanced over his shoulder at her. She remained standing behind the bar, leaning forward, holding a fresh shot of whiskey in both hands. She turned it slowly.

"Thanks for letting me know."

Comanche smiled, hiked a shoulder.

"What'd you have to tell him for?" complained Sorley from where he sat playing poker with his cowpuncher pards. He glared up at Stockburn. "I'd love to see a little daylight drilled through Mr. All-High-an'-Mighty."

"True, it might take some starch out of his drawers," opined Comanche with her devilish smile, still turning the glass in her fingers, "but I've already got three dead men to drag out to the turkey buzzards. Possibly a fourth, when Dad dies. I don't need a fifth."

Stockburn gave a droll chuckle then stepped into the second-floor hall. He turned and, closing one hand over the grips of the .45 Peacemaker holstered on his left hip, started walking slowly down the hall, heading back toward the front of the building.

The hall was lit by one window at the rear end of the hall behind him, and another window at the front end, before him. Five doors shone on each side of the hall, only one partway open. Hollis "Dad" Drago's room was the door just beyond it, on the hall's right side.

Stockburn approached slowly, wincing as some of the floorboards complained beneath his boots. He pricked his ears, listening. He could hear no sounds behind Dad's door. Comanche had warned the detective that Dad might have already saddled a golden cloud, for the old sinner had taken a bullet to the chest, close to his ticker, and she wasn't sure why he'd still been alive an hour ago, when she'd last checked on him.

Stockburn hoped the old reprobate hadn't expired. Not yet. If anyone knew where Red Bascom was holed up, Dad would. Bascom and Drago had been close pards back in the heyday of their outlaw depravities. Their reputations, as well as the law, had chased both men out of Texas after the war, and they'd for the most part confined their outlawry to Dakota Territory, ripe for the plundering after gold had been discovered in the Black Hills and rails were laid east to west starting at the now-prosperous Fargo on the Red River of the North and continuing right through Bismarck and on into Montana and clear across the country to the Pacific Ocean. In fact, President Grant had driven in the "golden spike" only a couple of years ago in Montana, in '83.

Settlements now abounded both north and south of the N.P. rails, and the bulk of those farm and ranch supply towns boasted a sweet little bank and sundry other well-off businesses.

Stockburn stopped and pressed his shoulder against the wall beside the door, which green paint on a dusty wooden plate identified as ROOM 9. He slid the Peacemaker from the holster on his left hip and tapped the barrel against the door. "Dad? You still kickin', you old scudder? It's Wolf Stockburn."

The query was answered by a thunderous roar. A pumpkin-sized hole was blasted out of the door. It was followed a second later by a second blast. The holes were, chest-level with any man who would have been fool enough to stand in front of it knowing that an old outlaw resided therein, armed with a gut-shredder.

From inside the room came the thunder of a heavy object crashing to the floor.

The pumpkin-sized holes were joined, making one large opening through which Stockburn glanced a second before kicking in what remained of the door. He didn't have to kick very hard. It was an old door with a rickety steel latch. He stepped forward as the rest of the door collapsed.

Hollis "Dad" Drago lay on his back on the bed before Stockburn. Gasping and grunting, Dad tried desperately to grab the pistol on the table to his left with his left hand. He had stretched the hand far out from the bed, and the maneuver was causing him great grief. Sitting up a little as he reached, his broad, fleshy face was as red as a Dakota sunset. He puffed his patch-bearded cheeks out, sweating and grimacing.

The double-barreled twelve-gauge shotgun he had ruined the door with lay on the floor beside the bed.

Stockburn picked up the old Remington conversion .44 and held it up in front of the dying old outlaw on the bed. "This what you looking for, Dad?"

Drago raised his hand toward the gun. His hand appeared to weigh a good ten pounds, giving him trouble with the maneuver. "Yes," he wheezed. "Yes . . . it is . . ."

"Here it is." Stockburn tossed it out the open window behind the washstand. It bounced off the porch's shake-shingled roof then thumped to the ground. "And now it's gone."

"Ah, hell," Drago said, defeatedly flopping back down against the bed. He gave a heavy sigh. "Damn you, Stockburn. How in the devil's own hell did you avoid my buckshot?"

"Not my first rodeo, Dad."

"No. No, it ain't, is it?"

Stockburn drew the single sheet and quilt down from the old man's lumpy chest, revealing the bandage and poultice Comanche had tucked inside the man's ragged longhandle top. The bandage was blood-soaked. The stain was widening, spreading, soaking the top where it bulged over the old man's fat belly.

The detective sucked a sharp breath through his teeth. "Doesn't look good, Dad."

"Don't feel any better 'n it looks."

"You're on the way out."

"Why don't you tell me somethin' I don't know?"

"You first," Stockburn said.

Drago frowned up at him. "Huh?"

"Where's your old pard, Red Bascom?"

Drago's frown lines cut deeper into the pasty skin across his forehead. "Red? Why?"

"The Devil's Horde."

That surprised the dying old outlaw. Or maybe the name alone caused even a man with Drago's reputation some awe and trepidation. His mouth opened a little, and his eyes widened.

"That's who I'm looking for. Red would know who and where they are, if anyone would."

"What about me?" Suddenly, Drago looked a little hurt. "Why wouldn't I know."

"Do you?"

Drago drew his mouth corners down. "No."

Stockburn wasn't surprised. Drago was no longer the outlaw he'd once been. He'd never been as feared as Red Bascom. They'd ridden together, but they'd never been equals. Red Bascom had cast a long shadow and likely still did, even dying from cancer.

Men feared him. Men even as poison mean as Bascom himself gave him a wide berth. His reputation had garnered him a lot of respect and power. It had also cost him and his old friend Drago their friendship a long time ago. Even before Stockburn had sent Bascom to the federal prison in Detroit, Michigan, the two had parted ways. It was hard on any man, especially one as prideful as Dad Drago, to get thrown on his back over and over again by the top dog of all Dakota outlaws, Red Bascom.

Still, if any outlaw in Dakota knew where Red Bascom was holed up, dying slowly, that old outlaw would be Dad Drago. And if any man knew where Stockburn could find the pack of bloodthirsty wolves known as the Devil's Horde, that man would be Red Bascom.

Through Drago, he'd find Bascom. And through Bascom, he'd find the Devil's Horde.

"Red knows," Stockburn told Drago again. "Tell me, Dad—where's Red? What does it matter? Hell, you're dying. He's dying . . ."

Drago was breathing hard. He swallowed. "He ain't dyin' as fast as me, the old scudder ain't."

"No, he's not. And that isn't fair, Dad."

"Hell, no, it ain't." Dago swallowed again. "But nothin's fair. I lived long enough to know that." He winced sharply, gave a little mewling wail. "Jesus, this hurts. Dyin' hurts . . . awful *bad*, Wolf. You don't ever wanna do it."

"We all gotta do it."

"Still . . . makes a fella wish he'd gotten right with the Lord . . . long time ago . . ."

"I bet ole St. Pete would feel a little more charitable toward you, Dad, if he knew you told me where I'd find Red."

"You think so?"

"Hell, I know so."

Drago gazed up at Stockburn. "I'll tell ya . . . iffen you do me . . . a favor."

"What's that?"

"Sit with me. Have a drink with me." Drago turned his head slightly to indicate the wooden chair on the other side of the table from the bed. "Stay here . . . till I give up my ghost. Would you d-do that, Wolf?"

Stockburn stared down at him. Fear haunted Drago's eyes. Given the old outlaw's depredations, Stockburn couldn't feel much sympathy. The regular law had hunted Dad Drago for some years, but the thing Drago had had going for him—up till recently, anyway—was luck. He'd always managed to slip away. Sometimes luck was worth as much as a coyote-like finesse, which was what Red Bascom had. That and a coldhearted savagery.

Since Drago hadn't robbed any Wells Fargo loot in recent years, he'd avoided finding himself shadowed by Stockburn. Mostly, county sheriffs and bounty hunters had hunted Drago.

No, Stockburn couldn't feel much sympathy for the old coyote. Still, somehow, he did. "All right." He dragged the wooden chair up close to the bed. "I'll sit with you."

There was a bottle on the table. One with a label. The big detective smiled. The dying old outlaw had even gotten to Comanche's normally stony heart. At least enough that she'd supplied him with a bottle of the good stuff to sip before he died, maybe take the sting out of the bite of that bullet in his chest.

Stockburn pried out the cork, splashed some liquor into the shot glass, and handed the whiskey to the outlaw. There was only one glass, so Stockburn would drink from the bottle.

He rested the bottle on his knee and looked at Drago. The old outlaw stared straight ahead at the wall to the right of the blasted out door. He was staring into space, but he appeared to feel better. Still pain-racked but relieved not to be dying alone.

"All right," the detective prompted him.

"One more thing." Drago turned to him with a wolfish smile. "Tell me your secret."

Stockburn frowned, puzzled. "My secret?"

"You know—your *secret*. The one secret we carry around in our soul and don't want no one else to ever know. It's all right. You can tell me. I'm dyin'. You tell me yours, an' I'll tell you mine. It'll lighten our hearts."

Stockburn pondered on that, scowling. Finally, he gave a dismissive grunt and said, "First—Red."

Bascom sipped his whiskey, smacked his lips, and set the glass on his sharply rising and falling chest. "Cold Water Wells. Holed up there at the old stage depot. Him and a handful of others leftover from our old gang and a few firebrands new to the owlhoot trail." He sipped his whiskey, coughed, and added in a strangled voice, "Least-ways, that's what I hear. I ain't seen Red in over a dozen years. Never cared to. Folks just tell me about him . . . to nettle me, if nothin' else."

"Cold Water Wells," Stockburn said, and took a drink from the bottle. The old hide-hunters' camp turned stage relay station on the old Fort Pierre Road was only a half-day's ride away. If he left here tomorrow morning, he'd arrive there by noon.

"Your turn."

"What's that?"

Drago smiled, closing one eye. "Tell me your secret, Wolf. An' I'll tell you mine."

"Why don't we just sit here and drink, Dad?"

"Ah, come on. Grant a dyin' old man's last wish."

Stockburn chuffed a wry laugh. "My secret, huh?"

"Yeah."

The detective stared down at the bottle on his knee. "My secret."

"You know the one. We all got one."

"Yeah," he nodded. "I know the one."

"Tell me."

Wolf took a deep pull from the bottle. The liquor soothed

his insides, but his mind was burning the way it always burned whenever his thoughts began probing that old bitter injury. The one he would take to his grave and, if there was a beyond, beyond it.

"All right." He nodded slowly, gazing down at the bottle again. "I'll tell you my secret, Dad."

Maybe it would give him some release. What could it hurt? Like Dad himself had said, the old man was dying. He wouldn't have the opportunity to tell anyone Stockburn's secret.

The secret.

CHAPTER 5

"About twenty years ago, I had a close friend—Mike Wayne," Stockburn said. "Mike an' I rode for the Pony Express together. We were just kids. When the telegraph an' the railroad drove the Express out of business, Mike and I hitched our stars together and we got jobs guarding bullion runs in the Sierra Nevadas.

"Mike an' I—we were inseparable back in those rollicking gold camp days. Like brothers." He chuckled. "We were like an old married couple. We knew what was on each other's minds before we said it. When you got a friend like that, you never feel alone, even when you are—know what I mean, Dad?"

"Yeah," Dad wheezed. "I know what you mean, Wolf."

"We hardly ever were alone—Mike and me. Like I said, we were inseparable. Until Mike got him a girl in Sacramento. We were deputy sheriffs then. Mike met Fannie in a bank. She was a teller. Well, they tumbled for each other. Tumbled hard. They didn't leave me out, though. Hell, no. We went on vacations together. Walked on the beach together. Dined together at night, gambled together, drank on the porch of my and Mike's rooming house till the wee hours of the morning.

"We doubled up on our jobs and brought in enough cash, supplemented by weekend gambling, that we decided to spend ten days together in San Francisco. Mike, Fannie, and me. Mike had asked for Fannie's hand, and she'd said yes, and we were going to celebrate. We stayed in the same hotel—The Palace."

Stockburn smiled. "Nothing but high-class for us. We made the nightly rounds of all the dancing and gambling joints. We were in the thick of it there in Frisco when Mike got called away on family business down in Pasadena. That's where Mike was from. He was from a rich family down there though he was sort of the black sheep of the clan, with an adventurous streak. Anyway, when he got called away, Fanny and I . . ."

"Yeah . . . ?" Dad said, a dreadful tone in his voice.

"Fanny and I continued stomping with our tails up and . . . we got drunk and . . . ended up in bed together."

"Shit."

"Mike came in early one morning, back to his and Fanny's room. Found me and Fanny . . . together."

"The hell."

"He stared at us. Just stared at us. None of us said anything. Fannie and I just stared at Mike. All the color left his face. I can still see it disappearing, being replaced by a sickly pale color. Sort of green and yellow combined. His eyes turned dark as coals. He stared back at us as though his soul had just dried up and withered away."

"Ah, hell, Wolf . . ."

"He turned around and walked back out into the hall. I lay there, thinking he'd left to get a gun. We'd had to check our weapons at the front desk. I figured he'd be back, and he'd shoot me. I wanted him to. That's how bad I felt. I lay there and just waited for him to end the misery. Fanny lay sobbing into her pillow beside me.

"Next thing I know, I hear a big commotion out on the street. A lady was screaming and a little girl was crying and a man was shouting for a doctor. I got up and ran to the window and looked out. A man lay on the cable car tracks. He was twisted and bloody, clothes torn and dirty. I couldn't see his face, so I dressed and ran out. Sure enough, it was Mike."

Stockburn drew a deep breath. "He'd walked out in front of a cable car. Struck him full on. He lingered in a hospital for three days. He was in and out. Then he died."

Stockburn cleared his throat and looked at Dad, who stared back at him, still breathing hard but his eyes riveted on the detective.

"That's my secret," Stockburn said.

"The hell. That's plain terrible, Wolf."

"The thing of it is, I don't know why I did it. Fanny wasn't particularly pretty. No more than most. Plainer than some. Not even much personality. I wasn't even sure what Mike saw in her. Yet I slept with her. I just don't know why I did. To this day, I don't know why."

He shook his head as he gazed out the window, the befuddlement over his own inner mystery plaguing him anew. "I never saw her again. Don't have any idea where she is now, and I don't care. But the memory of that morning . . . haunts me." He raked his hand through his roached hair and down his face, and he said in miserable frustration, "I betrayed the only true friend I ever had. And I killed him with that betrayal."

He drew a calming breath though it didn't calm him much. He lifted the bottle to his lips, took a deep pull. That didn't help much, either. Nothing helped when he got to reflecting on Mike Wayne and Fannie Albright. On the darkness and evil that must linger in his own heart, confounding him so. Repelling him. Making him want to reach in and tear the black organ out of his chest with a hand trowel.

Odd how the pain stayed with him even after all these years. Nothing seemed to soften it.

Not even talking it out like he'd just done to a dying old outlaw.

Stockburn gave a wry chuckle. "I never told that to anybody before. Not a word of it. No one else knows. Just me . . . and now you, Dad."

"You been carryin' around a heavy weight, Wolf."

"I 'spect I'll continue to carry it."

"You don't feel no better for having told it?"

"I thought maybe I would, but I don't."

"I'm sorry," Drago said, sounding like he really was.

Stockburn drew another deep breath and returned his gaze to the old outlaw who lay back against his pillow again, breathing hard, staring at the ceiling. "Your turn, Dad."

"Me?" Dad smiled as he studied the ceiling. His breathing sounded like an overpumped bellows. "My secret?" He winced again at the pain in his chest. Slowly, he turned his head toward Stockburn and stretched his lips back from his small, discolored teeth, few as he had left. "My secret is . . . I'm . . . I'm afraid of dyin' . . . Wolf . . ."

And all at once, just like that, the light left his eyes, and he stopped breathing. He was still staring at Stockburn, but he wasn't seeing anything anymore. His eyes were as opaque as isinglass.

Wolf stared at him for a time. Slowly, he rose from his chair, set the bottle on the table, and brushed his fingers over the old outlaw's eyes, closing them for good. "Now you won't have to worry about it anymore."

He stared down at the dead man, feeling hollow inside. He found himself envying old Drago. At least death had put an end to his suffering. He might have feared it, but he likely feared it no more. That was usually what happened when you faced things. Most often, anyway.

As for Stockburn, he had to live everyday with the knowledge of what he'd done to his best friend. The only real friend he'd ever had in the world.

Why in the hell had he done such a thing?

Would he ever know? Did he *want* to know?

Instead of relieving the weight from his shoulders, his confession to Dad Drago had only reminded him of the burden. It had gotten him thinking about it again, hating himself all over again for what he'd done.

Best not think about it, he told himself. *You don't have time to think about it. What you need to be thinking about is that twenty-odd-man band of kill-crazy cutthroats known as the Devil's Horde who've been stalking the Northern Pacific railroad of late—two big robberies with dozens killed, including the entire crews from both trains, in a little over three months' time.*

That's what you need to be thinking about. It's your job to run that band to ground. Or, barring that—since you're badly outnumbered and not even the storied Wolf of the Rails could bring down that many cutthroats on his own— your job is to locate the murdering plunderers and call in the deputy U.S. marshals and the U.S. army to cut them down or haul them in.

They'd be cut down, most likely. A band as savage as the Horde, who seemed to enjoy killing, would never be taken under rein. They'd go down fighting and, likely after a good many lawmen and soldiers were killed, they'd be kicked out with cold shovels themselves. And good riddance, too.

Who were they? Where in the hell did they come from? Who was their leader?

All questions Stockburn hoped to learn from Red Bascom tomorrow in Cold Water Wells.

He walked back into the hall and strode toward the stairs. He still felt pensive. He wanted to concentrate his energy on his job, which meant *the Horde*, as the local newspapers had dubbed the gang. But memories of Mike Wayne were slow to lift, like a stubborn morning fog after a hard rain.

He walked down the stairs, dark brows furrowed in thought, then stopped suddenly and glanced at the table at which Sorley and the other two punchers were playing poker. They were looking at Stockburn, and right away the detective sensed trouble.

Instantly, all three men's eyes grew bright. Just as instantly, their eyes flattened out, and they glanced at each other quickly, anxiously. Sorley slid his chair back and gained his feet, closing his hand over the grips of the Schofield on his right thigh.

The other two men gained their feet, as well. As Sorley took one step back from the table, the others took one step back and away from Sorley, giving themselves room. They also closed their hands over the handles of their holstered six-shooters.

All eyes were on Stockburn, fairly dancing with dark intent.

Stopped about two-thirds of the way down the stairs, he had his right hand on the right banister. His left hand hung straight down his left leg. He studied the men spread out around the table about thirty feet away, out beyond the stairs and to his left. They were the only ones in the saloon.

Casting his gaze out the front window, he saw Comanche brushing Smoke in the corral off the barn. She was currying the gray coat slowly, thoroughly, running her other hand along behind the brush. Stockburn could tell that she was talking softly to the horse, soothingly, lovingly, oblivious of the evil intent of the MacDonald riders.

Good. He was glad she was outside. Away from a possible errant round.

Stockburn looked back at the three men. His gray mustache rose slightly as he gave a knowing smile. Sorley had had just enough liquor to be dangerous. Dangerously stupid, but dangerous, just the same.

The ranch foreman smiled back. A few minutes ago, he wasn't sure. Fear had had a hold on him. After lowering the level on his unlabeled bottle by another third, the fear had gone. Courage had moved in to replace it. The foolish courage of forty-rod, but courage just the same.

Now, by God, he was going to do it. He was really going to do it. He was going to take down the legend himself—Wolf Stockburn. Get his own name in all the papers. Have every cowpuncher and train robber between here and Abilene saying his name around campfires and attaching to it an air of deep reverence.

He'd talked the others into throwing in with him. They didn't look as eager as Sorley, but they were going through with it. They'd had just enough busthead to have become stupid enough to throw in with the fool, Sorley.

"Three against one," Stockburn said, still smiling. "That don't seem fair to me." He really did find it funny. Dangerous, of course, but funny. Three drunken fools out in the middle of nowhere drunk with rotgut courage.

"Fair can go to hell!" Sorley shouted, slurring his words and jerking iron.

CHAPTER 6

The fool was slower than he might have been sober.

He might have had his hand on his pistol, but that quarter-second advantage didn't do him much good. Stockburn's left-side Peacemaker was in his right hand and roaring before Sorley cleared leather. The bullet punched dust from the center of the ranch foreman's shirt, throwing the man straight back with a clipped yelp but not before he'd fired his Schofield into the pile of pennies, dimes, and nickels on the table before him.

As the other two fools' hoglegs cleared leather, Stockburn tossed his Colt into his left hand and used his right hand to hoist his legs up and over the banister. He dropped to the floor beside the stairs as the other two went to work with their pistols, yelling and shooting.

The bullets plunked into the stairs in the general area where the railroad detective had been standing a half-second ago. One plowed into the stair rail, spitting wood slivers into his hair.

He landed on the balls of his feet then threw himself straight forward to the floor, his right-side Colt in his right hand. As he slid out clear of the stairs, he extended both poppers before him and slightly left. The cowpuncher who'd been standing to Sorley's right had tracked Stockburn's leap from the stairs.

Red-faced and yelling excitedly, he triggered a round over Stockburn's head. The detective returned fire, drilling one pill through the drunken fool's throat while the second .45-caliber round turned the man's left eye to strawberry jam.

Out he went through the sashed window behind him.

The other man ran forward, kicking chairs out of his way and firing over tables at Stockburn, who crabbed forward and left, past the front of the stairs, using a table in front of him for cover.

The cowpuncher's fourth and fifth rounds chunked into the table, throwing more slivers. As Stockburn moved to the left of the table, he saw the puncher swing toward him, wide-eyed and red-faced.

He yelped, knowing he was too late.

Both of Stockburn's pretty Peacemakers spoke loudly. Both .45-caliber rounds hammered into the fool's chest, picking him up and knocking him backward, where he lay atop a table, flopping his hands and arms like a bug impaled on a pin. "Oh!" he cried. "You killed me, you devil!" He rolled off the table and fell to the floor with a resolute thud.

Running footsteps sounded outside. Boots hammered the worn boards of the porch, then Comanche pushed through the quarter-open door, breathless and red-faced, looking around.

"Wolf?" she yelled. "*Wolf*?"

Stockburn gained his feet heavily. He, too, was breathing hard from exertion and the excitement of the lead swap. It was always frightening, but it was also exciting, though he didn't care if he was never in another one again. He'd been in plenty and was damn lucky to have come away from all of them with only a few minor burns and grazes. He'd once taken a bullet to the leg, but the flesh wound had healed in no time.

It was a damn good way to clear the crap out of your mind, though. Crap like having betrayed your best friend so he walked out in front of a cable car.

Comanche stared at him anxiously. "You good?"

"No," Stockburn said. "But I'm uninjured."

"I'm glad you came, Wolf. It's been a while. Cheers."

Stockburn picked up his half-filled whiskey glass. "Even despite the blood and broken glass . . . ?"

"Well, I'll admit you're a little hard on the clientele."

Chuckling, he touched his glass to Comanche's and sipped. The whiskey went down well, warming his insides and mellowing his thoughts, chasing Mike away. They sat together in the deep and ancient cowhide chair on Comanche's front porch, Comanche curled up on his lap like a small child, arms wrapped around his neck, cheek pressed to his chest, both of them covered by a heavy trade blanket.

After Stockburn had polished off the cowpunchers, he and Comanche had had a couple of drinks together. The storm had come up late in the afternoon, likely killing business for the rest of the day unless a mule team pulled in with a small crew of hungry, thirsty, and amorous skinners wanting shelter from the storm. Stockburn and Comanche had taken advantage of the peace and quiet by going up to her room and sheltering from the storm in their own special way, groaning and sighing and nibbling each other's parts while distant kettledrums banged in the skies over and around them.

It was a nice tumble, as tumbles usually were with Comanche. She had a tough, gruff exterior, but she was a tender lover. Also, she didn't have any expectations beyond that hour or so under the sheets, curling each other's toes and pausing to tell a few jokes and to laugh and snuggle. Both were old enough to know better than to fall in love with each other.

Afterwards, and during a lull in the storm, they got dressed, went downstairs, and tended to the dead men. They hauled Dad and the other three men in his gang out to a ravine after first stripping them of valuables, which Stockburn consigned to Comanche by way of compensation for the wreckage. They found a pair of money-stuffed saddlebags in the barn that was likely the loot they'd plundered from the bank in Pierre. There was a good bit there, meaning they probably hadn't had a chance to spend their booty anywhere but at Comanche's place.

The Pierre banker would be happy.

Stockburn considered giving Dad a proper burial the next day. The man had heard his secret, after all. *The* secret. But, why? The man had been a devil like all the others. Besides, grave-digging was one hell of an onerous task that Stockburn just didn't feel up for.

If you're bad, why pretend you're good? Why throw hypocrisy into the soup?

Stockburn hid the loot in the barn. When he got to a telegraph office, he'd cable the Pierre banker with the good news as well as the location of his money. The man and the Hughes County Sheriff could fetch it himself, as Stockburn was a detective, not a courier. Besides, he had bigger fish to fry.

The Devil's Horde.

It had started to rain and thunder again by the time Stockburn and Comanche got the cowpunchers loaded into the back of a buckboard wagon. She would have Billy Two Eagles, the beefy Indian who worked for her intermittently, when he was sober, drive the dead men out to George MacDonald's ranch along Big Owl Creek. Since they'd worked for the limey, the limey could bury them or toss them to the turkey buzzards, whichever he thought they deserved. Comanche had her own opinion on what the truculent cow nurses deserved. She kept their gambling money as partial closure of the trio's open drinking and whoring account.

"I don't know where they spent their money way out here," Comanche said, counting the money out atop her bar. "My place is the only watering and whoring hole in a hundred miles. But they never seemed to have enough to pay in full."

During the lull in the storm, the doxies next door had been thrown some business. Several ex–hide hunters who cut wood for a living rode up to the little whoring shanty in a rickety old prairie schooner. They were already three sheets to the wind, singing and passing a crock jug. The storm had apparently put an end to their woodcutting for the day. Let the party begin! Having paid Comanche ahead of time for their nights of frolic, as per her rules, they were over there drinking, dancing, and singing with the girls, one of whom played the fiddle.

Their shadows danced across the red-curtained windows.

One of the men loudly recounted the punchline to a joke, and the other men and "ladies" laughed raucously.

"I wish I could have heard the whole joke," Comanche said, nestled against Stockburn's lap.

"Must've been a dandy."

The rain had started again, lifting a low roar. The water pouring off the porch roof cut a long slender trench in the dirt of the yard below.

"You haven't mentioned her, Wolf," Comanche said after they'd sat listening to the rain. "How come?"

Lightning flashed in the sky to the south—a white witch's finger piercing a sphere of periwinkle blue.

He knew Comanche was referring to his sister, Emily. His farming family had been massacred by marauding Cheyenne in western Kansas Territory in 1858, and she was taken prisoner while the young Stockburn was spared only because in the chaos of smoke, blood, gunfire, screaming arrows, and billowing smoke and dust, the Indians had overlooked him.

He'd been clubbed in the head and knocked out, and had for years nursed only a vague recollection of his younger sister being carried off, screaming, over the pony of a howling brave.

The sole survivor of the attack, Stockburn had survived by his wits and hunting prowess until he'd been hired by the Pony Express in 1860. Over the years, in his spare time and possibly to help keep him from thinking about Mike, he'd ridden out to look for Emily in Kansas and Nebraska. His hope of someday finding her rekindled when a sodbuster in northern Nebraska had told him he'd seen a beautiful young black-haired white girl with cobalt eyes riding with a band of Sioux in the late '60s.

Emily had been a pretty young girl in pigtails when she'd been taken. Given the beauty of Stockburn's mother and other two sisters, Emily might very well be a beautiful young woman now—almost thirty years of age.

Stockburn thought it possible that the Cheyenne had traded or sold his sister to the Sioux, whose ancestral homelands lay to the north of the Oregon Trail in Dakota Territory. It was while looking for Emily several years ago that Stockburn had stopped at the intersection of two relatively busy trade routes and met Comanche.

The pretty half-breed woman had been an oasis in the prairie desert. An oasis of food, drink, pleasures of the flesh, and information. Travelers of all stripe passing through his neck of Dakota eventually passed through here, and while Comanche had as of his last visit heard no tales of a black-haired white girl with cobalt eyes living with Indians, he'd always hoped she would.

And that she'd eventually pass that information on to him.

"You always ask," Comanche said now after thunder had rumbled briefly. "Her name is usually the first word out of your mouth." She turned her head to gaze up at him probingly. "But not this time. Why?"

"Good Lord," he said, as surprised as Comanche. "I guess I've given up."

Comanche kept her eyes on him. "You have?"

Stockburn lifted his hand from her hip and set it back down. "Why else wouldn't I have asked? Sure enough," he said, studying the rain tumbling off the roof as if it was the tide of his own inscrutable motivations, "I reckon I have."

"Don't give up, Wolf."

Stockburn just shook his head. He hadn't thought he had. But he had. It saddened him to realize it.

"Too many years have gone by, Comanche. Good Lord, if Emily's still alive, she'd be near thirty. She was taken so young. Hell, she'd be more Indian than white. Probably wouldn't want anything to do with me. Probably couldn't speak English. Could've been killed in any number of ways. Might've even died in childbirth."

"Still, don't give up."

"Why not?" Stockburn frowned at the pretty woman in his lap.

"Because I know how important finding her is to you."

"Is it? I reckon it's been so long I don't even know anymore."

"Obviously it is, or you would have let her go long before now."

He lifted his glass and stared through it above the brown line of the whiskey, toward the intermittently glowing sky beyond the rain tumbling off the porch roof. "She's all I have. If she's still out there. All the rest of 'em . . . my family . . . gone."

His best friend, too. Gone.

Wolf took a hefty swallow of the whiskey.

"We are outsiders, you and me, Wolf. Loners and outsiders. That's why you never married and why you spent all these years looking for a sister who was taken when she was only eight years old. Long after anyone else would have given up. Because she's all you have. *Searching for her* is all you have. Look at you—pushing forty and no one to go back to Kansas City for. No one except Wells Fargo."

"They're my employer, Comanche. More loyal than any spouse. At least, the kind of spouse I would have married."

"Maybe you don't give yourself enough credit."

"You don't think?" He'd never told her about Mike. He never would.

"You're a handsome devil. You could have your pick."

Yeah, but what squalor lurked behind that handsome mug? "Look who's talking."

"Most men can't see beyond this." She reached up to indicate the patch over her left eye.

"If I'm out of line here, you'll let me know. But we've known each other going on eight years now, Comanche, and you've never . . . you know. You never told me how you lost the eye."

She arched her brows with customary insouciance. "You never asked."

"I reckon I thought I'd get a bullet for my trouble."

"I didn't know you were afraid of me, Wolf."

Stockburn smiled. "Maybe that's why I like you so much. I'm just a little bit afraid." He smiled more brightly and kissed her cheek.

She smiled, then, too. The smile faded but she continued to gaze directly at him, her face only inches from his. "My first husband. A hot-tempered Texan my foster family had warned me against."

"I see."

"No, you don't. Not quite." She looked away then looked at him again, and her dark-brown eye turned one shade darker. The distant lightning reflected in it flatly. "You see, he caught me sleeping with his friend. He shot his friend in an Abilene hotel and took a fireplace poker to my eye."

Stockburn stiffened. He stared at her, lips parted, chest rising slowly as he breathed.

"The story doesn't end there, though," Comanche said. "Rest assured."

"They never do."

She smiled brightly, and her eyes danced with glee. "I took the poker away from him and beat him to death with it. Then I stole out of Abilene and ran as hard and as far away as I could from Texas." She frowned, studying him. "Why are you looking at me like that? You didn't think I was a saint, did you?"

"No." Stockburn swallowed. "No, I didn't. None of us are." He drew his arms more tightly around her. For some reason, he found himself laughing. He kept laughing. He didn't know why, but he laughed and laughed.

She looked at him uncertainly. "What's so funny, Wolf? My Lord, I'm horrible!"

Stockburn laughed even louder, so that the ladies and their jakes could likely hear it over in the honey shack.

"Two peas in a pod, darlin'," Stockburn said, still laughing. "Two peas in a pod!"

CHAPTER 7

The next day around one o'clock in the afternoon, Stockburn leaned forward in his saddle and pressed his cheek taut against the side of Smoke's neck. A quarter-second later, he heard the ominous whine and felt the displacement of air where his forehead had been before he'd seen the glint of sunlight off metal atop the butte just ahead and on his right.

The bullet thumped into the sod behind him.

Moving fast, Wolf shucked his 1866 Winchester Yellow-boy repeater from the sheath jutting up from under his right leg. Swing-cocking the pretty rifle, he whipped his right boot over his saddle horn, dropped straight down to the trail, and slapped Smoke's left hip, yelling, "Go, Smoke! Get up the trail, boy!"

The detective dropped to one knee and raised the Winchester to his shoulder. The no-good peckerwood of a dry-gulching snake crouched atop the southwestern haystack butte, roughly a hundred yards from Stockburn's position. Wolf could see only the man's upper torso—hatted head and chest—silhouetted against the bright

Dakota sky behind him. He could also see the rifle the no-good peckerwood was leveling on him again.

The Wells Fargo detective had let the man get off the first shot. He would not get off a second one.

Stockburn lined up his sights on the man's silhouette and squeezed the trigger. The Winchester bucked and roared, smoke and flames jetting from the barrel. The bullet plumed chalky dirt from the face of the bluff, maybe two feet behind the dry-gulching no-account. It had, however, startled the man enough that his second shot flew wide of its intended target again, plunking into the sod behind Wolf.

"Come on, Stockburn, you're not that damn rusty!" the detective berated himself as he quickly worked the Winchester's cocking lever, pumping another round into the action.

He'd been traveling so much lately, from one job to the next, that he hadn't had time for a visit to the shooting range he'd set up behind his rooming house in Kansas City. He normally shot hell out of his empty whiskey bottles from time to time, just to stay in trim with the Yellowboy he'd bought new in Wichita when he'd been the town marshal of that fair city on the plains. He'd been known as the Wolf Who Tamed Wichita, or the Wolf of Wichita, back then by the half-drunk, shabbily attired, whore-mongering, ink-stained news scribblers. Ever since he'd ridden for the Pony Express and got the all-important mail from Three-Mile Ridge to Fort Laramie with the precious *mochila*, or mail pouch, intact despite a dozen war-painted braves hazing him every step of the way while throwing lead and arrows at him, the so-called *newsmen* seemed to follow him around, at least via the news cables, like hungry dogs looking for scraps from a soft touch.

He lined up the Yellowboy's sights again and fired. He lined them up again, fired again. Again . . . and again.

Between his second and third shots, the silhouetted figure atop the bluff jerked back and to one side. The man had turned his head to peer back toward Wolf as though in momentary shock, then drew back from the face of the bluff altogether, disappearing from Stockburn's sight.

"Got him."

Wolf reloaded the Yellowboy as he strode quickly up to where the gray stood a hundred feet up the trail. The horse turned to face him with a skeptical look, rippling one wither. Smoke didn't like being shot at any more than his rider did.

"I know, Smoke." Holding the Winchester in one hand, the detective swung up onto the leather. "Nothing worse than a dry-gulcher. There's a special place in hell for bush-whackers. The hottest damn corner!"

He turned the horse around and booted it on up the trail. Smoke quickly rocked into a hard gallop. Wolf turned the horse off the trail and around the backside of the bluff upon which the man had shot at him. The terrain around him was a wind-rippled sea of fawn-colored grass and scudding cloud shadows.

The bushwhacker was just then riding down the long, gently sloping southwest side of the bluff, heading away from Stockburn. Fifty yards away, the man rode slumped a little in the saddle and appeared to be favoring his left arm.

Stockburn reined Smoke to a halt and curveted the mount so that his shoulder was pointed at the fleeing gunman. Stockburn pumped a fresh round into the Winchester's action, raised the rifle to his shoulder, and settled the sights on the quickly dwindling figure of the horse and rider.

Smoke was well trained. The horse stood rock still, hardly breathing.

Stockburn allowed for the wind and the distance as well as for the fact that his target was riding away from him in a slightly wavering line. He drew a breath, held it, squeezed the trigger.

The Yellowboy bucked and roared.

The rider kept galloping away. One second . . . another . . . and another.

The man flinched, dipped forward at the waist. He sagged still farther forward until the wind blew his hat off his head. He slumped over his still-galloping mount's right wither for several more strides before sliding on down the side of the horse. He dropped to the ground, bounced, and rolled. The grass was so tall that Stockburn couldn't see the man himself, but he could see the moving brush.

The brush stopped moving.

The horse kept galloping straight across the prairie, growing smaller and smaller against the broad blue horizon.

"Let's go, Smoke. Hi-yahh!" Stockburn galloped toward where he'd last seen the grass move.

A minute later, he slowed Smoke to a walk then reined the horse to a stop. He stared down at the bushwhacker. He was still alive but hit hard. Blood oozed from a ragged wound in his left shoulder. He was tall and long-faced, with a big nose and bulging forehead bearing a star-shaped birthmark. The man's eyes angled up at Stockburn.

They were bright and sharp with pain; at the same time, they were dark with misery.

"Damn you, Stockburn. Look what you done. You killed me!"

"Leo Crabbe."

"That's right."

"How'd you know it was me on the trail back there?"

"Glassed you from a distance. I'd recognize the big man with the gray hair and the black sombrero riding that rangy gray anywhere."

"All right. Now that we got *that* covered, why'd you try to bushwhack me, Leo?"

Crabbed flinched as pain lanced through him. "You're after Bascom, ain't ya? The . . . gold . . . ?"

"I'm after Bascom. Just wanted to have a little chat with him."

"About the gold."

Stockburn swung his lean frame down from the saddle and dropped to a knee beside the hard-dying Leo Crabbe. "What gold?"

Crabbed scowled up at him, studying him skeptically, suspiciously. "You know what gold. Fixx didn't want no one complicatin' matters. That's why he posted me out here . . . on that bluff . . . to let him know who's ridin' into Cold Water Wells. To discourage them that don't look like they'd be wanted . . ."

"Fixx?" Stockburn flipped through the file of hard-cases stowed in his memory. "You mean Lonigan Fixx?"

"Yeah. Lonigan Fixx. Who else?"

"So Bascom really is in Cold Water Wells."

Again, Crabbe scowled up at Stockburn as though he thought the detective were playing some game with him.

"You knew that," he said through a dry chuckle. "That's why you're here."

Wolf was glad his trip out there hadn't been for nothing. That Lonigan Fixx was in town, as well, might complicate matters, however.

Fixx had been a member of Bascom's old gang, though Stockburn hadn't heard much about him in the decade since he'd put Bascom behind bars. When he'd thought of Lonigan Fixx, which hadn't been often, he'd figured someone else had put him away or beefed him, or maybe he'd hidden out down in Mexico, avoiding arrest warrants and bounty hunters.

It must have taken something big—mighty big—to have lured the old rat out of hiding.

"What about the gold, Leo? What gold are you talking about?"

He waited for a reply. It didn't come. It wouldn't come. Crabbe was staring up at him, but his face was expressionless and his eyes were cold and flat in death, though the cast of fear and befuddlement the man had felt at the prospect of his own imminent demise had not yet totally faded. It would in a minute or two. By the time he'd gotten into the rhythm of coal shoveling for Old Beelzebub, keeping the furnaces in Hell stoked, it would be gone.

Stockburn cursed. He gazed over the wind-rippled and shadow striped grass toward the southwest. Beyond the next jog of hills lay Cold Water Wells.

"What gold?"

Oh, well. Didn't matter. He was there to talk to Bascom about the Devil's Horde. He wouldn't be distracted by peripheral matters. He'd be distracted no further by Leo Crabbe, either.

If he ran into Lonigan Fixx in Cold Water Wells, he'd tell the old reprobate where he could find Crabbe. It figured that Stockburn would likely run into the old outlaw, since the last time he'd ridden through the little farm and ranch supply settlement it had been small enough that, standing on the east edge of town, you could practically hold a conversation with someone standing on the west edge without raising your voice overmuch.

CHAPTER 8

Stockburn dropped down the last jog of hills and entered the town roughly twenty minutes later. It hadn't grown much since the last time he'd ridden through. There were about a dozen business buildings—a rickety, sun-silvered lot of cottonwood structures with roofs of shake, tin, or tarred gravel. The Red Moon Saloon stood where it had stood last time he had stopped to wet his whistle and ended up ventilating the half-breed whiskey runner Charlie Crow.

Wolf hadn't been after Crow, but Crow had pulled a gun on him while he'd been standing at the bar, sipping a shot of Thunder Mountain and entertaining the sweet nothings whispered into his ear by a not-unappetizing young doxy. Crow had gotten his neck in a hump when Stockburn had killed Crow's older brother, Willis, who'd been part of a gang who'd robbed stock being shipped on the Helena, Dakota, and North Central Railroad. Since Wells Fargo had insured the shipment, Stockburn had been sent in to corral the stock thieves and the beef they'd robbed—thirty-five steers headed for Chicago.

He hadn't killed Willis, only winged him, but Willis's

horse had done him in when he had tumbled from the saddle and the indignant horse had kicked him in the head, splitting it wide open like an ax laid through a ripe cantaloupe. Wolf hadn't gotten a chance to explain the situation to Charlie Crow, however. Crow had stayed ominously silent for the first six or seven minutes after Stockburn had entered the Red Moon Saloon. Stockburn had spied the man glancing at him, however, from where Charlie had stood near the other end of the bar.

Sudden as a diamondback's strike, Charlie had slammed down his beer bottle, said, "Ah, hell!" and slapped leather. Stockburn had shoved the doxy aside and shot Charlie three times in the chest—a tight pattern right over the whiskey runner's heart. Charlie had triggered a shot through the brass rail running along the base of the bar. The ricochet had blown off the tip of his nose. It hadn't mattered. Charlie was done breathing by then, anyway. He was dead before he'd hit the floor.

Riding into town, Stockburn noted the half-dozen horses tied to the two hitch racks fronting the Red Moon. He tied Smoke to the rail beside a nice-looking sorrel with a Mexican-style saddle, then brushed dust from his clothes with his sombrero, returned the topper to his head, and pushed through the batwings.

He stopped just inside to see who'd he'd be sharing the environs with. It was always nice to know ahead of time, just in case he'd be drinking—and possibly swapping lead—with anymore Charlie Crows.

Six men sat at two tables to his right. Four at one. Two at another. The two were playing cards. The four were just slumped in their chairs, drinking. Some wore hats. Others had set their hats on the tables. The group of four wore deep suntans. The kind of dark-bronze tan the sun burned into a man down in Mexico. They were all dressed for the long winding trail, complete with one or two well-used and -cared-for six-shooters.

If one was Lonigan Fixx, Stockburn didn't recognize him. He'd only seen him once, and that had been a long time ago. He was one of the few who'd given the wily Wolf of the Rails the slip.

They all studied Stockburn shrewdly, some of them squinting through tobacco smoke.

Stockburn walked up to the bar running along the left-side wall. A stocky, apron-clad gent stood behind it, reading a newspaper spread across the wood. A bag of Durham tobacco sat on the bar to the right of the paper, near an ashtray cut from an airtight tin and in which a half-smoked quirley uncoiled feathery blue smoke into the air.

"What can I help you with, señor?" the barkeep said, grinning ironically. He was the type who liked to sprinkle a little Mexican into his talk whether he was talking to a Mexican or not. It amused him. His washed-out gray eyes glinted though it was hard to see them inside the heaped, ruddy, freckled flesh around them.

Stockburn placed his hands on top of the bar, fingers spread. "Where's Red Bascom?"

In the backbar mirror, he saw all six heads behind him swing toward him. He picked out Lonigan Fixx. He hadn't recognized him because of the full, salt-and-pepper beard he must have grown down in Mexico. With the dark beard and skin tanned nearly as dark as mahogany, he really did look like a Mexican.

A Mexican grown to middle-aged tallow.

He even had a sombrero on the table near his left elbow.

The Mexican kind with ornate stitching around the low, bullet-shaped, straw crown.

Fixx's gaze met Stockburn's.

The detective smiled and gave a little wave to the man in the mirror. "Well, I'll be damned," he said, chuckling and slapping the bar. "I'd have sworn you'd long since died of the Mexican pony drip somewhere along the shores of the Sea of Cortez, you ugly little pig fart!"

Fixx and the other five men, including the two sitting at their own table, leaped to their feet at the same time. They all slapped leather and skinned iron.

Stockburn had seen it coming. He'd seen it coming from the very second Red Bascom's name had left his lips. That's why he had a head start, throwing himself up and over the bar just as the six men clicked their hoglegs' hammers back. "Get down, apron!" he bellowed as he flew over the bar's far side and plummeted to the floor. "Unless you want daylight blown through you!"

The big man cut loose with a girlish wail and hurled himself to the floor. Already the hoglegs were roaring, bullets cutting into the bar and shattering the backbar mirror as well as bottles residing on shelves.

Liquor from shattered bottles rained down on and around Stockburn as, sitting up, he unholstered both Peacemakers. He'd lost his hat when he'd gone airborne and picked it up, whipping it to his left toward the front door off the end of the bar to keep from getting an inordinate amount of glass and liquor on it.

He was particular about his hat.

Holding both Colts barrel up in his hands, back pressed against the shelves beneath the bar, he waited. He was glad the front of the bar was paneled in wood heavy enough to keep the slugs from ripping through it.

The shooting quickly tapered off.

It stopped.

Silence save for the sobbing of the barman who lay facedown on the floor beside Stockburn, to the detective's right as he faced the backbar. The apron had a good bit of glass on him, and his white shirt was soaked with liquor so that Stockburn could see the man's soft, sickly white flesh through the cotton.

"Stockburn?" one of his assailants called from the far side of the room. A couple of seconds passed. Then, louder: "Stockburn?"

"Did we hit him?" one of the others asked quietly, voice pinched with apprehension.

"Only one way to find out," said the man who'd spoken first—probably Lonigan Fixx. Stockburn didn't know the man's voice. "Dick, you go around that way. Jimmy, you go around that—" Lonigan Fixx didn't finish the order. He saw Stockburn lift his head up above the bar and stretch both Colts over thc top of it, smiling his icy Wolf-of-the-Rails, cold-blooded, deadly smile.

Many men had gone to their graves with that grin emblazoned on their retinas. Six more were headed that way.

Stockburn shot Lonigan first.

The other five weren't as easy as Lonigan, who had realized a half second before he'd died with a bullet through his forehead that Stockburn had gotten the drop on him. The old outlaw had momentarily frozen, and before he could snap out of it, he was shaking hands with the fork-tailed devil.

The others panicked, as well, jerking around, trying to decide if they should duck and cover or return fire. Stockburn caught them all in that dark neverland of indecision. He shot them all like ducks on a millrace.

Bang! Bang! Bang-Bang-Bang!

One threw himself down behind a table, screaming. Stockburn had merely winged him. Panicking, the man gained his feet and ran toward the batwings.

He didn't make it three steps before Stockburn, tracking the target steadily with his right-hand Colt, calmly drilled a .45-caliber round through the man's right ear. The bullet exited the left side of the man's head and drilled the piano abutting the front wall to the right of the door.

The bullet plowed into an ivory key, making the piano *ping!*

Stockburn turned to face the room again. All five were down, one of them was still alive. Stockburn couldn't tell which one. Too many shadows. But he could hear the still-alive man saying—grunting, rather—"Oh, god; oh, god; oh, god . . ."

"Who's that?" Stockburn asked, squinting through the sifting, rotten-smelling powder smoke.

The apron remained belly down on the floor. He was reciting the Lord's Prayer.

"Stay where you are, barkeep."

Stockburn hoisted himself up and over the bar. He stepped forward, looking around, Peacemakers extended. He saw a hand reaching for a Smith & Wesson .44 with the initials T.J. engraved in the walnut grip. The hand was thick, brown, and hairy.

"T. J. Hanover?" Stockburn said. Another of Red

Bascom's old gang. Stockburn had honestly thought he was dead. He'd heard Hanover had been killed by a drunk whore in Phoenix some years ago.

The head belonging to the extended hand turned to gaze up at Stockburn. Coal-black eyes set too far apart in a long, horsey face under a cap of curly, black hair. The man had a silver upper front tooth. Hanover, all right. Never trust what you hear but haven't verified with your own eyes.

He opened his mouth and flared a nostril, but the curse that was likely coming didn't make it to his lips before Stockburn's Colt roared.

"Now, he's dead," Stockburn said. "And that's a fact."

CHAPTER 9

"Oh, lordy—look at my place! Look at my place! Just *look* at this place!"

"I have to admit it looked a whole lot better ten minutes ago."

"Just *look* at it!"

The stocky barman shambled out from behind the bar, the back of his shirt soaked with spilled liquor. Broken glass still clung to his shoulders and peppered his nearly bald head. He held his arms out before him as though in supplication. He was still sobbing from fright, but there was a good bit of grief for the condition of his business establishment mixed in with the fear.

"I see it, and I do apologize for my part in it, amigo." Stockburn walked around behind the bar and crouched to peruse the shelves beneath it. They were not only empty but bullet-shredded. When he found a labeled bottle—one of the very few bottles with labels on the premises, it appeared—he set it on top of the bullet-scarred bar and pried the cork from the lip. "There wasn't much I could do. I just asked a simple enough question . . . one that I'm still waiting for an answer to, by the way." He found an intact shot glass and set it on the bar beside the bottle.

"Look at the blood! My God, it's everywhere!"

"I see that. I can only say I'm grateful mine isn't down there, as well."

"It's going to take me two, three days to clean this up."

"I'd say you're right. Even with help. And, again, I do apologize. You had it looking real nice. Driscoll had let it go so that you could see daylight between the boards. That's some nice whitewashing you did to the walls. And those windows—were they new?"

"Yes, they were new! They cost me a purty penny, too! Had them freighted in from Bismarck. One hundred and twenty miles!"

Stockburn sipped the whiskey. Not bad bourbon for this neck of the feral prairie. "You must have bought the place from Driscoll since I last pulled through here."

The barman was still stumbling around as though drunk, wagging his head, his cheeks swollen and red from crying. "He called me out here to buy in with him. He was my brother-in-law. His wife, Mary, is my sister."

"He's still in town, then?"

"No." The barman was deeply distracted. He tripped over a chair leg then said, "I mean . . . yes, he's still here. He's in the cemetery. He's still here but he's dead. Quite dead, I'm afraid."

"Really? That's too bad. I liked Jim." Stockburn meant it. Jim Driscoll had been a nice fellow. Not very hard-working, though, which had been plainly evident by the fact that he had let the saloon disintegrate while he'd owned it. Stockburn remembered seeing rats nibbling food scraps near the piano, and a bird's nest on a ceiling beam. "What happened? Heart?"

Driscoll had complained to Stockburn of chest pains.

The barman stopped to gaze down at one of the dead men, then turned to regard the tall, gray-haired, gray-mustached detective standing behind the bar. The big apron frowned with annoyance. Understandably, he wasn't in a chatty frame of mind. "Huh?"

"I said did Jim die of heart trouble? Last time I passed through here he was complaining of chest pains."

"He was hanged by a local vigilance committee."

"No! Jim?"

"Yes." The barman picked up an overturned chair then wagged his head at the blood on the floor around it. "He was caught cattle rustling."

"I find that hard to believe."

"Well, truth be known, he'd been at it for years. He told me all about it after he lured me out here from Pittsburgh to buy in with him. He was stashing the money away in a box in his and Mary's root cellar. Turns out he had a lady on the side. He didn't tell me that part, but Mary found the notes they'd exchanged. *Love* notes. Rather descriptive. A local lady. Also married. She even had the *gall* to attend Jim's funeral."

"No!"

The barman turned to Stockburn again. "With her *husband*!"

The detective wagged his head, genuinely surprised by the tale, trying to marry it to the Jim Driscoll he'd known. "Just goes to show you can never tell about people."

"No, you certainly can't."

"Hanged him, huh?"

The barman accidentally stepped in a puddle of blood, lifted his foot to see the ooze on the bottom of his shoe, and made a face. "Played cat's cradle with his head, all right. Found him one night with eight head of stolen beef, and hanged him from a cottonwood."

"Frontier justice."

"Charming, isn't it?"

Stockburn threw back the rest of the bourbon, swallowed, and set his empty glass back down on the bar. He pulled one of his empty Colts and began reloading. "Well, my condolences to you and his wife. That's tough news. But if you wouldn't mind getting back to the original question . . ."

The barman had returned to the bar. He sighed and looked at Stockburn, scowling incredulously. "Original question?"

"Yeah, the one that touched the flame to the fuse of Lonigan Fixx and the other tough nuts lying dead down there."

The barman slapped the bar, flabbergasted. "I hope you'll forgive me, hombre, but after all that's happened in such a short amount of time—the ruining of my place, no less—I've forgotten what that was!"

Stockburn dropped a reloaded Peacemaker into its holster, refilled his shot glass, and slid it across the bar to the barman. "Red Bascom."

"Oh. Right." The barman winced and shook his head again, no doubt remembering the fiasco that had followed the first mention of Bascom's name. "What about him?"

Stockburn started reloading his second Peacemaker from the shells on his cartridge belt. "Where is he?"

The barman fingered the filled shot glass then turned warily toward the dead men lying crumpled around him.

"Don't worry," Stockburn said. "They've had their horns filed and their teeth pulled."

"Yes, yes . . . well." The barman drew a breath then picked up the glass and tossed back the entire shot. Instantly, his face, which had gone as pale as his wet shirt, flamed bright red. He set the glass back down on the bar, scrubbed his fat, freckled forearm across his plump-lipped mouth, and said, "He's at his daughter's place. She's taking care of him. He's dying, I hear."

"His daughter's place?"

"Yes. She lives here. She's married to the owner of the mercantile—Fred Lawton. An unhappy lady—Peggy. Never one to smile. She has even less reason to smile now after that old outlaw moved into her house, wanting her to take care of him in his last days."

Stockburn spun the cylinder of the second loaded Colt and dropped the pretty piece into the holster on his right hip. "So, Bascom came here so his daughter and her husband would care for him until he dies."

"That's about the size of it. At least, that's what I hear. I've never seen Bascom himself. Just heard the stories."

Stockburn looked at Lonigan Fixx and the other five expired owlhoots. "What were these men doing here?"

"They were after some gold that Bascom apparently has hidden somewhere."

"Ah." That was the gold that Leo Crabbe had been talking about.

"What?"

"Nothing." Stockburn dug his bag of Durham out of

his coat pocket and started building a smoke. "Tell me about the gold."

"I only know what I overheard those jackals talking about." The apron tossed his chin toward the dead men. "Apparently, before Bascom spent time in jail, he double-crossed one of his gang and ended up with a sizeable portion of loot, which he squirreled away for retirement."

"He had foresight. You gotta give him that."

"They"—the apron jerked his chin at the dead men again—"were hoping he'd tell them where he'd hidden the loot before he passed. They'd go over there occasionally, to the Lawton house, by ones and twos, their hats in their hands, and sit with the old curly wolf for a time, hoping to endear themselves, I reckon."

The barman splashed some more whiskey into his glass. "Seems to me he'd leave it with his daughter and son-in-law, but maybe he figured they didn't need it, since Lawton owns the mercantile and seems to be doing a brisk business thanks to the ranchers and wheat farmers. I overheard a couple of them"—again he nodded toward the dead men—"speaking the other day, though, and it sounded like they were going to get tough, if needed."

"Must be a helluva lot of gold to bring Fixx and the others out of retirement and up from Old Mexico."

The barman shrugged. "Must be." He sipped his whiskey. "Those miscreants put the whole town on edge, me included. I knew they were going to be trouble and, sure enough, they were." He beetled his brows incriminatingly at Stockburn.

"I just asked a simple question," the detective said.

"I heard nothin' stays simple when you're around."

Stockburn fired his quirley and arched a brow at the man. "You know who I am?"

"Wolf Stockburn. Your reputation precedes you. Least-ways, I read some newspaper articles about you not long ago. Business slows down in here in the afternoon, before the punchers ride in to stomp with their tails up. Gives me plenty of time to read the newspapers a couple traveling drummers always bring me from Bismarck and Fargo.

"Yessir," the apron continued, studying the big detective with reproof, "nothing stays simple when the Wolf of the Rails is in town. Violence follows you 'like a hind-tit calf on its mother's heels.'" He gave a lopsided grin. "That there is a direct quote."

"Hmmm." Stockburn took another deep drag off the quirley. "I missed that one. Has a ring to it."

"It does."

"Say, where's Pee-Wee Todd? I figured he'd be here by now. The shooting must have been heard from one end of town to the other."

Pee-Wee Todd was the cowpuncher turned town marshal. He'd worn the five-pointed star in Cold Water Wells for a good decade or more, though he wasn't much good. But then, the town was small enough that it really didn't need a good lawman. In fact, Stockburn had been a little surprised it had a lawman at all.

"Dead."

"You don't say!"

"Heart."

"Really?"

"Seized up on ole Pee-Wee while he was in the privy behind the jail. Went missing for over a week. The whole town looked high and low for him. Finally, someone thought to check the outhouse. This was last January. He was sitting there, frozen up like a marble statue with his baggy old denims pulled down around his ankles, a Montgomery Ward catalog open in his lap."

"Damn." Stockburn shook his head. "I reckon there's worse ways to go than sitting in the crapper with the Wish Book."

"The man had his dreams."

"There you go." Stockburn took another couple of puffs from his quirley then dropped it on the floor and mashed it out with his boot. "Well, if you'll give me directions to the Lawton house, I'll be on my way."

He got directions, refilled the shot glass, tossed back the bourbon, and headed for the batwings. "Good day, amigo."

CHAPTER 10

Wolf swung Smoke off the town's main drag and headed north along a secondary street that was merely a two-track wagon trail that continued on out of town and snaked off into the vast, grassy ocean of prairie beyond.

Two hundred yards from town it dropped into a bowl, then another two hundred yards beyond the bowl, looking like a brown thread from that distance, it climbed another low jog of buttes and disappeared down the other side.

It led out to the L. T. Connected, the Diamond J, and the Box 7, Stockburn knew, having traversed this country before while chasing train robbers and looking for his sister. In fact, he found himself looking for her even now, if only with one part of his mind. The part that was always looking for Emily made him rein Smoke to a halt when he'd ridden only the equivalent of one city block off Cold Water Wells' main street.

A woman in a simple gray sack dress was standing off the rear corner of a humble log shack with a sagging front stoop. Using a wooden stick, she was beating a pair of colorful rugs hanging on a line. Her hair was long and black and twisted into one thick braid. A colorful cambric scarf was tied under her chin; it rippled brightly in the prairie breeze, flashing in the sunshine. Two small children played with a spotted puppy in the brush near where several washtubs sat in the high grass around a pile of cut firewood.

Stockburn sat Smoke's back, studying the woman. She was mostly turned away from him as she beat the rugs, causing dust to billow on the sunlit air.

He couldn't see her face. He waited for her to turn toward him. Only then could he pass. He couldn't ride past her, just as he couldn't ride past any dark-haired woman roughly the age Emily would be if she were still alive.

Not until he knew it wasn't Emily.

But how would he know that? How did he ever know that? So many years had passed. How could he identify her after all this time? How could she identify him? She'd only been eight when she'd been taken. He'd been fifteen. He was a man now climbing into early middle age.

Still, he thought he'd know. Somehow, he thought he'd know . . .

One of the children, a small round-faced girl with a cap of straight brown hair, pointed a plump, wet finger toward Stockburn and said something he couldn't hear above the humming breeze. The woman glanced at the little girl.

She stopped beating the rugs and swung her head toward Stockburn, following the little girl's pointing finger.

The woman's eyes met Stockburn's, and she jerked back a little with a start and a gasp, dropping her stick and placing her hand on her chest.

"Oh mein Gott, du hast mich erschreckt!" she exclaimed. Oh my God, you frightened me.

Stockburn held up his hand, palm out, in apology. He

smiled, pinched his hat brim to the woman, nudged Smoke with the spurless heels of his boots, and continued north along the two-track trace.

That wasn't Emily. True, the Sioux might have sold her to a German family. This prairie teemed with Germans and Russians. But the face wasn't right.

He remembered his sister's eight-year-old face. It was blazed into his mind so that he saw it every morning upon waking; it was the last image he saw every night before slumber took him. Her voice—her high, screaming pleas as she was snatched away over the back of the warrior's painted pony—was the last sound he heard. They always took a long time fading.

No, that woman wasn't Emily. A German shopkeeper's wife, most likely. Not Emily. He'd know his sister if he ever saw her again, though the possibility of that grew more and more unlikely with every day that passed. That knowledge was an anguish that lingered inside of Wolf Stockburn. Not unlike the story about his friend Mike, it was a very slow-growing cancer, a pain that he tended daily, sometimes hourly. He knew he could never banish the ache completely.

No, not Emily. Still, he always had to check.

The Lawton house drowsed in the midafternoon sunshine.

It sat at the very edge of town, flanked by a small barn and a buggy shed, and was ringed with transplanted trees and flowers. The neat, stately, wood-frame affair was painted butter yellow with a white front porch. Two lilac bushes sat to each side of the porch steps. It being July, the lilacs had bloomed several weeks ago, but the dried-up remains of those flowers remained on the otherwise deep green shrubs.

A bird had built a neat little nest in the green branches. It remained even though all of the little ones had long since flown away to manage on their own.

Stockburn stopped Smoke at the edge of the yard, well outside of the freshly painted white picket fence, to admire the house, neatly trimmed grass, the pretty flowers and well-cared-for shrubs, and the perfect brick path that ran from the gate to the porch.

Nice. Damn nice.

It was the home of a virtuous, well-behaved town couple. The type who attended church every Sunday, whose kids—if they had kids—likely went to school and received all As and Bs and fished for catfish in the local creek on the way home. The man of the house was a civic booster, wore a tailored suit, had his hair trimmed weekly, and maybe blew a horn in the town band. The wife was likely president of a social committee and hosted Bible-study classes during which no one drank anything stronger than weak tea or coffee.

It was hard to reconcile these ideal digs to the old train robber and cold-blooded killer with Red Bascom.

Was he really here or had the barman been pulling Stockburn's leg?

Only one way to find out.

Wolf booted Smoke up to the fence and swung down from the saddle. He'd just finished tying the reins around a picket when the front door opened and a birdlike woman in a simple gingham dress stepped out onto the porch. She held a long side-by-side twelve-gauge shotgun and she aimed it in Stockburn's general direction as she pressed her back to the front of the house, just right of the door.

She was skinny and pale, and she looked very tired. Her brown hair, peppered with gray, was pulled back into a bun behind her head. Her voice was taut and weary as she said, "I told you men I don't want you coming around here anymore. I've had enough. I told you to stay away. My *husband* told you to stay away! I have a gun now, and my husband taught me how to use it, so you just get back up on that horse and ride away. For the last time!"

She almost sobbed on those last two words.

Stockburn turned to her and shaped an affable smile. "I'm not one of them, Mrs. Lawton."

She just stared at him, frowning. Even her eyes appeared washed out. She was so slight, her arms so thin, that she could barely hold the big barn-blaster, let alone raise it. If she were to fire it, it would likely kick her back off the other side of the porch and into the grass beyond.

"Stockburn's the name. Wolf Stockburn. I'm a detective with Wells Fargo." He reached slowly inside his coat, withdrew his black leather wallet, and held up the copper shield pinned inside. "See?"

Mrs. Lawton lowered the shotgun slightly, or maybe she just couldn't keep it raised anymore. She swallowed and licked her thin, chapped lips. "I don't know anything about any gold, Mr. Stockburn."

"I'm not here about gold, ma'am."

"Oh? Then what are you here for?"

"I'm here about the train robbers known as the Devil's Horde."

She gave a deep sigh, looking even wearier than before.

She was obviously exhausted. Anxious and weary and staggering from the enormous weight that her outlaw father had placed on her by coming to her home to die.

She let the shotgun hang down low at her side. "Oh, what a horror all of this is. I do apologize for . . . for this, Mr. Stockburn." She glanced at the Greener. "I never thought I would have to wield one of these. To threaten anyone with it, much less. But my husband isn't here. He's at the mercantile, and . . . with those awful men . . . my father's former cohorts . . . constantly coming around . . ."

"You won't have to worry about those men anymore, ma'am."

She frowned curiously, vaguely hopeful, at Stockburn.

"Do you mind if I come in, Mrs. Lawton?" Wolf gestured at the gate in the fence before him.

"Oh, of course, of course. Please." She made a weak beckoning gesture. "I'm sorry."

"No trouble, ma'am."

Stockburn flipped the gate's latch and stepped into the yard. He latched the gate behind him, then, politely doffing his sombrero, made his way along the level brick path. He stopped and looked up at the woman gazing curiously down at him, her thin, sandy brows beetled.

"They . . . left . . . ?" she asked.

"I reckon you could say that." Stockburn shaped a cockeyed smile.

She sagged backward a little as though under yet another burden. "Oh. Oh . . . dear . . ."

"At least they're out of your hair."

"Yes, yes. I will . . . I will say a prayer . . ."

"Won't do much good. Not for them. On the other hand, I reckon it couldn't hurt, neither."

"I feel as though I should. My husband and I . . . Fred . . . we're churchgoing people. We host socials and have formed a sobriety league."

Stockburn studied her. His befuddlement must have been obvious.

"Oh, yes, I know," Mrs. Lawton said. "How on earth did Red Bascom raise a pious daughter?"

"Took the thought right out of the air between my ears, ma'am."

"I don't know, to be honest with you." She shrugged a shoulder. "There must be some relatively good blood somewhere in the Bascom line. My mother wasn't much good, either, unfortunately. After my mother died, my father sent me to live with distant relatives back in Iowa. Council Bluffs, to be exact. Fred and I came out here after we were married, when his family's mercantile burned down and we needed a fresh start. Those distant relatives were good folk. They raised me well. I certainly wasn't prepared . . ." She lifted her eyes as though to indicate the neat little house's second story above her head. "I certainly wasn't prepared to see him . . . my father again . . . after all these years."

"You must have stayed in *some* contact."

"We exchanged brief letters now and then."

"I reckon it's been quite a burden. Taking him in, I mean. Quite the cross to bear, no pun intended, to take in your outlaw father here in a good Christian town. Being civic-minded, churchgoing folk, and all. I'm sure you'll be duly rewarded one day, Mrs. Lawton. I reckon even the likes of Red Bascom deserve a peaceable ending. After all, he did serve his time. Most of it, anyway."

"What else could we do—Fred and me? He has no

one else. I'm his only child. I make him as comfortable as I can."

"Cancer, I heard."

"Yes, it's in his lungs."

Suddenly, a loud voice thundered from somewhere above: "For cryin' in Grant's whiskey, stop that infernal chatter and send the man up here, Mary! I'm the one he wants to see. He didn't come here to have his damn ear chewed off!"

Stockburn hadn't thought it possible, but Mary Lawton's face turned a shade paler. She drew another deep breath into her flat sparrow's chest and let it out slowly. She gave a thin, brittle smile, and said, "Speak of the devil."

"I heard that!" thundered the voice of Red Bascom. He chuckled. The chuckle turned into a fit of violent coughing. The coughing turned so raucous that it made Stockburn's own lungs ache.

Mary stepped back and tossed her head toward the half open door. "You've been summoned, Mr. Stockburn. Take the stairs. You'll see them there at the end of the foyer. Just follow the din . . . and the stench, unfortunately . . . to the old devil's lair."

CHAPTER 11

Mrs. Lawton had been right about the stench. Stockburn smelled it well before he'd gained the top of the dimly lit stairs. He'd smelled the odor before, as had most folks who'd reached the age of forty.

Sickness. Cancer. Death.

More deep hacking reached Stockburn's ears from a partly open door at the end of the hall. A weary growling followed, a loud splat, and then: "Come on in, Wolf. I been waitin' on you, ya nasty old railroad dick!"

Stockburn stopped at the top of the stairs and canted his head slightly to one side. "You don't have a Greener to match your daughter's in there—do you, Red?"

Raspy, wheezing laughter was followed by another brief bout of hacking. "You're smart to be cautious. But if I'd wanted you dead, you'd be dead by now, Stockburn."

The detective continued forward, stopped at the end of the hall, and nudged the door wider. Bascom didn't have a shotgun. At least, none was visible, though he might be housing a pistol or two beneath the patchwork quilts that all but buried him.

Even if the old train robber did have a gun under there

somewhere, Stockburn doubted he could wield it. Red looked frailer than his daughter, who'd taken after him a little in the broad, high forehead and long jaw. The eyes were distinctly different. While Mary's were grave, hesitant, apprehensive, Red Bascom's eyes were amber-tan, glinting with devilish amusement.

His thick lips were curled upward at the corners. He had three or four days' worth of beard stubble on his sickness-ravaged, skeletal face, and a golden sheen of sweat glinted among the steel-colored bristles in the light from a near window with drawn back lacy pink curtains.

A porcelain thunder mug peeked out from beneath the bed. The wood-handled cover was only partway on. That was likely the source of much of the stench. Another source was the porcelain washbasin on the marble-topped stand to Red's right. It was covered in bloody cotton cloths.

The largest culprit, of course, was Red Bascom himself.

His egg-shaped head appeared too large for the rest of him . . . at least for the outline of his ravaged body outlined by the bedcovers. His curly hair was long and gray, brushed or smoothed straight back from where it began about halfway across the top of his head. His mustache, oddly, was still mostly red, with only a little gray in it.

His breathing was an irregular grumbling sound—half breathing, half strangling. The man's insignificant chest rose and fell heavily, sometimes shuddering or jerking a little.

"Sorry for the stink. I can't complain about it overmuch myself, on account of that was what finally got me furloughed. The warden was tired of the other prisoners and the guards complaining about my death stench, which began, oddly enough, before I really felt all that miserable."

"Go figure."

"Did you meet the apple of her daddy's eye?"

"I did."

"Mary's a gospel grinder. So is her husband. They spew it at me every morning and every evening. They swallow it down raw from the local sky pilot. Butter wouldn't melt in the mouth of either of them. They won't allow me whiskey, only laudanum prescribed by the local sawbones. But the laudanum gives me crazy dreams. In one I'm walking buck naked around the streets of some eastern city looking for a lady named Lil and doing all I can to keep my third leg from being discovered." Bascom started to chuckle, then hacked up phlegm, leaned to one side, and spat the large gob of bloody flotsam into the bowl with the nasty rags.

"It's the strangest thing, too. No one seems to notice this old gray-haired man stumbling around, naked as a Tonto Sioux at a sun dance." The old train robber clapped and laughed. A little blood bubbled out of a corner of his mouth but he didn't bother to wipe it or spit it away.

"Have a seat," he told Stockburn. "Pull up a chair." He gave the weakest of bony hand waves toward Stockburn's right to indicate a brocade-bottomed chair with arms scrolled into lion's paws. "Pull it up, pull it up. Let's have a chat. I get lonesome. Adam and Eve are tryin' to discourage the boys from visiting me anymore. They say my friends are *uncouth* and *dirty*. They also bring me whiskey and smokes. But the real problem lies elsewhere."

"The real problem?"

Bascom shrugged his spindly shoulders. "Never mind."

Stockburn dragged the chair up from the corner, slacked into it, and leaned forward, absently turning the sombrero in his hands. "How long you got left?"

Bascom studied the detective closely, obliquely, the corner of one eye twitching slightly. "Hell, I should be dead by now. The sawbones in the pen gave me three months a year ago. Sometimes I think I'm already dead and dreaming. *Nightmaring*, more like." He paused then brushed the blood from the corner of his mouth with a sleeve of his light-blue nightshirt. "Or maybe this is hell. Slowly dying. Stinking to high heaven. Hacking up the wreckage of my lungs. Just a little bit at a time. Making it harder and harder to breathe. Just lying here, suffocating and reflecting on my younger years when I was wild and free. Before the Gray Wolf ran me down . . . incarcerated me in that hellhole in Michigan."

"Sorry about that, Red."

"No, you're not."

"You're right. I'm not. You had it coming. I was shocked when they didn't hang you."

"That woulda been lettin' me off easy . . . after all I done."

"You have a point there, Red. Still, you're alive when so many you killed are not. Haven't been for a number of years."

"This is not living, Wolf."

"Again, you do have a point, Red."

"Go over to that bureau back there, will ya? Open the top drawer. Lonny Fixx left me a little present last time he visited."

Stockburn set his sombrero at the foot of Bascom's bed, near Red's long, bony feet pushing up the covers. "Ah, the devil's brew," Stockburn said, wrapping his hand around the labeled bottle of whiskey that had been concealed under socks, folded hankies, and a cedar jewelry box. Two shot glasses nestled against the bottle, wrapped in a red handkerchief with white polka dots. He took the bottle and the two glasses over to the bed, set them down on the washstand, filled the glasses from the bottle, and handed one of the glasses to Bascom.

"Devil's brew." Bascom chuckled. "That's what she calls it, all right. Strictly off-limits."

Stockburn picked up his own glass and sat back down in the chair. "What're you going to do if she kicks your wretched ass out, Red?"

"Oh, she won't do that." Hungrily, Bascom sucked whiskey off the top of the glass then licked it off his overgrown mustache. He winked. "Trust me on that!"

"Oh?"

"You know that gold Mary mentioned? When you just rode up to the house?"

"Yes."

"She figured you was here for it, because my old gang is here for it. They're hopin' I'll tell 'em where I stowed it before I expire. They come in here—leastways, they did—puckerin' up to my behind, askin' if I need anything to make my passing more comfortable. Ha! Now I reckon they're just waitin' like buzzards over at the Red Moon to hear that I've saddled a golden cloud."

"Would you tell 'em?"

"Nah." Bascom suppressed another cough. "Mary ain't as pious as she lets on. She knows all about that gold. In fact, I gave her an' her fancy-dan of a husband half up front to let me die here in peace."

Stockburn chuckled remembering the so-called pious woman's denials downstairs. "Boy, she sure fooled me."

"She did, didn't she?" Bascom cackled. "She ain't all that different from me, when you get right down to it. I told her an' Fred they'd get the other half after I died. I left a map to its whereabouts amongst my papers in here. They can look for it once they've given me a proper burial. I made 'em swear on a Bible, an' you know what?"

"They did."

"They sure enough did!" Bascom slapped his thigh as he cackled out more laughter that promptly turned into what sounded like a lung-shredding fit of raucous coughing. The harder he laughed the more blood he spit up until one whole arm of his top was soaked with the rancid-smelling stuff.

"Damn," he said when he'd finally settled down. "Gospel grinders . . ."

"Yeah."

Bascom frowned. "What did you mean by *would* I tell them? Why not say 'was I *going* to' tell them?"

"Would you tell them if you got another chance, I meant. Purely speculative. They're all layin' dead over at the Red River Saloon." Stockburn smiled.

"Oh, ho-ho-ho!" The old outlaw flopped his arms, incredulous but also genuinely amused. "Oh, boy! Ain't you somethin', though, Wolf?"

"I like to think so."

"Oh, ho-ho-ho!"

Stockburn chuckled then sipped his own shot. He leaned forward again, holding the shot glass between his spread knees. Glancing at the half-open window, he said, "All right, Red. You know why I'm here."

Bascom took another hungry swallow of his whiskey

like a man who'd stumbled across the desert to drink at a cold running spring at long last. "Yes, I do," he said raggedly. He turned to Stockburn and grinned his coyote grin, eyes flashing again with devilish delight. "The Devil's Horde."

"Who are they? You know, don't you?"

Bascom studied Stockburn for a long time, teasing, tormenting. The old reprobate had the upper hand at long last, and he was going to exploit the hell out of it. He was going to enjoy it.

"Yeah," he wheezed finally. "I know who they are. Who their leader is. Where they come from. Why they do what they do."

"They do what you used to do, Red."

"What's that?"

"Come in from all points of the compass and retreat in the same directions. Confusing their sign. Making them almost impossible to track. They took a page out of your book. That's how *I* knew *you* know who they are. Or that there was a good chance you do, anyway. And I can see I did not miss my guess."

"No, no. You didn't miss your guess, Wolf."

"Who are they, Red? *Where* are they?"

"Why should I tell you?"

Stockburn shrugged. "Maybe it'll keep you from going to Hell."

"Nah. Too late for that."

"Maybe it'll make you rest a little easier, knowing that at long last you did one good thing before you die."

"I don't care about that."

Frustration was building in Stockburn. He was growing desperate. Desperate enough to try to mine another vein.

"Please, Red. Innocent people are dying. Surely, lying

here all these months, rotting from the inside out, you must have done some reflecting."

Bascom laughed. "Me? Nah." He shook his head. "Not a bit."

"Tell me."

Bascom sat up a little, red-faced with anger. "Tell me why I should, and I will!"

Again, Stockburn shrugged a shoulder. "Call it a nod toward old times."

"Old times? You hunted me down and put me away. For twelve years!"

"You had fun. You enjoyed the cat and mouse."

Bascom narrowed a skeptical eye at the rail detective. "Did you?"

"Of course. I enjoy this racket. I like working this side of the law as much as you enjoyed working the other side of it."

"We're really not all that different, are we, Wolf?"

"Yes, we are." Stockburn threw back the last of his whiskey. "True, we're both tough men. Hard men. *Uncompromising* men. But you're a cold-blooded killer, Red. When I kill, it's justified. When I ran you down and sent you up the river, I enjoyed putting you away. Just another wild dog off the streets." He set his empty shot glass on the washstand and climbed to his feet. He pulled the Colt from the holster on his left hip, and aimed it down at Bascom's head. "Tell me who ramrods the Devil's Horde. Tell me where I'll find him. Or I'll kill you, Red."

Bascom arched a brow. "That'd be cold-blooded murder, Wolf."

"Justified murder, the way I see it."

Bascom laughed his wheezing, liquid laugh then spat

a gob of bloody phlegm into the washbowl beside him. Sinking back against his pillows again, he said, "You've always kind of rewritten the laws to suit you—haven't you, Stockburn?"

"Sometimes . . . out here on the frontier . . . it's necessary."

"So, you're gonna murder me in my own bed . . . in my daughter's house . . . if I don't tell you about the train robbers . . . ?"

Stockburn narrowed his right eye as he aimed down the nickeled barrel at a large liver spot on Bascom's forehead, just above the man's right eye. "You got it."

"Ha!" Again, the dying outlaw laughed. "No, you won't." He reached up with his clawlike hand and shoved the Peacemaker aside. "You're right, Wolf. We are different. I'm a cold-blooded killer. You, however, are not. You rewrite the laws some, but mostly you walk the straight an' narrow. Pride yourself on it. That's what makes you respected and feared. It's also what makes you incapable of pulling that trigger."

Respected, maybe, but not respectable. This is one dying outlaw who is not going to hear about Mike.

Bascom grimaced, shook his head. "God, how I wish you could pull that trigger, though, Wolf. I'd love nothin' better than a sudden end to this misery. But you won't give it to me. You don't think I deserve it. You're bluffin'. You want me to die slow, drowning in my own bitter juices. Wolf—you shouldn't tease a man like that!" He gritted his teeth, throwing his head back and groaning in frustration, blood dribbling out both corners of his mouth. "Damn you, Stockburn!"

Cheeks warming with the embarrassment of having

been so transparent, Wolf holstered the Colt, grabbed his hat, and strode toward the open door. He'd had enough. He'd been a fool to have thought he'd be able to coax information out of the old sinner. He should have known he'd get nothing out of him. Why would he?

Stockburn had put him away for over a decade. All those years in jail hadn't reformed him a bit. If anything, they had shrunk his heart even more, made it even blacker.

A damned wasted trip.

"Go to Hell, Red," Stockburn said as he stepped out into the hall. "I mean that literally."

"Hold on."

The detective stopped. Frowning, he turned back to the room. Bascom stared at him from his deep eye sockets—a skeleton of a man already shaping a death grimace. The old outlaw just stared at Stockburn. The expression on such an emaciated face was impossible to read.

Red gave a feeble wave, beckoning.

Wolf sighed and walked back into the room.

Bascom grinned his droll death's-head grin. "I won't tell you who they are."

"Maybe you don't know."

"Oh, I know, all right. Their leader was here . . . to see me . . . before he started hitting the Northern Pacific. Being the longtime professional I am, he wanted my help."

Stockburn waited. He didn't expect much, but he waited, just the same.

"I do all the planning."

"What?"

"I planned the two previous robberies. The gang leader comes to me with all the information, and I help him plan when and where."

Stockburn's heart thudded. He'd had a feeling Bascom was in on the planning. The strikes had had his marks on them.

"Who is he, Red? Where will I find him?"

Bascom only smiled, delighting in Stockburn's consternation.

"All right. If that's all you have, I'll hunt him down on my—"

"Hold on."

Stockburn had started toward the door again, but stopped and turned back around. "Look, Red, I get it. You're enjoying the turning of the tables. You're the cat now. I'm the mouse. All right, but—"

"They're gonna strike the Northern Pacific two miles west of the Weatherford Station."

Again, Stockburn's heart thudded as the blood moved more quickly through his veins. "When?" He expected the old outlaw just to lay there, grinning at him, teasing him.

But then Red opened his mouth and wheezed out slowly: "Seven o'clock tonight." His smile broadened. His eyes drew up at the corners.

"Seven o'clock?" Stockburn's heart pumped faster. "*Tonight?*"

Bascom winked.

Stockburn backed up then turned to gaze out the window, digesting the information. He reached into his vest pocket and pulled out his old windup railroad Ingersoll. He studied the black gothic hands through the cracked glass. Two minutes after three in the afternoon. If Bascom wasn't telling a big windy just to jerk his old nemesis's chain, that meant the train would be held up . . . and a good many more innocent people killed . . . in less than four hours.

"Four hours," he said aloud. "Four hours."

"Yep."

Stockburn turned, breathing hard. Somehow, he had to stop that train. Immediately, his thoughts went to the nearest telegraph office. Did Cold Water Wells have a Western Union? He glanced at Bascom.

Red lay back against his pillows, grinning like the cat that ate the canary. Slowly, he shook his head. He was reading the detective's mind. "Nope. There ain't a telegraph within a hundred miles of here, Wolf." His raspy voice and his gaze were taunting, jeering.

But Stockburn had already known there was no Western Union there. The telegraph system did not connect the little backwater towns.

What the hell was he going to do? The Devil's Horde was going to pull another robbery, but being a hundred miles away, without any way to alert the station agent in Fargo, Stockburn was powerless to do anything about it.

Anything at all . . .

He looked at Bascom again. The man was telling the truth. He wasn't lying. And he was enjoying every second of Stockburn's consternation.

The detective started for the door again.

"I reckon I had the last laugh—didn't I, Wolf?" Bascom wheezed behind him.

Striding down the hall, Stockburn said again, "Go to Hell, Red. I mean that literally."

The old outlaw's only response was more elated, wheezing, strangling laughter.

CHAPTER 12

Stockburn walked down the stairs. As he crossed the foyer to the front door, the kitchen door slammed on his left. He stopped with a start, automatically stretching his right hand across his belly to close it around the grips of the Peacemaker holstered on his left hip.

He kept the gun in its holster. The door's sudden closing had been no threat. Mary Lawton had likely heard Stockburn and her father talking upstairs. About the gold. She'd closed the door in shame and was likely cowering away in her kitchen, trying to hide from her own hypocrisy.

"Don't worry, lady," the detective muttered, continuing through the door and onto the porch. "I don't give a damn about your gold. You should, though—given how many people your father had likely killed when he'd stolen it." He paused on the porch, his feet suddenly growing heavy. His plight was an anvil on his shoulders.

The train. How in the hell was he going to stop the blasted train? How was he going to alert the crew? He looked around as though for an answer. None came. There was only the tidy yard with the bright, cheery flowers and shrubs tended by Christians with blood on their hands.

He walked down the steps, stopped on the third step, and sat down. He dug the makings out of his coat pocket and pensively rolled a smoke. He scratched a lucifer to life on the porch rail, lit the quirley, and sat puffing it, thinking.

Desperately thinking.

He wanted to scream.

Four hours.

A hundred miles.

No way to cover that much ground in that little time. Just no way. If he tried, he'd kill his horse before he got even halfway. He'd ruin the stallion long before he even reached the midway point, for sure.

Come on, Stockburn. Think!

He puffed the cigarette, removed the sombrero, and ran a big, sun-bronzed hand through his roached gray mane. He tugged at the hair in frustration.

You were a Pony Express rider, fer chrissakes!

Wait.

That's it!

He dropped the cigarette on the step and gave it a cursory mashing with his boot. He reached into a coat pocket, withdrew a small notebook with a brown pasteboard cover and a pencil stub. Flipping to a clean leaf, he did some scribbling, starting with a short squiggly line reaching from the page's bottom left corner to within an inch of the middle. That was Montpelier Creek. He drew another squiggly line above it, slanting toward the left and with a severe upward dogleg at the very end near the top of the page. That was Cottonwood Creek. Across the very top of the leaf, from left to right, he drew a relatively straight line with hatch marks through it—the Northern Pacific rails.

He returned the pencil to the leaf's bottom left corner and started scribbling Xs along both creeks on each side until he'd worked his way back up to the top of the page and the line indicating the Northern Pacific rails. He'd scribbled five Xs.

Each of those Xs was a ranch or a stage relay station where he knew he could find a good horse. Several farms were scattered along those creeks, but Stockburn knew he could count on the ranches and one relay station for good horseflesh. He knew he'd find a horse with Morgan blood at Jordan Walsh's L.T. Connected.

He knew every ranch and most of the farms along Montpelier and Cottonwood Creeks, stretching from just outside of Cold Water Wells to the Northern Pacific line. The ranches he'd marked lay anywhere from ten to twenty miles apart—roughly the same distance the Pony Express relay stations had been laid out on the old cross-country trail.

Having been through this country several times over the years, searching for Emily. he'd gotten to know the ranchers and farmers and relay station attendants. Some he even counted as friends.

All, he knew, would lend him a horse on his wind-splitting relay run to the Northern Pacific line.

He closed the book and returned it and the pencil to his pocket. He rose, hope lightening his heart. He hadn't ridden for the Express in a good twenty years. Not quite twenty back then and still a kid, now he was pushing forty. He didn't know if he had that kind of a hell-for-leather ride in him anymore, but he sure as hell was going to try. He had no other choice.

He swung up into the saddle, rode back into the heart of town, and let Smoke have a good long drink and a bait of oats while Stockburn filled his canteen at the city well. He chewed some jerky he found in his coat pocket. That's all he'd have to eat for a while. It would have to do.

Horse and rider fortified, Stockburn swung up into the saddle, trotted the horse to the mouth of Montpelier Creek, picked up the trail that lead to the northern ranches, and booted the stallion into a hard run.

The L.T. Connected was twenty-five miles nearly straight north of Cold Water Wells. By the time Stockburn reached it, Smoke was blowing and sweat-lathered, but he wasn't blown out. The horse could have gone farther. He was one-quarter Morgan with a deep bottom, and he loved to run. What's more, he loved to show off, and he loved to please his owner.

But Stockburn valued good horseflesh in general and Smoke in particular far too much to blow him out. It was time for Smoke to rest. His leg of the job was done. Time for the detective to acquire a fresh mount.

The L.T. Connected's owner, Jordan Walsh, was walking away from the three men sitting on the corral fence when Stockburn thundered under the ranch headquarters' wooden crossbar into which the L.T. Connected's brand had been burned. Walsh jerked around quickly, opening his mouth with surprise and dropping the cigarette that had been clamped between his lips. It shed sparks as it bounced from his wool shirt to the dirt at his worn boots.

The rancher automatically brushed his right hip with his right hand; a few years ago, when the Sioux were running roughshod over the hard-fought-for country, a hogleg would have bristled there.

A couple of the hands on the corral fence—those sporting six-shooters—reached for their holstered shooting irons before Stockburn held up his gloved right hand, palm out, and reined Smoke to a stop near the startled Walsh.

"Good Lord, Wolf!" the rancher said, scowling at the dust-caked detective and sweat-lathered horse. He waved off the hands. "What the hell brings you here on a bolt of greased lightning?" He chuckled, apparently relieved that he was not under Indian attack. "You do the wrong woman wrong, did you? Or did Miss Comanche try talking you into marriage again?"

The rancher and his hands chuckled.

Stockburn swung down from the leather. He was pleased to note that he still felt relatively fresh. Sun- and windburned, and a little stiff through the shoulders, but relatively fresh.

Blinking dust from his eyelashes, he looped his canteen over his head and right shoulder. He stripped his tack off the mount and dropped it in the dirt. "Jordie, I need a fresh horse pronto. I'm headed north to the Northern Pacific line. There's gonna be a holdup at seven tonight, and I need to stop that train!"

The rancher didn't need to be told twice. He glanced at the hands gathered on the corral fence, where they'd been overseeing another hand gentling a fine-looking sorrel pony at the snubbing post, and said, "Stump, rope Wild Blue and lead him out here!"

"You got it, boss!" The young cowhand leaped off the fence and ran toward the corral to the north of the round breaking corral.

"Little Bill, tend Smoke here, will you? Let him cool down some, then give him all the water he wants. Follow that up with a feed sack then brush the filth off him and give him a nice pile of hay."

"You bet, boss!"

As the smallest of the hands, wearing a bright red billowy neckerchief, leaped off the corral and strode toward the sweating gray, Walsh turned to Stockburn. The rancher was a whipcord lean, tall, rugged-looking man in his late fifties. He sported a thick, gray, soup-strainer mustache and blue eyes that were forever smiling.

A recent widower, Walsh had become a good friend of Stockburn over the years, forever keeping a sharp eye out for a young white woman who might have been raised by Indians. He'd written a couple of letters to Wolf in Kansas City, relaying possible leads that had, alas, not turned up the detective's missing sister.

"Wild Blue's full-blood Morgan," Walsh said. "He'll get you to the Diamond J faster 'n you could fly!"

Stockburn walked over to the water tank ringing the windmill. "That's what I was counting on, Jordie."

Walsh walked toward him, his features grave. "The Devil's Horde?"

"You got it."

Walsh clucked his disdain for the robbers.

Stockburn removed his hat then dunked his head in the tank's tepid, brackish water. When he came up for air, the refreshing water as well as what felt like a shovelful of trail grit cascaded from his head and shoulders, soaking his suit.

Walsh said, "You got a lead on 'em, I take it?"

Stockburn nodded. "I found Red Bascom in Cold Water Wells."

"Well, I'll be damned. I thought he was in—"

"Yeah. Me, too." Stockburn ran his hands back through his short hair then pressed the excess from his mustache. "He has cancer. He's dying slow."

"Good for him." Walsh scowled his disdain for the old outlaw.

Bascom had been a cattle rustler back before the railroads had come that far west, and he'd sold rifles and whiskey to the Indians. That had gotten him crossways with the local ranchers like Walsh.

"How'd you get him to tell you about the holdup?"

"I didn't." Stockburn grinned. "He doesn't think I can make it."

Walsh glanced at the angle of the sun. That's all he needed to know the time within a minute or two. "Do you think you can?"

"If Wild Blue's as wild as his name, and I can find equal or near-equal mounts farther up the creeks, I should make it just fine."

"Old Hamer's got him a chestnut with wild Arab and Morgan blood. He'll get you as far as the Box 7."

"I'll ask for it."

Stockburn strode over to where the hand called Stump was just then leading a big, blue-ebony Morgan through the gate of the second corral. The Morgan was a sleek, rangy beast with big, prominent eyes and well-rounded jowls. The long neck jutted from well-angulated shoulders.

The body was compact with a short back, broad loins, and deep flank. The flat-boned legs were straight with short cannons. The pasterns had sufficient length for a light, springy step.

The former Pony Express rider and current frequent imbiber of Kansas City horse races knew good horseflesh when he saw it.

Big Blue looked like a firecracker, to boot. He had his head up, blue mane rippling, and he was rolling his eyes, the whites flashing wildly, the pupils glinting as though flames burned inside.

Now, if Stockburn could just stay on him . . .

"I appreciate this, Jordie. I'll be back for Smoke." Stockburn helped Stump saddle Wild Blue then shoved his rifle into its scabbard strapped to the saddle's right side.

"Wolf, just what in the hell are you gonna do once you reach the rails? I mean, when the Horde converges on that train?"

Stockburn turned to the rancher, who equaled him in height. He frowned, briefly pensive, then grinned. "I got no idea. I reckon I'll cross that trestle when I steam up to it." He winked at his old friend then swung into the leather. "Good-bye, Jordie. Thanks for the hoss!"

"Anytime," Walsh yelled as Stockburn and the wild-eyed blue-black Morgan raced out under the ranch portal. "Just don't turn buzzard bait up there!"

Stockburn waved then grabbed the saddle horn, holding on for dear life as the stallion shot like a seven-hundred-pound black bullet straight up the trail along the creek.

CHAPTER 13

Stockburn exchanged the appropriately named Wild Blue for the lean, spring-footed chestnut Arab-Morgan at Franz Hamer's Diamond J ranch twenty miles north of the L.T. Connected.

He stormed into the headquarters of the Box 7 just as Lauren Reed and his wife, Jackie, were sitting down to supper with their three sons and two daughters. Reed's foreman, Kelly Alexander, roped and saddled a stocky dun quarter horse named Lucky Sam, and after taking a couple of pulls from the hide-covered whiskey flask proffered by Reed with a twinkle in his eyes, Stockburn caromed up the trail, following Cottonwood Creek to Bill Davis's Cottonwood Ranch.

Davis outfitted him with another quarter horse, this one named Devil. The name was explained when the horse bucked Stockburn off as he kicked toward the main gate, crow-hopping.

"Let him know who's boss, Wolf!" Bill Davis called from the brush arbor fronting his bunkhouse, where he stood with the three old grinning cowhands, smoking a pipe.

"Trouble is I think he already knows," the rail detective

grumbled, spitting dirt from his lips as he grabbed the reins and leaped back into the hurricane deck.

Devil tried bucking off his unfamiliar rider three more times as he and Stockburn headed north. But when the horse wasn't airing his spleen, it was a relatively smooth ride, and the colicky horse even seemed to enjoy the frantic pace as he and his rider raced up and over the buttes rising on both sides of the muddy ribbon of water that was the Cottonwood at that time of the year.

Stockburn exchanged Devil for a palomino named Golden Nugget, Nugget for short, at the stagecoach relay station on the sandy bank of Charlie's Wash. The Scottish-brogued Ma McDougal, who ramrodded the station as well as her three hostler sons, shoved an antelope sandwich into Stockburn's hand just before Nugget lunged off his rear hooves and thundered up the trail. Wolf ate half the sandwich while hunkered low in the saddle then threw the rest away. He was too desperate to reach the Northern Pacific rails to realize he was hungry. Besides, the pitching deck of a half-wild bronc wasn't the best place to digest a greasy meal.

Stockburn left the trail about twenty minutes after leaving the relay station and headed straight north, following the map in his mind. He wasn't sure how far away he still was from the rails, but according to his old railroad turnip, he was making good time. When the chalky buttes fell away behind him, he slowed to rest Nugget as well as himself and pulled the timepiece from his pocket once more.

Six forty-three.

With little time left, he crouched low and rammed his heels into the horse's loins again. The deep-bottomed mount lunged into another ground-chewing lope.

Stockburn gazed ahead and to his right and left, looking for the rails. They were near somewhere. No way that, heading north, he could miss them.

The horse's hooves thumped across the short-grass prairie. Stockburn could hear him blowing now, tiring. Oh, lordy, he was tired, too. He hadn't ridden like that since he'd been but a wet-behind-the-ears sprout riding for the Express. His rump, back, and neck all ached as though he'd been caught in a storm of Sioux arrows. His eyes and nose were dried out, and his face had been burned raw by the sun and wind.

"Come on, Nugget," he rasped into the horse's laid-back ears. "Just a little farther . . . keep going . . . keep going . . ." He spoke to himself as much as to his horse.

Finally, dead ahead, something glinted in the foreshort-ening shadows and angling sunlight. He looked for it again, but the glint was gone. He slowed the palomino to a walk. Again, the horse gave a weary blow. Stockburn knew how it felt.

He and the horse climbed a low knoll. He drew the horse to a halt and stared north.

The rails stretched from right to left before him. From left to right. Straight as twin carpenter's rules laid side by side. They came out of the grass and sky to his right and disappeared into the grass and sky to his left. Maybe two hundred yards away. He could just barely make them out. The sunlight glinting off the rails made them stand out from the tawny prairie, atop the mounded, cinder-paved bed corduroyed with stout wooden ties.

The problem facing him was that he didn't know his exact position along the Northern Pacific. He knew the little settlement of Weatherford, mostly just a small station with a water tank for the railroad as well as a catcher arm for the U.S. mail, was in the general area. But he wasn't sure if he was east or west of it.

He thought it was directly north, give or take a few miles, of Cold Water Wells, but those few miles made a big difference. If he was east of the town, the train might have already passed him, which would mean he was too late to help.

He nudged the poor, worn-out Nugget on ahead, gazing east. If the train was heading toward him as opposed to already having passed his position, it would come from that direction—from Fargo, likely having left around five-thirty or six o'clock. An hour to an hour and a half ago.

If it was still on its way, Stockburn could stop it and alert the crew of what they were in for. They could go back to the closest station in the east—he thought there were three stations between Fargo and Jamestown—and send a telegram to Fargo for help from the county sheriff, and send another wire ahead to Bismarck, summoning deputy U.S. marshals and a contingent of soldiers from Fort Lincoln.

Stockburn just hoped Red Bascom hadn't hornswoggled him. If so—if the train wasn't really due to be struck tonight—he'd look like one hell of a fool. On the other hand, it was a chance he was willing to take. Better safe than sorry. If the gang did strike tonight, many innocent people would die.

He checked his watch again and winced. Thirteen minutes past seven. "Damn."

He rode north another hundred yards then swung slightly off course toward a haystack bluff another hundred yards to the east. Stopping Nugget at the base of the bluff, Stockburn swung down from the saddle, struck the ground with a groan, and leaned forward, doffing his hat and pressing his forehead against the side of the tall horse. Aware he and the horse might have stopped moving, he realized his head hadn't. He felt like a drunk Irish sailor. One who'd been beaten on the New Orleans docks.

Such pain and exhaustion he hadn't felt in years. He blinked his eyes. They felt filled with sand. He unscrewed the cap from his canteen, took a long drink then poured the water into his eyes, blinking, trying to wash away the trail grit. The canteen he'd filled at Ma MacDougal's station hadn't yet gone completely warm. He took another long drink.

When he'd had his fill, he lowered his hat to the ground in front of Nugget and poured several inches of the water into the hat. While the horse drank greedily, Stockburn loosened his belly strap, making room for the water. The gesture was the least he could do after the stalwart runner had tried so hard to get him to the rails on time.

He pulled his field glasses out of his saddlebags, looped the lanyard around his neck, and climbed the bluff. Slipping on the sun-cured grass, he grunted with each miserable step.

Sweating and breathing hard, he gained the crest and spit out a bug that he'd nearly inhaled. It tasted bitter on his tongue, aggravating his surly mood.

He found a place to sit down on the bluff's relatively flat top, removed the glasses from their leather case, and scrutinized the eastern horizon. Nothing out there but grass and sky.

To the west, same.

Damned confounding.

Wolf lowered the glasses and leaned back against a hump of ground, resting. Below, he could hear the palomino chewing grass and occasionally rippling its withers and flanks against the pesky prairie flies. Soon, when the sun drifted farther down in the west and the air cooled, the mosquitoes would come out and make life truly miserable.

The breeze rose, brushing the tawny grass. It subsided then rose again, making sporadic whooshing sounds. The sounds were soporific, making Stockburn, in his worn-out state, sleepy. The breeze and the palomino's chewing were the only sounds he could hear.

A train's whistle rose slowly above a breeze gust—a long, mournful wail.

Instantly, Stockburn came alive.

He grunted and groaned himself back to his unsteady feet and peered to the east. Nothing was visible, but the wail sounded again, shorter this time. As the breeze fell again, the whistle grew clearer.

His pulse quickened. He'd made it in time. The train hadn't yet passed. It was only late. Not uncommon.

Raising the glasses to his eyes, Wolf peered east and adjusted the focus to bring up the two silver lines of the east-stretching rails. They reached off to infinity, to invisibility, but as he held the glasses steady, a feather of black smoke rose into the circle of magnified vision.

The feather grew in size and length. It wavered. As the seconds passed, it became a long, tattered black guidon stretching back and over the growing black bug of the locomotive, more and more of it spewing from the Baldwin engine's diamond-shaped stack to roll over the train as yet unseen behind it.

The locomotive grew larger, its bullet nose taking

shape and definition, the soft copper sunlight glinting off of the round number plate.

Again, the wail rose.

Gradually, Stockburn could hear the deep *chuga-chuga-chuga*.

He could see the black iron tender car trundling along behind the locomotive and swung around, heading down the bluff toward the palomino. He had to get to the rails, wave down the train, and inform the engineer and the conductor about the threat.

Only three long strides down the incline, his fatigue fading with the hope and relief building in him, an enormous roar made the air shudder. The palomino whinnied shrilly. Stockburn was only partly aware of the sound of hoofbeats as the horse, frightened by the sound, ran off.

He turned around and returned to the top of the bluff. Staring east, he saw an enormous smoke plume rising above the silver rails somewhere between him and the train. The smoke was threaded with long, bent black tendrils that he knew were the rails.

His brain was slow to comprehend what he was looking at. His eyes knew. His heart knew. But his brain would not be convinced.

As his ears picked up the distant squeal of the train's brakes, his heart thudded a frenetic rhythm against his breastbone.

"They did it. The dirty rats did it," he heard himself mutter as he watched the drifting smoke and heard the clatter and the thuds of the rails dropping back to the ground. "They blew the rails!"

As hoof thuds rose on his right, Wolf jerked his head in that direction. A horse and rider were galloping across a shallow wash maybe fifty yards away from Stockburn's position atop the bluff. Horse and rider were making a beeline for the train and the blasted tracks. Tall and dressed all in black—black hat, black suitcoat, black duster, the rider was crouched low over his horse's neck, the wind basting the front brim of his hat against his forehead.

"Hi—yah!" Stockburn heard him yell into the horse's ear. "Hi-yahhh! Go, horse. *Gooo!*"

The detective reached for both Peacemakers, but by then the man was past him and racing off toward the smoke plume still billowing over the rails. Too far away for a short gun.

More thuds sounded to Stockburn's left. He whipped his head to the northwest and spat out a bitter curse. Another rider was galloping from the west. Skirting the bluff from about a hundred yards away, he raced toward the train whose brakes were still screaming as the engineer tried to stop it before it reached the blown rails.

Stockburn wheeled again and started down the bluff, taking long strides, almost falling. He needed the Yellowboy. But when he reached the bottom of the butte and saw the palomino still running off toward the southwest, a hundred yards away and still fleeing, trailing its reins, he remembered hearing the horse flee earlier on the heels of the explosion. The two galloping devils had likely further added to the horse's distress.

Nugget had fled with Stockburn's rifle.

What the detective wouldn't give to have Smoke with him! The horse had been trained by one of the best trainers in Kansas not to shy from loud sounds like explosions and gunfire.

Cursing loudly, Wolf ran around the base of the bluff, heading northeast. "No," he said under his breath, increasing his pace until he was fairly sprinting across the prairie. "No, dammit! No! No! *Nooo!*"

Then he heard the shooting.

Shouts rose.

More shooting. A horse whinnied. A young woman screamed.

More shooting accompanied by the sharp clanking sounds of bullets ricocheting off iron and steel. Windows shattered.

Stockburn tried increasing his pace but he was running as fast as he could on the coarse grass footing.

Another blast rose—not as loud as before. That would be the express car. They'd blown the door open. He saw the pale powder smoke rise from midway down the train though he was still a good quarter of a mile away. The Devil's Horde was milling around it—some men on horseback, others running, some down on knees and firing into the passenger cars.

More shouts and screams. A baby wailed.

The killers were whooping and hollering like mooncrazed coyotes.

It was just like the survivors of the two previous holdups had described it in the reports Stockburn had read—a bloodbath! Only a handful had survived from both attacks, but that's what they'd called it.

"It was like they didn't want to leave anyone alive to identify them," one man had said while recovering from several bullet wounds. "Or maybe they just enjoyed the killing. Yes, that's it—I think they just plain enjoyed murdering innocent people!"

Wolf stopped abruptly. The cut of a creek—a narrow, deep slash through the fawn-colored brome and wheat grass—had opened before him. He hadn't seen it until he was right up on it. In the cut, he saw the tracks of the first rider he'd seen from the butte. The horse had leaped off the bank and into the cut, splashed across the muddy stream then leaped up the other side in three long, muddy strides. A sure-footed beast. Likely well-trained, too.

Still hearing the shouting and the screaming as well as another blast—that would be the express car safe being blown open—Stockburn leaped into the cut. He took two quick-plummeting strides. Too quick. His right boot came down on a slick rock, his foot slipped out from beneath him, and he went airborne, landing hard on his shoulder then rolling down the incline and into the muddy water.

His head struck a rock—a hammering blow that instantly trimmed his wick.

CHAPTER 14

Stockburn opened his eyes, squinting against the hammering in his head, to see two small, mud-black eyes regarding him flatly.

At first, he thought he must be dreaming. But then the blackbird canted its head slightly, incredulously, and opened its pale-yellow beak. Three loud "caws" echoed around inside Wolf's tender brain like bullets inside a stone cavern.

That jarred the detective's marbles back into place, and he instantly remembered what he was doing out there—the train, the killers, his tumble into the creek in which he lay on his back, half-submerged in the shallow, muddy water.

Stockburn sat up quickly. "Get off me, you winged viper!" he wheezed out. "I'm not dead. Not yet, anyway!" he added miserably, clutching his head as the bird lighted from his chest and winged up out of the creek bed, joining several more of the carrion-eaters.

The birds had likely sensed they were about to get a large meal courtesy the Devil's Horde.

Trying to suppress the agony in his head, Stockburn heaved himself to his feet and sleeved sweat away from his right temple, which he decided, after a quick probing with his fingers, wore a two- or three-inch gash from his meeting with the rock. He'd live but he'd have one hell of a headache for a while.

He'd just have to endure it.

He scrambled up the side of the bank, breathing hard and gritting his teeth against the pain. Back atop the prairie, he straightened, vaguely noting the creaks and pops in his aching lower back, and stared toward the train.

It sat there like a dead dinosaur in the waning, copper light. Nothing moved around it except wafting smoke and steam. An eerie silence enshrouded it.

"What the hell . . . ?" Wolf drew his left-side Colt and strode forward. A tender heart throbbed in his right temple. Again, he brushed blood away from that eye.

The gun was straight down along his right leg. There was nothing to shoot at. "What the hell?" he muttered to himself again. "Are they already gone?"

He kept walking, closing the distance between himself and the train stalled on the tracks about fifty feet east of the blown rails and torn-up bed. Bodies lay in crumpled heaps around the motionless cars. Some bodies lay hanging from the two passenger coaches' blown-out windows. Another body—a stout man in pinstriped overalls—hung over the side of the locomotive, gauntlet-clad hands hanging straight down toward the ground.

That would be the engineer.

Steam jetted from the locomotive's pressure release valves, snaking out around the large iron wheels. The big iron engine panted like some dying, giant beast, the heated water gurgling and groaning inside its huge black belly.

Stockburn stepped over and around dead men and even a few dead women as he approached the train at an angle, the train and tender car to his left, the two passenger cars in front of him. Those were flanked by two freight cars, a stock car for the horses. The red caboose brought up the end of the combination roughly seventy yards to Stockburn's right.

The only people he saw lay unmoving.

The only sounds were the heavy sighs of the locomotive. High overhead, turkey buzzards circled.

Lordy, what a bloodbath . . .

"Hello?" Stockburn called.

Nothing but funereal silence.

He moved to the first passenger car. Using the brass handrail, he mounted the front vestibule and ducked through the door as he entered the car. A deep grimace creased his features. The grimace grew as he walked along the center aisle, stepping over bodies. Around fifteen passengers were in the car. All were dead.

He didn't even bother to check for a pulse. Most had been shot twice. Some had been shot three times, just to make sure. Even a chicken in a portable cage had been shot, the cage resting on the floor beside a dead farmer with half-closed eyes and a death snarl creasing his sunburned face.

Stockburn stepped out of the car's back door and stopped on the rear vestibule. A man in the navy-blue wool uniform of a conductor was bent forward over the brass rail of the next passenger car's front vestibule. The top of the man's bald head faced Stockburn. The man's leather-billed cap with the *NP* insignia stitched on the low brim lay on the ties between the cars, beneath the man's dangling hands.

One of those hands twitched. Probably a death spasm. To make sure, Stockburn strode onto the vestibule of the next car and placed his finger on the side of the man's neck. A faint throb.

Quickly, he pulled the conductor off the rail and eased him to the vestibule floor, leaning him back against the rails. Recognizing the man, he said, "Jack? Jack, you still with me?"

Conductor Jack Towne was usually assigned to the 333 Flier out of Minneapolis, a twice-weekly passenger train with through-service to Billings, Montana. A good man with a family. Towne didn't deserve that bullet in his chest or the other one in his left thigh. The man was still bleeding, which meant his heart was still beating.

"Jack?" Stockburn reached into his coat pocket for a handkerchief to shove into the chest wound to stop the bleeding before the conductor bled out.

The man lifted his head. His blue eyes appeared to have trouble focusing. He made a face against the pain and licked his lips. "They came . . . so fast . . . Wolf."

"I know. I know they did, Jack. Did you recognize any of them?"

"Nah." Towne's voice was barely above a whisper. "Too much shootin' . . . confusion . . . smoke. I didn't get a good look . . . at any of . . ." He didn't finish the sentence. He gave a long, loud exhalation and dropped his head forward.

Stockburn cursed, shoved his handkerchief back into his coat pocket, and then eased the poor man's head and shoulders down sideways to the vestibule floor.

"Rest in peace, Jack." He patted the conductor's shoulder. "Rest in peace."

Stockburn rose. His head was still pounding. He felt sick to his stomach with sadness, revulsion, and rage.

What kind of men could be capable of such cold-blooded murder? He had been doing law work for many years, and he'd never seen anything as depraved as this.

Thirty or forty people, dead.

He made his way through the next car, stepping over more bodies, young and old. A baby had been shot. Among the dead was even an old nun. She'd been shot from point-blank rage in the center of her forehead. The bullet had blown out the back of her head. Still, she appeared to be smiling up at Stockburn through a cracked lens of her wire-rimmed spectacles.

He continued to the end of the car, fighting off his nausea, and stopped suddenly when he heard a rifle being cocked behind him.

A woman's angry, quavering voice followed. "Stop right there!"

Stockburn stopped.

"Give me one good damn reason why I shouldn't shoot you!"

Slowly, Stockburn raised his hands. "Easy, miss."

"Don't 'easy, miss' me! Who are you?"

Stockburn kept looking straight ahead. "I'm not one of them."

Her voice was brittle, shaking. "How do I know that?"

"Now, sweetheart." Stockburn smiled. "That wouldn't make sense, now, would it? The gang left. Why would they leave one behind?"

"Don't 'sweetheart' me, either! All I know is you weren't on the train before the attack, and I want to know what you're doing on it now!"

"Can I turn around?"

"What?" she asked uncertainly.

"Can I turn around?" Wolf thought there might be less chance of her shooting him if she saw his eyes. She was just terrified, not a cold-blooded killer.

She seemed to study on the question for a few seconds. "All right," she said finally, backing up a couple of steps. "Slow. Try anything funny, and you'll get a bullet!"

Stockburn slowly turned until he found himself facing a tall, slender young woman in a long wool skirt and a black leather vest over a purple silk blouse with puffy sleeves. Long, thick, curly red hair tumbled over her shoulders. A black felt hat hung down her back from a cord around her neck. She was a pretty girl with delicate features and a long, clean nose, her face awash in freckles.

Her shaking hands, clad in black leather gloves, held a Winchester repeating carbine, angled up sharply. While a tall girl, she stood several inches shorter than Stockburn's six-foot-three. She raised the carbine to her right shoulder, canted her cheek to the stock, and narrowed one green eye as she planted the carbine's sights on Stockburn's head.

The confident way she handled the rifle told the detective that she was no stranger to firearms. She may have been beautiful enough to shred a man's heart with a first look, but she was no kitten.

"Who are you?" she asked again, more sharply, shaking her mussed hair back from her eyes.

"Wolf Stockburn. Railroad dick for the Wells Fargo Company."

She studied him from over the barrel of the cocked Winchester, frowning. "No, you're not." She almost laughed.

"Sure, I am."

"No, you're not."

"I am, miss."

She stomped one of her black boots in anger. "No, you're not! You're a bald-faced liar!"

Stockburn gave an impatient chuff. "Can I reach for my credentials without you coring me, young lady?"

She opened and closed her shaking hands around the Winchester, shifting her feet a little, balancing her weight in the narrow aisle. "Take your hat off. Slow!"

Stockburn looked at her dubiously then slowly removed his hat. She frowned up at his short cap of coarse gray-white hair. Her freckled cheeks flushed a little.

Frowning, she slowly lowered the carbine. "It is you." She studied him skeptically, apparently not sure she could believe her eyes.

Stockburn reached out with his right hand. "Can I have the rifle?"

"Hey!" She raised the rifle again, fire in her eyes. "Don't do that!"

"All right." The detective opened his hands in surrender, smiling at her reassuringly. "It's all yours."

She pointed the barrel down. Her eyes flickered with hesitation. "S-sorry." She lowered the rifle again. "You just . . . you frightened me . . . Mr. Stockburn."

"It's all right. You've had quite a shock." He paused, studying her. Her eyes were glazed. "What's your name?"

She depressed the Winchester's hammer and lowered the barrel. She took another step back and to one side, her face bleaching a little as she said, "I'm Hank, uh . . . Henrietta Holloway. Ex-Express guard . . . for Wells Fargo."

"You?" Stockburn looked her up and down. She was the prettiest express guard he'd ever been acquainted with, since most—no, *all*—of the express guards he'd ever been acquainted with had been men.

She glanced behind her at the old nun lying in the aisle. Hank's eyes filled with tears and her lips trembled. She raised the back of a hand to her mouth as though to quell a sudden onslaught of emotion. "They . . . they came so fast . . . blew the . . . blew the express door. The blast blew me clear to the back of the car . . . buried me under gunnysacks full of mail. They must not have seen me."

She brushed her left hand across her ear. "I have an awful ringing in my ears, and . . . and I can't hear very well . . ." She shook her head as she looked at the carnage around her . . . the dead baby . . . "Good Lord—look what they did!" She squeezed her eyes closed and sobbed, tears rolling down her cheeks. She stepped back again, staggering, dragging the rifle barrel along the floor. She appeared about to faint.

"Here, here . . ." Stockburn grabbed her and picked her up.

She clutched the rifle by the end of the rear stock, letting the barrel drag along the floor.

He carried her out of the car, down the vestibule steps, and over to a small cottonwood about ten feet beyond the base of the rail bed.

"I'm so ashamed," the young express guard said in a trilling, forlorn voice. "I lost . . . I lost the treasure in my charge . . . the three other guards were killed . . . and . . . and here I am . . . with a ter . . . a terrible ringing in my ears." She sobbed, more tears rolling down her cheeks.

"Shh, shh." Stockburn set her gently down on the ground by the tree. "You've had one hell of a shock, Miss Holloway." He crouched over her, smiling reassuringly at the young woman who leaned back against the tree with her rifle resting across her legs. She wasn't going to let the rifle get too far away from her. "You're addled by it, but you got fire, I'll give you that."

She'd mistaken him for one of the killers, and she'd been going to take him down all by herself.

"No." She shook her head. "I don't have fire. I'm sobbing like a child who lost her kitten." She glanced back at the train and the several men who lay dead along the rail bed.

Stockburn recognized one of the brakemen, Earl Gunderson, another family man.

"Those people lost their lives. Those devils stole them . . . right along with the treasure." She looked at the detective. "They really are devils, Mr. Stockburn. They were aptly named. They were fast . . . and deadly. So very deadly." She shook her head and sleeved tears from her freckled cheeks.

Hoof thuds rose from the east, along the steel rails dwindling off against the dimming horizon. Automatically, Stockburn closed his hands over the grips of the Colt on his left hip. He turned to see three horseback riders moving toward him—man-shaped silhouettes wearing Stetsons. Something flashed on the shirt of one of the riders. A badge, most likely.

As the riders continued their approach along the grassy prairie on the north side of the railbed, he turned back to Miss Holloway, who had stopped sobbing now. She gazed off with a deeply dejected air on her pale, tear-streaked face. She was in shock.

"Miss Holloway, are there horses in that stock car?" The detective canted his head toward the wooden-slatted car that stood about halfway down the eleven-car combination, behind the second of the two freight cars.

The young woman brushed another tear from her cheek with her gloved hand and nodded. "Back in St. Paul, I saw several army remounts being led into the car. Likely from Fort Snelling headed to Fort Lincoln. A couple of ranch hands led some stock ponies into the car, as well. I'm surprised the killers didn't shoot the stock, too."

"Horses can't identify them . . . or sic a posse on them."

Henrietta Holloway nodded dully.

"Sit tight, Henrietta."

"Hank."

"All right—Hank." Stockburn squeezed her shoulder and rose to his feet.

She frowned up at him skeptically. "What are you going to do, Mr. Stockburn?"

"Wolf."

She smiled weakly.

"I'm gonna talk with these men over here," he said. "You sit tight, rest."

Wolf walked over to where the three riders were approaching. Within thirty feet and closing, they gazed in hang-jawed shock at the stalled train, the dead men, and a few dead women lying around it. The man riding in the center of the three-man pack was the shortest of the three—a dark-bearded, middle-aged man wearing a five-pointed star that read CONSTABLE

The man straddling a stocky dun gelding to his right wore a white shirt, suspenders, and a bowler hat. He was older, maybe in his sixties. The third man was tall and thin with thin gray hair and a thin gray mustache. He wore town clothes including a striped, collarless shirt and worn black brogans. A townsman. Maybe a shopkeeper. His glazed eyes told Stockburn he'd a few drinks before supper and maybe a couple more afterwards.

"Good Lord, they struck again!" said the man wearing the badge. He'd turned his astonished eyes on Stockburn. "Anyone left alive?"

"Just the young lady," Stockburn said, turning his head slightly to indicate Miss Holloway. Returning his gaze to the three newcomers, he said, "You're from Weatherford, I take it."

"I'm the Weatherford station agent—Wilford Holte," said the older man sitting to the right of the one with the badge. "I heard the blast . . . the shooting. I went over and pulled Cal an' Carl out of the Blackbird . . ." He glanced at the man wearing the badge.

The badge-wearer colored a little. "Cal Jenkinson. Weatherford Town Constable. When we need one, that is . . . which ain't that often." He returned his shocked gaze to the train. His eyes were also a little shiny, and he had crumbs in his mustache.

"I'm Wolf Stockburn, Detective for—"

"I know who you are, Mr. Stockburn," said the station agent. "Wolf of the Rails." The corners of his mouth shot up a little. "Pleased to make your acquaintance, sir. Were you on the train?"

Stockburn shook his head. "I rode up from Cold Water Wells hoping I'd get here in time to stop the attack." He tightened his jaws. "I didn't."

"Cold Water Wells is over a hundred miles away," said the constable.

"Will you men see to loading the dead back on the train?" Stockburn asked, ignoring the man's comment.

"Yeah, we'll get 'em on board," Jenkinson said, turning toward the dead once more. "Poor souls."

Stockburn gazed pointedly at the station manager. "Can you back this beast as far as Weatherford?"

Holte nodded. "Yes. I was never an engineer, but I was a fireman and rode with enough engineers to know how to back the train. I'm probably going to need some time to power back up, but I should have it back to Weatherford in a couple of hours."

"Good," Stockburn said. "When you get back to the station . . . well, you know what to do."

"I'll cable Fargo and Bismarck for the law . . . the U.S. marshals . . . the army." He narrowed a skeptical eye at the detective. "What are you going to do?"

"I'm going to take a horse out of the stock car and start tracking those killers. Don't report this is as a robbery, Mr. Holte. This was a massacre. A mass murder of innocent men, women, and children. Yeah, they blew the express safe and cleaned it out, but this, first and foremost, was cold-blooded murder. I'm going to run those devils to ground before they can do it again."

"All by yourself?" exclaimed the constable and the man called Carl at nearly the same time.

"Before their trail goes cold!" Wolf swung around and strode toward the stock car.

He paused when he saw the young express guard, Hank Holloway, leading a big bay gelding down the stock car's wooden ramp. The horse was bridled and saddled and ready to go. Her rifle was in the scabbard.

In response to his skeptical expression, she said with cool defiance, "I'll be going with you, Mr. Stockburn. I've already saddled my horse."

CHAPTER 15

Stockburn grabbed the reins out of the young woman's hands. "Thanks, Hank. You have a good eye for horseflesh."

She held out her hand, her face coloring with anger. "Hey, give those back! This is my horse. You can saddle your own!"

"You don't need a horse, Hank. You're not going anywhere except back to where you came from." He shucked her Winchester and handed it to her.

"I told you"—she stomped her boot down hard on the bottom of the loading ramp, and her lovely cheeks colored again—"I'm going with you!"

Stockburn adjusted the saddle stirrups to accommodate his long legs. "No, you're not."

"Mr. Stockburn, the Wells Fargo company, our mutual employer, put me in charge of that safe. It is my duty to get its contents to its destination, and that's what I intend to do. But first I have to reacquire it from the men who took it. Since you are going after them, I will be riding with you whether you like it or not. If that means picking out another horse, that is exactly what I shall do!" Hank turned in a snit and started back up the ramp.

She stopped and looked over her shoulder when Stockburn said, louder, "No, I don't like it. And, what's more, it's not going to happen. I've been with Wells Fargo for damn near fifteen years, little girl. You were still a suckling when I first pinned the copper shield to my vest."

He pointed an admonishing finger at her from over the saddle—a regular stock saddle as opposed to a cavalry McClellan—strapped to the bay, and narrowed his long faded blue eyes with authority. "That means you abide by my orders."

She drew a calming breath and bent forward at the waist. "You are *not* my supervisor. Mr. Winthrop is my supervisor. Mr. Winthrop and only *Mr. Winthrop* will tell me what to do. He charged me with the responsibility of getting that safe and all contents therein to the First Stockmen's Bank of Billings, Montana, and that is what I still intend to do."

The three men from Weatherford stared in mute silence at the two verbal combatants as the pretty express messenger continued. "There was over a hundred thousand dollars in banknotes in that safe, not to mention another twenty or thirty thousand in gold and silver coin. That money belongs to a ranching cooperative who sold several thousand head of beef to the J.H. Nelson Meat Packers in Chicago. The Nelson company insured that money with Wells Fargo. Our company is responsible for its safe delivery. That means *I* am responsible for it!"

She raised her voice still louder, shriller. "Say! Say there, *where are you going?* You wait for me, damn your ornery hide, Mr. Stockburn!" She stomped her boot in fury. "I'm going with you!"

But Stockburn was already far enough away, crossing

the tracks in front of the stalled engine, that he barely heard her last words beneath the thudding of the bay's galloping hooves. He glanced behind and gave a wry chuckle then turned his head forward and set his mind to the formidable task that faced him.

His first step was tracking down Nugget, who'd fled the region with Stockburn's prized Yellowboy repeating rifle. He didn't have a snowball's chance in hell of going up against the Devil's Horde without it. Not that he intended to face the killers on his own. He was neither stupid nor suicidal. But he did intend to learn where they holed up between jobs, and that meant there was a chance he'd encounter them unexpectedly. If that happened, he sure as hell didn't want to be wielding only six-shooters, as powerful as the ivory-gripped Peacemakers were.

He hurried to find the palomino, for the light was waning quickly, cloaking the prairie in deep purple shadows. The air was cooling, which meant the infernal mosquitoes were coming out. He slapped several as he rode back across the wash in which he'd encountered the rock then around the haystack butte atop which he'd spied the two riders deadheading toward the train.

As he started west of the bluff, he was relieved to see that Nugget hadn't absconded far with his Yellowboy. The horse stood just ahead—a horse-shaped silhouette, reins drooping, head lowered as he cropped prairie grass, taking little mincing steps forward, following the feed. As Stockburn approached, the palomino lifted his head and turned toward Stockburn, wary.

The horse rippled his withers and switched his tail at the bugs.

He let the detective get to within fifty yards, calling gently, trying to soothe his apprehension. Then he cut and run. Stockburn galloped after him, cursing at the renewed pounding the hard travel kicked up in his head not to mention his sore behind.

He was glad the bay was well-trained, for he responded well to his strange rider's commands, and he took only a few minutes to ride up parallel with the palomino. The horse didn't have much more run in him, thank God, and made only a half-hearted attempt to flee as Wolf reached over to grab Nugget's reins.

When both horses were stopped, he swung down from his saddle and retrieved the Yellowboy from the boot. He slid the rifle into the boot strapped to the bay. Ma MacDougal, bless her otherwise contrary Scottish heart, had tied a small grub sack to the horn. He left the grub sack on the palomino and climbed back onto the bay, keeping Nugget's reins in his hand, and led the handsome golden horse along behind him.

Nugget didn't have any more hard travel in him, but Stockburn didn't, either. Even if he did, the light wasn't obliging. While tracking the Horde tomorrow, a spare horse would come in handy. Besides, he needed to get it back to its rightful owner. He didn't want to cross Ma MacDougal. Nobody did.

With Nugget trotting along behind the bay, the detective returned to the wash and tied the palomino to a cottonwood sapling. Gritting his teeth against the pain still throbbing in his head, he was pleasantly pleased to register it was growing duller. He walked back down into the wash and scoured the sand and gravel for the tracks of the Devil's Horde rider.

The Horde's previous strategy had been to flee the train in the same direction from which each man had attacked it. That meant the man he'd spied earlier from atop the bluff had likely retraced his route to the southwest.

Sure enough, he had.

Stockburn picked up the return set of prints, separate from the ones he'd made with the bay a few minutes ago, where the galloping rider had recrossed the slender stream and mounted the western bank.

Wolf climbed up out of the wash, pulled the palomino's slip-knotted reins from the sapling, and mounted the bay. He followed the devil's tracks across the grassy prairie, heading generally southwest, until darkness finally concealed them. Camped on the open prairie near the killer's sign, he took comfort in the knowledge that he had at least picked up one of the fleeing devils' trail. That was a start.

He'd rest tonight, and hopefully shed the ache in his head and backside. Tomorrow was another day.

When he'd built a small, smoky fire to ward off the mosquitoes, he led both horses over to a shallow creek to drink their fill then pulled a pair of hobbles from his saddlebags and used those on the bay. The less-predictable Nugget he tied to a tree near the camp. He left Nugget's bridle on, but slipped the bit so the horse could crop grass.

In Ma MacDougal's grub sack Stockburn found a loaf of crusty brown bread, some jerky, and a small wheel of cheese. Exhausted, with his head pounding, he didn't have much of an appetite.

Still, he forced some of the bread and cheese down his gullet, for he'd need the sustenance come morning. He had no coffee or anything to cook it with since he'd left his war bag with trail supplies in Cold Water Wells, owing to his need to travel light. That was all right. He didn't have much of an appetite for coffee, either.

He wanted only to sleep, to let the night pass, and to rise tomorrow, fresh for the killers' trail.

He rose, all right. But he was far from fresh.

He'd be damned if he didn't feel even worse than he had last night before he'd hunkered down in his coat and plunged into a deep, exhausted sleep against his saddle. His head was considerably better, though the goose egg that had risen on his temple was sore as hell. That paled in comparison to the rest of him.

The rest of him felt as though he'd been long-looped and dragged over rough rocks by some lunatic saddle tramp on a bronc even greener than Wild Blue. He knew he wasn't as young as he used to be, but this was ridiculous. He was so stiff that merely sitting up made him feel as though his spine was going to crack at the base of his back, reminding him of a broken comb.

Using his rifle, he finally hoisted himself to his feet and took inventory of all his sundry aches and pains. His hips and neck felt broken. His ass was chafed raw. He could barely turn his head. Both shoulders felt as though he'd taken bullets to them. His feet were so stiff he stumbled around his camp for fifteen minutes like a little old man about two days away from his deathbed.

Boy howdy, age was a nasty thing!

Back in his days riding for the Pony Express, he used

to wake as fresh as a spring colt, ready to climb into the hurricane deck and do it all again.

By the time he led the horses back from the creek where they'd filled up on water, he was feeling slightly better. He'd loosened up a little so he could at least turn his head from side to side and he was no longer limping like a cripple hunchback. He had another bite of bread and cheese, which he washed down with cool though brackish water from the creek, then hauled his aching behind into the saddle.

He continued following the killer's trail, which he assumed would meet up with the trails of the other killers and—thunder and lightning!—he'd know where they holed up between jobs.

However, the tracking didn't go all that well, either.

The killer he was following had left a clear trail of bent and broken grass for roughly two hundred yards beyond where Stockburn had camped. But as the man continued southwest, his trail led into drier country. The grass was shorter. He continued into bluff country, and the ground between bluffs was harder, and in some places it turned to coarse gravel.

Several times, he lost the trail and had to slow down and scour the ground more closely to pick it up again. The farther southwest he rode, the thinner the soil and the shorter and curlier the grass until it seemed for a time he was riding on a giant buffalo coat stretched taut from horizon to horizon.

The man he was following was expert at covering his trail and at traversing terrain that covered it for him. If the man had camped last night with a fire, Stockburn had found no trace of it. He had a feeling the man, a tough customer indeed, had stopped for a few hours without bothering with a fire, rested his horse, then continued riding.

Still, Wolf managed to spy part of a shod shoe print here and there, the scrape where a shoe had kicked a rock, horsehair snagged on prickly hawthorn branches, and sporadic tufts of relatively fresh horse apples, to keep him going. He did, however, get a good understanding of the frustration felt by the earlier posse riders who'd ridden after these cagey devils. He hoped that, like them, he wouldn't eventually ride into the proverbial rock wall and have no choice but to give up the trail altogether for lack of sign.

The low point of his day came just after noon.

He lost the killer's trail in a jog of rocky buttes that looked like ancient, badly eroded volcanoes that had spewed up their guts in the form of rocks of all shapes and sizes and flung them for miles in all directions. Damned little grass there. Adding to his vexation were the many alkali washes that cut up into a veritable devil's playground. The killer he was after had likely followed one of those washes, but lacking sign to show him which one the devil had chosen, Stockburn had no idea.

Still, he kept riding, switching from the bay to the palomino then back again.

He'd ridden through a low, brushy area late in the afternoon when he spied three riders sitting their horses at the base of a tall pinnacle of chalky white rock. Stopping his horses, he studied the men.

One of them saw him and widened his eyes in surprise. He poked another man's shoulder and pointed. The man jerked with a start. The third rider turned toward Stockburn, as well, and gave a similar start, lurching slightly back in his saddle and giving his horse a fright. He drew back sharply on the horse's reins, settling the animal. His gloved right hand crept toward the stock of the rifle jutting from his saddle scabbard.

"That won't be necessary." Stockburn nudged Nugget ahead with his heels and jerked the bay along by its bridle reins. "I'm looking for information, not trouble."

They stared at him. They were lean, dark-eyed men, so sun- and windburned that they almost appeared Indian. But they were dressed in the rough trail garb of the run-of-the-mill cowpuncher, right down to their weathered and worn felt sombreros and brush-scarred chaps. They were not part of the Devil's Horde. That was plain to Stockburn right away. Their clothes were old and ragged, and the pistols in their holsters and rifle scabbards were aged, worn, and not well cared for.

They were range riders, all right. They'd likely been born out there, and they'd likely die out there, too.

None said a word as Wolf drew up before them. They were sitting in a semicircle, conferring. One was smoking a loosely rolled cigarette. One had his right leg hooked over his saddle horn but slowly lowered it back down to the stirrup. That man's face had been badly burned at one time. The grisly scar stretched across his right cheek, jaw, and forehead and extended back to include the twisted knot of his right ear.

Stockburn said, "I'm wondering if you saw a rider pass through here a few hours ago. Maybe around midday, if I don't miss my guess. Probably appeared in a bit of a hurry."

The three dark-eyed, long-faced men studied him

skeptically. The one with the scarred face said through a dull grunt, "Why should we tell you?"

"I have a real good reason," Stockburn said.

The three just stared at him, a dark suspicion building in their eyes. They sat their saddles tensely; they were like coiled rattlesnakes. Not your run-of-the-mill cowpuncher, after all. They were too nervous. Too scared.

Wolf switched his gaze to the man sitting a coyote dun pony ahead and slightly to his left—the man whose hand had started to slide toward his rifle. "You answer my question and I won't inform Lucien Stark about that runnin' iron I suspect you're packing on your saddle there, partner." He glanced at the bedroll strapped behind the cantle of the man's saddle. He could see the branding iron rolled up in the double blankets and rainslicker, all but concealed.

The faces of the three men tightened.

"It's really hard to hide those damn things," he said in a mock voice of complaint. "If old Stark found that on you, I reckon you'd be stretching some hemp, dancing the midair two-step, no questions asked."

The three men looked at each other.

The one with the burned face turned to Stockburn and pointed with his right arm. "Seen a man in a black duster pull through here around noon, like you say. I glassed him, seen him swing back east when he reached Taylor's Bluff another mile south."

The answer had been too detailed to be a lie. At least that's what Stockburn thought. Those three knew very well the punishment for rustling, and they were too desperate to lie to a man who had their fates in his hands.

He smiled, tapped two fingers to the brim of his black sombrero, and pulled straight back on Nugget's reins. He hoped the palomino had been trained to back up and was relieved to see that he had. Backing away from the three men still studying him darkly, tensely, Stockburn continued smiling.

When he was twenty feet away, he reined the palomino south and put the boots to him. The bay followed, its reins clasped in the detective's gloved left hand.

He glanced back over his right shoulder.

Those three could be trouble now that he had their fates in his hands.

Chapter 16

Stockburn picked up the killer's trail at Taylor's Bluff. It was the highest peak for miles around on the vast, lonely prairie tufted with buckbrush, buffalo grass, and occasional wildflowers showing their bright reds, purples, and yellows among the summer-cured fawns and ochres.

The devil's sign came in the form of part of a horse apple lying near a prairie dog hole. The rest of the horse's discharge had been kicked into a thicket of willows and honeysuckle growing up around a seep. Prairie dogs stood before the round entrances to their underground houses as Stockburn poked around in the brush. The little varmints stood on their hind feet, wringing their front paws like fat, ugly old men standing on their porches, threatening visitors.

They chuckled and chortled and prattled their anger at the interloper—the second one today. They flicked their tails and jerked their nervous little comical heads and black button eyes.

Stockburn studied the grassy-green horse apples that the rider had kicked into the brush. The man had purposely covered his trail, overlooking the spoonful of the stuff he'd left out in the open. He'd overlooked part of the pile because he'd stepped on it, flattening it out against the grass.

Wolf had simply lucked into spotting it after scouring the ground around the chalky pedestal base of the butte for nearly a half hour. If the Fates hadn't cast his gaze downward at just the right moment, he would have ridden right on past the sign.

His concern now was: *Why has my quarry covered his trail?*

The obvious answer: *He knows he is being shadowed.*

Taylor's Butte was a good thirty miles south of the Northern Pacific tracks. The man wouldn't still be covering his trail this far south of the charnel house he'd made of the train unless he knew Stockburn was dogging him. *Wolfing* him, more like.

He gave a dry snort at the old joke, a fleeting bit of levity to temper his concern. The devil he was tracking was close. Maybe real close.

Despite having to slow his pace and scour the terrain for the killer's sign, Stockburn had gained ground on his quarry. By switching his two horses often, he hadn't needed to rest all that frequently. He'd been able to keep pushing.

On the other hand, the man he was tracking had only one horse. He couldn't push his mount too hard or he'd end up afoot. That's how Stockburn had caught up.

Something told him that the man had glassed him from a distance. In most places, it was wide-open country. He could have been spotted riding along the killer's back trail at nearly any time over the past several hours.

Thinking the killer might be glassing him from the next

butte to the southeast, Stockburn cast his eagle-eyed gaze to the pale, conical formation that lay in that direction. That butte appeared a slightly smaller version of Taylor's Butte. *The killer could be anywhere out here,* he thought, searching in nearly a complete circle around him.

How close was his man to the other killers?

They'd all rendezvous in one spot sooner or later. The others were out there, too, somewhere, gradually switching their individual courses to come together at some point to split their plunder. Stockburn's man had switched his own course slightly, heading southeast. He was likely making the turn to gather with the others . . . somewhere.

Or maybe he'd made the turn to lose his shadower . . .

No telling. All the detective could do was keep tracking the man whose trail he was on and hope he'd lead him to the others. At the same time, the killer knew he had a shadow—or *probably* knew he had a shadow. Wolf had to be careful not to get dry-gulched, shot out of his saddle.

He switched to the bay and continued following the killer's course.

The man's trail had become easier to follow since he was no longer traversing ground on which he left little or no sign. Either he thought he'd eluded all pursuers, or he'd resigned himself to his pursuer.

Now, he'd try a different tack. That likely meant ambush.

Stockburn loped both horses across the sea of wind-brushed grass swept by cloud shadows. Several times he crossed the trails of the once-great buffalo herds—they were like broad valleys cut by thousands of hooves—and skirted their enormous wallows, which were deep craters in the prairie. They became veritable lakes during rains. The ghosts of the old Sioux warriors—members of the Seven Council Fires—rode with Stockburn, as they always did when he found himself on the vast and haunted plain.

He'd once known a smattering of the three main Sioux dialects—the Yankton, Lakota, and Santee—and imagined seeing brightly painted, dusky-skinned warriors in buck skins adorned with beads and porcupine quills fording this sea of wither-high grass, quivers of brightly fletched arrows hanging down their broad backs, ash bows dangling from heavy shoulders. He had once encountered parties of the legendary hunter/warriors. Each time, he'd been filled with awe and what can only be called a calm sort of awestruck terror.

Encountering the old Sioux war parties had been like happening upon some magnificent wild beast stepping through a curtain in time, out of the shadows of the long-dead ancients—untainted by civilization, untrammeled and pristine in its savagery. The Sioux were so impressive and ethereal that Stockburn had often thought he might feel a little honored, being sent to his reward by one.

The Lakota, especially, were fierce fighters. As fierce as the Chiricahua Apache, some said. Most of his encounters with those aboriginal lords of the plains had been friendly despite his purpose there—his search for the sister a Cheyenne war party had kidnapped after massacring his family. He'd dined and slept in a few Sioux villages, powwowing—to no avail, as it had turned out—about the whereabouts of his sister. He'd sweated with war chiefs and shared the blankets of several young smooth-skinned and firm-breasted maidens of the Hunkpapa and Santee.

All gone now.

Or at least they'd been relegated to reservations, which came to about the same thing. Once in a while a small war party would jump the reserve and wreak havoc with the farmers and ranchers, much like the Apaches did down in Arizona and New Mexico. But they were not so fierce anymore. Mostly, they skipped the reserves to hunt the white man's whiskey, which they were plagued with such a weakness for.

They were easily corralled.

Now they were gone and the buffalo that had sustained them over the centuries were gone save a few thin scattered herds. They, too, were ghosts of their former selves.

Wolf imagined how it once had been not all that long ago, back before the coming of the iron horse that made his own employment possible. The unceasing wind spoke to him of the ancient times, of less complicated times before the coming of his own people, but it only hinted at the secrets it held close to its breast.

He no longer harbored the vengeance fury he had as a younger man, on the heels of the massacre and his sister's kidnapping. Time had dulled the rage as well as the pain. Also, with the years had come the knowledge that his own people were the interlopers. He'd tried to get to know the Cheyenne, but he'd failed beyond learning some of their rites and tongue.

As a civilized man, he would never truly understand the people who had taken his sister. Maybe that's why he might never find her. Maybe Emily had become one of them and had been lain to rest on a feather-trimmed scaffold somewhere on the prairie, her most prized possessions and even food laid out around her, to sustain her on her journey to the next world.

Wolf reined up suddenly. He'd come to the lip of another unexpected wash. A shallow canyon, rather. What lay before him, roughly fifty feet below, were several dry creek beds intersecting in a badlands area, like the knotted veins in an old man's leg.

He was about to boot the bay down off the lip of the canyon, for outlined against the sky he made an easy target for a dry-gulcher's rifle, but something he saw or heard or sensed unconsciously made him wheel the bay abruptly and back away from the canyon.

A bullet screeched through the air beside him, thudded into the ground behind him, and was followed close on its heels by the crashing belch of the ambusher's rifle.

Stockburn dropped Nugget's reins and rammed his boots into the bay's flanks, whipping his rein ends against the mount's right hip. More bullets sliced the air around him, tearing up sod beyond him, the crashing reports of the rifles following half a second later.

He couldn't get away from the lip of the canyon fast enough.

When he thought he was out of sight of the men who'd fired at him, he swung the bay onto a parallel course with the canyon and traced a broad circle around it. He'd work his way around behind the bushwhackers. He was sure there were two men. The speed at which those shots had come at him told him there had to be two shooters.

Where had the other man come from?

Gradually, he turned the galloping bay to the east, then the south, the horse lunging easily across the grass. Wolf kept the canyon roughly fifty yards away on his right. As he gained the opposite side of the canyon, he slowed the bay and turned directly toward the chasm.

Abel Wilkins watched the blackfly land on the barrel of his 1873 First Model Winchester .44-40 rifle, then brushed the bug away in irritation with his buckskin-clad right hand. From where he hunkered behind a mossy granite rock on the south side of the pale, intersecting washes comprising the isolated badlands area, he cast his gaze along the rim of the canyon to the north.

Then the west. Then the east.

The fly buzzed around his right ear. He brushed it away, cursing under his breath. The fly was an added vexation. The shadow rider had vexed him enough, consarn it. Now he and his partner, Bryce Cade, had blown their attempt at scouring the man from their trail, which made him twice as dangerous as he'd been before when he'd only been a vexing shadow keeping pace along Wilkins's back trail.

He turned to where Cade knelt behind another rock just down the grassy slope to his right and roughly forty feet away. "You see him, Bryce?" he called.

Cade turned to glower at Wilkins over his left shoulder. "Hell, no, I don't see him!"

"It's too damn windy to hear him!"

Again, Cade looked at Wilkins over his shoulder. "Maybe he done lit a shuck."

Wilkins brushed the vexatious fly away from his other ear and pondered on what Cade had said. "I reckon one of us better walk up and find out."

"You do it," Cade said.

Wilkins snorted a wry laugh. "Why don't we *both* do it?"

Just then the fly bit into the back of his neck. It was a hungry, angry bite, a fierce jolt of grinding pain.

"Damn your winged hide!" He slapped at the fly but missed. He watched the winged viper wheel jeeringly away in the air, a very small chunk of flesh in its mouth or whatever bugs used to nip a man with.

"Will you shut up?" Cade berated his partner. "You're giving away our position!"

"Fly bit me. Damn, that hurt!"

"A lot more than that's gonna bite you if you don't—"

A faint rumbling rose.

Cade lifted his gaze toward the rim of the canyon to the north. Wilkins looked around, as well.

"Hear that?"

Cade didn't reply. He and Wilkins jerked their nervous gazes this way and that, trying to find the source of the low rumbling sound that quickly grew louder. The wind swirled the noise so that it seemed to come from the left, then the right, and then behind.

Sure enough, it was coming from behind!

The realization that the man had flanked them had just brushed across Wilkins's blackfly-addled brain when he rose from his crouch, stepped away from his covering rock, and turned toward the south rim of the canyon. As he did, a great black bird rose up from the canyon's lip and flew toward him.

Only, it wasn't a bird.

CHAPTER 17

"Hi-yahhh!" Stockburn roared as he ground his heels into the bay's flanks.

The bay loosed a shrill whinny as in full gallop it leaped over the rim of the canyon and shot downward at nearly a forty-five-degree angle. One of the killers stood straight out in front of them, just as Stockburn knew he would be after his quick, furtive reconnaissance only two minutes earlier, crabbing toward the lip on his belly.

The killer screamed, only just starting to raise his rifle when the bay's forward-reaching hooves slammed into him and hammered him straight down to the ground, the hooves following him and slamming him once more when he lay supine in the thick, pale grass.

"Oof!" Stockburn heard the man say beneath the full force of the horse's weight, as the air and probably most of the life was slammed out of him.

The bay continued straight down the slope, taking long, deep strides. The other man on his right gave a shocked scream, having seen his partner pancaked by the hard-charging bay. The second killer slammed his Henry repeating rifle to his shoulder. The rifle crashed as the bullet plumed dust in the wash beyond where Stockburn had stopped and wheeled the bay, bringing up his own Yellowboy.

He laid a bead on the second shooter just as the man slid his own rifle toward the detective, tracking him, ejecting his spent cartridge, and ramming a fresh one into the breech. He was moving quickly but calmly, focusing on his target—a practiced killer—but he didn't get the next shot off before Stockburn's Winchester roared. The bay flinched but didn't take a step as Wolf cocked and fired two more times, all three slugs punching the second killer back across the shoulder of the slope as he threw his Henry high into the air, his black hat wheeling away on the wind.

The flaps of his black duster whipped like a crow's wings as he flailed around on the ground, gasping and groaning, dying hard.

Stockburn cocked another round into the Yellowboy's action and turned to the man the bay had wrecked. The killer lay with the soles of his boots pointed toward the canyon's south rim. The top of his head faced the bay directly below him, near the bottom of the canyon where the pale washes intersected. The man had thick, coarse hair the washed-out blond color of flax straws. His broken chest rose and fell quickly as he sucked air in and out of his lungs, whimpering like a whipped dog.

Grinding sounds came from his chest, the sounds of his broken ribs and sternum grinding together as he breathed.

Stockburn booted the bay up the slope toward the dying man. He swung down from the saddle and walked over to the man, letting the Winchester hang straight down against his right leg. "Where were you headed?"

The man's pale face with long, thin, blond side whiskers and thin blond mustache was a mask of harrowing pain. He stared straight up at the turquoise sky vaulting over the prairie. His gray eyes reflected the sunlight sharply. They were bright with torment. His lower jaw hung slack.

Stockburn poked the Yellowboy's barrel against the man's forehead. "Where were you headed? Where's the rendezvous point?"

His eyes rolled toward Stockburn and seemed to study the tall, gray-mustached detective in the three-piece black suit for a time, as though he had only then realized he was there, standing over him, gazing skeptically down at him. "If I tell you, will you kill me?" he croaked out. He ground his teeth together against the pain of his shattered ribs that were no doubt stabbing his lungs, opening grisly wounds, filling the lungs with blood. His breathing was sounding more and more liquid.

"Be glad to," Stockburn said.

The man moved his lips but no words came out. Blood appeared at the corners of his mouth. He licked his lips, coating them with blood. He gave a weak smile, then said, "Not . . . necessary . . ."

He died right then. His eyes rolled up into their sockets. His chest ceased moving and making the bellowslike wheezing sound that caused Stockburn's own lungs to ache. Both hands slid down from the dead man's chest to lie in the grass, palms up, as though in surrender to whatever gods or demons were waiting for him.

Demons, most like, Wolf thought. *Definitely demons.*

* * *

Stockburn laid out the dead killers side by side in the grass near where they'd breathed their last breath, and went through their pockets, looking for anything that would identify them.

He found nothing. He wasn't surprised. The Horde might have been made up of black-hearted devils, but they were not stupid black-hearted devils. Leastways, whoever ramrodded the group wasn't stupid. Their holdups were elaborately staged and planned, leaving few if any witnesses, and they had the knack of avoiding posses down to a fine art. No, whoever was heading up the group had likely made sure none of his charges carried anything on his person that might identify him in the event of what had just happened to these two.

Identifying individuals might very well lead to identifying the entire group.

He found nothing but timepieces, a comb, a pencil stub, sulfur-tipped matches, a corncob pipe, tobacco and rolling papers, and some greenbacks and coins. He found their horses tied to scrub brush not far from where he'd made his plunge into the canyon. Going through the gear he discovered on their mounts, a mouse-brown grullo and a charcoal gray, he learned that these two weren't carrying any of the train loot. They were probably lesser lights, men hired mainly for their gun skills.

Mercenaries.

All of which led to no answers to Stockburn's burning questions regarding who the gang was and where they hid between holdups. He'd botched his job. He'd intended to take one of the men alive. At least long enough to get that information out of him. That's why he'd run the first man down instead of shooting him. Odds were he'd only injure him, not kill him.

He'd killed him.

What he did get from the killers was food, cooking supplies, and an extra canteen. They'd each been well stocked for the long trail back to where they'd come from. Not elaborately stocked, but stocked with beans, side pork, cornmeal, jerky, hardtack, baking powder, salt, sugar, coffee, a coffeepot, and a small skillet for whipping together a quick, basic but nourishing meal over a cookfire.

He gathered the gear into one war bag, unsaddled the killers' horses, and turned them loose to find a new home. He left the killers' guns with the bodies but he took a box of .44 shells for his Winchester. He didn't need their weapons.

He left the dead killers to the carrion eaters who would likely descend on them later that evening after the sun went down, snarling and cawing and howling and generally kicking up one hell of a greedy, proprietary fuss, as carrion-eaters were wont to do.

Riding a stretch along his own back trail astraddle Nugget, with the bay hauling the extra gear, he saw where the second killer's trail intersected that of the first. It was only a half a mile or so north of the canyon. Stockburn had been so intent on following the first man, he'd overlooked the second man's trail, which lay several yards to the left of the first man's—a slender swath of bent and broken grass parallel to the sign of the man he had followed.

He stopped, rolled a cigarette, and pondered on the meeting of the two killers.

Maybe the rest were joining up around there somewhere, as well. The gang had ridden far enough south of the train. Maybe, according to plan, they were meeting by ones and twos and threes, possibly at preplanned points around the compass, and were turning for home.

Home. Where was home, anyway? Their temporary home away from home. Likely nearby.

Or not.

Maybe they'd only holed up out here to strike the Northern Pacific a few times. Maybe yesterday had been their last time and they were going to hightail it out of here now, out of the territory. Out of possible danger.

If so, the onus was on Stockburn more than ever to run them to ground before they forted up elsewhere and possibly preyed on another line. They'd been successful here. They'd come up with a proven strategy. Pillage, plunder, slaughter, scatter to the four winds, come together again . . . do it all again.

Or maybe they weren't finished here. It was coming on to roundup time on the northern plains. That meant fat payrolls heading toward the big ranches stretched across the territory and into Montana. Maybe they'd wait a few months, make a play for those payrolls come fall.

Whatever their plans were, they were going to be mighty surprised when two of their pack didn't show up back at the den.

They might even come looking for him, Stockburn thought as he set up camp along a big slough laced with bulrushes and cattails, maybe five miles southwest of the canyon in which the dead men moldered.

Wouldn't that be nice?

He smiled at the prospect as he leaned back against his saddle, rolling a smoke while his coffeepot steamed and his beans and side pork cooked in the skillet he'd placed on a rock at the edge of the small cookfire. He'd like nothing better than to tear into those killers with his Winchester. They'd grown far too confident. Time to wipe the smiles off their merciless faces.

He remembered the carnage inside the train. Men, women, children. A baby. An old nun.

Who were these men? Never before had he encountered anyone so depraved. Part of it likely came from running with the pack. Men would do with other men what they otherwise would not do on their own. The larger the gang, the more frenzied they often became. Like coyotes after a doe with a fawn.

Speaking of which . . . he could hear coyotes yapping in the far distance.

Stockburn yawned, stretched, looked around. He'd set up his camp on a low hill fifty yards away from the slough that stretched away to the south. The ten-acre pan of water, ringed by low hills, sat in a broad, shallow bowl on the prairie offering the only cover. He hadn't seen any trees in a long while. He'd passed only three or four small farms on his way down from the Northern Pacific rails—sod hovels flanked by leaning sod barns and ringed by meager patches of half-dead wheat or corn. Such homesteads were swallowed by the sky and the vast grassy, windy prairie stretching around them.

He'd seen only a couple of weary-looking people

around those places, a few bony cows. Such homesteads, haunted by the unceasing wind and the endless stretches of grass around them were breeding grounds of prairie madness—a very particular and brutal form of insanity spawned by the relentless rush of the wind blowing across a vast and empty land. He'd seen it many times on his journeys crisscrossing the territory, looking for Emily.

That part of the territory was still relatively unsettled. The railroad would bring more people, but so far, most emigrants gravitated toward the little towns that sprouted along the rails. Comfort in numbers. Distraction from the wind, from the bending sea of grass. From the void.

Stockburn gave his beans a stir then poured a cup of coffee. He sat back against his saddle again, sipping the coffee and drawing on his quirley. The sun was still an hour from sliding into the prairie to the west. The light was soft, the shadows long.

Red-winged blackbirds flew around him, catching bugs. They were little splashes of bright red darting here and there. You didn't see the black until you saw the red. Then you saw the whole bird. The gray and yellow meadowlarks rode the bending cattails, singing their chortling songs while mourning doves lent their own forlorn refrains from farther out across the slough.

His mind turned to Emily.

Had she enjoyed such a quiet time of day on the plains? Was she enjoying these very moments somewhere, possibly nearby? Or was she dead? For all he knew, she might have died—been killed—not long after she'd been kidnapped. Possibly after the howling braves had taken their pleasures with her . . .

Wolf shook his head as he exhaled smoke from his nostrils.

No. He wouldn't think about such a possibility. He'd thought about it before, been haunted by it, in fact, and it had gotten him nowhere. Why not cling to hope? Without Emily herself, hope was all he had. The hope made him feel not quite so alone, as he almost always did, even around other people. He wondered if he'd have been a different man if his family had not been taken from him so young. More amenable to the herd. Better company to others. Maybe he would not have betrayed Mike with Fannie.

As it was, he felt more at home out in the wild, alone, than he did anywhere else. Hunting bad men or searching for his sister.

He ate his meager meal and watched the sun go down. He thought about tomorrow. He no longer had a trail to follow to the lair of the Devil's Horde. He'd have to turn to investigative work to find their hideout.

It was nearby. Somewhere. He was close. He could sense it. He could almost smell the fetor of such a place that men like that would call home, however temporary. It was a town, probably. A small one that had been forsaken by the railroad, the comfort of the herd.

The madness had likely infested the place.

Or it was a ranch. A very isolated spread where men could hide without fear of harassment.

Stockburn would find them and he'd chop off their head. That's how you killed a snake, after all. He'd kill the ramrod, the head man. Then he'd pull out and leave the others to the marshals or to the army at Fort Lincoln.

"Piece of cake," he said, taking a last sip of his nearly

cold coffee, grinning wryly. Then strode off a few feet from camp to evacuate his bladder.

He gave a deep, weary sigh. His body still ached but not as badly as before. Maybe he'd become one with the pain, or maybe the hard ride had toughened him, like the tough kid he once was. A scrappy Scot with a chip on his shoulder.

But, then, he'd always had a chip on his shoulder. He was just older now. Pushing forty. My God . . .

He returned to the camp, tossed some brush on his fire to kick up smoke to fight off the mosquitoes that were coming off the slough, then lay back down against his saddle. He crossed his legs at the ankles, tipped his sombrero down over his eyes, and almost instantly was asleep.

A girl screamed.

Stockburn sat straight up, knocking the sombrero off his head. His heart pounded. He listened intently, gazing into the inky darkness.

She screamed again.

"Emily?" he yelled.

CHAPTER 18

Stockburn's sleep-fogged brain believed that his long-lost sister was calling him even as he pulled on his second boot and grabbed his rifle. As slumber slid farther and farther away from him, like water tumbling off his body after a swim, he half-believed it.

Running toward the sounds of the girl's cries, leaving his dark camp behind him in the darkness, the realization that the cries were not Emily's took hold. Of course, they were not his sister's cries. Nevertheless, the crying and the pleading were real. He hadn't been dreaming them.

He ran up the low rise west of where he'd camped, stumbling over tufts of buckbrush and small hummocks of grassy ground in the darkness. He hadn't taken time to strap his belt guns around his waist. He'd only grabbed the Winchester. He hadn't even grabbed his hat.

As he reached the top of the rise, flickering stars arching over him, he looked around, listening. The screams had stopped. He hadn't heard them for over a minute. They'd come from the west, he was pretty sure. As he stared in that direction, he caught the pinprick red glow of a distant fire.

Another cry pierced the otherwise silent night. An anguished plea for help cut short by a sob. Stockburn barely heard it. But he *had* heard it. Something awful was happening to the woman.

The fire was maybe a mile away. He jogged westward, moderating his speed to save his wind.

There were more hills than he'd realized. Hillocks, actually—low swells in the sealike prairie. As he crested one rise, he saw the fire growing a little larger. The blaze disappeared as he continued running, dropping down into the next trough so shallow as to be hardly noticeable.

Minutes later, the fire reappeared, slightly larger than before.

After ten minutes, he crossed yet another rise. He was close enough that he could more clearly see the fire's individual flames and the glowing cinders rising on the plume of gray smoke. Figures moved around the fire— human figures silhouetted against the flames.

They were men. Crouching men. He couldn't tell how many but more than one.

The camp was on a slight rise backed by a fifty-foot bluff. A patch of sandy, gravelly ground lay around the fire. Gear was spread out. Something else lay on the ground by the fire.

Winded from the run, Stockburn dropped to hands and knees. He was maybe sixty feet from the camp. Crawling, the distance became fifty . . . forty . . .

He sleeved sweat from his left eye, wincing against the peppery sting, and looked toward the fire again.

He could see what lay on the ground between him and the flames. A young woman, her limbs tied to wooden stakes that had been driven into the ground. She'd been stripped naked, her clothes strewn around her. She sobbed as she struggled against the ropes tying her wrists and ankles to the wooden stakes.

Her bare breasts, lit by the orange light of the fire, jostled as she fought to free herself. Her thick, curly red hair was a pillow of burnished copper spilling about her pale shoulders.

Three men sat around her. Two sat, rather. One was moving around her, crouching, chuckling while the others watched him, also chuckling and laughing. Stockburn recognized them. They were the three lean, hawklike, cow-eyed rustlers he'd run into the day before. One of the two sitting and watching the festivities held a pair of the woman's bloomers up close to his face, fondling them, sniffing them.

As the crouching man—the man with the burned face—snickered and jeered at the girl, he lowered his right hand to her bare belly. Clutched between his thumb and index finger, he held a half-smoked cigarette. He pressed the hot end of the cigarette against the girl's belly and snickered through his teeth.

The girl drew her body taut, tipped her head far back until the cords stood out in her neck, and loosed an agonized wail.

Stockburn had seen enough. What's more, he'd caught his breath. He strode forward, holding the Winchester up high across his chest. He'd taken only three steps when the two sitting rustlers saw him. Their eyes widened in astonishment.

"Hey!" one of them bellowed, lurching to his feet.

Burn Face had just crouched over the young woman once more, intending to lower the cigarette, when he looked up just in time to see the tall man with the rifle step into the firelight and thrust his right foot forward. The toe of Stockburn's boot caught him on the point of his chin.

He flew backward and screamed when he hit the flames.

The other two were shocked into inaction for half a heartbeat then couldn't seem to make up their minds if they wanted to reach for a six-shooter or turn and run. Both decided too late to reach for their six-shooters. Stockburn had already stepped beside the girl, slammed the butt of the Winchester to his shoulder, and drawn a quick bead on the wide-eyed man facing him on his left.

Boom!

The man screamed and flew back.

The other man got his Colt halfway out of its holster.

Boom!

He yelped as the bullet punched into his throat. Clawing at his neck with his eyes rolling around in their sockets, he then turned around and staggered toward the darkness beyond the fire.

Boom!

Another round to the back of his head finished him though he didn't deserve the mercy.

Stockburn racked another round into the Winchester's breech and turned toward the man-shaped torch flailing on the ground beyond the fire, flames coating nearly every inch of him.

Burn Face screamed shrilly like a young child. "Sweet Lordy Jesus, I'm burnin'. I'm burnin'!"

"Second time around, I reckon." Stockburn drew a bead on the center of the flames and hammered two more rounds into Burn Face—who had burned considerably more than his face—though he wasn't worth the lead.

Stockburn looked down at Henrietta Holloway staring up at him, her green eyes glazed with terror. She had one cigarette burn on her cheek, one between her breasts, one *on* each breast, and four more in a straight line across her belly. Several cuts and bruises were evident on her face.

Her belly and chest rose and fell quickly as she breathed.

"Good Lord, girl." He leaned the Winchester against a rock, then dropped to a knee beside her and pulled his Barlow from a pants pocket. "That's some damp powder you done got into."

"Quaint expression, but you're right."

He sawed through the rope tying her left hand to the stake.

"Stop looking at me."

"I was looking at the burns," he said, flinging the cut rope into the darkness and starting on the rope tied around her right wrist.

"I know what you were looking at."

"Can't blame a man for appreciating a well-turned body. Not too many out here in the tall and uncut."

She glared at him as he cut through the rest of the ropes and tossed them into the darkness. "You're little better than them."

"Not by much, no." He stood and extended his hand to her, but she did not take it.

She gained her feet of her own accord, gathered her clothes from where they were strewn around the camp, then stood holding the big wad against her nakedness.

Her hair was a tangled red mess hanging about her dirty shoulders.

"Would you mind turning away while I dress?" she said with restrained exasperation.

Stockburn gave her his back. "What in holy hell are you doing out here?"

"Same thing you are."

"I told you to stay with the train."

She was breathing hard as she dressed. He could see her in the corner of his eye, bending and crouching as she drew on her tattered undergarments.

"I don't take orders from you."

"Don't be a fool!" Stockburn laughed caustically. "You're going to get yourself killed, young lady!"

"Stop patronizing me," she bit out. "I am a professional woman. You will not condescend to me."

"Is that what this is all about?" He glanced back at her. She'd covered all of her personal parts, so he turned to face her. "You thought I condescended to you, so you're out here to prove a point?"

She looked down at her torn blouse, holding the tattered pieces across her breasts. Her camisole remained on the ground. It had been cut so badly that it could no longer perform the function it had been designed for. "Don't be ridiculous. I am out here to retrieve the treasure those devils stole from the express car."

"And look what it got you. You were nearly killed!"

She still had her head down.

He thought she was still trying to figure out what to do about her purple blouse and the torn chemise beneath it, but then she sniffed and staggered back a little.

Stockburn said, "Oh, now . . ." He extended his arms to her, but she slapped one of his hands away.

Brushing a tear from her cheek with the back of her hand, she said, "No! Keep your hands off me. I made a mistake, is all. I let my guard down." She gazed up at him, jade eyes blazing defiantly. "It could have happened to anyone."

"Not just anyone is a beautiful young woman."

That seemed to have caught her by surprise. Her cheeks colored a little, and then she took another step back. "I'll thank you not to treat me like I'm some fragile object in the queen's boudoir. I am a professional woman. I am an employee of Wells Fargo and Company, same as you, and I am only trying to do my job."

"You followed me here?"

She nodded. "As soon as you had ridden out of sight, I saddled another one of the horses." She glanced at the saddle near the smoldering ruins of the fire, which still glowed despite the battering it had taken from Burn Face. "There was another regular stockman's saddle in the stock car, so I strapped that to its back . . . since the cowpuncher who likely owned it wouldn't be needing it anymore."

Stockburn assumed that the saddle she had strapped to the bay had also belonged to some drifting cowboy whose horse and gear had been stowed in the stock car with the army remounts. She knew tack well enough to know that McClellans were notoriously hard on a man's . . . and a woman's . . . rump.

"I knew you'd make me go back if you saw me, so I stayed far enough back as to be out of your field of vision."

Stockburn felt a little chagrined. He'd been so intent

on following his own quarry that he hadn't given due attention to his own back trail.

She shook her head quickly, stubbornly, and slid a lock of her dirty red hair back behind her ear, where it would not remain stowed. "There you have it. I am here now. I am here to help. I was raised with firearms. I know how to shoot that rifle. True, I've never shot a man, but I've brought down plenty of game, and how much harder can it be to shoot a man—especially such a man as them"—she pointed to her abusers—"than a running pronghorn at two hundred yards?"

He scowled at her. "You've shot a running pronghorn at two hundred yards?"

She gave a noncommittal shrug, her pretty cheeks coloring once more. "Give or take."

"Where did you grow up?"

"Colorado. On a ranch. My mother died when I was very young, and my father only knew how to raise boys. He raised me like he raised my brothers, and that included teaching me how to trap and shoot and even how to fight with my fists." She made a tough, determined expression, narrowing her eyes, pursing her lips, and raising her fists.

In spite of himself, Stockburn chuckled as he gazed at her. "You sure don't look like no boy."

She huffed, face clouding up again. "Would you please stop doing that?"

"Doing what?"

"Condescending to me so. Not taking me seriously!"

"I'm sorry, Henrietta. I mean Hank. It's just that I've never seen an express guard . . . well, uh . . . like you."

"I usually ride undercover in one of the passenger cars, keeping an eye out for possible trouble. On this run, they were short guards for the express car . . . and with the Devil's Horde having preyed on this route of late . . . I was otherwise assigned. Mr. Winthrop would not have given me such an assignment if he hadn't been confident of my skills with a shooting iron, Mr. Stockburn."

"Call me Wolf, remember?"

"Wolf, then." She looked up at him from beneath her dark-red brows, jade eyes twinkling hopefully in the light from the fire. "Does that mean . . . ?"

Stockburn sighed his defeat. "Yeah, I reckon it means we're riding together. I mean, since you're here an' all." He glanced around at her camp. "I've seen what happens when you're left to your own devices."

"*Really?*" The young woman's dirt-streaked face blossomed into a relieved and grateful smile. "Oh, thank you, Wolf!" She bounded forward and wrapped her arms around his neck, giving him a tight hug.

"Say, now . . . say, now . . ." Stockburn wasn't sure what to do with his own arms. He didn't want to encourage her by returning the hug. He was still mad at the fool girl, dammit.

"You won't regret it—I promise!" Smiling, she pulled her face out of his neck and planted a kiss on his cheek. Immediately, she blushed again with embarrassment, then rubbed the kiss off his cheek with her thumb. "I'm sorry. I do apologize. That wasn't professional."

"No, it wasn't," Stockburn growled.

Still, he'd rather enjoyed the texture of her lips against his cheek.

CHAPTER 19

"Here," he said later, when he'd helped her transfer her gear as well as her borrowed horse to his camp. He extended a small tin of Brooks' Bear's-Foot Ointment to her. "Put that on your . . . you know . . . your—"

"Burns. On my *body*?" She looked up at him and again her green eyes flickered in the firelight.

It was his own fire, which he'd built up with dead willow branches he'd found around the slough.

"Yes. The burns. I didn't want to seem too forward, Henrietta."

"You're calling me Hank, remember? Since you've already seen more of me than the rules of polite society would allow outside of holy matrimony, and since we're partners now, and all."

"Whoa," Stockburn said, leaning back against his saddle with a cup of the coffee he'd brewed. "I didn't say anything about us being partners, Hank."

"Of course, we're partners. We work for the same company, don't we? We're in the same camp, aren't we? Following the same bunch of killers. "

Wolf sipped his coffee. "Be that as it may, if we run up

against them devils, you make yourself scarce. Go to ground and keep your head down until the smoke clears. Anyway, all I want to do is find out where they're forted up. Since I'm so badly outnumbered, I'll leave that bunch to the marshals and the army."

"You mean since *we're* so badly outnumbered," Hank said with a sly grin. "Now, if you'll excuse me"—she heaved herself to her feet—"I'm going to apply some of your salve here to the burns . . . on my body . . ." She chuckled throatily then flounced off into the darkness.

"Don't go far," Stockburn warned her. "There might be more where those three long-loopers came from, and they might have gone as long as the others probably had without a woman."

"Don't worry—I've learned my lesson about dissolute long-loopers!" she piped back good-naturedly.

Stockburn chuckled again, this time in amazement at how quickly the young woman had recovered from the torture she'd endured at the hands of the depraved rustlers. She was pretty, but she was not soft. And he had to admit to himself, begrudgingly, that he'd found himself enjoying her company despite her penchant for ribbing him just to get a reaction from his otherwise stoic countenance.

He couldn't let on, however. He should *not* be enjoying her company. Having her along on such a hunt was not only dangerous for her, but dangerous for him. Now he had to look out for her as well as for himself, and at such a time, he couldn't afford distractions.

He doubted very much that her supervisor, Mr. Winthrop, would have approved of Henrietta "Hank" Holloway going after a good twenty or thirty of the most depraved cutthroats to ever rob a train west of the Mississippi. They made the

James and Younger gangs look like ladies' sobriety societies.

"What's the matter?" Hank had just walked back into the camp.

"How's that?" Stockburn said.

"You're scowling." She walked over and gave him back the salve.

"Never mind. You're here now, and there isn't anything I can do about it."

"I won't be a problem, Wolf. I assure you."

Stockburn finished the last of his coffee, then shoved his cup into his possibles bag. He glowered up at the girl, who'd sewn her blouse and skirt with needle and thread she'd packed in her carpetbag. "See that you aren't." He rolled up in his blankets. "Getting late. We both need our shut-eye. Go to bed."

She sighed her frustration at his colicky nature then walked across the fire to her own bedroll.

He closed his eyes but as soon as he did he saw her staked out by that fire, those perverts ogling and torturing the poor girl. Again, in spite of himself, he opened his eyes and lifted his head. She was just then rolling into her own blankets.

"Hank?"

She glanced over at him. "What is it?"

"They didn't hurt you too bad, did they? I mean, they didn't . . ."

Hank shook her head. "No." Then she smiled. "Thanks to the Wolf of the Rails."

Stockburn gave a caustic snort then rolled onto his side, giving the girl his back.

* * *

"Where are we going, Wolf?" Hank asked the next morning, after they'd had a quick breakfast and strapped their gear to their horses. "How are we ever going to find those devils out here?"

Already mounted on her handsome dun whom she'd named Tom, after her father, she looked around the grassy prairie stretching away in all directions under the soft morning sun. Morning dew dampened the grass, flashing like sequins. Canada geese honked contentedly where they fed on the grassy slopes.

Stockburn told her about having to shoot the man he'd been following in hopes the devil would lead him to the others, thus no longer having a trail to follow to the devils' lair. He slid his freshly cleaned, oiled, and loaded Yellowboy into his saddle boot. "Your guess is as good as mine, Hank." He swung up into the saddle with a weary grunt. His night's sleep had been cut short. "But the man, which turned out to be two men, I was following were headed generally to the southeast. So, I'm thinking to keep riding in that direction. Maybe we'll pick up more sign."

He booted the bay around the slough, which smelled gamy this late in the year, then swung southeast, climbing a long, low hill. They rode out side by side, both scouring the ground with their eyes but also keeping an eye on the knolls around them, on the scout for possible riders or the telltale flash of a gun barrel.

They didn't want to ride into an ambush like Stockburn had almost done the previous day. If his sixth sense hadn't kicked in when he'd needed it most, he'd have given up the ghost.

After they'd ridden for almost an hour in silence, finding no sign, Stockburn glanced over at Hank and said, "So, tell me—how does a pretty young lady end up working for Wells Fargo as an express guard?"

Hank smiled at the compliment. "When I was sixteen, my father sent me to a Methodist school for girls in St. Louis. I think he was afraid he'd raised me more boy than girl, so he wanted me to spend some time with other young ladies my age, preferably those who were educated. I think he also hoped that by sending me to St. Louis, I would find a husband. I did not. The idea of marriage, truth be told, made my stomach roll. To be tied to a man, well . . ." She looked over at Stockburn and curled her upper lip disdainfully.

"You don't like men?" he asked with an incredulous raise of his brows.

"Oh, I like them just fine. As long as I'm not living with them. Having been raised by an overbearing father and three overbearing brothers, I am pleased to live independently now, thank you very much."

"Well, that's a damn shame. A pretty girl like you would make some man very happy."

"You don't know me. And looks aren't everything, Wolf."

"No, but they help. Anyway, go on . . ."

"While I did not find a man in St. Louis, I did find a good education. Good thing that I did, too, because after I graduated from Mary Elizabeth College, I returned home to find that my father was dying of cancer. He gave me no indication in any of his letters, as he didn't want me to, quote, fret, so of course it came as quite a shock. He died three months later."

"I'm sorry, Hank."

"Turns out that over the past few years, he'd gone into

deep debt. He'd never been a good business manager, and with the fall of stock prices and a bout of blackleg, he suffered enormous losses and mortgaged himself silly. In short, the bank owned the ranch, so as soon as my father was buried beside my mother and one of my brothers who'd died when a horse kicked him in the head, I was escorted—very politely, of course—off the property by two representatives of the Durango Bank and Trust."

"What about your other two brothers?"

"While I'd been away, Theo had moved to town and married the daughter of the man who ran the mercantile. He'd never liked ranching. My younger brother Eddie . . . well, Eddie went outlaw. Last I heard he was holing up in the mountains of Arizona, on the run from a murder charge. Apparently, he killed a teller when he and three of his friends held up a bank in Flagstaff."

Stockburn clucked his dismay at the girl's misfortune.

"So, I took a couple of steamer trunks and a carpetbag as well as my diploma from Mary Elizabeth College and hopped the train back to St. Louis, where I looked for a job. I worked for an attorney for a time, and then I answered an ad placed by the Wells Fargo Company. They were looking for express guards." She cast Stockburn a saucy smile and mock haughtily tossed her hair back behind her shoulder. "Of the female variety."

"Well, I've known they used a few women now and then." Stockburn smiled at her. "I just never met one . . . till the other day."

Her playful smile made her eyes sparkle again as she turned to him sidelong. "I've met a few detectives, but not you . . . till the other day. Heard about you, though."

"Don't believe everything you hear, Hank. Those ink spillers get paid by the word."

"You're quite the legend, Mister Wolf of the Rails. Formerly the Wolf Who Tamed Wichita." Her smile broadened coquettishly, making her pretty cheeks dimple beautifully.

Stockburn's ears warmed. How was it this girl seemed so adept at making him blush? He was not ordinarily the blushing sort. He covered his embarrassment with an acidic chuff. "Like I said, don't believe everything you read, Hank."

"Someday I'd like to hear your version of those stories, Wolf."

"Put you to sleep."

"I doubt that. I think you're just being coy."

Knowing he was at risk of blushing again, Stockburn ignored her impudence and cast his gaze across the ground around him, looking for sign.

"Um, Wolf?"

He turned to her. "What is it?"

She wrinkled the skin above the bridge of her nose with consternation. "Can we stop just for a minute?"

"Again?" he said, incredulous. "We stopped only twenty minutes ago!"

"I know—it must be the saddle. I haven't sat one this long since roundups back home, and I think I must've drunk too much coffee this morning."

Wolf gave a disgusted snort and stopped the bay. "All right, all right. Make it fast. We're burning daylight."

Hank swung down from her saddle, tossed her reins to him, and hurried off into a patch of wild berries growing on the side of the low slope. She glanced over her shoulder, a ripe berry in her lips. "No peeking!"

"No promises," he growled, looking away.

After a minute, she called, "Hey, Wolf!"

"You can't blame a man for—"

"Come here."

Stockburn turned toward her. "What is it?"

She peered at him from over the tangle of brush, and beckoned. "Come here and take a look."

Stockburn gave a ragged sigh and swung down from his saddle. He dropped both sets of reins and walked down the grassy slope, swinging wide of the brush then turning back toward where she stood twenty feet below the shrubs. As he approached, she turned toward him and raised something she held between her thumb and index finger.

"Horse apple," she said, arching one brow. She drew it to her nose and sniffed. "Fresh. Two hours, maybe three hours old, I'd say."

He stopped, drew her hand to his face, and sniffed the scat. "Impressive," he said, referring to her skill at dating the age of a horse apple. He was also mildly impressed that she would hold such a thing in her bare fingers. Most girls would not. But then, Hank Holloway was not most girls, he'd already concluded.

"Where'd you find it?"

"There." She pointed out the trail of apples some horse had dumped as it had passed, leaving prints in the shin-high prairie grass.

Stockburn walked down the slope a few more feet, studying the bent grass as well as the tracks of the shod horse. Looking around, he spied another set of tracks a few feet lower on the slope, laid out parallel with the first set.

"Two riders. They came from the north." He looked back over the crest of the slope then turned his head to follow the two faint, shadowlike trails of bent grass with his gaze. "They crossed the shoulder of this hill and continued to the southeast."

He shaded his eyes, studying the southeastern distance. He could see little in the sun glare except more fawn-colored prairie brushed by the soughing breeze. Heavy clouds had gathered, and their unwieldy, ragged-edged shadows moved like clipper ships across the sea of grass. Occasional cattle from area ranches peppered the low ridges, but this was mostly farm country. A few miles back, they'd passed a couple of forlorn-looking homesteads with sod shanties, and seen a farmer in striped overalls and a straw hat hoeing weeds from around his sad-looking cornstalks.

"What do you think?" Hank said, stepping up beside Stockburn.

"I think you stumbled on the trails of two riders."

"Could be cowpunchers." The young woman shrugged her slender shoulders. "Could be anyone, really."

Stockburn nodded. "Could be. I reckon we won't know who made those tracks until we run them down. And since they're the first tracks we've seen in a while, let's run 'em down."

Feeling hopeful again, he strode quickly back up the slope and swung into the leather.

Hank did the same, turning her playful, dimple-cheeked smile on him again. "See what I mean about two pair of eyes being better than one?"

"Yeah, yeah," Stockburn grunted, booting the bay down the slope.

"Guess you're not so mad at me for taking that nature walk anymore," she called as she put her own mount into motion behind him.

Chagrined, Stockburn muttered under his breath.

He urged the bay into a rocking lope, no longer needing to lead Ma MacDougal's palomino. Nugget and the bay had made friends, and horses being some of the most social of animals, Nugget wanted to stick close.

He had a feeling he was getting close, very close, to the hideout of the Devil's Horde, and soon would no longer need the extra mount. He had another feeling that the two sets of tracks that Hank had picked up would lead him to the front door.

After another half hour's hard ride, more clouds closed over the sky and hunkered low. They were the color of bruised plums. The wind picked up, turning cold. Stockburn smelled the fresh aroma of rain and saw a blue curtain streaked with white that meant heavy showers laced with hail.

It was getting darker and darker.

"Not good," he said aloud, raising his voice to be heard above the wind. "Not good at all."

Soon, it got worse.

A deep rumbling rose. If they'd been anywhere near the Northern Pacific rails, he'd have thought it was a fast-approaching train.

"What is that?" Hank called from where she rode her dun to his right. "Sounds like a big Baldwin locomotive deadheading down a steep decline!"

"It does at that." Stockburn checked the bay down and peered to the southwest. "But it's not."

Hank stopped her own mount and turned toward where a giant, rotating twister was bearing down on them. The young woman's lower jaw dropped. "Oh . . . my . . . *God!*"

CHAPTER 20

"Ride like hell, Hank!" Stockburn shouted.

"You don't have to tell me twice!" she returned, booting her dun into a lunging gallop off Stockburn's left stirrup.

Riding hard, he looked southwest toward the pale funnel looming to his left. It grew gradually larger as it rotated, shepherding a great cloud of dust around at its base. It had to be a good mile wide, he silently opined, a cold stone of dread dropping in his belly. And they were right in its path.

Suddenly, the air around them went still. Eerily still. A sickly yellow-green color, like some atmospheric jaundice, dropped around them.

"What are those black things in the funnel?" Hank called, glancing warily toward the cyclone as she rode crouching low against the dun's mane.

Stockburn glanced at the swirling storm again. A second cold stone dropped in his belly. "Cows."

"What?" Hank yelled, looking at him skeptically.

"Those black shapes are cows, Hank! Ride like hell! You don't want to go the way of those cows!"

They couldn't outrun the storm. It was probably moving

twice as fast as any good Thoroughbred could gallop, and it stretched a good mile. But what else were they going to do?

A mile or so back, he'd thought he'd spied a draw ahead of them. Maybe, if they could reach the ravine before the tornado swept over them, they could find cover. Low ground was always safest in a cyclone. At least, that's what he'd heard. He'd never been unfortunate enough to find himself in the path of a tornado before, but he'd known those who had and who'd lived to tell the hair-raising tales.

He'd spied several from a distance when he'd been scouring the northern plains looking for his sister. None of those, however, had been as large nor as angrily threatening as the enormous pale funnel growing larger and larger before him, swooping toward them with the thunderous and deeply ominous chugging sound that seemed to rumble up out of hell's bowels.

Stockburn hunkered low in the saddle, his sombrero pulled down low over his eyes. He gave the bay its head. The palomino galloped along beside him, eyes wide and white-ringed, wanting in no way to face the storm alone. He peered around the bay's neck and was grateful to see the cut he'd been looking for opening before them.

"Ravine ahead!" he told Hank galloping on his left. "We'll take cover there!"

"I see it!"

Reaching the lip of the draw, they drew rein. The horses were breathing hard, sweat-lathered, and blowing, shifting their weight edgily, as aware as the humans were of the massive death cloud swirling and rumbling toward them.

Stockburn gazed at the storm in hang-jawed astonishment. It was a white mountain looming over them, churning, ripping, tearing up sod and shrubs and trees, and still more cattle, whipping them frenetically hundreds of feet above the ground. It was a mindless, enraged giant, as destructive as it was indifferent to that which it destroyed.

Hank looked toward the massive funnel and cursed.

"Come on!" Stockburn said, putting the bay over the lip of the draw and down the steep slope.

The ravine was around a hundred feet deep. Deeper in some places than in others. It had been cut by the forks of several creeks that were mostly dry in the late summer. Bluffs and hills and slab-sided outcroppings of sandstone and granite rose from the floor, like dinosaur teeth.

He spied what he hoped was a cavern on the side of one of those bluffs and headed for it. "Follow me!"

The bay ran sure-footedly down the steep, chalky slope, reached the ravine floor, then, obeying the light tug on the reins, galloped east along a creek bed. The gash narrowed when two bluffs pushed together from both sides. The gap was maybe a dozen feet wide, offering at least a modicum of shelter. Wolf drew rein, swung down from the saddle, grabbed his rifle and saddlebags, and paused to stare up at the ridge from which he'd come.

The funnel was turning northward. He and Hank and the horses were on its southern edge, but the winds were still pulling at them like the claws of some enormous and powerful beast. The detective held his hat in his hands or he would have lost it. A black shape caromed toward him, quickly growing in size as it swooped toward the canyon. The cow, caught by the invisible arms of the wind, was hurled in a semicircle to the north, away from the draw, flailing its hooves, its tail curving out like a thrown rope.

He gritted his teeth when he heard the poor beast's horrified lowing.

Hank's dun lunged up beside the bay. Her hair was being blown violently around her head, and the wind was snatching at her skirt and blouse, threatening to tear them off her body as violently as the three depraved rustlers had.

Stockburn reached up and pulled the young woman down off the terrified horse. "This way!"

"Oh god, Wolf!" she cried as Stockburn half-dragged her up the steep slope, heading toward the round, black maw of the cave, "It's taking me!"

"Keep your legs moving!" he shouted above the wind.

Even the horses were having trouble staying grounded, he saw with a quick glance back into the ravine. Their hooves were sliding around, sometimes rising two to three inches off the sandy creek bed. All three bucked, whinnied in terror, then took off running east along the cut and on away from the cave—which was good, he thought. They needed to save themselves just as he and Hank were trying to do.

They continued climbing the slope. He had his saddlebags draped over his right shoulder, his rifle and sombrero in his left hand. In his right hand he clutched Hank's right wrist, but the wind was pulling her with such ferocity he had trouble maintaining his hold on her. The wind was trying to suck them both off the slope and up into the funnel. It pulled Hank off her feet several times. She screamed and reached for Wolf's hand with both of her own, her blouse ripping open to expose one pale shoulder and all but the tip of a plump breast.

He had to thrust himself forward, dropping to his knees,

to maintain his hold on her. Fortunately, he was just heavy enough that he managed to stay grounded.

Meanwhile, all sorts of flotsam were being hurled around them—mainly, dirt, cow pies, grass, and willow and chokecherry branches. Even a few good-sized chunks of sod as well as a wagon wheel which had likely been torn off some sodbuster's buckboard. Stockburn wasn't sure, maybe it was only his imagination, but he thought he saw a garter snake go hurling past him and off up the creek bed in the direction the horses had fled. It had resembled a flying bullwhip.

Finally, he threw himself forward, landing belly down at the base of the cavern. He grunted, grinding his teeth as he gave Hank another hard pull, drawing her up beside him. He thrust himself onto his hands and knees and crawled into the cave, pulling her along behind him. He rolled over, drawing the young woman over him and onto her back on the other side of him, farther into the cave.

He lay just inside the cave on his back, drawing air in and out of his lungs, thoroughly exhausted, trying to catch his breath.

Hank rolled partway onto him, wrapped her arms around his neck, sobbing. "Oh god!" she cried. "Oh god—it was trying to suck me away!"

"It's all right." Wolf gave her shoulder a half-hearted pat. "Wind's dyin' now. It's passing. We're . . . all right . . ."

The resounding chugging sounds were indeed fading. The cyclone was like a train whipping past a station and racing off into the distance, only this train was leaving one hell of a broad swath of destruction in its wake. They would have been part of that destruction if they'd been only a few feet closer to the eye of the funnel. As it was, the mountain of wind had swerved at the last second, changing course and heading more north than east.

Otherwise, Wolf Stockburn and Henrietta Holloway would be no more.

Hank pressed her cheek against Stockburn's chest, shuddering with every breath she took. "I've . . . never . . . been . . . so frightened!"

"Yeah," he said wiping grit and bits of grass from his face. "I gotta admit I was a mite shaken myself."

She rose onto an elbow, gazed down at him. "You saved my life."

Suddenly, she lowered her face to his and pressed her lips to his own. "Oh, my God!" she said, lifting her face from his. "Please forget I did that! I did not do that! Please forget I did that!"

"All right, all right," he said, stunned by not only the storm in the form of the tornado but the one in the form of his pretty young partner, as well. "It's forgotten."

"Really?" she said, incredulous. "That fast?"

Stockburn sat up, still feeling the girl's lips on his. "Well, you told me to, didn't you?"

"Yes, but . . . of course, I did! All right. I'm glad. I don't know what came over me. It was the cyclone . . . so near death . . ."

"That's what I figured, Hank." He placed his hand on her knee. "Don't worry about it."

She looked down at his hand, then at him. He removed his hand from her leg.

Blushing again, she turned away quickly and stared out through the cave opening. "Is it over?"

It had become still as death. The light had turned a washed-out yellow. Thunder rumbled.

"The wind's over. Now we're in for the rain."

No sooner had the word left his lips than rain fell straight down from the sky. It was as though someone had opened a floodgate. The rain was nearly as loud as the tornado had been.

Stockburn watched the torrent, which was like a wavering white screen pulled down over the cave mouth. "Damn," he said through a sigh.

"The rain's going to wipe out the killers' sign, isn't it?"

Stockburn grimaced, nodded. "Afraid so. Damn the luck."

"Maybe we'll pick it up again if we keep riding."

"Maybe . . ."

Stockburn looked around the cave for the first time. It was maybe ten feet deep by eight feet wide. Critters had holed up in there. He saw coyote and fox prints and some old rabbit bones to which a few tufts of cottony fur still clung. What caught most of his attention was the small, neatly piled stack of brush and branches abutting the cave's wall to Stockburn's left. In front of the brush and wood was a ring of fire-charred rocks.

Some passing pilgrim had been thoughtful enough to leave the fire makings for the next passing pilgrim. Or, in this case, pilgrims.

"Our luck's not all bad," he said.

"There—ya see," said Hank. "Maybe that's a sign we'll pick up the killer's trail later today, after the storm passes."

Wolf looked back out at the rain. The sky had settled low. He couldn't see individual clouds, just a hunkered-down mass of gray. Thunder rumbled sporadically, occasionally crashing violently. Bright bolts of lightning cut through the gloom.

"I doubt we'll be pulling out of here today," he said. "Almost four o'clock as it is. These prairie storms can stay awhile, sort of roll around in place. This one has all the markings of just such a squall. I grabbed my saddlebags, though. Not much in them but some beef jerky and coffee. We won't starve."

"Is your pot in there, too, Wolf?"

"It is."

"Fish it out, and I'll make some coffee. I could go for a hot cup myself." Hank clutched herself, shivering. "Getting cold."

He handed her the coffeepot. "Here you go."

"Thank you." She avoided looking into his eyes, took the pot, removed the lid, and held it out to catch the rain gushing down over the cave opening, splashing onto the ground then rolling into the creek bed below. She was feeling self-conscious about the kiss.

What had gotten into the girl? He was old enough to be her father. Or nearly so, anyway. Like she'd said, she'd just been frightened and in need of comfort.

He decided not to think about it anymore. He'd forget it had ever happened. What the hell? It was just a kiss.

The pot filled quickly. Hank built a fire in the ring, brewed the coffee, and poured them each a cup. They sat at the opening, just inside the curtain of steadily falling rain, watching the storm in intimate silence.

By the time they'd drained the first pot, the rain had slowed, but the mist continued. The ravine beneath the cave was roughly one-quarter filled with churning, muddy water roiling off toward the east.

Even if the rain stopped, the travelers wouldn't be going anywhere till morning. There was no point in trying to negotiate floodwaters that high, nor ground that muddy. Especially when they no longer had a trail to follow.

Hank made another pot of coffee, poured them each a fresh cup. Stockburn pulled his traveling flask out of his coat pocket and held it up, one brow arched in question at his traveling companion.

Hank chuckled. "Why not?"

He dumped some of the whiskey into her steaming cup then added a liberal jigger to his own. They sat back, each against an opposite wall of the cave, and sipped their whiskey-laced coffee, bodies facing each other, but their heads turned toward the opening, watching it rain.

They said nothing for a time, then Hank took another sip of her coffee, set the cup down on the cave floor, and drew her knees to her chest. She wrapped her arms around them, rested set her chin on them, and turned to Stockburn, gazing at him from beneath her brows for nearly an entire minute in continued silence before her full mouth shaped a devious little smile. "I have a confession to make."

"Oh?"

"I've been an ardent admirer of yours for some time."

Again, Stockburn said, "Oh?"

"I'd read about you in the newspapers even before I saw the Wells Fargo ad in the St. Louis newspaper. I guess I had a schoolgirl crush on you from early on." Her smile broadened, and another flush rose from her neck into her cheeks. She looked demurely down. "I saw you as a white knight, riding the untamed West, running down and slaying savage highwaymen to make the rails safe for all."

Stockburn sipped his coffee, swallowed, and smiled. "You have a romantic turn of mind, Miss Holloway."

"You were a big reason I joined Wells Fargo."

"Sure—blame me."

"No, it's true," Hank said. "I wanted to be the female version of you, I guess. After I joined, I listened intently to the stories the other agents told about you. They, too, hold you in high esteem, and my own esteem grew. I hoped I'd get to meet you one day"

"Sorry to disappoint you."

She gazed at him intently, pursing her lips as she smiled. "You haven't."

"Nor you me, Hank."

She narrowed an eye skeptically. "Really?"

"Absolutely."

"Even after, you know, the rustlers . . . ?"

"I've been in a tight spot a time or two myself, due only to my own carelessness. It can happen to anybody, but," he added with a grin, "as regarding that particular incident, it helps when you're pretty."

She blushed again, looked down, looked at the rain, and then turned her head back to face him. Her eyes were suddenly serious, almost grave. "Why did you rebuff my kiss?"

CHAPTER 21

Wolf sipped his coffee again and returned Hank's gaze with a direct one of his own, narrowing one admonishing eye. "Because I have too much respect for both of us to have done anything less."

Deep lines of anger cut across her forehead. "What's that supposed to mean?"

"When you're older, you'll know."

"I hate that answer."

"I know." He set his coffee cup down, dug his makings out of his coat pocket, and started building a smoke.

She scowled at him, but he ignored her. Finally, she changed the subject. "I haven't heard anything about a woman in your life."

He smiled as he dribbled chopped tobacco on the Rizla paper troughed between his index finger and thumb. "You'll never see a ring on this finger."

"Why not?"

"I'm contrary."

"That I believe!"

Stockburn chuckled as he rolled the cylinder closed

and twisted the ends. "Too set in my ways. Besides, I move around too much."

"There must be someone," Hank prodded him, stretching her legs out before her and crossing her ankles. She crossed her arms on her breasts. "Don't tell me you don't have a sweet-smelling letter or two in your saddlebags."

"No sweet-smelling letters, but you're right." He was thinking about Comanche. "The lady's as contrary as I am, so we let each other breathe. Otherwise, we'd probably get into a shooting war." He smiled at the fond memory of the half-breed woman as he scraped a match across the holster on his left hip and touched the flame to the quirley sagging between his lips.

"I heard about your sister."

Stockburn took a deep drag off the cigarette and blew the smoke out into the drizzle. "You've investigated me pretty thoroughly, it seems."

"You go out looking for her from time to time. So far"—she shook her head, her eyes grave—"you haven't found her."

"No." He raised a knee, rested an arm on it, and stared out into the rain. "I likely never will. Too much time has passed."

"I'm sorry, Wolf."

"Don't be. I have a good life."

"You're lonely."

Stockburn turned to her, a brow arched skeptically. "Am I, now?"

"Yes. You don't fit in."

"You're right insightful for a girl so young."

"A woman so young."

"Forgive me. But you're wrong. Just being alone don't mean a man is lonely."

"You are, though. I see it in your eyes. You like to think you like being alone, because you have a contrary and pessimistic nature. You don't like most people. You don't have any faith in them or in society, which is just a fancy word for more than one person in a room."

"Listen to this!"

"But, really, when you get right down to it, you're lonely." Hank lifted her cup to her lips, took a slow sip, swallowed, and looked over at him again. "You know how I know this about you, Mr. Wolf of the Rails?"

"I got a feeling you're gonna tell me whether I want to hear it or not."

"Because I'm just like you."

Stockburn studied her through the gloom in the cave. His cup in one hand, his cigarette in the other hand, he crawled awkwardly over to her side of the cavern. He settled himself down close beside her, leaned back against the cool stone wall, then set his cup down. Taking her hand in his, he held it and caressed her knuckles with his thumb.

She looked at him tenderly, smiled, and rested her head against his shoulder. They sat watching the stormy night descend.

Stockburn didn't know when he'd ever before slept so deeply.

It must have had something to do with the rain that had continued off-and-on all night, the distant and soporific rumbling of thunder, and the tranquilizing sounds of the water churning below the cave. Also, the coolness and the deep darkness of the night.

The cave had been a restful cocoon, a brief escape from tumult. He felt its healing powers despite not having had a comfortable blanket to sleep on, for his and Hank's bedrolls were still on their horses—wherever they were.

The sun was already lifting its head above the horizon and angling its first buttery rays into the canyon.

He rose from where he'd slept leaning back against the cave wall and nudged Hank, who lay asleep beside him. As she stirred, groaning and stretching, he grabbed his hat, strapped on his guns and slipped and slid down the slope and into the wash, which was no longer flooded. The water had receded during the night, leaving a muddy mess.

The buttes were still dripping.

Negotiating the mud, he found the horses roughly a quarter mile beyond the cave, grazing peacefully in a grassy, willow-spiked meadow between two branches of the creek. The bay and the dun were still saddled. He led those two mounts back to the cave and unsaddled them, giving them a break from the tack while he and Hank ate the rest of their jerky and drank coffee.

They left the cave a half hour later. Stockburn wished he could return the favor of whoever had supplied the fuel for a fire, but under the sodden circumstances, that was impossible. Maybe, if he ever passed this way again—and there was a chance he would—he would resupply the cavern for the next passing pilgrim. He'd been grateful to find the wood there himself.

Of course, there was no longer any sign of the killers' trails . . . if it had been two of the Devil's Horde they'd been trailing the day before. All sign had been thoroughly wiped out by the wind and rain.

Still, Stockburn and his pretty companion continued riding southeast across the great, grassy plain, hoping to pick up the trail again soon. It was a long shot. Something told the detective he'd lost the trail for good, but he was too stubborn to turn back. Not yet. Not until he'd scoured every last canyon and draw and buffalo wallow within a hundred square miles would he admit defeat and head back to the district office in St. Paul with a report detailing only hard luck and missed opportunities.

They rode side by side, Stockburn on the bay, Hank on her dun. The palomino followed like a loyal dog.

The sun climbed, its light intensifying, burning off the fog that had cloaked the terrain in a gauzy murk. The humidity was thick and stifling.

By noon, the fog had finally burned off and Stockburn could clearly see a figure standing on a knoll maybe a half mile away, to the northeast. "Whoa, horse," he said, reining in the bay.

Hank halted the dun. "What is it?"

"Look there. Someone's waving . . . I think." He squinted, shading his eyes with a gloved hand. Sure enough, the slender figure on the knoll was waving.

It was a woman. She appeared slender and blond from that distance. She wore a white blouse and a dark green skirt. A billowy-crowned poke bonnet sat atop her head, tied beneath her chin. She waved both arms high above her head.

Beckoning.

"Looks like she might need help, Wolf," Hank said with concern.

"It does, indeed." Stockburn turned to his trail partner and narrowed one eye commandingly. "We're gonna ride in slow. You stay behind me in case it's a trap."

"All right."

"Be ready for anything, Hank."

"I will."

He booted the bay toward the waving woman, keeping his right hand on his thigh, near the ivory grips of the Peacemaker holstered on that side. He rode ahead slowly, looking around for possible trouble. He wouldn't put it past the Devil's Horde to spring a trap on him. They certainly wouldn't be above using a woman to bait it, either.

Slowly, he started up the knoll, the fawn grass waving around him, brushed with cloud shadows. The woman continued to wave, appearing to grow more and more excited as he approached, the wind battering her bonnet and tossing her long blond hair about her head and shoulders. She rose up and down on her bare feet, thrusting both hands high above her head and waving them. She appeared about to burst with excitement.

"Hi!" she yelled. "Hello! Hello! Hi, there! Hello!"

Stockburn could see her more clearly. Her clothes were badly worn. She wore a soiled apron around her slender waist. She appeared to be in her late twenties, maybe early thirties, and was very thin, almost bony. Her blond hair was nearly white, and it hung straight down past her shoulders. Her face was round and sort of cherub-like inside the cambric bonnet, with a very light dusting of freckles across her cheeks. Her eyes were a striking cornflower blue. They fairly danced with joy at the strangers' approach.

"Hello! Hello, there! Hello!"

"Hi," Stockburn said as he reined up ten feet in front of her.

In the broad hollow behind her he could see a little farm with a couple of patches of what appeared to be dead corn and another of wheat. The fields seemed old, untended, and unharvested. Set back and to one side of the little sod shack that seemed to slump under an enormous weight was a cottonwood—an old, half-dead cottonwood with a massive tangle of tendril-like branches. A sod barn flanked the shanty and flanking the barn was a paddock with one cow in it. A milch cow. A few chickens pecked around a coop near the house.

"Hello, there!" the woman said, pulling her arms down and drawing her hands together in childlike delight beneath her chin. "Welcome! Welcome! What's your name?"

Stockburn looked around and behind the woman again. Seeing no one crouching in the brush or wielding a rifle near the shack or barn, he returned his gaze to her. "I'm Stockburn." He glanced at Hank riding slowly up beside him. "This is Henrietta Holloway."

"Hello, Mister Stockburn." She bounded forward so quickly that the bay gave a start, a reaction the women seemed oblivious to. She reached up toward him with her right hand, fingers splayed desperately. He wrapped his hand around hers and then she closed her other hand around his, as well, and gave it a resolute, affectionate, delighted couple of pumps. "Hello, hello, hello! How nice to see you here!"

She broke away from him and ran on her soiled bare feet to Hank, startling the dun, as well. Again, she appeared oblivious.

"Whoa, whoa," Hank said as the horse flinched, pulling his head sharply back and to one side. When she'd calmed the mount, she extended her left hand to the woman, because she was on that side of the horse, and let her give Hank's hand the same treatment she'd given Stockburn's.

"*Velkommen, Henrietta!* Hello! *Velkommen!* I'm Beret! How nice to see you both here! Welcome, welcome!"

CHAPTER 22

The woman stepped back, shading her eyes with one hand up around her bonnet's visor, and looked up at Hank and then at Stockburn. She spoke with a pronounced Scandinavian brogue, which figured, since she appeared straight out of the fjord.

"Are you all right, Miss, uh . . . Miss Beret?" Stockburn asked. "By the way you were waving us down, I thought you might need help."

"Help? Oh, no, no, no—I just wanted you to come in for coffee and crumb cake. I just made a fresh batch for my husband, Hans Kristian, and myself. We usually stop with our chores and sit down for coffee and crumb cake at this time every morning."

Stockburn and Hank shared a fleeting, skeptical glance, then Hank smiled curiously at the woman and said, "Crumb cake?"

"A Norwegian sweet," Stockburn told her. He'd sampled the thin, rolled-up wafflelike cookie on previous visits to this land homesteaded mostly by Scandinavians and Germans.

The woman said, "I just finished baking a fresh batch.

The coffee should be cooked now, as well. Please, do come. Sit for a spell and visit with me and Hans Kristian. We do so love to visit with guests, though I'm afraid it's been a while since anyone has ridden over here. We're out a long way from the other farmers. Mrs. Kittelsen drives over now and then in her carriage to buy my eggs—they are very delicious eggs; my hens are spectacular!—but I haven't seen her in a coon's age. *Herregud*—what a beautiful horse you have! Oh, what a beautiful animal!"

She'd started to pat the snout of the bay, but the horse shied away. Her ebullient nature seemed to make both horses a little skittish. She laughed as though in delight at the horse's reaction, and again Wolf and Hank shared another curious glance.

Extreme loneliness, he thought. Almost to the point of prairie madness. The isolation caused it. He'd spied a deeply worn trail leading up the far side of the hill from the sod shack below. The trail stopped at Beret's bare feet. He felt a deep pang of sympathy for her. It appeared she came up often—maybe every day—to watch for passing visitors.

Could she really be that desperate for company?

"Please, do come," Beret urged, clenching her small, work-scarred hands together beneath her blunt chin. "*Komme, komme*—there is water in the tank for your horses!"

He glanced at Hank, then back at Beret, and smiled broadly. "Of course, we will. I was just thinking it was time to stop for a belt or two of coffee and a sweet snack. We saw you just in time, Beret." Chuckling, he swung down from his saddle.

Hank followed suit, saying, "I could use a cup myself. And crumb cake sounds wonderful!"

"Oh, Hans Kristian will be so pleased!" Beret flushed with delight as she swung around and began walking down the hill with childlike litheness, almost dancing. Twisting and turning made the hem of her sorry-looking dress swirl about her legs.

Walking backward along the path, facing the detective and the express guard following behind her, leading their horses by the reins, she said, "Hans Kristian has been feeling poorly. He spends some days in bed. Some days, like today, he gets up and milks the cow and does a little hoeing in the corn, but he gets worn out easily and returns to bed. He's in bed now, napping, but I'm sure he will join us for crumb cake and coffee. Hans Kristian says I make it even better than his mother." Beaming, she pressed two fingers to her lips. "Shhhh! *Må ikke si det!* Mustn't tell!" She blushed again, laughing girlishly, then turned forward as she continued down the trail.

"Feeling poorly, is he?" Stockburn said. "What seems to be the trouble, Beret?"

"The doctor in Jamestown told him there is something in his lungs. I don't know what it is, but he coughs a lot, and, *herregud*, he has been losing weight. I keep trying to put meat back on his bones by cooking a big meal every night."

"Is it working?" Hank asked.

"It is working! And I think I see more and more color in my beloved Hans Kristian's cheeks every day. Oh, what a handsome man he is—my Hans Kristian. The most handsome and the strongest of all of his brothers, and they are quite an impressive pack, the Andersson boys are!"

As they entered the yard at the bottom of the hill, Stockburn glanced at the patch of corn on his left. Most of the stalks still appeared to have ears on them, though badly shriveled and bird-pecked. The stalks themselves were skinny and badly withered, with hardly any leaves remaining. Green weeds—crabgrass, quack grass, pig-weed, lamb's-quarter, and dandelion—grew tall among them. Same with the wheat patch, in which the weeds were even higher than the wheat in places.

Around the coop to the east of the sod shack, there didn't appear to be many chickens. Maybe a half dozen at the most, unless others were pecking around in the tall brush behind the coop.

"Water there!" Beret pointed toward the stock tank to the right of the shanty and which was probably filled from the well that stood roughly thirty feet straight out from the shanty's front door. The water inside the stock tank looked fresh. It felt fresh when Stockburn dipped his hand.

He and Hank loosened their horses' saddle cinches to let the mounts drink freely. Ma MacDougal's palomino pushed its own way up to the tank, dipped its head, rippled its withers, and drank.

Beret stood just outside the shanty, oohing and ahing at the beauty of the three horses, her face flushed with the vigor of her vehemence. As they stepped up to the shanty, Stockburn and Hank shared a concerned glance. They shared another one when Beret opened the rickety wooden door and a foul odor drifted outside to assault their noses.

"Come, come—please!" the woman said, beckoning as she flounced into the earthen-floored hovel.

Stockburn doffed his hat as he stepped inside behind Hank. He had to duck his head, for the door frame was considerably shorter than his six-foot-three. Just inside the door, she stepped to one side and he stepped to the other side.

"I can't wait to tell Hans Kristian that we have guests!" Beret intoned, doing a bizarre little-girl's dance again as she headed for a curtained doorway in the shanty's rear wall on the far side of a small, rough-hewn eating table outfitted with two handmade, straight-back, hide-bottom chairs. A small, flat tin sheet sat on the table bearing six neatly folded and intricately patterned waffle cookies. "I know he will bounce right up and come out and greet you both warmly! He does so love conversation, Hans Kristian does!"

She pushed through the curtain. As the curtain—two trade blankets sewn together and caked with dust—jostled back into place behind her, they heard her talking quietly to someone in the bedroom. They could hear Beret's voice but not a man's.

Hank nudged Stockburn with her elbow and leaned toward him. "What's that smell?"

He shook his head. "I don't know. Smells like an un-emptied trash bin or rotten meat."

"It's making me feel a little sick."

"I know what you mean."

"Do you think she doesn't smell it?"

With his right index finger, Stockburn made a whirling motion near his ear. "Addled."

"Prairie madness?"

"Close to—"

He stopped when Beret reemerged from the bedroom. She was still smiling though not as brightly as before. She wrung her hands together in front of her flat belly. "Hans

Kristian would like me to extend his kindest regards, and his appreciation for stopping, but he will be unable to join us this morning. Unfortunately, he feels too weak to rise. Please wait here. I will fetch some cream from the springhouse." She turned and strode rather than danced out the hovel's back door, which scraped badly across the earthen floor so that Beret had to give a little grunt as she opened it.

Stockburn looked around the cabin. A small kitchen area with cupboards and shelves made from old steamer trunks and packing crates lay to the left. A small sheet-iron stove was there, as well. Heat from the stove had turned the little sod shack into a sauna. He was sweating inside his shirt and coat. A small tin pan of what appeared coffee was boiling atop the range—boiling furiously, the dancing brown bubbles oozing up out of the pot and splashing onto the ring of the stove lid beneath it.

Hank walked over to the range, found a thick scrap of cloth, and used it to pad her hand as she slid the pan to the side, where it immediately stopped boiling.

Stockburn walked around the table and glanced at Hank who regarded him incredulously from the range. He hesitated, then reached out and slid the curtain aside. He winced, then released the curtain and turned to Hank who was gazing at him with a question in her eyes.

"Well, I know what the smell is," he said.

"What?"

"Hans Kristian."

Hank gasped and raised her hand to her mouth, which opened to shape a nearly perfect O. "How long?"

"Long time. He's practically a skeleton, sitting up in bed in his nightshirt and night sock, plates of rotten food on a table beside him. Looks like she's been trying to feed him."

Footsteps sounded beyond the open back door to Stockburn's right. Beret entered holding a stone jug with a cork stopper in it. She was bright and cheerful again as she held up the jug and trilled, "Fresh cream from my lovely Corinne. Such a good and loyal cow! What would Hans Kristian and I do without the lovely milk, cream, and butter she provides each day?"

She set the jug on the table and gestured with her hand to Hank and Stockburn. "Please, sit down! Sit down! Oh, what a lovely talk we will have! I will just fetch down some cups and saucers that we carried all the way from home across the sea, and we will be all set to enjoy some fresh coffee and crumb cake! Oh, to have guests! The men who stopped here last night—and what a surprise that was!— insisted in staying in the barn. They didn't say two words, and they were gone this morning before I could even take them porridge and coffee!"

Stockburn looked at Hank sitting across from him at the table. Hank looked back at him, her eyes wide and round.

Turning back to Beret, he said, "You had visitors, ma'am?"

"If you could call them that." Beret retrieved three delicate cups and saucers from a shelf above the dry sink and set them carefully onto the table. "They didn't seem to want to have anything to do with me. The shy types, I suppose. They probably spend a lot of time out on the range and don't know how to get on with others. You know—make the *samtale*, conversation."

"They looked like cowpunchers?" Hank asked.

Stockburn saw a flush rising in her cheeks. She was getting as riled as he was. She was thinking, as was he, that there was a good chance that last night's visitors had been the devils they were after, likely seeking shelter from the storm. The time and distance would be about right.

Beret turned to retrieve the pan of coffee from the range. "Yes, they said as much. That's about all they said before they decided to spend the night in the barn. They were going to set down to table with me and Hans Kristian, but at the last minute they had second thoughts and said they'd stay in the barn. Said they didn't want to put me out any. I assure them that Hans Kristian and I—"

"Beret, were those men wearing long, black dusters, by any chance?" Stockburn interrupted the woman.

She had just filled one of the delicate cups, which had butterflies and wildflowers of many colors painted on the inside and out, with coffee from the pan. Looking over at Stockburn, surprise showing in her strangely lucid blue eyes, she said, "Why, yes, they were. How on earth did you know that, Mr. Stockburn?"

He glanced at Hank again and said with a hike of a shoulder, "Just a guess."

"What time did they leave this morning, Beret?" Hank asked, trying to keep her excitement in check. "And what direction did they head—do you know?"

"*Takk for sist!* It must have been early, because Hans Kristian and I were still asleep." She carefully set cups in front of Wolf and Hank and appeared to have forgotten Hank's second question.

Stockburn placed his right hand on her left one, smiled gently up at her, and asked, "What direction did they go . . . did you notice . . . ?"

Smiling obliviously, Beret sank onto a stool she had pulled up from a corner of the shanty. "I don't know where they went. Back to their cows, I suppose. They are probably happiest most with the *kyr*!" She tittered an enchanted laugh, then, wrapping both of her small, red, callused hands around the delicate cup, lifted her coffee to her lips.

CHAPTER 23

Stockburn felt as restless as a willow in a windstorm. He was champing at the bit to light back out on the stalking trail. The killers had been at the Andersson farm only last night! That meant they were not far away. After the rain they'd probably left a clear trail, to boot. One that would be easy to follow—possibly right up to where the whole gang of fork-tailed devils was holing up.

But he and Hank could not simply rush out of the little shanty despite how hot and fetid it was inside, with the range stoked and Hans Kristian rotting in the next room. They couldn't run out on Beret like that. The poor woman had been driven mad by grief and loneliness. Her only other recent visitors had been three of the Devil's Horde. The three riders who'd stopped last night had to have been them! Three more of the killers had rendezvoused. They'd likely left the woman alone because she was so obviously crazy.

They'd likely also gotten a good whiff of Hans Kristian, or maybe even taken a peek through the door curtain, as he had.

Funny how lunacy will put a man off, Stockburn silently

opined while he and Hank did their best to make small talk with the lonely woman. Beret Andersson was a nice-looking gal, still relatively young, but her insanity had probably prevented her from being raped and her cabin burned.

Odd how lunacy will put even a depraved man off when nothing else will. There was something about insanity that turned a man's gut cold. Stockburn felt it himself—the fear of an unmoored mind, the implication that it could, under the right circumstances, afflict him, as well.

What did we have without our sanity?

He and Hank forced themselves to stay for over a half hour in that hot, stinky little cabin, chinning with the woman whose mercurial, childlike mind leapfrogged from subject to subject, like the butterflies painted on her cups dancing from one pretty flower to the next. Finally, after they'd both eaten two of the delicious crumb cakes and downed two cups of the potent coffee, they bid adieu to the lonely woman despite her begging them to stay for dinner—and despite her assurances that Hans Kristian would likely join them by then for sure!

They mounted up and rode over to the barn while Beret stood outside the shanty, waving and calling "goodbye!" and "farewell!" The killers' trail was easy to pick up in the still-muddy yard. The three sets of tracks angled away from the barn and out of the yard to the southeast. Hearts skipping beats of anticipation, Stockburn and his pretty trail partner followed them, hearing Beret calling "*Ha det!*" and "*Farvel!*" until they were nearly a mile away and the farm behind them was little larger than a postage stamp.

As she and Stockburn trotted their horses through the stirrup-high bromegrass, Hank turned to him and said,

"Wolf, don't you think we should have done something about her?"

He glanced over his shoulder at the little farm disappearing behind a low upswell of grassy ground. "If there were anywhere else for her to go, she'd likely be there by now." He turned his head forward. "For now, she's happy. Or thinks she is, anyway. She'll end it when she's ready. When she realizes she's alone, most like."

"By *end it*, you mean . . . ?"

Stockburn shot her a grim glance. He answered the question with his eyes, adding, "It's a tough life out here, Hank. Some think the mountains are harder. They're wrong." He looked around at the nearly featureless prairie extending around him, cloud shadows scudding over him, one after another. "Out here it's the wind. Never stops. Drives people mad. Then you add in the remoteness . . . the loneliness . . ."

Hank sighed. "Still, there must be something someone could do for that poor woman."

"You think a madhouse would be better than where she is now?" Stockburn wagged his head. "Not a chance."

"Her family . . ."

"Likely all back in Norway. Her neighbors will do what they can do, then . . ."

"She'll end it," Hank said forlornly.

He shook his head at the grim cards life had a habit of dealing, especially out there.

For the moment, at least, his own cards were looking better. As far as tracking the killers went, that was. The tracks of the three horseback riders were clearly delineated in the long, blond grass. A child could have followed them.

A little farther on, the two came upon a fire ring in which the killers had likely brewed coffee. Around the ring were cigarette butts and an empty peach tin. Stockburn found a single playing card in the grass near the ring and held it up to Hank.

"Joker," she said.

"Right fitting."

Apparently, the killers had taken time for a quick game of cards with a new deck.

He dropped the card and swung up onto the bay's back. The palomino grazed nearby, keeping close. The prairie was too vast for him, as well. He didn't want to be alone.

"Let's keep going. We're close, Hank. Real close. Judging by the heat left in those ashes, they didn't stop here much over an hour ago."

They rode on ahead for a while, and then Hank said, "Do you think we're getting close to their lair, Wolf?" Her voice was low, pitched with apprehension.

"I do."

"What makes you think so?"

"We're a good hundred miles south of the Northern Pacific rails. I don't think they'd hole up much farther away from their target than that. I could be wrong, but I don't think so." Stockburn booted the bay into a trot, pondering. "Their hidey-hole is around here somewhere. We'll find it soon." He turned to Hank. "And when we do—"

"I know, I know," Hank said. "I'll keep my head down."

They followed the trails of the three killers into a broad bowl in the prairie. It took them a half hour to cross the bowl, skirting a small lake at the very bottom, and to crest the ridge on the opposite side, where they reined their mounts to a stop.

Staring into the long valley to the south, Stockburn whistled his surprise.

"A town," Hank said, staring at the little settlement nestled in the valley through which a creek or a river wound, sheathed in heavy brush and trees. She glanced at Stockburn. "Did you know there was a town out here?"

"Indeed, I did not. Don't remember seeing one way out here. On the other hand, I may not have wandered through here. It's a big territory, and there's still a lot of it I haven't searched." Stockburn turned his head to stare toward the eastern horizon. "If we're generally where I think we are, the Red River should be over that way maybe forty, fifty miles. Fort Abercrombie's on the river. So's the town of Wahpeton. I've been to both looking for Emily, but I don't know that I ever rode straight west. Mostly north or south along the Red and then west along the old army trail that the Northern Pacific rails now follow."

He looked at a two-track trail that stretched toward the little settlement below from the east, following the somewhat meandering course of the river, which looked like a river out of a romantic prairie landscape. "That would be the freight trail between Wahpeton and Bismarck. A little farther west it branches southwest toward Fort Pierre and the Black Hills. That river down there must be the Sheyenne."

"I'm so dirty and stinky," Hank said, "the Sheyenne is beckoning me to a long soak."

Stockburn raked his gloved thumb down the long line of his unshaven jaw. "No, I don't know that I've ever been through this country before. Looks like the trails we're following are heading right into town, so let's ride down and have a look around. Only . . ." He cast Hank another admonishing look.

"I know, I know," she said, rolling her eyes in frustration. "If trouble rears its ugly head, I'll keep my own head down!"

"You'll do, my dear." Stockburn smiled as he booted his horse ahead. "You'll do just fine . . . in a pinch," he added, broadening his ironic grin at the pretty young Wells Fargo messenger.

They rode on into the valley and onto the trail that stretched from east to west across it, following the picturesque stream. The three men they were following had turned their mounts east, so Stockburn and Hank turned their own mounts east, and followed the trail toward the little settlement that grew gradually before them—a small town with the usual broad main street sheathed in false-fronted buildings but with several new wood-frame houses going up around it, amid the original sod shanties and slumping log shacks.

When a sign poked its head out of the brush ahead, on the trail's right side, the two riders checked their mounts down once more. The sign leaned to one side. The wood was old but the paint on it had been refreshed lately—a single word in bright red proudly announcing PARADISE.

Below the town's name was POPULATION 161 GOOD SOULS.

"Good souls," Hank said snidely, casting a sidelong glance at Stockburn. "I just bet!"

"Yeah, I've never found that many good souls together in one place," he said with typical cynicism.

He booted the bay ahead, and soon they rode into the outskirts of the town, past a church that was getting a fresh coat of white paint. With his eyes, he followed the sounds of pounding hammers to a wood-frame house being built behind the church. The house was a mere skeleton of green lumber at the moment, but three beefy men in dungarees and suspenders were standing atop wood scaffolding, hammering siding onto the south-facing wall.

One of the men, black-bearded and stocky, was smoking a pipe and speaking around it in what Wolf recognized as German. A dray half-filled with lumber waited below the three carpenters, a beefy Percheron standing hangheaded in the tugs and traces.

The stocky German stopped talking and turned his head toward where Stockburn and Hank had stopped their horses on the street fronting the church. He nudged one of the men beside him with his elbow, then all three carpenters turned to gaze toward them with a vague suspicion in their eyes.

Hank looked at Stockburn, one brow arched skeptically. He gave a faint smile, pinching his sombrero brim to the carpenters, then nudged the bay on down the street. Hank gigged the dun ahead, staying just off Stockburn's right stirrup.

The newcomers passed a dozen or so false-fronted business buildings. A few were of old log construction but the others were wood-frame, and most were painted. Freshly painted. One of the buildings on the trail's east side—the trail had become Main Street in town, according to a crisply painted sign—was getting a new front porch. Or at least having the previous old and rotted one refurbished.

A bib-bearded older man and a younger man were doing the hoisting and nailing. A green buckboard wagon with RASMUSSEN & SON CONSTR. painted on its side and mounded with fresh lumber and a couple of nail kegs, stood on the street before them. A short-haired yellow dog with a black muzzle stood in the wagon, its front paws up on the wagon's side panel as it yipped softly and growled deeply, regarding the two strangers warily with its small, black eyes.

Stockburn rode on past the mercantile with its new veranda then again stopped the bay. Hank followed suit, and they turned their heads left and right and back again, surveying the buildings around them.

Men and women had stopped on boardwalks or in shop doors to study the two newcomers critically. A couple of old ladies in bright print dresses and felt hats tied beneath their double chins, and wearing long, black gloves, had stopped chatting out front of Haugen's Grocery Store, on the street's left side. They stared at the strangers and muttered between themselves, their tones furtively hushed.

To Stockburn's right, a man in a striped shirt, sleeve garters, and a white apron stood between the open batwings of the Sheyenne River Saloon. He leaned against the door frame, slowly smoking a hand-rolled quirley, narrowing his eyes at the pair who'd stopped their horses on the street between his saloon and the grocery store.

"Excuse me," Hank said to the apron-clad gent. "You

haven't seen three men ride into town recently, have you? Three men in long, black dusters, perhaps?"

The apron-clad man slowly lifted his quirley to his lips and drew on it deeply. Lowering his hand back down to his waist, he exhaled the smoke through his nostrils, saying quietly but firmly, "Nope."

The two old ladies to Stockburn's left muttered to each other a little more busily, regarding the two strangers with obvious disdain, as though the pretty young redhead mounted on the handsome dun had uttered something the reverend wouldn't approve of.

Hank turned to Stockburn.

He returned her look with a chastising one of his own. "Let me ask the questions—all right, Hank?"

She glowered in exasperation. "Isn't that who we're looking for?"

"Just let me do the asking—all right, Hank?" He nudged his horse ahead.

"All right, all right," she said woundedly, muttering beneath her breath as she nudged her own mount forward. "Just saw no reason not to get to the bottom of things straightaway is all."

"Getting to the bottom of things straightaway might just get us blown out of our saddles," Stockburn said, watching a shopkeeper step quickly into his shop and draw a shade down over the window in his door.

CHAPTER 24

Stockburn and Hank passed a log cabin that appeared long abandoned, with moss growing on the badly slouching roof, and weeds growing tall around it and through the boardwalk fronting it. Beyond the cabin sat a small stone shack, also with weeds growing up around it. A sign over the front door read PARADISE TOWN CONSTABLE.

While the yard was untended around the building, the building itself did not appear abandoned. A half-filled stock tank fronted it, and a saddled paint horse was tied to the hitch rack next to the tank. The saddle's latigo straps hung loose below the horse's belly. The paint turned to see the two strangers and the three horses approaching it, and gave a curious whicker as well as a ripple of his right wither. It stomped its right rear hoof.

Stockburn's bay gave an affable switch of his tail as the detective stopped the horse beside the paint and swung down from the saddle.

"What're you going to do?" Hank asked, furrowing her brow curiously as she brought her dun to a halt beside the bay.

"Figured I'd check in with the local law. He might know something."

"Funny," Hank said, hipping around in her saddle to gaze back along the street down which they'd just ridden. "Those three must be here, somewhere. I figured we'd find three saddled horses—hard-ridden ones—tied to a hitchrail outside a saloon."

"They might've stabled them," Stockburn said. "They've come a long way."

"Or maybe they rode right through town," Hank opined. "And back to their lair."

"Could be. Anyway, I'll check with the local law. He might have his own suspicions about—" He stopped as the constable's office door opened with a caterwauling of dry hinges.

A fetching young woman with long, straight, sandy-blonde hair stepped out onto the stoop, a steaming tin cup in her hand. She wore tight black denim trousers and a red-checked wool shirt a little too small for the size of the swells it had to cover. Two snakeskin suspenders holding the trousers up on her lean but nicely curved hips made that shirt look all the more inadequate.

"He might have his own suspicions about what?" the girl said. *Woman*, rather. She appeared roughly Hank's age. Gray-eyed and pretty in a country sort of way, her expression was stonily disinterested. Pinned to the shirt was a five-pointed badge into which the single word CONSTABLE had been stamped. Around her lean waist was strapped a shell belt and holster. The holster was filled with a Schofield .44 revolver with worn walnut grips. She hiked her left hip onto the rail to the right of the door as she studied the two newcomers with a vague disdain. Her high-topped brown boots were worn nearly to the texture of Indian moccasins.

Stockburn returned her gaze. As soon as he'd seen her, a lump had grown in his throat. He hadn't expected to see a woman this pretty in a town this size and this far out in the tall and uncut, let alone a woman this pretty wearing a badge.

"He might have his own suspicions about what?" the blonde repeated louder and with a growing annoyance. Her voice was deep, husky but as fetching in its way as the rest of her.

"About three men who might have ridden through town an hour or so ago," Hank answered for Stockburn, her voice pitched with its own pique. "Wearing long black dusters."

Wolf gave his partner another look of reproof. "Hank, what did I say about letting me ask the questions?"

"Well, don't just stare at her—get down to it, then!"

"I was about to!" he said, feeling his ears warm with embarrassment.

Hank wrinkled a nostril at him.

He returned his gaze to the pretty young lawwoman who appeared to be regarding him and his fiery, red-haired, jade-eyed partner with cool amusement. She wasn't smiling. He had a feeling she didn't smile a lot.

She looked at Hank and then at him, arched a brow, and said, "Hank?"

He smiled. "That's her name."

"Short for Henrietta," Hank put in cheekily.

"I think I'd go ahead and stick with Henrietta," the young lawwoman said, blinking once at Hank, "even if it takes longer to say."

Instantly, Hank's cheeks turned as red as her hair. "Thank you very much. I will take your suggestion under consideration. There, I did. I'll stick with Hank since it's my father's term of endear—"

"All right, all right," Stockburn stepped in, holding up his hand to his saucy partner, palm out and smiling at the pretty, expressionless lawwoman. "So, you're the, uh . . . the law here in Paradise."

She pulled her shirt out away from a very nicely formed breast to show the badge. "Says so, don't it?"

"Uh . . . yes, it sure does, Miss . . ."

"Lockwood. Belle Lockwood." She cut her coolly sneering gaze back to Hank. "Belle is short for Belinda." Hank fashioned a smile as cold as a frosty window in January in those parts.

Disregarding the redhead, Belle turned back to Stockburn as though he were the only one of her visitors worth addressing. "My pa, Rowdy Lockwood, is the actual constable. But Pa's on a tear, as he's wont to do, as an old army buddy came to town to visit him last week, and I haven't seen neither of 'em since. Likely over in Wahpeton seeing the elephant. Appropriately named, my Pa."

"What elephant?" Hank said, casting deep lines of incredulity across her forehead. Her face was still bright red.

Belle rolled her eyes up and to one side but did not look at Hank, much less deem her question worthy of a response. She said instead to Stockburn, "When Pa's on a tear, I take over for him until he comes back to his senses."

"By tear, you mean . . ."

"Bender." Belle Lockwood extended her thumb and raised it to her mouth, tipping her head back a little to pantomime a good healthy pull off a bottle of forty-rod. She did not smile. She made no expression whatever. Her face, which was somewhere on the knife-edge between stunning and plain as to be truly intoxicating—was as flat as slate. Still, somehow, she'd just made one of the sexiest, alluring, and erotic gestures Stockburn believed he had ever witnessed a female make in his forty long years.

She returned her gaze to his once more, and gave a single, slow blink.

He swallowed down the knot in his throat, brushed a fist across his nose, glanced around him, then returned his gaze to Belle. "Miss Lockwood . . . er, I mean, *Constable* Lockwood . . . could we step inside for a private word?"

"Hah!" Hank raked out, glaring at him.

"All right," Belle said, nodding slowly. She slid her gaze back to Hank. "I don't keep the place up like a city-lady would, so if you get the fantods at the sight of dust and maybe some mouse droppings . . ."

Hank fashioned that half-frozen smile again and said, "I assure you I don't."

Belle rose from the rail and stepped into the building. "Come on, then," she said with a weary sigh.

"I don't know what you hope to learn from her," Hank said with a caustic chuff, swinging down from the dun's back. "Her father's a drunk and she's just filling in for him because she probably doesn't have anything else to do out here on this canker on the devil's behind. I doubt she's qualified." She started toward the stone building, glancing up and over her shoulder at Stockburn and saying snidely, "Pretty, though, isn't she?" She turned her head back forward, adding half under her breath, "In a backwards sort of way . . . if you're attracted to that sort of thing."

Stockburn choked back a laugh and followed Hank up

onto the boardwalk. He doffed his sombrero and ducked his head to pass through the low opening as he stepped into the office.

It was roughly ten feet by ten feet, with a hard-packed earthen floor. A small table serving as a desk sat against the wall to the left. Three empty cells were lined up against the back wall. A black potbelly stove sat in the middle of the room. To the right was an old velvet armchair and a horsehide sofa draped by a couple of moth-eaten trade blankets. On one end of the sofa was a wooden packing crate stuffed with straw. On the straw lay a liver-colored puss with a half-dozen or more fuzzy little newborn kittens pulling on her teats, purring up a storm.

"What can I help you with?" Belle asked, sagging into the chair behind the cluttered desk. She raised her long legs and crossed them at the ankles atop the desk, leaning back in the chair, lifting the front legs up off the floor and lacing her fingers behind her head.

Stockburn stood next to the potbelly stove, which was ticking against the heat inside it and making the room stuffily uncomfortable though not as stinky as the Andersson shack, thank God. Belle didn't offer either of her guests a chair or a cup of coffee, though she raised her own cup to her lips and took a generous sip.

He glanced at the cat and her kittens and said with a smile to Belle, "Cute kitty-cats."

"Mousers," was all Belle said, closing her lips over the rim of the cup once more.

Since the girl obviously didn't cotton to idle chitchat, he got down to business. "Miss Belle, I'm Wolf Stockburn. This is Henrietta Holloway."

"I know," Belle said, sliding her snide glance toward Hank standing to Wolf's right. "Hank for short."

Hank wrinkled her nose at the young woman.

"We work for Wells Fargo. Hank's an express messenger and I'm a detective. We're here looking for the Devil's Horde. Have you heard of them?"

Belle shook a lock of her long blond hair back from her cheek and frowned up at him, pooching her lips out in idle, vaguely skeptical contemplation. "The Devil's Horde?"

"That's what the gang that's been robbing the Northern Pacific train up north has been informally dubbed by the newspapers."

"It's a fitting name," Hank put in sourly.

"They're robbers and cold-blooded killers," Stockburn said. "Hank and I tracked three of them right here to Paradise."

Belle gave a little grunt and shifted around in her chair. "I never heard of any Devil's Horde."

When Stockburn stared at her, one brow raised in disbelief, she said, "Look, Mr. Stockburn, we're a bit off the beaten path. We got no newspaper and we got no telegraph. What happens outside of shouting distance we usually don't hear about. The only news from the outside usually comes by way of a traveling tinker and a whiskey drummer from Fargo. Howell Lewis ain't been to town in several months, not since he came down with a case of the clap from one of the whores at Mrs. Stonewell's place down by the river, and Dudley Udder over to the Sheyenne River Saloon started brewing his own rotgut. So I'm sorry if I've disappointed you in knowing nothing about this Devil's Horde of train robbers."

"And cold-blooded killers," Hank slipped in.

"And cold-blooded killers," Belle said, without acknowledging the pretty messenger with a glance.

"We tracked three of them here," Hank said, her voice pitched with accusation.

"So you did," Belle said, incredulous. "And if you can find 'em, they're yours."

"Belle, folks didn't seem all that happy to see me an' Hank ride into town," Stockburn pointed out from the open doorway, where he stood staring out at the street before him.

A bald man was too-busily sweeping the boardwalk fronting Vance Johnson's Tonsorial Parlor back down the street about thirty yards, on Main Street's opposite side from the constable's office. The bald man stared toward Stockburn, the sunlight glinting off the barber's round little steel-framed spectacles.

The detective turned to regard Belle curiously. "You have any idea why?"

She shrugged. "We don't get many visitors. Naturally, when we do, folks are going to get suspicious."

"Well, they sure do seem suspicious," he said, pensively raking his thumb down his cheek.

The barber glanced up at him again, saw the detective staring back at him, then quickly drew his eyes down and quickened his sweeping, lifting a thick plume of dust around him, in front of his candy-striped barber pole.

"Almost like they're hiding something," Wolf added.

"Hiding what?" Belle asked, frowning.

"Those three killers," Hank said.

"Look here." Belle's suntanned cheeks grew a shade darker, and her pale eyes grew even flintier. "Don't you go throwin' accusations around, Hank. This is a good, peaceable town. Hardly any crime to speak of. About the only trouble that ever breaks out is when a coupla punchers from area ranches get into a foo-foo-raw over a whore or a card game. When that happens, this usually works just fine for either me or Pa."

She reached down and pulled a club up from where it had been leaning against the wall behind her. It was a four-foot-long oak branch roughly as big around as one of Stockburn's forearms. A stout knot about the size of a wheel hub lay at one end. The other end had been wrapped with rawhide to make it easier to wield. It was a well-worn, shiny, intimidating-looking thing. Stockburn wouldn't want to get brained with it. Likely no puncher, however drunk or peeved over a two-dollar doxy, would, either.

"When that doesn't do it"—Belle set the branch on the desk and slid the old Schofield .44 from the holster on her right hip and held it up for Stockburn and Hank to get a good look at—"this *always* does. Hah!"

Hank gave a start at the young constable's sudden yell. Belle flicked open the Schofield's loading gate and gave the cylinder a savage spin. The .44 sang like a coiled diamondback about to strike. Smiling—actually grinning ominously—for the first time, she slowly returned the revolver to its holster and snapped the keeper thong into place over the hammer.

Stockburn smiled at the gal. "Impressive."

Hank glowered at him. "She's just showing off for you!"

"I don't show off for no man, sweetie," Belle fired at Hank.

"You were just now showing off for him. I saw you. You may think you're very tough and capable, Miss Constable, but you are very transparent. And I wonder just how much of a hold on this town you really have!"

Belle dropped her feet to the floor with a bang and sprang up out of her chair, glaring at Hank. "What the hell is *that* supposed to mean?"

"All right, all right, ladies!" Stockburn said, stepping between the two female firebrands facing off like a couple of she-bears sparring over the same rogue bull. "Hank, I reckon we'll be running along." He gave his pretty partner a hard shove toward the door. "Now!"

Hank stumbled toward the door then got her feet beneath her and swung a withering glare at Stockburn.

He turned back to Belle and said, "I hope you don't mind us poking around for a while, Miss Belle. I got a feeling those train robbers are holed up somewhere around here—the whole damn gang. I got a feeling the three we followed into town are still here, maybe intending to spend the night."

She narrowed an eye and canted her head to one side skeptically. "Are you sure they rode into town. *My* town?"

"We're sure," Hank said crisply from the door.

Stockburn cast her a commanding stare. "Wait for me outside, Hank!"

Chapter 25

Hank cursed under her breath then stomped through the door, across the boardwalk, and into the street.

Stockburn turned back to Belle. "You haven't heard of any suspicious activity lately in or around Paradise?"

"What do you call suspicious activity?"

"Oh, I don't know—large gatherings of men. Horseback riders crossing farmland or ranch land? Possibly late at night."

Belle laughed. "If folks reported large gatherings of men on horseback crossing their land, that's all I'd be investigating. This is ranch country out here, Mr. Stockburn. Beef country. Lots of cowboys. Just east of here is farmland. But around the Sheyenne, we grow beef and mostly beef. Some corn and oats, but that's mainly to feed the beef. So large packs of horseback riders is a common sight out this way."

"No sightings of a large gang holed up somewhere—a remote farm or abandoned ranch?"

Belle sucked in her cheeks and shook her head.

Stockburn pondered on that then asked, "What are

some of the largest ranches in this country? Fairly close
to Paradise, I mean."

Belle had plopped back down in her chair and hiked
her left boot onto her right knee. Running her index finger
around the rim of the coffee cup on the desk to her right,
she said, "There's the Box Star five miles north of town.
That's run by old Jason Miller. The old bastard and his
sons ramrod it along with a passel of men, most of 'em
gunhands. Eight miles southwest of town, there's Mrs.
Thornburg's Bittersweet Creek ranch."

Stockburn raised a curious brow. "A woman runs a
ranch out here?"

"We women can run a lot of things out here, Mr. Stockburn."

"I didn't mean the question as an insult—I assure you,
Belle."

"I'm just sayin' the women in these parts is right special."
Belle dipped her chin and looked up at him coquettishly
as she made the remark. He hadn't expected the salty,
rough-hewn girl capable of such a tone. "If you were to
play your cards right, maybe you might find that out for
yourself." She smiled faintly, sucking in her cheeks
again. Her eyes fairly glowed from a light from within,
and she gave the knee of her leg resting atop the other one
a single, alluring wag.

Stockburn stared down at her in silent shock.

Before he could say anything, she tossed her head
toward the window over the desk, indicating the street.
"What's she to you?"

"Hank's my colleague."

"Fancy word. What's it mean?"

"It means our relationship is strictly professional."

"I can see why. Kind of a harpy, ain't she?"

Stockburn wasn't sure how to answer that, so he said nothing, though a chuff of amusement escaped his lips. If Hank overhead either of them, they might get a bullet for their impudence, Hank already being sore at them and all.

"Yeah, she sure as hell is," Belle said. Boldly, she raked her gaze up and down the body of the tall man before her. "How tall are you, anyway, Mr. Stockburn? I personally like a tall man. You're a nice dresser, too. Sort of like a drummer, but not really. You're no fancy dan. I bet you could make a girl right happy . . . under the right conditions." She gave a boldly insinuating smile.

Suddenly, Stockburn wasn't sure who he was talking to—the Constable Belle he'd first met when he'd walked up to the place, or her previously well-concealed but brazenly outlandish alter ego.

No, he did know which one, after all. Just as he rarely ever blushed, the cat rarely got his tongue. However, he found himself suffering from both afflictions.

Belle stared up at him, chewing on the nail of her left index finger and giving her left knee another wag.

Stockburn gave another wry chuckle and, quickly composing himself, made his best effort to steer the conversation back into the realm of the professional. "Belle, I wonder if I could get you to draw me a map of the area. Just a simple one showing me the routes out to both the Bittersweet Creek Ranch and the Box Star Ranch?"

"Oh, hell!" Apparently, she hadn't been ready to get professional again. "All right! I don't think you're gonna find anything at either ranch but a peck of trouble. Especially if you get crossways with either old Jason Miller *or* Mrs. Thornburg. Colicky, both! And they don't like each other. Leastways, Mrs. Thornburg don't like Jason Miller. Not a bit."

Belle was hastily sketching away with a pencil on the back of what appeared to be an old court summons.

"Really?" Stockburn said. "How so? Land dispute?" A common enough problem among ranchers.

"No, no—nothin' like that." Belle was still scratching away on the leaf, hunkered low over the desk and pressing her tongue to her lower lip in concentration.

Scratch—scratch—scratch-scratch—scratch. Scratch-scratch-scratch.

"There!" She slapped the pencil down on the desk and slid the paper toward him. "If that don't get you to both places, I might've just saved you a bad case of lead poisoning. Jason Miller's colicky, but his oldest son, Reynolds, has got his own drawers in more of a twist than the old man does. Probably runs in that old German blood, but Reynolds and his old man are right upset on account of how Melissa Ann Thornburg refused his marriage proposal."

"Wait." Frowning, Stockburn folded the map and stuffed it into his shirt pocket, inside his frock coat. "Didn't you call her *Mrs.* Thornburg just a moment ago?"

Belle turned to face him again. Leaning back in her chair, she hiked her left boot on her right knee again. "Her husband up and died on her two years ago. Ansel Thornburg. He was a good fifteen years older than her. A wealthy man. Owns a good ten thousand acres back in the Sheyenne Bluffs. Prime stock graze. Deep ravines for winter shelter. Plenty of water all year long. Yes, sir— prime graze. He left it all to her."

"Let me guess—old Jason Miller wanted his oldest son, Reynolds, to marry her and join the two spreads."

"Or take all Mrs. Thornburg's land and money in return for a wedding certificate." Belle gave a throaty, caustic laugh to show which side she was on.

"That's getting right down to it."

"That's what I do." Belle wagged her knee and shaped her brazen grin again, color rising into her beguiling, heart-shaped face with country-direct eyes that flashed with a heedless light residing deep within. "I get right down to it."

He puckered up his forehead into a corrugation of deep lines as he said with ironic castigation, "Miss Belle, I bet you're right hard on the male population in these parts."

"If you wanna see for yourself, I'll be over to the Sheyenne River Saloon later this evening." Again, she wagged that knee and chewed her nail.

Stockburn smiled. "I could use a drink, sure enough. But first, I reckon I'd better secure rooms for me and Hank. Any suggestions?"

"You can't go wrong with the Prairie Inn . . . if you don't mind a few bedbugs, I mean. Besides, it's the only hotel in town." She jerked her head to indicate east.

"And for a bath . . . ?"

Belle dipped her chin at the barbershop she could see through the open door. The barber was no longer sweeping. He was sitting in a Windsor chair on the boardwalk fronting his wood-frame, yellow-painted shop, legs crossed, staring toward the constable's office. "Vance Johnson will fix you right up. Even give you a shave if you don't mind a nick or two. He's a nervous man, that Vance."

"Hmmm." Stockburn caressed the several-days' growth

of bristle on his cheeks. "Might be just what the doctor ordered." He pinched his hat brim to the beguiling young constable, smiled, and said, "Much obliged, Belle. Maybe see you later on this evening."

"Oh, Mr. Stockburn!"

He stopped on the boardwalk and glanced back at her. "Please, Belle—call me Wolf."

"All right. Wolf, I think you ought to accept one more word of my advice." She gave a cold smile and shook her head, making her long, pale blond hair dance about her slender shoulders. "Don't go around asking too many questions. Like I said, Paradise is a small town. But to strangers—especially snoopy strangers—it can be considerably less than—"

"Paradise?" Stockburn finished for her. "Thank you for that counsel, Miss Belle." He winked and stepped down off the boardwalk.

Hank stood in the middle of the street before him, facing east, opposite the direction from which they'd ridden into Paradise. She had her boots spread wide, fists on her hips, looking frustrated but determined. Also, a little angry. She turned to Stockburn and wrinkled the skin above the bridge of her nose. "What was that all about?"

"Private conversation," he said shortly, untying his reins from the hitchrail.

She hardened her jaws. "That woman is trouble."

"She's not the only one." Stockburn swung up into his saddle.

"What's that supposed to mean?"

"You know what it means. How you acted in there." He tossed his chin toward the constable's office where Belle stood in the doorway, resting her shoulder against the jamb, arms crossed on her chest, smiling at the two Wells Fargo agents arguing on Main Street. "Right unprofessional."

"Oh, I suppose—" Hank stopped when she saw Belle. Cheeks coloring, she swung up onto the dun and turned her horse to follow Stockburn, who was slow-walking his bay to the east. The palomino followed them, tossing his head playfully, the bay switching his tail at the unsaddled mount. They had some sort of game going, as horses would do now and then, oblivious to what was going on with their riders.

"I suppose you sparking that wild girl is professional," Hank snapped.

"I wasn't sparking her," he said, glancing at the buildings they passed as they headed toward the far end of the town. "I was getting information out of her . . . which I finally did after I gave you the bum's rush."

"I don't think you should trust anything she says."

"Oh? Why's that? 'Cause she's pretty?" He cast his angry partner a wolfish grin.

"Pretty? Hah! Maybe if she'd take a bath and put on clothes befitting her sex."

"Now, you see here? This is why I don't like working with women."

"Oh? Why, pray tell?"

"Too emotional. Downright unprofessional." Stockburn stopped his horse and turned to Hank. "And you're all a bunch of harpies, to boot!"

He glanced around him then flushed. Several people stood on boardwalks or sat in farm or ranch supply wagons, regarding them skeptically. A man loading feed into the back of a buckboard wagon gave a snicker then spat a wad of chaw into the dirt out front of the feed store on the street's north side.

"Now, if you'll forgive me," Stockburn continued to Hank, booting his horse on up the street, "I have a job to do."

Hank stayed where she was, scowling incredulously at him. "What are you doing? Where are you going?"

He glanced back at her. "I'm gonna check out the trail at this end of town, see if the three men we're looking for left town heading east."

"I already did," Hank said with a caustic sneer.

Stockburn jerked back on the bay's reins. "Huh?"

"While you were inside chatting up the so-called constable of Paradise, I checked out the trail leading out of town. Nothing. Only a few sets of wagon tracks, and one horseback rider. No three sets of shod horse tracks running parallel."

"Oh." Wolf felt his cheeks warm again. He was getting tired of blushing not to mention being read to from the book by a woman. "Well, good," he said, quickly recovering from his chagrin. "I'm glad you're finally doing something productive. You keep this up, you might even earn your keep."

Hank glared at him, flaring her nostrils.

He rode back to her. Frowning, he glanced toward where Belle was still standing in her open doorway. The pretty constable still had her arms crossed as she leaned against the doorjamb, but she was no long smiling. She was scowling. Evidently, she had something on her mind. Something that wasn't making her happy.

Halting the bay close to Hank's dun, and keeping his

voice down, Stockburn said, "Why do you think she's trouble?"

"I just do, that's all. We women might be emotional, but we're also quite prescient. Especially when it comes to other women." Hank peered over her shoulder at Belle. "Especially women who are up to no good."

He glanced toward Belle again and sighed. "Well, I reckon we'll see."

"What are we going to do now?"

"First thing? Stable our horses. Second thing, get a hotel room. We'll be spending the night."

"What about the three devils we tracked here?"

"If they didn't leave town to the east, they might have followed some secondary trail out in another direction. He looked around warily. "Or—

"They're still here," Hank finished for him, also looking around with an apprehensive expression creasing her eye corners.

"Yep." Stockburn reined his horse over to a nearby livery and feed barn. "Watch your back."

"Oh, believe me"—she tossed Belle another look of bald scorn—"I will."

CHAPTER 26

Their welcome at Nils Bergman's Livery & Feed Barn was no warmer than the welcoming they'd received in the rest of Paradise.

As they rode up to the ramp rising between the big barn's open front doors, they'd heard the Swede bawling out one of his hostlers somewhere inside the barn's deep shadows. Cussing up a storm in English. So they knew that Bergman—a big, round-faced, yellow-haired and bearded Swede—spoke English, albeit brokenly.

But when Stockburn asked the man if he'd put up three trail-worn horses within the last couple of hours, the hostler threw up his hands and grinned sympathetically, feigning incomprehension.

"We heard you speaking English very well just a moment ago, Mr. Bergman," Hank told him, adjusting the saddlebags she'd tossed over her shoulder.

Bergman stared down at her, his heavy blond brows forming V-shaped birds' wings over his blue eyes, all but hiding them from view. He threw up his hands again then led the two saddled horses into the barn, the palomino following of its own accord, no doubt smelling the oats and fresh hay residing inside.

"So that's it?" Hank scowled up at Stockburn, whose own saddlebags were draped over his left shoulder. He held his Yellowboy in his right hand. "You're just gonna let him get away with that?"

"What the hell would you like me to do, Hank? Sit him down and pistol-whip him?"

"If that's what it takes! You're the detective here. Remember, I'm just the lowly messenger."

"I'm glad you finally figured that out!" he said with a chuff, heading west along the street in the direction of the Prairie Inn, which they'd passed on their way into town. "I think you an' me are like an old married couple, Hank."

"How so?" she asked as she hurried along behind him.

He gave her a lopsided smile. "We need a little time apart."

"I've done nothing to justify your rancor," she said, snootily.

"We need to get you your own room so you can caterwaul privately. And a bath. Maybe a bath will take that hump out of your neck. At least, I'll be free of you for a time. I'm due!"

The Prairie Inn sat on the street's south side roughly a block or so from the west edge of town. It was a humble two-story building in the process of getting a fresh coat of white paint. Almost half of the building had been painted, and the wooden scaffolds were still up on one side, but there were no painters at work at the moment. The brush growing up around the building's stone foundation had taken a good bit of paint spatter from above.

Stockburn stomped up the front porch steps. As he

pushed through the front door, a little man in a green
eyeshade turned quickly away from the plant he'd been
watering. Seeing, them he gave a little strangled cry, dropping down off the short stool he'd been standing on to
water the plant, and fell back into a corner.

"Oh, lordy—it's you!" he chortled, pushing off the wall
and awkwardly regaining his feet, flushed and breathing
hard. He stood behind an oak desk flanked by ten or so
pigeonholes, a gold-washed key residing in each hole. The
plant he'd been watering hung from a hook in the ceiling
behind the desk, in the corner where the stairs rising to
the second floor slanted over the desk and the pigeonholes.

"Hell, little friend," Stockburn said with an ironic
chuckle, "you look like you just seen a ghost!"

"Or a pair of strangers he's not too fond to see on the
premises," Hank said in her sharply accusing tone. "Isn't
that right, mister?"

The man hemmed and hawed, puffing out his round
cheeks and blinking his little suety eyes. "I, uh . . . you
startled me, and I have a weak heart!"

"Or a guilty conscience."

"Hank!" Stockburn reprimanded his hot-blooded
partner.

She pursed her lips and averted her gaze, successfully
cowed.

"What would I have to feel guilty for?" the man behind
the desk asked with a keen air of self-righteous indignation.

Stockburn stepped up to the desk and swung the open
ledger book around to face him. The last date with a
name next to it was two days ago. The last name on the

page, scribbled in blue-black ink, was Titus McCormick. *Probably a drummer*.

Looking up at the indignant, little, red-faced man in the green eyeshade still glaring at him from behind the desk, he said, "Who do you have lodging here?"

"No one at the moment," he said forthrightly, lifting his knobby chin on which a white spade beard tufted.

"Well, now you have. Her and me. Separate rooms. Far, far apart. She'll have a bath."

The little old man—he couldn't have stood much over five-two or -three and was probably in his hard-earned early seventies—looked pained. He swallowed, shook his head slowly, and said, "You, uh . . . you want rooms, do ya? *Here?*"

"You are a hotel, aren't you?"

"Yes, yes . . . it's just that . . . well, I wasn't . . . I wasn't expecting any business this evening. My, uh . . . my wife has been sick and since . . . well, since I have no one working for me, just Bertha and myself, I was going to stay at home . . . with Bertha . . . since she's not feelin' well an' all . . ."

"Do it." Stockburn scribbled his and Hank's names in the ledger book then said, "How much?"

"Two dollars for each room. An extra fifty cents for the bath. It will be a while. I have to carry the water up there myself and I have—"

"Yeah, I heard—a weak heart." Stockburn flipped some coins onto the ledger book then extended his hand to the little man, who looked at the pigeonholes for a time, pondering, before choosing two keys. He turned slowly and with a vaguely guilty expression on his puffy, red-cheeked face, blinking his tiny eyes in their fat little sockets, deposited both keys into Stockburn's open palm, one after the other, with great care.

Then he stepped back and smiled weakly.

"What's your name?" Stockburn asked him.

"Samuel Schumacher. I am the owner and proprietor," he added proudly.

"I see your last guest was two nights ago," Stockburn said, frowning at the man. "You do much of a business here in Paradise, do you?"

"Certain times of the year," Schumacher added, again proudly. "Enough to make a fair living for Bertha and myself." He didn't add: *As if it were any of your business.* At least not out loud. He added it quite plainly with his eyes, however.

Stockburn grunted, turned to give Hank her key, then tramped on past the desk and mounted the stairs. It creaked beneath his boots. The handrail wobbled a little. Hank came up behind him. He could tell she was miffed because she wasn't saying anything—not characteristic of her. He was enjoying the peace and quiet.

He walked on down the second-floor hall, saying, "I'll take Six. You can have Nine."

She only grunted her general anger at him as well as her pique specific to his having asked Schumacher for rooms far apart. As he walked, he glanced at the floor at the base of each door. Gray light pooled there, reaching maybe a half inch into the otherwise dark hall from windows inside each room. As he passed Room Four on his left, the gray light beneath that door wavered a little.

The detective stopped. He gazed down at the gray light at the bottom of the door. Had a shadow passed through it? The shadow of a man moving inside the room on the other side of the door, perhaps?

"What is it?" Hank asked, standing behind him.

Stockburn took his rifle in his left hand, slid his right hand to the doorknob before him, and tried to turn it.

Locked.

Hank nudged him, giving him an exaggerated frown of curiosity.

"Thought I saw a shadow move behind this door," he whispered. He looked at the door, frowning. "Odd it's locked if no one's in there."

"You think— ?" Hank whispered.

"I don't know."

"Kick it in. Let's see who's in there."

Stockburn gave her a dubious look. She arched a quizzical brow at him.

"I'm not gonna kick the door in, Hank," he said with strained patience.

"Why not? You're a Wells Fargo detective and three train robbers might be behind that door."

"I don't know that. I'm not going to kick in Schumacher's door with nothing more to go on than I thought I saw a shadow move. It could have been a bird on the other side of the window." He moved off along the hall, raising his voice slightly as he said, "I'll keep an eye on it."

"What're you going to do?" she asked from the door to Room Six.

Stockburn poked his key in the lock of the door to room nine and said, "I'm gonna get a shave and a bath, talk to the barber. Barbers are usually a wealth of information, and they're usually good conversationalists."

"You can't keep an eye on that door"—Hank glanced

at the locked door just across the hall from her own room—"from the barbershop."

"All right, you keep an ear skinned, but keep your door closed. If anybody comes out of there, you leave 'em be and fetch me. Don't try anything stupid. You know the kind of men we're dealing with."

She drew her mouth corners down and nodded contritely, an odd disposition for her, then pushed her door open and stepped inside. Stockburn stepped into his own room then stepped out a minute later with only his saddlebags. He'd left the rifle on the bed. In town, his six-shooters would likely serve. If he ran into trouble, that was. Given the hostility he and Hank had been met with so far, that wasn't an inside chance.

As he passed Hank's room, her door opened. He stopped. She stared at him through the two-foot gap. Again, her eyes appeared contrite. Sincerely contrite, not just faking it.

"Wolf?"

"What is it?"

"I want to apologize. You know. For earlier." She jerked her chin to one side. "At the constable's office. Like you said, I was behaving unprofessionally. I don't know . . . I guess I was . . ." She dropped her chin and stared down at her hands, which she entwined in front of her belly. "I was jealous. Of Belle." She lifted her eyes to his again. "I didn't like how she was flirting with you . . . you with her."

"Ah, hell. That's all right. A fella can't get too colicky over a pretty gal feelin' jealous over him." He smiled, nudging her chin with his thumb. Have a long, hot bath. Take a nap. It's been a long ride."

Hank nodded. "I'll do both."

"And stay away from that room yonder, all right? Bad men we're dealin' with. If they're in there . . . well, you just stay away, that's all."

"Don't worry. I will, Wolf."

"And lock your door. Don't get too far away from that Winchester, neither."

"I will." Again, she tugged her mouth corners down in contrition and slowly closed and latched the door.

When he heard the key scrape in the lock, sending the bolt home, Stockburn continued down the hall and down the stairs. In the small lobby, he found the hotel owner cleaning the hotel's front windows with a rag, breathing hard and grunting with the effort.

"Mr. Schumacher, I thought you said you had no other guests besides me and my partner."

The diminutive oldster stopped shoving the rag around on the glass and turned to his tall guest, giving another sour expression. "I don't!"

"How come room five is locked?"

"Oh," Schumacher said, turning back to resume cleaning the window. "That's storage. One of these days I'm going to finally get around to cleaning it out. Thanks for reminding me of the rather extensive job facing me, Mr. Stockburn." He glowered at his annoying guest then shook his head as he continued with the window.

"Storage, huh? I see." It seemed a reasonable enough answer, and a genuine one, to boot. "All right, then. Good day, Mr. Schumacher," Wolf said as he opened the door and went out.

The little old hotelier only grunted.

When Stockburn had closed the door behind him,

Schumacher stopped cleaning the window and cast his ominous gaze toward the ceiling above his head.

Upstairs, the door to Room Four was unlocked with a raspy click. The door was pulled slowly open, the hinges squawking faintly. A man poked his head out—a big head with curly brown hair and a matching mustache. The face was all hard lines and severe planes, with a long hooked nose.

When the man saw that no one was in the hall, he drew the door open wider and stepped out. He moved on stealthy cat feet to the door nearly straight across the room from his—the door to Room Six. As he did, two more men stepped out into the hall behind him. They were both tall. All three men were tall and rawboned. All three wore rough trail gear beneath long, black dusters. Black hats topped their heads.

The first man, the one with the severe features and hooked nose, glanced at the others then, shouldering up beside the door to Room Six, softly rapped his knuckles against the door's upper panel.

"Who is it?" a girl's voice asked from the other side of the door.

The man cast his two cohorts a snide look then shoved his face up close against the door. "Stockburn," he said in a voice just above a whisper.

A floorboard on the other side of the door squeaked. A shadow moved through the gray light at the bottom of the door. The locking bolt slid open with a grating click. The door latch gave, and then the door opened a few inches.

The young redhead peered through the one-foot gap between the door and the jamb, saying, "What is—"

Those were the only two words she got out before the hook-nosed man hurled himself at her, closing his big right hand over her nose and mouth and shoving her back into the room.

His two cohorts followed him into the girl's room, hearing her muffled cries.

The third man, tall and thick-set, with a heavy, savage brow, turned to look cautiously up and down the hall then stepped back into the room and drew the door closed behind him.

CHAPTER 27

The barber, Vance Johnson, was a thin, bald, fidgety fellow whose hand shook slightly as he scraped the whiskers from Stockburn's face.

At one point, the detective reached up from beneath the starched barber cape to grab the man's hand with his own—the hand holding the straight razor with an obsidian handle. The razor-edged blade was coated in snowy white Dubois shaving soap, which, in turn, was flecked with the gray cuttings from the detective's beard.

"You're a mite on the shaky side, Mr. Johnson," Wolf said.

The barber, who had close-set, light-brown eyes and nearly a full single brow the same, mud-brown color of the hair forming a single, semicircular band around his head, just above his ears, looked down at his hands and smiled. "Don't worry, Mr. Stockburn. I haven't lost a patient yet." He looked at his hand holding the razor again.

Stockburn kept his own hand wrapped around the man's wrist, looking up to study the face of the obviously nervous gent. Perspiration had beaded along the single line of his brow.

"What's on your mind, Mr. Johnson?"

Johnson smiled again. His teeth were very small and square and ivory-colored. "Nothing, nothing."

"When a man shakes so, he's usually got something on his mind. Something devious, maybe."

"Me? Devious? Pshaw!" Johnson laughed. "Mr. Stockburn, I don't have enough imagination to be devious. Just ask my wife." He laughed again.

Stockburn released the man's hand. Johnson wiped the blade on the towel draped over his own shoulder then set the freshly stropped, razor-edged blade up the left side of his client's neck, right over the jugular and then up and over the jaw.

Hearing the soft scraping sounds of the quarter-inch beard being cleaved from his skin under the foamy layer of the mint-smelling Dubois, Stockburn was well aware that if the man wanted to kill him, he could do it in a heartbeat with one quick slice. He had considered the risk already, and decided to take it. Barbers knew things about towns that most folks, save the ladies of the evening, did not. Besides, Vance Johnson was not a killer. He had obviously not been thrilled to see Stockburn enter his shop a few minutes ago, but he was not a killer. At least, Stockburn didn't think he was. He'd missed his guess in that department in the past, but he didn't think he was missing it now.

"Tell me about your town here, Mr. Johnson," Wolf prodded the barber as he once again wiped the soap from the razor-edged blade on his towel and started cutting a fresh swath up from the base of Wolf's neck to his chin.

"Oh? Well, what would you like to know about Paradise, Mr. Stockburn?"

"Seems right prosperous for being so far out in the high and rocky. That's just an expression of course. Nothing but grass in these parts. Grass and mosquitoes." He laughed as the man wiped the blade on the towel again.

"Yessir, grass and mosquitoes, Mr. Stockburn. We got 'em both in spades. And wood ticks earlier in the year."

"I picked a few off of me recently."

"You don't say?" intoned the barber with exaggerated, conversational surprise. "Well, there you go. There's no end to 'em. As soon as the snow is gone—hell, the very next day!—then here come the ticks, an' the skeeters ain't far behind."

"Back to the town."

"What's that? Oh, yes, the town." Pressing the tip of his tongue to his lower lip and stretching his lips slightly back from his small, square, ivory-colored teeth, Johnson ran the blade up the right side of Stockburn's neck to the jaw. Shakily, he wiped the soap off on the towel.

"Seems right prosperous," Wolf prompted the man.

"Well, it is, it is. You see the freight road between Wahpeton and Bismarck runs through here from east to west. And there's a dogleg cutoff that heads down through Fort Pierre and into the Black Hills." Johnson wiped the bade again and straightened, staring down at Stockburn. "Now, there's not near the freight teams on it as there used to be, back ten, fifteen years ago, before the railroad. But it's still an easy shot from Minneapolis and St. Paul through Wahpeton to Fort Pierre or on to the north and west to Bismarck and Mandan. Sometimes, you know, it's faster and cheaper to haul by mule team than by that crazy iron hoss, yessir. I don't think the railroad's all it's cracked up to be, if you ask me. I think they got so much money tied up in rails and right-of-ways and bridges and the like, they're all gonna go broke and we'll be back to hauling by mule again, after all!"

"You might be right, you might be right," Wolf said as the barber crouched over him to go back to work with the razor. "But the freighters can't be the reason Paradise has prospered so."

"Oh, no, no. Not just the freighters. This is ranching country, Mr. Stockburn. Paradise is a supply town for the two largest ranches in the area."

"Those belonging to Mrs. Thornburg to the south and Jason Miller to the north," Stockburn put in.

"Yes, yes, exactly." Johnson was trimming the left side-burn with a small scissors, wincing with his concentration. "Those two spreads buy a lot of feed . . . harness . . . groceries . . . whiskey on the weekends"—he smiled and winked at Wolf—"haircuts."

"Hmmm."

"And there are a few smaller ranches, also a few farms."

"Still," Stockburn said, scowling his skepticism and shaking his head. "Seems like a lot of new buildings going up, a lot of repair on those already up and running."

"Yes, well, be that as it may, nobody's getting rich, Mr. Stockburn, I assure you."

"Oh, someone is."

"How's that?" Johnson handed Stockburn a damp towel sprinkled with medicinal-smelling skin tonic.

He used it to scrub his face clean of the excess shaving soap. "Whoever's robbing the Northern Pacific up north of here is hauling it in hand over fist!" He laughed darkly and watched the barber's long face turn the deep red of a

Dakota sunset. "You wouldn't know anything about that—would you, Mr. Johnson?"

Johnson looked as though he'd just swallowed a turtle. Trying to force it down, swallowing and wincing and shaking his head and smiling like a donkey with a mouthful of foxtails, he said, "The, uh . . . the, uh . . . train's been robbed? You're telling me that, Mr. Stockburn ?"

Stockburn wasn't going to get any more out of the nervous fellow. Obviously, he knew something. It was written all over his face and in the palsy in his shaving hand. But he'd choked it down so deep it wasn't going to rear its ugly head today no matter how much Wolf prodded the man. As it was, the barber appeared on the verge of suffering a heart stroke.

Changing the subject, Stockburn said, "How much for a bath, Mr. Johnson? I could use a soak."

Minutes later, armed with a clean towel, he followed the barber into the room behind the barbershop, just off a narrow outdoor dogtrot. A clothesline was strung between two awning support posts of the dogtrot. A single pair of wash-worn longhandles and a pair of socks hung on the line, buffeting slightly in the humid breeze.

On the other side of the dogtrot lay the bathhouse part of the tonsorial parlor. Through two sashed windows in the rear wall, Stockburn could see the big stove, which was situated outside under a wooden awning. The stove had a couple of large copper pots on it, steaming and bubbling away. Mixed with the steam was smoke from the chimney pipe that pushed up through the roof's broad overhang but which had gaps in its joints. Blue smoke bled out of the gaps and slithered around with the steam in the wind.

The bathhouse had a single tub in it. Stockburn had been expecting a corrugated tin tub just large enough for him to sink his big carcass into but small enough that he'd have a devil of a time climbing out of. That was usually the case out in the wild and woolly. He was pleasantly surprised to see that Johnson had outfitted his place with a deep cast-iron tub with high sides and a wide ledge on the right for accouterments like soap and a washcloth as well as a scrub brush, all of which were there.

The thing was too heavy to lift, of course, so Johnson had put a drain in it. The steel drain dropped straight down into the floor and then doglegged sharply to run straight out into the backyard, well beyond the stove. He had a patch of potatoes out there. Leastways, he'd had one. But, of course, the drainage from the bathhouse, which contained lye soap, had promptly killed off the patch, so, having learned the error of his ways, Johnson had allowed the patch to grow up in mallow and musk thistle.

"Live and learn," Johnson said, topping off the tub with a bucket of cold water after he'd poured in three buckets of near-boiling hot. "Live and learn." He left the washroom, chuckling and wagging his head with feigned joviality. "Enjoy your bath, Mr. Stockburn. Give a yell if you need anything!"

Stockburn skinned out of his duds, hung them on wall pegs over the single bench running along the front wall, and stepped into the steaming water. The water was damned hot; he watched the red line work its way up his body as, gritting his teeth, he eased himself into the tub, from which steam rose in vapor snakes. When the water had cooled a little, or he'd at least gotten accustomed to the near-scalding temperature, he went to work scrubbing and rubbing the trail filth from his broad, tall body, from the tip of his head to his toes.

Then he sank back in the still-steaming, sudsy water that had grown considerably murkier over the past couple of minutes, dug into the makings sack he'd placed on the iron shelf to his right, and rolled a smoke. He fired a lucifer match on the outside of the tub, touched the flame to the quirley, dropped the match in the water, and inhaled the peppery smoke deep into his lungs.

"Ahhhh . . ." he said, his voice echoing around the unpainted, plank-walled, wood-floored room that smelled of steam and wood smoke from the range outside. "That feels damn good."

Not just the smoke but the warm water and the absence of the ground-in grit on his skin. Stockburn was not a fancy man. He didn't mind a little trail dirt and sweat grit, but it sure felt damn good to have it scrubbed away, just the same.

He sank back, lounging in the water, relaxing, enjoying his quirley, and thinking about the problem at hand.

The Devil's Horde.

They were nearby. Somewhere close, at least. The folks in the town knew it, too, but they were keeping their own counsel. The signs were all there. The suspicious stares as Stockburn and Hank had ridden into town. Half the folks on the street probably had sore necks from watching the two strangers so closely as well as tensely.

Johnson had been as nervous as a rabbit at a rattlesnake convention.

The town was hiding something. It had a dirty secret. That secret was likely the whereabouts of the cold-blooded gang of train-robbing killers.

But why? How were they tied to them? Was Belle tied to them, too? She was a tough, proud gal. Was she a crooked one, to boot?

Wolf lifted the quirley to his lips, took another drag.

Something snapped outside of the thin-walled shack.

He held the smoke in his lungs, pricking his ears to listen intently. Nothing. He exhaled the smoke and turned to his left.

He heard it again—the very faint crunching sound of a foot being set down on brittle, late-summer grass. It came from his right. Turning in that direction, he saw movement through a knothole in a bare pine plank. He saw more movement in the gaps between the planks.

Slowly, he lifted his right hand out of the murky, tepid bathwater and placed it atop the Colt Peacemaker he had placed on the iron shelf with the soap and the rag and the brush.

Out of the corner of his left eye, he saw something move and swung his head in that direction quickly—just in time to see an unshaven face grinning at him through the sashed window. The man in a funneled brim of a black Stetson stepped back and moved his shoulders, raising something in both hands toward the window. Something moved in the window to Wolf's right, but he knew that if he took the half second to look, he'd get a bullet to the head.

He did the smart thing and grabbed the Peacemaker off the shelf and plunged backward into the water. Even underwater, he heard the deafening roar of a rifle—two rifles, rather, being triggered at nearly the same time.

Bang! Bang!

The bullets clanged like cracked bells off both sides of the cast-iron tub.

Good thing it's cast iron, Stockburn vaguely thought, his ears ringing from the deafening clangs. He rose quickly from the water and, hoping his cartridges were watertight, whipped the Peacemaker toward the window on his left. The man peering into the bathhouse widened his eyes and dropped his lower jaw in frozen dread, watching flames leap from the Colt's barrel.

Stockburn saw the bullet punch a hole in the window's upper right slash and bury itself in the ambusher's forehead, right above his brow. Dropping back down in the water caused the suds to lap up over the sides and onto the floor. At the same time, the second shooter fired another round through the right window. The bullet skimmed off the top left side of the tub, kicking up another ringing in Stockburn's ears under the water.

He rose from the brackish water again, blowing out his held breath before holding it again and lining up his sights on the right window. Too late. The second ambusher had pulled his head back away from the window.

But Stockburn could see him through the cracks between the perpendicular boards. The devil was running toward the front of the bathhouse. The detective punched a conical, high-powered round through a board.

The man yelped.

Stockburn curled his upper lip in a devilish grin and blasted two more holes through the boards, tracking the ambusher toward the front of the bathhouse. The man yelped again. There was the thud of the devil falling and striking the ground.

Wolf clambered up out of the tub. Foregoing his clothes

or even a towel, not wanting the second shooter to get away, he ran to the front door, shoved it open, and stepped out onto the dogtrot, wheeling left and extending the Peacemaker straight out in his right hand.

He moved to the east end of the dogtrot and stopped.

The second ambusher lay in the brush and strewn trash—a twisted heap shrouded in a long, black duster. The man's hat was on the ground beside him, as was a Winchester carbine. Blood coated his white shirt and string tie as well as the broadcloth waistcoat under the duster.

He wasn't moving. He'd taken all three shots. He wouldn't move again.

The first man wouldn't be moving, either, where he'd fallen on the opposite side of the bathhouse. Stockburn remembered seeing his bullet blast through the glass and into the man's forehead.

Still, he looked around—back toward the rear of the bathhouse then up along the barbershop toward the main street. Where was the third devil?

Heart thudding, naked as a jaybird and dripping wet, Stockburn strode to the other end of the dogtrot, sweeping the longhandles down from the line with his left hand. At the end of the dogtrot, he looked around once more.

Nothing out there but the first ambusher lying on his back straight out from the window through which he'd been drilled. He lay spread-eagled, still clutching his Spencer repeater in his outstretched right hand. He had curly blond hair and curly blond side whiskers as well as a good week's worth of blond beard stubble. His black hat lay on his chest over his heart as though someone had set it there out of respect for the dead.

But there was no one else out there.

"Where the hell are you, dammit?" Stockburn growled to himself. "You gotta be—" Then he remembered the locked door nearly directly across the hall from Hank's room in the Prairie Inn. His heart leaped.

The third devil was likely after Hank.

CHAPTER 28

Wolf ran back into the bathhouse, gathered his clothes, and dressed quickly, desperately, pulling on his long-handles, cotton trousers, and boots. He didn't need his tie or his vest or black frock coat or sombrero. They could wait. He ran back across the dogtrot and into the barbershop, holding both revolvers straight out before him, in case of another attack.

All he found in the barbershop was the barber sitting on the floor behind the barber chair, knees drawn up to his chest. He sat back against the shelving behind him trimmed with brightly colored bottles of many shapes and sizes. He shook his head, moaning, saying, "I'm sorry . . . I'm sorry . . . they said they'd kill me if I warned you!"

Stockburn cursed and hurried out of the barbershop through the front door.

He ran west down the main street, angling to his left. Folks had come out of shops to stare toward him skeptically, warily, some shading their eyes with their hands. Several horses were tied to the hitch rack fronting the only saloon in town, the Sheyenne River Saloon, and a couple of men in dusty range gear including chaps stepped out through the batwings, scowling curiously beneath the broad brims of their uncreased hats at the tall, half-dressed man running past them.

Stockburn mounted the hotel's front porch and fairly flew inside. He paused and raised both Peacemakers again.

The only man in the lobby was Schumacher. He stood back in the corner where Stockburn had first met him, but he wasn't watering the plant hanging there. He stood beneath the plant, hands entwined in front of his narrow chest, staring down at the floor several feet in front of him. The expression on his face was of deep chagrin, like a young schoolboy who'd been caught tossing a snake through the half-moon in the girls' privy.

Without looking at Stockburn, he shook his head slowly and said, "They threatened me. They told me they'd kill me." He turned as the detective ran past him toward the stairs. "I swear!" his voice cracked out.

Stockburn ran up the stairs taking the steps three at a time, not using the rail but holding both Colts in his hands. Reaching the top of the stairs, he yelled, "*Hank?*" and strode quickly down the dingy hall between unpainted board walls.

On his right, a door opened ahead of him. Hank's door. He stopped.

A man stepped out of the room—a tall gent in a black duster. On his long, craggy face was a scraggly washed-out mustache, goatee, and long, hooked nose. He wore no hat, and his thin hair was mussed.

As the man turned toward him, Wolf raised both thunderers and yelled, "Hold it!"

The man stumbled a little then walked toward the detective. Wolf held his fire. The man's hands were empty.

He stumbled again but quickly regained his balance. He was like a drunk who was trying very hard to appear sober. As he approached, Stockburn saw that the man wasn't looking at him. His glassy eyes appeared to be focused on something behind Wolf. The man's long, ugly face was stiff. Sweat glistened on his forehead.

Slowly, he raised his hands to his belly, and it was then that Stockburn saw the blood on his black waistcoat, behind the long, flapping duster. Blood oozed out of the man's belly, right around his bellybutton, and dribbled down over the gold buckle of his cartridge belt.

Stockburn stepped to one side, and the man walked straight on past him. He was breathing hard, making gurgling sounds in his throat.

Ahead of Stockburn, Hank stepped out of her room. Her blouse was torn again. Her long hair was mussed, several curls hanging in her face. She stopped just outside of her open door and turned toward him. Something glistening red in her right hand hung down low by her side, along the folds of her skirt. Thick red blood ribboned off the knife in her hand onto the rough wooden floor. "It's all right," she said. "He's not going anywhere but to Hell!" Her angry voice echoed around the hall.

Stockburn turned to see the gutted man stop at the top of the stairs and stare down as though considering the steps before him. He swayed backward then forward. He swayed backward again before leaning forward once more, leaving his feet and dropping straight down the stairs and out of sight. The thudding of his body on the wooden risers sounded like an earthquake. Stockburn could feel the reverberations through his boot soles.

The man piled up at the bottom of the steps with one

final *bang!* He sighed raggedly as the last breath left his lungs.

Hank strode up to Stockburn, a question in her eyes. "The other two?"

"Dead."

"Did you learn . . . ?"

"Nothing. You?"

Hank sucked in her cheeks and shook her head. "They overheard us talking in the hall. That's how they knew you were at the washhouse. The other one stayed with me. He was supposed to kill me but decided to get friendly first." She hardened her jaws as she stared toward the dark mouth of the staircase. "He found out the hard way that I carry this little pigsticker concealed in my skirt in a handy little sheath I sewed myself." She held up the bloody, pearl-handled stiletto with a five-inch blade.

"Handy." Stockburn tucked her hair back behind her shoulder. "You all right?"

She nodded, her features still hard. "Never better. I just wish one of them would've talked. About something important, I mean."

"Yeah." He walked back over to the stairs and stared at the dead man lying in an unnaturally twisted heap below.

He appeared to have broken and dislocated one arm and a leg in the fall. Stockburn didn't think his head should be turned that way, either. Schumacher must have been thinking the same thing. He stood over the dead man, staring down at him and slowly shaking his head.

"Couldn't have happened to a nicer fella," Hank said, standing beside Wolf.

Harried footsteps sounded, growing louder—boots angrily pounding the floorboards.

A shadow moved beside Schumacher and then Belle Lockwood stepped up beside the hotel owner. She stared down at the dead man then looked up at Stockburn and Hank.

She gave a caustic little half smile and, eyes firing darts of barely suppressed fury, said, "This was once a peaceable town, Paradise was. That's how it acquired the name. It was peaceable. Everyone was friendly and everyone got along. The only killin's were mostly accidental gunshot wounds." She placed her hand on her hip, jutting one elbow out to the side. "Till you two rode into town. Now I got three dead men."

"Who are they, Belle?" Stockburn asked.

"Never seen 'em before in my life," she spat out with customary defiance. "And you!" She pointed an angry finger up the stairs. "I want you two out of town tomorrow before sunrise. You understand me?"

Stockburn walked slowly down the stairs, one heavy step at a time. "No."

"No, you don't understand me, or—"

"No, we won't be leaving before sundown tomorrow."

"All right. I'll give you till after breakfast. It's a long ride to anywhere."

Continuing slowly down the stairs, brushing his right hand along the rail, he said, "I won't be going anywhere, dear Belle. Not until I've found out who and where the rest of the Devil's Horde is holed up."

"You'll do as I say!" She unsheathed the Schofield from the holster on her right hip, aimed it up at him, and clicked the hammer back. "Now, are you gonna leave or aren't ya?"

"No." He stopped near the bottom of the stairs, looking

down at Belle with her fiery eyes and cocked Schofield aimed at his head from three feet away.

"Yes, you are—or I will kill you, Stockburn!" she fairly screamed, lips stretched back from her teeth, which were white but endearingly imperfect.

"No, you won't," he said. "Belle, you're tough as whang leather, but you're no cold-blooded killer. I know what they look like. Something in the eyes. You don't have those eyes."

He calmly reached up, wrapped his hand around the Schofield, and tugged it out of the young woman's hand.

"No, damn you!" she said, stumbling forward and nearly falling onto the dead man. "You can't do that. You can't just take my gun away. I'm the goddamn constable of Paradise, damn your rancid hide, Stockburn!"

She was almost crying. Sobbing with rage.

He opened the Schofield's loading gate and turned the wheel, shaking the shells out. They tumbled onto the floor around the dead man. He closed the loading gate, spun the wheel, and handed the gun back to Belle.

She accepted it angrily and held it down at her side, staring up at Stockburn in silent, crimson-faced rage. "Damn you!" she screamed, slamming one boot down on the floor with a resounding boom.

Stockburn stepped over the dead man, brushed past Belle and Schumacher, and walked to the front of the hotel and outside.

"Damn you!" Belle fairly screamed behind him, again slamming her boot heel down on the floor. The report was nearly as loud as a pistol shot, echoing around the hotel lobby.

Wolf walked back over to the bathhouse and down the

side of the building. At the rear, three men were standing around the dead man on that side of the bathhouse, the second bushwhacker Stockburn had ventilated. They were talking in hushed, furtive tones. One was the barber, Vance Johnson, who flushed when he saw Stockburn. He looked as though he'd rather be anywhere else.

Ignoring him, Stockburn looked at the other two men—both middle-aged, one tall and lanky, with long hair and patchy beard. The other was short and gone to middle-aged tallow. "Undertakers?" Wolf asked.

The tall one just stared at the detective as though he hadn't heard the question. The other one nodded faintly. "We heard the shooting."

"Load this one and the other one on the other side of the building into a wagon. Load the one you'll find in the hotel, as well. Take the wagon over to the livery barn. I'll pick it up bright and early tomorrow."

The tall one licked his upper lip and said dully, "What're you gonna do with 'em?"

"I'm gonna see they're disposed of properly." Stockburn stepped up onto the dogtrot and walked into the bathhouse to collect the rest of his gear.

He came out five minutes later fully dressed, his saddle-bags slung over one shoulder. He'd put on a fresh pair of underwear to go with the rest of his clean self. He might have been frustrated and angry, downright colicky over the pickle he was in, but at least he and his underwear were clean. That was something, anyway.

The shorter of the two undertakers was dragging the first man Stockburn had shot by his ankles across the dogtrot, intending to lay him out with the other one, apparently. The tall undertaker was gone, probably fetching the wagon. The shorter man didn't say anything, and he avoided meeting Stockburn's gaze.

The barber had made himself scarce.

Everyone was uncomfortable, moodily holding their secrets.

When Wolf got back to the main street, it was mostly deserted. Shops were closing, but a few faces still regarded him warily from behind dusty glass. Belle was walking along the north side of the street, opposite him, heading back in the direction of her office. She turned her side-long gaze toward him and slowed her pace, a deep scowl cutting ladder rungs across her forehead. She stopped behind an awning support post, holding the post with one hand, and half turned toward him, regarding him shyly, warily, angrily.

He'd injured her pride, and she was a prideful gal. Stockburn was sorry about that, but he wasn't going to take any guff from anyone in Paradise. The citizens were harboring secrets. He wanted someone to spill the beans before he was driven into a rage and shot up the place.

He looked to his right. The Sheyenne River Saloon was calling him. Nothing like a saloon for spilling secrets. Maybe he'd get some clue as to where the rest of the Devil's Horde was holing up, cooling their heels, possibly planning another massacre.

He headed that way and a minute later mounted the boardwalk fronting the watering hole. He paused and looked to his left. Belle had turned toward him, staring at him from a block away. Her boots were spread a little more than shoulder width apart, her thumbs were hooked behind her cartridge belt. There was a challenge in the set of the girl. She looked as though she were ready to slap leather on him.

But not from a block away. She wanted to. She was thinking about it. But the distance kept her from trying anything stupid.

He'd have to watch her, though.

Stockburn grunted as he pushed through the batwings, stepping quickly to one side in case someone was bearing down on him with a rifle or something just as debilitating. To the right, five men in range gear were bellied up to the ornate bar and mirrored backbar running along the wall. Several others sat around a single table straight out from Stockburn maybe fifteen feet away. Those fellas were playing poker.

All faces turned toward the detective. Two of the men standing at the bar glanced at each other. They had a quick, silent discussion then threw back their whiskeys, grabbed their hats, and pushed away from the bar. With only a couple of quick, furtive, sheepish glances at Stockburn, they brushed past him and pushed out through the batwings.

Their stench of sweat, leather, and whiskey lingered.

"Now, that was downright unfriendly," he said.

He had a feeling Paradise wasn't going to get any friendlier anytime soon.

CHAPTER 29

Stockburn looked at the five cardplayers. All five were looking back at him with blank expressions on their faces as he sauntered over to the bar on his right.

Dudley Udder, a very tall man with coal-black hair and matching waxed mustache, stood behind the bar, looking like he might be more comfortable in a fancier watering hole in Denver, say. Or even San Francisco. But there he was in Paradise, wearing a three-piece suit without the coat. The sleeves of his pinstriped shirt with a celluloid collar, like Stockburn's own, were rolled up to his bony elbows. A foulard tie was around his neck and a red apron was tied around his waist.

Stockburn turned sideways, resting his right elbow on the bar and his right boot on the brass rail running along the base of the mahogany, and faced the three men drinking at the bar, roughly ten feet away from him. They, too, were dressed in the worn, rough-hewn gear of cow nurses.

They and Udder were looking at him with expressions ranging from mild skepticism to severe suspicion bordering on open rancor.

Stockburn said, "You fellas got any idea where that

dead beef out there belongs?" He canted his head to indicate the barbershop, figuring everyone in town already knew about the dead devils turning cold in the hotel and outside the bathhouse. Word got around fast in a town as small as Paradise. Especially word about killings. Especially word about the killings of such men as those from the Devil's Horde. Likely, the two by the bathhouse were already being loaded into the buckboard he had requested.

The cardplayers were also looking at him. They'd resumed their game for a minute or two, but after he had asked such an impertinent and shockingly direct question, they were wide-eyed, he saw by glancing quickly into the backbar mirror.

The two punchers nearest and farthest away from Stockburn were almost as tall as the bartender, who must have stood six-five or more. The puncher between them was short, with short thick arms and broad shoulders. The top of his hat came to only the shoulders of the punchers on either side of him. He stared around the man nearest Stockburn, glowering darkly at the detective, hardening his jaws until the muscles over their hinges bulged.

The clock on the far wall ticktocked.

Outside, a couple of horseback riders clomped past at fast walks. A wagon with ungreased wheel hubs squawked past. A long way away, a dog was barking.

Hearing a long, slow scraping sound, Stockburn turned his head slightly left. One of the cardplayers—a bearded man in spectacles and a brown bowler hat—fired a lucifer and lifted it to the long, black cheroot drooping from between his mustached lips. He kept his eyes on the detective as he touched the flame to the cheroot.

The little puncher turned to face the bar, picked up his shot glass, and threw back the half shot of whiskey. He set the glass down hard, angrily, then patted the shoulder of the tall puncher standing nearest Stockburn, and said, "Come on, Dutch." He glanced at the man on the other side of him. "Pecos . . ." He stepped out away from the bar, keeping his glare on Stockburn, and headed for the batwings.

Dutch and Pecos finished their own drinks, and Pecos, leaving a half-smoked quirley still smoldering in an ashtray near his empty shot glass, headed out after the glowering little bulldog.

Stockburn glanced at the five poker players still staring at him. He turned to the dour-faced bartender. "Was it something I said?"

The man stared back at him without blinking.

"Whiskey," Wolf said.

The man tucked his mouth corners down slightly and, keeping his eyes on Stockburn, reached under the bar and pulled up a bottle. The detective was glad it was a bottle. He'd thought maybe a shotgun. A twelve-gauge sawed-off would carve a mighty big hole through him. That was often what you got when you asked impertinent questions in a town that already didn't like you overmuch.

Udder pulled a shot glass down from a nearby pyramid and, still keeping his vaguely reproving gaze on Stockburn, filled the glass without look at the glass or the bottle even once. Filled it all the way to the brim, not one bit more or less, and didn't spill a drop.

That takes the talent of a man who should be working in Denver or San Francisco.

"Ten cents," he said, barely opening his mouth.

"Why don't you start me a tab? I intend to be here awhile."

"I don't start tabs for dead men, mister."

Stockburn smiled. He was getting to people. That was good. That's what he'd intended. When you offend people, they either start talking or shooting. He hoped at least one told him something before he started shooting. Maybe it wasn't the most subtle detective work, but he was an impatient man, and subtlety was an art Wolf Stockburn had not mastered. Likely, he never would.

"You run a hard bargain, friend." Wolf reached into his trousers pocket, pulled out a Liberty Eagle, and slapped it down on the bar. "Ten dollars oughta cover the night. Give me a bottle of Thunder Mountain if you got it."

"I got it," the barman said, mildly indignant. He set the bottle on the bar.

"Hold it for me. I'll be back for it." Stockburn took a sip of his whiskey then turned to regard the five card-players.

They were playing again—betting and raising and calling and tossing cards and coins on the table—and speaking in quiet, furtive tones.

He watched them for a time, finished his first shot of whiskey, and nodded at the barman, who pried the cork out of the Thunder Mountain bottle and refilled Wolf's shot glass. Reloaded, Stockburn sauntered toward the poker table. All conversation at the table stopped and all heads turned toward him.

He stopped near the table, flashed an affable smile at the five men clustered there, some looking up at him with cigarettes or cigars smoldering between their lips.

"Wondering if I could squeeze in," he said. "Nothing

like a friendly game of poker to relax and distract a man after a hard day's travails." He smiled again.

They all stared at him for about five ticks of the clock on the opposite wall.

Finally, one of them slapped his cards down and said, "You can have my place. I was just about to fold, anyway. Florence will beat me with her broomstick if I'm not home for supper."

"You can have my place," another one said, dropping his own cards and scooping a small stack of nickels off the table. "I gotta get home an' eat the slop Ethel calls cooking."

"Here, take my chair," said yet another. "If it hadn't been for bad luck tonight, I'd have had no luck at all." He, too, rose from his chair.

A half minute later, the table was cleared of everything but a nearly empty whiskey bottle, a half-finished mug of beer, an overflowing ashtray, and five shot glasses. All five poker players filed out through the batwings, the last two casting skeptical looks behind them.

Stockburn turned to the bartender, who stood regarding him dourly from behind the bar.

Udder thrust up a long arm and jutted an angry finger at his last remaining customer. "You're bad for business."

"What was your first clue?" Wolf walked back to the bar. "Oh, well. I'll take the bottle and settle into a table. You serve supper?"

"I have beefsteak and beans in the back."

"I'll take it." He grabbed the bottle and started for a table off the front end of the bar, where he could sit with his back to the wall. Of all places, and of all nights, he felt certain he'd be wise to sit with his back to the wall. He saw the batwings open and turned to see Hank step into the saloon.

She wore a fresh shirt she'd either just purchased or had taken from her carpetbag. Her long, red hair was slightly wet and freshly brushed. She looked scrubbed clean, fairly glowing from a long, hot soak, though the bridge of her nose was valleyed with deep concern.

"I expected to find you on Boot Hill," she quipped, walking toward the table Wolf had chosen. He kicked out a chair and turned to the bartender who was about to disappear through a door in the wall at the far end of the bar. "Apron, bring another plate for the lady."

The dour man didn't say anything, just disappeared through the swing door into the kitchen.

"I'm not hungry," Hank said.

"You have to eat."

She stood looking around at the empty room then turned to Wolf with an ironic half smile. "You can really clean a place out."

"I even had a bath." He sank into his chair beneath an oil painting of woman clad in only a little white dog and a come-hither smile, lounging on an ornate velvet fainting couch. He popped the cork on the bottle and filled his glass.

"You're in a bad mood," Hank observed.

"Yep."

"Considering the state you're in, I don't think you should be drinking."

"It sharpens my senses."

"After what you did to Belle, she's liable to come gunning for you." Hank, who had slacked into a chair to Stockburn's left, nearly brushing shoulders with him, reached over and closed her hand around his wrist. "I really think you should stay alert."

"I will be alert."

"If not Belle, then someone else. This town isn't safe. It's . . . it's got secrets," she said darkly, glancing through the front windows at the street touched with the muted colors of early evening.

"You can say that again." Stockburn removed her hand from his wrist and set it down on the table.

She looked down at her hand, flushed a little, and said with quiet urging, "Please, don't get into anything tonight, Wolf. I sense you're angry. I'm angry, too, but we must not throw caution to the wind."

"Me?" he said, knowing she was right but fearing his inner wolf was going to snap its chain, anyway. "Hell, I'll be as soft an' fuzzy as one of Belle's newborn baby kittens." He winked at the pretty redhead. "Just the same, if lead starts flying, you remember to keep your head down and hightail it back to the hotel pronto."

She gave an ominous sigh and cast another wary gaze toward the windows and the ever-dimming street. Stockburn knew what she was thinking. He was thinking the same thing.

Once the sun went down and darkness closed over Paradise, all hell was liable to pop.

CHAPTER 30

The steak was tough and chewy but the beans were good. At least they had nice big chunks of bacon in them.

While Stockburn and Hank ate and shadows slowly replaced the green evening light in the street outside the saloon's dirty windows, customers pushed in through the batwings by ones, twos, and threes. They had the look of townsmen thirsty enough or hungry enough to patronize the only saloon in town despite the two undesirables sitting at the table near the bar.

A few more came in to stand at the bar and nurse a beer or a whiskey or both. A poker game started up again near the table at which the previous one had been situated until Stockburn had waltzed over like a rattlesnake poking its head into a rabbit hole and scattered the poker-playing rabbits.

Five ranch men rode into town on dusty cow ponies, which they tied at the hitch racks fronting the saloon, and jostled into the Sheyenne River Saloon, laughing and cajoling and elbowing each other, cowhide chaps buffeting about their denim-clad legs, before bellying up to the bar. The other customers had all cast Wolf and Hank dark, vaguely sheepish glances, but not this bunch of ranch hands. They likely hadn't heard about the earlier dustup after which three devils lay dead.

The punchers were blissfully unaware of the danger as they sipped their whiskies and beers before ordering supper and, still laughing and cajoling and slapping each other with their dusty hats, drifted over to a table to eat it.

Later, a girl appeared from seemingly nowhere—maybe a room in the saloon's second story?—and sat down at the piano on the room's far side and began playing and singing. She had a good voice, though a little out of tune. Or maybe that was the piano.

Stockburn couldn't decide if she was just a singer and a piano player or if she plied the world's oldest trade upstairs, as well. What she wore—a lot of silk and satin around a lacy corset and bustier—was cut to show off as much of her as possible. Fishnet stockings and high-heeled red shoes also drew attention to her. Bright feathers had been braided into her hair that had been rinsed with red henna.

Wolf decided that dressed like she was, she wasn't just a piano player and singer. He guessed that if one of the men walked over and tapped her on the shoulder, she'd likely take him upstairs. She wasn't much to look at in the face, however—she had a mousy look with a pronounced overbite and a nubbin chin—so she likely wouldn't get the ol' shoulder tap until later in the evening after the townsmen and cow nurses had had enough liquor to pretty her up a bit.

One of the townsmen eventually got up and walked over to the piano and Stockburn thought he'd likely had enough forty-rod to give her the tap but, no, the short, pudgy man in a shabby derby hat and equally shabby suit just stood there, resting one elbow on the piano. Sipping from the beer bottle in his right hand, he talked and laughed with the gal a little, like they were old friends. She wasn't singing, just playing, and she seemed able to talk and play at the same time without it hurting her performance any, since it wasn't that great of a performance to start with.

As he watched them, Stockburn thought the pudgy man might just be working up the courage to give her the tap. Then the detective was given a reprieve in his desultory thinking, for Belle Lockwood pushed through the batwings.

"Oh-oh," Hank said, pushing her plate away.

"Get ready to duck," Stockburn quipped, taking a sip from his shot glass.

Belle strode into the room with aplomb, kicking her booted feet up high and throwing her hair and shoulders back and striding for the bar. She turned her head toward Stockburn and Hank just enough that he knew she saw them. She didn't give them her full attention, however. Pointedly ignoring them, she strode at a left-to-right angle and over to the bar.

"Belle, come on over here and sit down," Wolf called to her above the piano. "Let me buy you a drink."

"I buy my own drinks, thank you," she said, not looking at him but keeping her nose pointed toward the backbar mirror where she appeared to study her reflection, making sure she was fashioning the right mix of snooty disdain on her comely, suntanned features. Her tomboy face, so fresh and natural, wouldn't have been half so distracting if she didn't fill out her shirt so well and her hips hadn't been sculpted with just the right amount of female fullness.

Belle Lockwood was the kind of gal who could break a man's heart while stomping the stuffing out of him.

"Oh, come on," Stockburn said. "Let me buy you a drink by way of apology."

Hank cast him a fiery glare. "She said no, Wolf. Let her go. Besides, I think she's already drunk!"

Belle must have heard the young express messenger's haughtily spoken words. She swung around to face them, resting her left elbow atop the bar and lacing her fingers together. She considered the pair for a moment, her eyes glassy, that devilish smile in place.

Yep, she'd had a few, all right, drinking and licking her wounds. She plucked a shot glass off a pyramid on the bar then flounced over to their table.

"Oh, what the hell—I do hate to make a man beg." Belle set the glass down on the table, kicked out a chair, and dropped into it. She slid the glass toward the bottle and looking at Hank with cold disdain, said, "Fill me up."

Hank glared back at her, frozen in her own chair. "You've had enough."

"You go to hell!" Belle fired back.

"Easy, ladies." Stockburn filled Belle's glass and slid it over to her. He lifted his own glass and smiled across the table at her. "Salud!" He threw back the shot.

"Salud!" Belle tossed back her own shot. She frowned at Hank, who had not joined in the salute, then switched her gaze back to Stockburn. "She's not drinking?"

"I've had enough," Hank said, glancing down at her empty shot glass.

"Probably can't hold your liquor," Belle said with a jeering smile.

"I can hold my liquor just fine."

She leaned forward, grabbed the bottle, and filled Hank's shot glass. "Prove it."

Hank flushed and glanced at Stockburn.

"Don't do it, Hank. The constable is just trying to get your bloomers in a twist. She's got a lot on her mind, the constable does."

"Oh, do I? What do I have on my mind? If you're talking about the incident in the hotel—I let you take my pistol away from me."

"Of course you did."

"I did!" Belle slapped the table with her hand and leaned forward, glaring at him.

Some of the din died around them as others in the saloon turned toward them. The doxy—or whatever she was—playing the piano let her playing almost dwindle to a stop before she picked it back up again, pattering away at "Little Brown Jug" and singing along jovially. The pudgy man in the suit and derby hat hadn't tapped her shoulder, after all. He'd gone back to playing poker.

Belle looked around then returned her angry, defiant gaze to Wolf. "I did," she repeated, more quietly this time. "If I hadn't let you take it, I'd have had to shoot you. I'm the constable here in Paradise." She thumped her thumb against her chest. "I decide who lives and who dies, dammit!"

Hank turned to Stockburn and rolled her eyes.

"I saw that!" Belle accused her, loudening her voice again.

"You're drunk," Hank said. "I don't think the constable

of Paradise should be pie-eyed. Especially when you got—"

Stockburn cut her off with: "Where are they, Belle?"

She was slow to slide her angry eyes from Hank to him. She was still chewing on that last slight, wondering what to do about it when she said, "Where's who?"

"The train robbers."

"What train robbers?"

"You know what train robbers. The pack the dead three belong to."

Belle refilled her glass. "I got no idea."

"You don't know who those dead men were?" Hank asked her.

"I do not." She looked at Stockburn. "Salud!" She threw back the shot and slammed the glass down on the table. Running the back of her hand across her mouth, she looked at Hank. "I don't go poking my nose into other folks' business. My jurisdiction stops at the edge of town. Outside of town is up to the sheriff—Glenn Divine—over in Wahpeton. If you can get his fat ass out here, ask *him* where the train robbers are."

"Your father was a deputy," Stockburn pointed out.

"Yeah, well, my father ain't here!" She'd spoken the words fiercely, but a sheen of emotion shone in her eyes and she quickly blinked it away.

Stockburn studied her closely. He canted his head to one side and said, "You really don't know?"

"I do not. If I did, I'd tell you."

"Really?" Hank asked, also frowning deeply, curiously.

Belle did not deem her worthy of another look, apparently. She kept her eyes on Stockburn. "I have no idea." She leaned forward, crossing her arms on the table and pressing her chest against them, shoving up her cleavage into the open V of her plaid work shirt. "All right—that's not true." She looked down, ridging her brows and chewing her rich bottom lip, pensive.

"What *is* true?" Wolf prodded her, refilling her glass and then his own.

Belle looked at him, glanced around furtively as if checking to make sure they were not being eavesdropped on, and returned her gaze to Stockburn. Keeping her voice low she said, "Throwing speculation around about this is likely gonna get me back shot. Or, if not *me, you*, but—"

"But . . ." Hank said, prodding Belle.

Belle ignored her. It was like Hank was no longer sitting at the same table.

Keeping her eyes on Stockburn, Belle said, "I think it's Jason Miller. There's a big bunch of men out there at the Box Star. They come to town now an' then. Not together but in smaller groups, like the three today. Some of the old salts in town have recognized Miller's men as Texas shooters."

"From Texas, eh?" Stockburn said, slowly turning his filled shot glass on the table.

Belle continued. "Miller's had business trouble. He doesn't manage his range well and his sons are worthless. He's been frustrated because the Widow Thornburg—Melissa Ann Thornburg—refused to marry Reynolds and merge their ranches." She glanced around again, suspiciously, studying a couple of faces as though making sure no one was trying to read her lips. Finally, she turned back to Stockburn. "What I'm thinking is that if trains are being robbed up north and you think the robbers are from around here, then Miller is probably sending them."

Again, Stockburn turned his glass in a slow circle on the table. "Miller, eh?"

"Knowing what I know," Belle said, "it makes sense. Those three men you just beefed . . . ?"

"Yeah?"

"Miller's men."

"Hmmm," Stockburn said, hope growing in him. Hope that he was at last reaching the end of the trail. Tomorrow, after he'd delivered the dead killers to the Box Star, he'd likely know for sure. The trick was getting back off the Box Star without giving up his ghost.

Belle smiled and reached across the table to wrap her right hand around Wolf's left wrist. "Happy now? You like me a little better now, Wolf?"

Stockburn smiled back at her. "I do indeed, Miss Belle."

Her smile grew lusty. "How 'bout if you shake your shadow here"—she jerked her chin at Hank—"and you and me go and spend the rest of the evening somewhere private . . . and quiet?"

A loud bark of chair legs raked across the wood floor. Hank was on her feet and glaring down at Belle, hands clenched into tight fists at her sides. *"Get your hands off him, you backwater whore!"*

CHAPTER 31

The screamed insult rocketed around the saloon like the echo of a gun fired inside a stone-walled cave. It stopped all conversation and silenced the piano after the plain-faced young doxy playing it banged out a grating note with a gasping start. She turned her head full around to stare in wide-eyed shock and dismay at the pretty redhead confronting the Paradise town constable.

Belle sat back in her chair for several seconds, glaring up at the impertinent young Wells Fargo messenger glaring down at her, fists tightly clenched at Hank's sides. The blood in Belle's face rose like mercury in a thermometer, only it did so much, much more quickly than mercury ever could in Dakota, even on the hottest summer day.

"All right, now, ladies," Wolf said, placing both hands flat on the table, preparing to push himself to his feet. "Let's not get— "

Belle gave a strangling wail, bounded up out of her chair, and slammed her left fist across Hank's cheek. Hank screamed and staggered backward and sideways, hair flying. She fell into a table between Stockburn's table and the big front window.

"Whoa!" one of the men sitting at the table exclaimed, leaning far back in his chair and raising his shot glass high to avoid having his whiskey spilled.

The other two men laughed and cheered.

"Good one, Belle!" said a man on the far side of the room. "Let her have it!"

Hank pushed off the table, shook her head to clear the cobwebs, and turned to see Belle closing on her, swinging both fists. "Why, you . . . !" Hank cried, bounding forward and slamming her right fist into the constable's face.

Belle's head turned sharply to one side, and then she was the one staggering, hair flying over her face. Hank cursed shrilly and threw herself on Belle, and then they were sort of wrestling on their feet, fists flying.

"All right—that's enough!" Wolf bellowed, pushing himself to his feet. He started moving toward the two savagely fighting females but stopped when a long-barreled Smith & Wesson was pressed to his forehead, and the hammer ratcheted back.

The man wielding the weapon was one of the men who'd been sitting at the table between Wolf's own table and the window—an older gent with cottony white hair and drink-glistening eyes. He stretched his lips back from scraggly teeth and said, "Let 'em go, big man. Just blowin' off a little steam is all." His drunk-eyed grin widened, and he winked.

Rage burning in him, Stockburn glared at the smaller, older man who kept the Smithy snugged taut against Wolf's forehead. Wolf knew the man could easily shoot him and in the morning not even remember doing so. The detective had little choice but to keep his boots in place.

He watched in deep frustration as Belle and Hank

continued their fight in the middle of the saloon. Several men scattered from a table as the fighters approached, punching each other, screaming, cussing, wrestling, and pulling each other's hair.

Hank rammed her right fist into Belle's gut. Belle grunted loudly and bent forward. Hank whipped up her right knee. Wolf winced, knowing that if the knee hit home, Belle would be carried out of there. Fortunately, the knee merely glanced off of Belle's left temple as she lurched to one side, straightened, cussed shrilly, and landed a right haymaker against Hank's left cheek.

It was a solid smacking blow, evoking several loud mirthful groans and exclamations from the crowd of men standing in a ragged circle around the two fighters, cheering and laughing and offering advice to the hometown favorite—Constable Belle Lockwood.

She rolled off a table, scattering bottles and glasses. Hank followed her across the table on hands and knees. Kneeling at the table's edge, she swung her right fist, connecting solidly with Belle's mouth. Belle groaned and cupped both hands to her mouth as she staggered backward, blood oozing from her split lips.

Stockburn winced again and shook his head. He tried to step forward again, but the man holding the gun on him said, "Uh-uh," and pressed the gun barrel more firmly against his head. "Let 'em have their fun, big man. And let us have ours. I ain't been so entertained in a month of Sundays!" He laughed then turned his attention to the two fighters.

The man was distracted, but Wolf knew that if he moved overmuch, the drunken old sot would drill a bullet through his brain.

He winced again as Belle, recovered from the punch to her mouth, leaped on Hank and drove her to the floor, snarling like an enraged mountain lion with a den full of cubs. Hank screamed and cursed and then they were rolling across the floor, Hank on top, then Belle . . . then Hank . . . then Belle . . .

A chair went flying. The two fighters ripped the feet out from one of the onlookers and he fell into others who caught him, and, laughing, lifted him back upright. The one who'd almost fallen made a sad expression and complained about the beer he'd spilled. The others ignored him and returned their attention to Belle and Hank wrestling around on the floor, twisting and turning and slapping and punching and kicking and biting and howling.

Good Lord, Wolf thought. *They're gonna kill each other for certain-sure!*

Belle rolled off Hank and climbed to her feet, breathing hard. Her hair was a mess. Her mouth and nose streamed blood and one eye was already puffing up. She leaned forward to smack Hank with a roundhouse, but either because she was too addled from all the clubbing and slapping or because she couldn't see clearly because of her swelling eyes, she swung and missed though Hank hadn't even ducked.

Belle grunted as her fist whooshed through the air, her own momentum whipping her nearly full around and sending her staggering.

Hank looked up and saw Belle staggering backward toward the big plateglass window on the right side of the batwings.

Oh no, Wolf thought. *Don't do it, Hank. For all that's holy . . . don't do it!*

Hank gave a guttural wail and shot up off her heels. She rammed her head and shoulders into Belle's chest, picking Belle up off the floor and driving her backward . . . right through the big plateglass window.

Both women screamed shrilly. So did the plain-faced doxy who'd been playing the piano. She covered her face with her hands as the glass shattered and both women dropped onto the boardwalk fronting the saloon and out of sight.

The crowd roared merrily. Except for the dour-faced bartender. Dudley Udder wailed a blubbering cry of deep sadness. "Ah, no. Why'd they have to go and break my consarned window for?

Stockburn involuntarily lurched forward.

"Hold it, mister," said the man still holding the gun on him. "They ain't done!"

"Yeah, they are." Wolf jerked his head back and whipped his right arm up, slamming his fist into the Smith & Wesson. The gun roared as the shooter screamed.

The bullet blew out an eye on a grizzly head mounted on the wall over the bar. Stockburn ripped the pistol out of the old man's hand, flipped it into the air, caught it by its barrel, and slammed the butt against the old man's left temple. He hit the floor hard, out cold.

Gritting his teeth, Wolf pushed through the crowd, heaving men aside angrily, and bulled through the bat-wings and onto the boardwalk. Both girls were climbing to their feet, shaking dust and broken glass out of their hair.

They were staggering badly, both battered and bloody, clothes torn. Belle's shirt was nearly entirely ripped away from her body, revealing her pink, bloodstained chemise, which was also torn. She stood straight out away from Stockburn, facing Hank, who was just then gaining her feet and breathing hard.

"I'm gonna finish you off, you crazy lady!" Belle spat out, breathless. She pulled her Schofield from its holster.

"No, you're not." Wolf walked up behind her, ripped the pistol out of her hand, and tossed it into the nearest water trough with a plop. He picked Belle up in his arms, carried her over to the trough, and dropped her in after the gun.

She screamed as the water closed over her, sloshing over the sides of the trough.

Stockburn turned to Hank. She was still snarling though she was obviously spent. Her face was battered and bruised, blood dribbling from one nostril. She too would be sporting a pair of shiners in the morning. Her hair hung around her cheeks like a tattered red velvet curtain.

"I'm not finished with her yet!" Hank yelled as the rest of the saloon crowd watched from behind the broken window. Some of the men pushed out through the bat-wings, watching in wide-eyed fascination at likely the most fascinating spectacle to have visited Paradise in many a year.

"In fact," Hank continued, stumbling toward where Belle was lolling, only semiconscious in the rippling water, "I was just getting started!"

"I don't think so, honey." Stockburn stepped toward her.

Hank stopped. Her eyes seemed to grow heavy. She

fought to keep them open. She shook her head, took another weak-legged step forward, then stopped again. Her chin lifted and her eyes rolled back into her head. She started falling backward but Wolf reached for her, grabbed her right hand, crouched, and heaved her up. She hung over his shoulder like a sack of grain, arms and hair dangling toward the boardwalk, out like a blown lamp.

"Come on, you crazy polecat," Wolf said with a grunt. He started back in the direction of the hotel. "All good times must end. It's time for bed!"

Wolf sent Samuel Schumacher out for two bottles of whiskey—one with a label and one without.

"Do I look like your errand boy?" the hotelier asked from behind his desk as Stockburn started up the steps with Hank flung over his shoulder.

Wolf stopped and glanced over his shoulder at the man, narrowing one eye threateningly.

The man pulled his mouth corners down then reluctantly strode out from behind the desk and shambled toward the door.

Stockburn took Hank upstairs, into her room, and dropped her on the bed. "Crazy polecat!"

Regaining consciousness, she lifted her head and pressed the heels of her hands to her temples. She rolled onto one side and drew her knees to her chest. "Oh!" she groaned. "Oh, oh, oh!"

"You can say that again." He left the room to fetch his saddlebags back to Hank's room.

When Schumacher brought the whiskey, he paid the

man for the busthead but not for the errand. He still held a grudge against the man for not telling him about the three devils who had been holed up in the room with the locked door. He didn't tip men who conspired against him with killers.

The hotelier left in a snit.

Stockburn pried the cork out of each bottle and took the bottle with the label over to the bed. Hank lay on her back, eyes closed, only half conscious. Her bloody lips were stretched back from her teeth in misery.

"Here," Stockburn said, helping her sit up. "Take a couple swallows of this."

"Why?"

"Ease the pain."

She glared up at him. At least, he thought she was glaring. It was hard to tell with her eyes so swollen.

"It's whiskey that got me into this situation in the first place."

"Here, I thought you were fighting for my honor!"

Hank just stared at him.

He shook the bottle. "Go on—take a pull. It'll ease the pain. You're gonna beg me for more when I start to stitch that cut on your cheek."

She touched the first two fingers to her right cheek. "It doesn't need stitches."

"Believe me," Wolf said. "It needs stitches."

Hank took a couple of small sips from the bottle then lay back against the pillow. Stockburn set the bottle on the table beside the bed then poured the whiskey from the unlabeled bottle into the washbasin on the marble-topped stand under the room's single, curtained window and tossed a washcloth into the basin.

"I feel like a fool," Hank said tonelessly, staring up at the ceiling.

"You are a fool."

"Thank you very much."

Stockburn took the basin of whiskey over to the bed and set it on the table beside the labeled bottle. He reached into his saddlebags for his small leather sewing kit, which had saved him from a good bit of blood loss on multiple occasions when there'd been no sawbones handy. Being a railroad dick could be hazardous to one's health.

Hank watched him as he threaded the needle with catgut. "Are you going to write this into your report? Will Mr. Winthrop read about my display this evening?"

"I won't tell him on one condition."

Hank arched an expectant brow.

Wolf tied a knot in the end of the catgut, pulled it tight. "You don't fight over me anymore." He looked sidelong at her and gave a droll, one-quarter smile. "I'm not half pretty enough."

Hank grunted.

"One more thing."

"What's that?"

"You keep low tomorrow. Stay right here in your room. You're not going to feel like dancing in the streets, anyway. Stay here. Keep the door locked, your rifle handy. I'll send Schumacher up with your meals."

Hank sat up a little farther, scowling at him again. "What're you going to do?"

"I'm gonna pay a little visit to the Box Star north of town."

She crossed her arms on her chest. "Not without me you're not!"

Stockburn cast her a threatening look and said, "Winthrop's gonna get his drawers in a twist over that fight tonight, I reckon. Prob'ly won't fire you, but he'll write you up, no doubt. Nasty blemish on your work record."

Hank let out disgusted breath and sagged back against her pillow again, keeping her arms crossed on her breasts. "All right, all right. Have it your way. Get yourself killed without me."

"There's the spirit!"

He wrung the cloth out in the whiskey then set to work cleaning the cuts and bruises on her face. She moaned and groaned from the pain. Stockburn gave her more whiskey; that quieted her down a little.

It took eight stitches to close the cut on her right cheek where Belle had delivered a wicked left hook. During the procedure, Hank was admirably stoic, apparently finding a single spot on the ceiling and staring at it in silent meditation.

When he finished, she gave a heavy sigh and said, "I think I'll take another drink of that whiskey." She slurred her words drunkenly.

When Stockburn had given her more whiskey, she sat up and started unbuttoning her blouse. Her fingers weren't obeying the commands her brain was sending it. She turned to him where he sat on the bed shoving his sewing kit back into his saddlebags and rubbed her right leg against his back. With a mock-fateful sigh, she said, "I guess you're going to have to undress me, Wolf." She flopped back against her pillow, stretching her arms out to the sides invitingly, grinning at him lustily.

Wolf buckled the strap on his saddlebag pouch. "Not a chance." He rose and started for the door. "Good night, Hank."

"Sidewinder!"

Stockburn stopped at the door, his hand on the knob. "You got no idea, darlin'."

She sat up again, her swollen, drink-rheumy eyes studying him morosely. "What have you done that's so bad you can't let anyone get close to you, Wolf?"

He only smiled, winked, and glanced at the door. "Lock this when I'm gone." He left.

CHAPTER 32

Despite how pleasant it was to sleep in a bed, albeit neither all that comfortable nor lacking in bedbugs, Stockburn rose early.

The dawn was still a lavender streak in the east when he let himself out of the hotel and walked over to the only restaurant in town, the Bull Buffalo Café. It was a small, unpainted plankboard shack with a bleached buffalo skull complete with horns mounted over the front door. It was run by a stout, taciturn German woman. At least, she was taciturn with Stockburn. But, then, everyone in Paradise had been taciturn with him, so maybe the woman was quite friendly, just not to him.

He smoked his first cigarette of the day sitting at the oilcloth-covered table at the front of the earthen-floored café, his back to the wall, the front window on his left. His Yellowboy leaned against the wall behind him. He was the only customer in the café at that early hour. Maybe that was the reason the German proprietor had only scowled at him and said, "Ja?" when walking over to take his order. Maybe she hadn't been ready to start cooking yet.

Nah, that wasn't it. The town didn't like him.

As he smoked and sipped a white stone mug of hot, black coffee, a couple of shopkeepers passed on the boardwalk fronting the café. They must have seen him walk over here, for they glanced in at him through the warped glass window, churlish expressions in their eyes. When he turned his head toward them, they glanced away quickly.

People were keeping track of him. They didn't want him there. He felt he was on the brink of finding out why. Either that or on the verge of taking a pill he couldn't digest. One in .44 or .45 caliber, say.

When his food came, the sullen German woman topped off his coffee cup then disappeared into the kitchen. He didn't see her again. No other customers entered the place.

He was bad for business. If he wasn't careful, he was going to get stigmatized.

When he finished his three eggs, potatoes, a thick slab of ham, and four pieces of dark rye bread, he dropped coins onto the table, grabbed his rifle, and headed over to the livery barn. Smoking his second cigarette of the morning, he looked around warily for someone possibly bearing down on him with a rifle from an alley mouth or a second-floor window. It was still early. The sun had only started to rise, and the street was cluttered with thick, purple shadows laced with the blue smoke of breakfast fires.

Fifteen minutes later, he drove out of town in a buckboard wagon, the three dead devils lying in the low-sided box covered in several horse blankets. The Yellowboy rested on the seat beside him. Belle's map resided in the breast pocket of his shirt, but he'd memorized it over breakfast. He knew where he was going. There weren't that many trails in the big, empty country.

He'd saddled Nugget and tied the mount to the back of the wagon. The horse clomped along behind, tossing his head friskily in the fresh morning air, the intensifying sunlight flashing in his mane.

He passed a cluster of sod shanties, all likely belonging to the same family, or extended family. Often, brothers would migrate together, homestead in the same general area, and raise their families within a few miles of each other. A young boy and a girl, both clad in overalls though the girl also wore a faded checked bonnet, waved to him from near a water tank. They ran toward him, thrilled at the prospect of a visitor, but stopped and grew long-faced when Stockburn rode on by, only tapping two fingers against his hat brim.

Soon, he entered ranch country. The hills around him became spotted with cows—mainly cow-calf pairs lounging in the sun of a grassy hillside. He rode down into a creek bottom then swung west to follow the creek. He came to a barbed wire fence with a gate. Fronting the gate was a post to which three signs had been nailed. From top to bottom, they read BOX STAR RANCH. STAY OUT! RUSSLERS WILL BE SHOT ON SITE.

Not an overly educated lot, the Millers, Wolf thought as he opened the gate. He drove the wagon through the gate then walked back and closed it. He continued on his way, wondering if he'd been seen yet. If this was the Devil's Horde's hidey-hole, he likely had been. Unless they were so confident in the secrecy of their hideaway that they didn't trouble with pickets.

Keeping a close eye on the terrain around him, he kept

the wagon moving along the two-track trail. Cows grazing to either side of him broke and ran at the clatter of the wagon wheels. They were good-looking cattle, with several white faces in the bunch. Others had been bred from Texas longhorns—hardy enough to endure the harsh conditions while providing good-quality beef. Several times, Wolf studied the double ruts separated by shaggy prairie grass. Neither rut showed signs of many shod riders. A few but not, say, twenty or thirty. That didn't mean much. Passing showers might have washed away the sign or the riders might have covered their own trails to their hideout.

He stopped the wagon, dug the map out of his pocket, and studied it. Returning the map to his pocket, he swung the wagon off the trail and put the rented claybank up a steep hill stippled with post oaks and cedars. When the dun had made it to the hill's crest, Stockburn drew back on the reins, stopping the wagon. He stared down the hill's other side.

Below lay the headquarters of the Box Star.

The trail he'd been following curved around the hill he was on and entered the ranch yard from the right, roughly a quarter mile ahead. The headquarters was customary for the area. It consisted of a rambling, two-story log shack with a wraparound front porch and a large fieldstone hearth abutting one wall. The lower story was faced with whitewashed rock. The porch sagged a little from neglect, and missing shakes on the roof of the house had been replaced with rusty tin.

A large log barn and bunkhouse sat to the left, a windmill between them. A fenced paddock flanked the barn. Several smaller outbuildings and a couple of corrals sat directly across the barren yard from the house. A half-dozen horses milled inside the corrals, switching their tails. Two were playing like colts, kicking up salmon-colored dust. The windmill's blades were not moving, for there wasn't much of a breeze so early in the day. The wind would pick up around ten or so and blow its lungs out for the rest of the day, until the sun sank once more into the oceanic prairie.

A big man in an apron was moving around outside the open doors of the small blacksmith shop near the corrals in which the two horses played. A few other men were just then walking into the barn while two more were working with the horses in the paddock flanking it. Stockburn couldn't tell what the two in the corral were doing. He was too far away.

He didn't see signs of twenty to thirty men down there. That was a little disappointing. On the other hand, maybe they didn't all hole up together. Maybe they'd already met up and split up. That would be unfortunate.

But maybe the leader was there.

Anyway, he was about to find out if the Devil's Horde headquartered there.

He set the wagon's brake, grabbed his Winchester, and stepped into the wagon box behind the seat. Making his way around the dead men, he untied the bay's reins from the steel ring on the inside of the box beside the tailgate. He pulled the horse up close to the wagon, curveting him, then stepped lithely into the saddle.

He cocked and raised the Winchester, aiming skyward, and triggered off three thundering shots, spacing them roughly two seconds apart.

Resting the Winchester across his saddlebows, he then

galloped the bay back down the hill a half-dozen yards. He turned the horse and galloped west another fifty yards, pulling up behind a wagon-sized, lone, pitted, and moss-mottled boulder. A gnarled cedar grew up alongside the large rock.

Stockburn dismounted, tied the bay to another cedar, then walked up behind the rock. Peering around the left side of the boulder, he could again look down at the ranch headquarters.

Two men were standing outside the barn, looking toward the hill. They were tall and slender and dressed in the garb of your average range rider—work shirts, neckerchiefs, broad-brimmed hats, and leather chaps over denim jeans. One was smoking a cigarette. Another man stepped out of the barn and looked up the hill toward where they could no doubt see the wagon.

The man who'd been working in front of the blacksmith shop walked around to the side of the shop and raised his hand to shield the sun from his eyes as he, too, gazed up the hill at the wagon.

No one was moving with any urgency.

Then the cabin door opened. A rotund woman with black hair and wearing an apron stepped out, holding the door open behind her. Through the door came a man in what appeared a pushchair with wheels. He appeared bald, and he had a plaid blanket draped over his legs despite the warmth of the summer morning. He wheeled himself onto the porch then sat staring up the hill toward the wagon.

Wolf stared back at them, frowning. "What in tarnation," he said, feeling a little exasperated. "Is anyone going to check out the wagon or the fired shots?"

He'd expected to see a whole horde of men come riding

up hell for leather. He'd hoped one of them would be the leader of the bunch—the one who wore the white hat as opposed to the black hats the rest of the bunch wore. He'd figured he'd shoot the leader, thereby cutting off the snake's head, then hightail it out on the bay. He'd ride to the nearest town with a telegraph—probably Wahpeton over on the Red River—and summon help. He and the county sheriff as well as a posse would ride back and give the what-for to the Devil's Horde before they could scatter again to the four winds. Or at least keep them occupied until the deputy U.S. marshals and the cavalry arrived.

Four men stood outside the barn, conferring. The fourth was a bandy-legged little cowboy much shorter than the other three.

Stockburn was flabbergasted. They were just standing there, chinning like four men waiting for a train!

The man in the pushchair on the porch must have said something, because the four in the yard turned to him. The four walked into the barn and then back out into the corral and soon they led four saddled horses out of the barn. They swung up into the leather and, looking at each other, hesitating, owning apprehensive airs, booted their mounts out of the yard and up the hill toward the wagon.

About damn time, Wolf thought. He'd dropped to one knee and was leaning on his rifle, staying out of sight.

Something was wrong. Where were the other men? Why wasn't an entire horde storming out of the yard, riding hell for leather toward the wagon?

The four riders, strung out in a ragged Indian-file line, galloped up the hill. A tall, dark-haired man wearing a black felt Stetson and boasting a thick mustache rode ahead of the others on a claybank mare. The second man was sandy-haired and sharp-featured, also with a mustache. The third was the bandy-legged little fellow on a roan gelding that appeared far too large for him though he handled it adroitly, leaning forward in the saddle.

The fourth man hung back, hesitating, looking wary, downright fearful, keeping his mount to a shambling trot, drawing back on the reins and keeping the bit snug in his zebra dun's mouth. The dun fought the bit, snorting.

Stockburn watched them from his position behind the rock. He turned his head from left to right, tracking them up the hill toward the wagon, which was forty yards beyond the rock.

When he came to within a stone's throw of the wagon, the first man slowed his horse then stopped it altogether. The horse stomped and snorted, swinging sideways. The man studied the wagon skeptically, looking around. When he turned his head toward Stockburn's boulder, Wolf drew his head back behind the rock.

He waited a few seconds then poked his head out around the side of the rock again. All four riders sat their horses in a tight cluster, studying the wagon. The wind had kicked up, so Wolf couldn't hear what they were saying, but he could tell they were in no hurry to approach the wagon. They were looking around warily, the wind buffeting their hat brims and tearing at their horses' tails.

He could tell by the rough tones of their voices they were arguing about which one would approach the wagon. Finally, the lead rider turned to the fourth man in the pack, the hesitant one, and said, "Riley, get your ass up there and check out that wagon!"

"Nah, I ain't gonna do it, Rey!"

"I told you to check it out. You check it out now!"

Riley shook his head. He appeared younger by a few years than the lead rider and the sandy-haired one. He was younger than the small, bandy-legged gent by a long shot. "I ain't gonna do it, Rey! You think you can boss me around cause I'm the youngest, but I ain't gonna do it, Rey! You can go to hell!"

"Oh, fer corn's sake—I'll do it," said the sandy-haired rider who wore a green bandanna knotted tightly around his neck.

"Yeah, you do it, Chick," said the bandy-legged gent. He shucked an old-model Winchester carbine from his saddle boot and cocked it one-handed. "We'll cover you in case it's an ambush." He spat a wad of chaw and looked around from beneath the brim of his badly weathered high-crowned Stetson.

Wolf jerked his head back behind the rock again.

"If it's rustlers," the bandy-legged man snarled around a cheek full of remaining chaw, then by God they came to the wrong damn outfit. They know what we do to rustlers at the Box Star! What're you waiting for, Chick—*Christmas*? Haul your ass up there, boy, or I'll tell your pa you proved yourself a coward. Go on—we'll cover you!"

"I'm goin', Uncle Billy!" Chick said.

Stockburn poked his head out around the rock again. Chick shucked his own old carbine from its scabbard, cocked it, then set the hammer to half cock. He nudged his skittish steel dust forward, swinging wide around the wagon to his left, to approach the box from behind.

He stopped the steel dust about ten feet behind the wagon and rose up in his saddle to cast a look into the box. He glanced over at the others, scowling.

"What is it?" Rey asked.

"It looks . . . it looks like . . ."

"Like what?" asked Uncle Billy.

Chick licked his lips. "There's, uh . . . there's somethin' under some blankets in there."

"What's under the blankets?" Rey asked.

"Uh . . . I think . . ."

"Go check it out!" ordered Uncle Billy, looking around sharply with his deep-blue eyes that kept Stockburn jerking his head back behind the boulder.

Chick cursed and nudged his horse up to the side of the wagon. Grimacing as he looked down into the wagon, he leaned out to his left and lowered his gloved left hand into the box. He lifted up a corner of one of the blankets and yelped as he dropped the blanket quickly, jerking so violently back in his saddle that his horse lurched forward and to one side, away from the wagon.

Unprepared for the horse's sudden movement, Chick cried, "Oh, for pity's sake!" as he tumbled out of his saddle and into the wagon. He hit the box with a thud, disappearing behind the low side panel.

"Oh, fer the love of Mike!" said Uncle Billy.

"*Dead men!*" Chick wailed, sitting up and casting his horrified gaze at the three other men on horseback. "There's dead men heaped in there. It's a wagonload o' wolf bait!"

CHAPTER 33

Cursing and grunting, Chick bounded forward to clamber out of the wagon. He moved so fast that he ended up tumbling down the side of the buckboard and with another yelp, piled up on the ground in a heap.

"There's dead men in there?" yelled Rey.

"Oh, damn," Stockburn grunted, stepping out from behind the rock. "Nobody move!" He looked at the dark-haired Rey and old Uncle Billy. "Sheath those rifles!" Loudly, he cocked the Yellowboy in his hands. "Sheath 'em now!"

The men turned to Stockburn and froze, staring wide-eyed at the cocked Winchester in his hands. Two had frozen, anyway. Riley gave a terrified scream, wheeled his horse, and galloped back down the hill, headed for the ranch yard below. Chick had left his rifle in the wagon and he wasn't wearing a gun belt.

Wolf kept his eyes on Rey and Uncle Billy. "Sheath 'em!" Stockburn repeated, louder.

Rey and Uncle Billy glanced at each other darkly. Slowly, keeping their eyes on the big man with the rifle, they slid their rifles into their saddle sheaths.

"All right," Uncle Billy said, raising his gloved hands shoulder high, palms out. "There you go. We done did what you asked." His ruddy forehead creased. "Who are ya? And what are you doin'—bringin' a load o' dead men to the Box Star? This some kinda sick joke or somethin', mister?"

"It's not a joke." Stockburn off-cocked the Yellowboy, rested the barrel atop his shoulder, then walked over and helped Chick to his feet. Chick was a raw-boned, round-faced fellow in his early twenties. Nearly as tall as Wolf, he was all bone without a lick of fat on him. He cradled one arm before him, his unintelligent hazel eyes riveted on Stockburn, wary. "It's a mistake."

The detective looked at Chick. "You all right, son?"

"I hurt my arm," Chick complained, glancing at Rey as though for commiseration.

Rey kept his eyes on Stockburn.

"I apologize," Wolf said.

"Who are you?" Rey said, scowling. He was an unattractive fellow in his mid-to-late twenties. He had no chin to speak of and a pronounced overbite that he obviously tried to hide with his ostentatious mustache. His eyes were too far apart, and they would have been depthless and dull if not puzzled and enraged just then. His cheeks were pocked with old acne scars.

Stockburn could see similar, unfortunate family features in both him and the younger Chick.

Uncle Billy was the pleasantest-looking of the bunch, and he was old and grizzled.

"The name's Stockburn. Railroad dick."

"What's a railroad dick doin' way out here?" asked

Uncle Billy. He glanced at the wagon, and his befuddled scowl deepened. "Bringin' us dead men . . ."

"I thought they were yours."

"You thought they were *our* dead men?"

"That's right," Wolf said. "I was led to believe they belonged to you. Or out here, at least . . . somewhere." Frustrated, feeling foolish, and downright embarrassed, he said, "What I'm trying to say is I thought you were running an outlaw operation out here, and I thought those men were part of it."

"Why'd you think we was runnin' an outlaw operation?" Rey asked.

Stockburn studied him. "You're Reynolds Miller?"

Indignantly, the tall, chinless man said, "That's right."

Stockburn studied him again. Belle had led him to believe he'd be riding into a bailiwick of formidable men. Cold-blooded killers. From what she'd told him about Jason Miller trying to get the Widow Thornburg to marry his son, Reynolds, Wolf's image of Reynolds had been far, far from the tall, chinless, bucktoothed, cow-eyed saddle tramp sitting before him. In fact, he'd figured all of the Millers would be the kind of men who could lead the Devil's Horde.

These three were not. Four, if you counted the younger brother who'd cut and run. Jason Miller must have been the old man in the pushchair on the front porch. If he'd been forbidding at one time, he was far from that now. Men like those in the Devil's Horde would ride circles around an old man in a pushchair. And around his sons, to boot.

This was not a noble bloodline.

"Why'd you think we was runnin' an outlaw operation out here, mister?" asked Uncle Billy in exasperation.

"Belle Lockwood led me to believe you were. She led me to believe those three dead men belonged out here."

"Belle did?" said Rey, stunned. He doffed his hat and beat it against his thigh in anger. "Well, that's one dirty damn trick! But she's full of 'em—that's for sure."

"She is?" Stockburn asked.

"You can't trust that catamount as far as you could throw her uphill drippin' wet!" said Chick, still cradling his injured arm in front of his belly. "She gave her poor old man, Constable Lockwood, seven kinds of hell over the years. I'm surprised she didn't drive him to drink, just tryin' to keep up with her. Not to mention all the heartache she's caused him, runnin' with the wrong sort o' fellas."

Stockburn turned to him sharply. "I thought he *did* drink."

Uncle Billy said, "Rowdy Lockwood? *Drink?* Are you joshin', mister? No man was more misnamed than Rowdy. Oh, at one time he'd turn a town inside out and paint it red, for sure. That was a long, long time ago. Rowdy became a changed man after he found the Lord fifteen, sixteen years ago, after his wife died."

They all had a good chuckle over the idea of Constable Lockwood taking a drink.

"Rowdy Lockwood never touched the stuff," said Chick. "And he often read from the Good Book to those who did. He was a lay preacher, don't ya know? A straight an' true fella. Honest as the day is long and just as religious."

Wolf stared at them in disbelief. "Wait a minute," he said, deeply troubled, trying in vain to marry what these men had said about Belle's father to what Belle herself had said about him. "Why are you talking about Constable Lockwood in the past tense?"

All three looked at him as though he'd broken out in a language they didn't speak.

"I mean," Stockburn said, changing course and looking at Chick, "you said he was a lay preacher? Why *was*? I heard he was off on a bender with an old army buddy."

All three studied him again, hanging their jaws.

"Off on a bender . . . ?" said Chick.

"With an army buddy . . . ?" said Rey.

"*Rowdy Lockwood?*" put in Uncle Billy. "Hah! That'd be the day!"

"All right, all right. I get that part," Wolf said in annoyance, keeping his befuddled gaze on Chick. "Why did you say he was a lay preacher? As if he wasn't one anymore."

"'Cause last time we was in town, which was just a few days ago, we heard he was still missin'. He's been missin' for over a month and we figured he still was." Uncle Billy wrinkled his shaggy, gray-brown brows. "Ain't he?"

Wolf rubbed his chin, pensive. "Missing . . ."

"That's right," Uncle Billy said. "He went out trackin' rustlers south of town and never came home. Belle went out to look for him. Never found nothin'. Purty broken up, Belle was, I heard, even though she an' the constable never really got along. Maybe she loved him more than she let on. Felt bad for all the trouble she was to the old man."

"Why was he out looking for long-loopers?" Wolf asked. "He's the town constable. Or, was. Constables don't usually have jurisdiction outside of the town limits."

Uncle Billy spat another long, wet stream of chaw then dug a parfleche pouch out of his shirt pocket. "Unofficial deputy sheriff. It's a big county, and the sheriff over in

Wahpeton only has two official deputies, an' that ain't near enough to take care of all the trouble in this county." He tucked a pinch of chopped tobacco between his cheek and gum, adjusted it with his brown tongue, and said, "We've had rustlin' problems from way back, an' they continue to this day. Bane of the whole damn country. Makes it damn tough to make a livin'."

"That's what we figured you was, maybe," Chick said. "Rustler. Or one of Mrs. Thornburg's men. Here to stir up more trouble." He'd added that last sentence bitterly.

"Oh?" Wolf said. "Trouble between the Box Star and Mrs. Thornburg?"

Reynolds Miller flushed. "She's just pure contrary, she is. As contrary as she is easy on the eyes."

"You mean she's contrary because she refused to marry you?"

Young Miller's flush deepened. Uncle Billy and Chick snickered, glancing at Rey, who bunched up his ugly face in anger. "How'd you know about that?"

"Again, Belle."

"Well, you know now not to believe everything she says—don't you?"

"That wasn't a lie, though, was it?"

"It was Pa's idea," Chick said. "These has been hard times for both outfits. Didn't help that the railroad didn't come through Paradise like they said they was gonna do. That would've changed everything around here, brought prosperity. Since our ranges rub up against each other to the west, he figured . . . well"—a mocking grin flashed in the younger Miller brother's eyes—"maybe ole Rey and Mrs. Thornburg should rub up against each other, too.

Combine herds an' maybe a few other things . . . for the benefit of both outfits." Again, he snickered.

"Shut up about that, Chick, or I'll climb down off this hoss an'—"

"Calm down, calm down!" Wolf said. "I'm not here about you and Mrs. Thornburg or about your rustling problems, either."

"What are you here for?" asked Uncle Billy. "And who are them dead men inside the wagon?"

"Train robbers."

"Train robbers?" said Chick, scowling uncertainly. "Way out here?"

"I followed them down from the Northern Pacific rails." Stockburn looked at each man in turn. "You fellas know anything about a group of train robbers and cold-blooded killers known as the Devil's Horde?"

The three men looked at each other, brows beetled, shaking their heads.

"Nope," said Uncle Billy. "Right colorful name, but we never heard about 'em till now."

Stockburn believed them. They weren't smart enough to tell a convincing lie. He looked at Chick. "What's this you said about the railroad not comin' through Paradise?"

Chick shrugged. "What's to tell? It never happened. The railroad sent men in tailored suits through town a couple years ago, promised to buy up land for the rights-of-way. Even signed papers. They said prosperity was headed our way just as soon as they brought their railroad right through the heart of town! They said Paradise would live up to its name, that it would double in size, grow rich! They said we was gonna need more hotels and saloons for all the travelers, stock pens for all the cattle that would be shipped through here. Pshaw!" He glowered, shaking his head. "One big fat lie!"

"They rerouted farther north, laid rails through Fargo instead," Uncle Billy added grimly.

"The Northern Pacific?" Wolf said.

Uncle Billy nodded. "Lyin' noodleheads."

Wolf pondered the information. "All right, then," he said. "I reckon I'll be getting back to town." He walked back behind the boulder and returned a minute later, leading his horse toward the wagon.

Uncle Billy and Chick and Reynolds Miller remained where they'd been a minute before, regarding him skeptically, curiously.

"So . . . where you headed now?" asked Uncle Billy.

Stockburn tied the bay's reins to the back of the wagon then climbed up onto the seat. "Back to town." He released the brake with an angry grunt. "I want to know why the pretty young Belle Lockwood sent me up here on a wild-goose chase!"

He booted the claybank around the Millers and back toward the trail to Paradise.

Hank Holloway switched the raw steak she'd been holding to her swollen left eye to her swollen right eye, and glanced out the front window of the Bull Buffalo Café. Her nemesis and bare-knuckle opponent from the previous night—Belle Lockwood—was just walking past the café, striding with purpose as though she had somewhere she needed to be in a hurry.

She stopped suddenly as though she'd sensed Hank's eyes on her and turned to peer through the dirty glass, holding her hands up to her own swollen eyes, shading them from the midmorning sunlight. The front of her hat brim pressed flat against the glass and her eyes locked with Hank's.

Belle wrinkled her nostrils, pulled her head back away from the glass then gave a taut, taunting smile as she lifted her gloved right hand and extended one finger in a most unladylike salute. She held the finger up a good five seconds before lowering her hand and continued marching past the café, her long, straight blond hair billowing down her rail-straight back.

The three men sitting at the back of the café behind Hank snickered. One laughed out loud, briefly. Hank's face warmed with fury as she cowed all three with a look. She dropped the raw steak to her plate where it resided with the remains of the cooked one she'd eaten with two eggs and fried potatoes. She'd been surprised by how hungry she'd felt upon awakening from her long, drunken night's sleep, despite the thudding inside her tender head and the pain around her swollen eyes and the many cuts and bruises on her cheeks and lips.

Wolf had told her to stay in her room, but he wasn't her boss. Mr. Winthrop was her boss. Besides, she didn't like it when men tried to order her around. True, Stockburn had vastly more experience than she, and she felt honored to ride with such a legend, as well as a hero of hers. But she wasn't about to let herself be ordered around like a child.

She was a Wells Fargo express guard, by God. A professional. The treasure in her charge had been stolen, the other guards murdered. She was not about to cower in a hotel room.

She had to do her part in running those robbing killers to ground.

How she was going to do that in a town that obviously didn't want her here, she didn't know. But she would get nothing done by hiding in her room. So, first things first, she'd tended to her hunger. Now that she'd eaten, she would get to work.

How? She considered the question as she sipped the last half of her lukewarm coffee.

She'd nearly drained the cup when again the irascible Belle Lockwood passed the café, moving in the opposite direction as before, and she was mounted on a saddled paint gelding. She was heading east, her revolver on her hip, a rifle jutting from her saddle boot.

She rode stiffly, reins held high, chin down, hat shading her bruised face with swollen, discolored eyes. Hank leaned to one side, following the young constable along the street with her gaze. Just a few yards past the café, Belle nudged her horse from a trot to a gallop, thudding hooves kicking up dust.

Hank rose clumsily from her chair and walked to the window, keeping Belle in her field of vision until the young constable had ridden out of town and was consumed by the prairie beyond.

"Hmmm." Hank tapped the coffee cup in her hands. "Where's she off to . . . ?" Thinking on that, Hank walked back over to her table.

The three men sitting in the shadows at the rear of the room were whispering among themselves, casting furtive glances toward her. They'd entered the café after she had and had chosen a table well away from hers. Several other men as well as a couple of older ladies in picture hats had started to enter the café for breakfast, but soon after they'd stepped through the door and seen Hank, they'd done an about-face and vacated the premises.

No one wanted to be near her. Of course, everyone in town knew she was an agent from Wells Fargo. Word of her dustup with the town constable had spread, as well. Like a wildfire, most likely.

Hank finished her coffee and set the cup on the table. She looked down at the empty cup, but her mind was on Belle Lockwood. Her heart quickened. Belle had ridden out of town with a distinct purpose. She'd left in a hurry. Where was she off to, and why?

Hank had a feeling it had something to do with the Devil's Horde. She had to follow her. Not doing so would be a missed opportunity.

Quickly, the Wells Fargo express messenger withdrew a small leather purse from her skirt pocket, set some coins on the table, and picked up her rifle from where it leaned against the wall behind her. She grabbed her hat off the table and set it on her head, letting the drawstring hang loose on her chest, and hurried out of the restaurant's front door.

She walked quickly to the west, toward the livery stable, her boots clomping on the boardwalks fronting the several shops. In the corner of her eye, she saw several men watching her furtively from the opposite side of the street. They stood on boardwalks in clumps of two or three or gazed at her through sashed windows.

She crossed a gap between shops then stepped up onto the boardwalk fronting Herman Hartford's Butcher Shop and Grocery. A big man thick through the waist and shoulders stepped out of the shop and onto the boardwalk in front of her, blocking her way. His considerable paunch bulged out against a bloodstained white apron. The sleeves of his pinstriped shirt were rolled up past his pale, bulging forearms carpeted in long, dark-brown hair.

"Stockburn's not here, little lady," he said, keeping his voice low and pitched with menace. "You're . . . all . . . alone." He dragged the words out slowly, apparently thinking they sounded more threatening that way.

Deep furrows cut across Hank's forehead, and an angry burn rose in her cheeks. "Are you threatening me?"

"I'm just sayin' . . . you're all—."

"I heard you the first time—I'm all alone. Stand aside, guttersnipe!"

Flushing, the big man stepped forward and reached out with his fat right hand. Blood was crusted under his fingernails. He set that hand against Hank's cheek and slid a lock of her red hair back with his thumb. "Might wanna go on home . . . before something bad happens, pretty little lad—*OAFFFF-UKK-AHH!*"

She'd rammed the butt of her Winchester soundly into the big man's crotch.

CHAPTER 34

Herman Hartford bent forward sharply at the waist and dropped to one knee, cursing under his breath and groaning. His big, fat head swelled and turned red.

Hank swung the rifle back around and cocked it. Placing the barrel against the top of his head, right in the center of his bald spot, she said, "You think because I'm a woman and you're bigger, you can intimidate me. Well, you just found out it takes a lot to intimidate me."

"Oh god . . . oh, you hurt me bad!"

Hank remembered the rustler pressing the burning end of that cigarette against her skin, and her face grew hotter. Her blood pumped faster. "If you ever try to intimidate me again, or just look at me crossways, Mr. Hartford, I'm going to do way more damage to you down there than what you got away with today. Understand?"

The grocer held his head low, groaning and cursing under his breath. He held both hands firmly against his crotch.

"Nod your head if you understand, or I'll finish you right now." Hank pressed the Winchester's barrel harder against his bald spot.

The man glanced up at her with bloodshot eyes and nodded his head. "I . . . understand . . ." he raked out.

"Good." Hank pulled the rifle away from the man's head and grinned. "That will make life much simpler . . . and less painful . . . for both of us."

She off-cocked the Winchester's hammer, rested the rifle on her shoulder, stepped around the ailing grocer, and continued along the street. Several men were still watching her, their gazes cast with a good degree more wariness than before. One round-faced bald man stepped off the stoop of his shop and, wiping his hands on his apron, crossed the street, heading over to help the grocer.

"Good god, Herman," Hank heard him say behind her. "What'd that catamount do to you?"

As Hank approached the livery barn, she saw the liveryman—also a big man but with straw-yellow hair and a matching beard—standing between the barn's open doors, watching her and pensively puffing a briar pipe.

Hank said, "Mr. Bergman, I'm going to need you to saddle—"

"Now, Miss Holloway," the Swede said in a heavy accent, smiling mockingly, "You know I don't speak English!" He laughed then turned and walked into his barn, puffing his pipe.

"*Oh!*" Hank said, enraged. She strode into the barn and peered into the heavy shadows.

Bergman was walking down the main alleyway, heading toward the open doors at the barn's opposite end. He'd left a trail of aromatic pipe smoke behind him to mingle with the sour smells of urine and the green smells of fresh hay and straw.

"Fine, then," Hank said, forthrightly striding toward the

stall in which Bergman had housed her handsome dun. "I'll saddle him myself!"

Keeping his back to her, Bergman said in Swedish: "*Gå hem, ung dam. Eller du kommer bli ledsen.*" Shaking his head darkly, he sighed and puffed his pipe.

She didn't know what he'd said. She didn't know a lick of Swedish. It turned out she didn't have to know the language. As she led the dun out of the barn and mounted up ten minutes later, the big Swede yelled the translation at her: "Go home, young lady . . . or you'll be sorry!"

Stockburn drove the wagon into Paradise, dead devils still heaped in the back, nearly an hour later. He pulled the wagon up in front of the livery barn.

Nils Bergman was outside replacing the wheel on another wagon and didn't look happy. He was sweating in the midday summer heat and cursing in what was likely Swedish. It wasn't English. The problem seemed to be the wagon jack he was using.

He didn't look any happier when Wolf rolled the wagon to a stop beside the wagon Bergman was working on. The liveryman shaped a deep scowl, flaring his nostrils, then lifted his chin to peer into Wolf's wagon. "Good Lord, man. You still have those dead men in there, and they're stinking to high heaven!"

Stockburn grabbed his rifle and stepped over the seat into the box. "Your English is improving, Mr. Bergman. You must've been taking lessons while I was away."

"What am I supposed to do with all that human beef?" Bergman asked, his big face flushed with exasperation.

"Bury 'em."

"Who—*me?*"

The detective stepped to the back of the wagon then crouched to free the bay's reins from the iron eye. "I don't care who buries 'em. In fact, I don't care if you *don't* bury 'em. Do what you want with 'em. But you better get 'em off the street, 'cause the way they stink, I fear they're gonna scare away your customers." Wolf swung up onto the bay's back and shoved his rifle into the saddle boot.

"I'm not the undertaker!" Bergman bellowed at Stockburn's back as Wolf galloped over to the constable's office.

He pulled up in front of the squat stone building, swung down, and tossed his reins over the hitch rack. Mounting the rickety front porch, he tapped once on the door, flipped the steel latch, and poked his head into the office. "Belle?"

The office was empty. A fly caught in a spiderweb was the only sound or movement except for the kittens still purring as they pulled at their mother's teats.

Wolf stepped back outside, drawing the door closed behind him, and cast his gaze up and down the street. Several people on boardwalks were staring at him dubiously. That was all right. He was accustomed to being stared at dubiously in Paradise. As long as no one was drawing a bead on him.

He saw no sign of a bushwhacker.

He also saw no sign of Belle.

Stockburn swung up onto the bay's back then rode over to the barbershop on the street's opposite side. The bald barber sat in a Windsor chair outside his shop and the bathhouse flanking it. His legs were crossed, and he was holding a newspaper up in front of his face.

"Have you seen the constable, Mr. Johnson?"

Johnson didn't respond. He didn't do anything. He just continued holding up the newspaper, pretending to be reading it.

"I say, there, Mr. Johnson," Stockburn said a little louder though he knew the man had heard him the first time. "Have you seen Belle Lockwood?"

Johnson lowered the newspaper. He did not look at Stockburn. He merely folded the paper, rose from his chair, cleared his throat, stepped into his shop, and closed the door behind him. A shade was drawn over the door, announcing CLOSED.

Stockburn hardened his jaws as he looked around the street. No one stood on the boardwalks. Well, a medium-sized, short-haired yellow dog did, but the dog didn't count. It was licking the boards of the walk fronting the grocery store, not purposefully avoiding the Wells Fargo detective like the rest of the town was.

On the bay again, Wolf booted it up the deserted street to the hotel. His bad feeling about Paradise was growing worse. He wanted to check on Hank, make sure she was still safely stowed in her room.

He swung down, tied the reins, and entered the hotel. The lobby was empty. "I saw you duck down behind your desk as I rode up, Schumacher," he said as he strode through the lobby.

A startled chirp sounded from behind the desk.

Stockburn gave a caustic snort then mounted the stairs. On the second floor, he tapped on her door. "Hank, it's Wolf."

On the other side of the door, silence.

Wolf frowned. "Hank?" Then, louder: "Hank, are you all right?"

He tried the door. Locked.

Even louder, he said, "Open up, Hank—it's Wolf!" His voice thundered around the near-dark hall.

Still no response. Anxiety raked through him. He stepped back, shucked his Colt from the holster on his left hip, raised his right leg, and slammed the heel of his boot against the door panel beneath the knob. The door burst open, the locking bolt as well as a good bit of wood from the jamb flying into the room. He stepped inside and looked around.

Just like Belle previously in the jailhouse, no Hank was in the hotel.

Wolf looked around closely, glad to find no signs of violence. "Dammit, girl," he said, holstering his Colt as he left the room. "I told you to stay put!"

He strode back down the hall and down the stairs. The diminutive Samuel Schumacher stood behind his desk, looking a little green around the gills. He lowered his eyes as well as his mouth corners, looking like a man who wished a trapdoor would open beneath his worn brogans.

"Where is she?" Wolf asked, turning to face the man at the desk.

"Where is who?"

"You know who. My partner—Henrietta Holloway. She's not in her room."

The little man raised his hands in a dismissive gesture. "It is not my job to—" He stopped abruptly when Stockburn grabbed the little man's necktie with his left hand and drew his head across the desk.

With his right hand, Wolf pressed his Colt to the little man's forehead, clicking back the hammer.

"Oh!" Schumacher screamed. "Oh, my . . . *ohh!*"

"You got a good view of the whole town from your desk here, Mr. Schumacher. I haven't found Belle Lockwood, and I haven't found my partner. I got me a really good feeling you know where they both are, and I'm gonna give you three seconds to—"

"They left!" the little man wailed, his eyes as large and round as teacups. "They rode out of town, one after another, about an hour ago!"

Stockburn arched a brow. The interrogation had been easier than he'd expected. "On horseback?"

"Yes!"

"Which way?"

"East!"

"Where were they going?"

"I don't know! Please don't kill me—I beg you!" The man looked at the big silver revolver pressed against his head then squeezed his eyes closed and sobbed.

"East, huh?" Stockburn pulled the Peacemaker away from the little man's head, leaving a dime-sized indentation just above the bridge of his nose. "One after another you say?"

Schumacher continued to lean forward across his desk, eyes squeezed shut.

Stockburn holstered his Colt and walked to the door. His brow furrowed in thought, he opened the door and stepped outside. He looked east along the street, toward the rolling prairie opening beyond. He swung his gaze to the west, toward the livery barn. Both women had likely fetched their horses from Bergman's place. The liveryman might know where Belle was headed.

It was a lead-pipe cinch that Hank was following Belle,

which was a crazy thing for her to do alone. But that was Hank, all right. She had a mind and a will of her own.

And her only boss was Mr. Winthrop, four hundred miles away.

Damn her.

Bergman might know where the women were headed, but he wouldn't be as easy as Schumacher. And Stockburn doubted he'd get it out of him, anyway.

With no time to waste, he needed to get onto their trail before the sign grew cold. He grabbed his reins off the hitch rack, swung into the saddle, and booted the horse up the street, heading east.

The prints of the two shod horses were easy to follow. Aside from one wagon drawn by two heavy mules—judging by the size of the shod horse prints in the finely churned dirt between the twin furrows made by the wagon wheels—they were the only tracks.

Wolf booted the bay into a rocking lope. He had to catch up to Hank fast, before the foolish young express guard got herself into another rough patch—one that he couldn't pull her out of.

CHAPTER 35

The echoes of three gunshots clattered around the buttes ahead of Hank Holloway. Two were fired quickly. After a three-second pause, the third one vaulted skyward. All three sounded like the sneezes of angry gods.

The shots were still swallowing their own echoes when the dun, apparently not trained to gunfire, reared back suddenly. She hadn't been prepared for the move though she should have been. Raised in the saddle, she'd ridden every kind of mount imaginable. Her grip on the reins had loosened as her ears picked up the gunfire and, when the horse pitched, it ripped the ribbons from her hands.

The dun followed the pitch, and before Hank could grab the horn, she was flying over the mount's right wither. She struck the ground and rolled, the wind hammered out of her lungs. Rolling off her left shoulder and onto her back, she looked up to see the dun galloping off through a narrow crease between the chalky buttes that stippled the country like the spires, towers, and turrets of some giant medieval castle. The bridle reins bounced along the ground behind the beast.

Her rifle was in the boot.

Hank stifled an exasperated curse only because she wasn't sure she was alone or that the shots hadn't been aimed at her, though no bullets had plunked into the ground around her. Although she ached in several places—namely, her left arm and left hip that had taken the brunt of her tumble—she didn't think she'd been shot.

Looking around at the narrow horse and cow trail she'd been riding along to follow Belle, Hank realized they'd been on the trail a good hour, crossing mostly rolling grassland before entering the badland of chalky buttes roughly a half hour ago. Still on Belle's trail, Hank had wended her way through the buttes apparently cut by a river a long time ago and then eroded by wind and more water.

Wincing at the pain in her hip and shoulder, she heaved herself to her feet, removed her hat hanging by its drawstring over her right arm, set it on her head to shield her eyes from the relentless prairie sun, and then turned south. The direction Belle had ridden was the same direction from which the gunshots had been fired.

Something told the young messenger that the shots had been fired by Belle herself and hadn't been intended for Hank. By staying far enough behind the Paradise town constable, Hank didn't think Belle had spotted her. No, the shots hadn't been meant for her.

They'd been signal shots.

Bang-bang. Three seconds of silence, then *Bang*.

Signal shots, all right. Belle had been alerting someone of her arrival.

Hank's heart quickened. Was Belle meeting the Devil's Horde?

Wincing again, Hank hurried forward in spite of

aggravating the ache in her hip. Her heart thudded with
fear, but curiosity compelled her to keep moving along
the trail, clearly marked with Belle's mount's shoe prints.
Around a couple of cone-shaped buttes it continued
through a trough splitting two more buttes and forming a
V-shaped gap.

Sitting just beyond that gap, her back to Hank, was
Belle.

Hank's heart hiccupped, and she gave a short gasp of
surprise. Quickly, she stepped to her left so Belle wouldn't
see her if she glanced behind her.

Hank scrambled up the side of a high bluff to the right
of the V. It was steeper at the top, and she had to crawl on
all fours, grabbing at roots and small, wiry plants clinging
to the bluff's chalky face. A few feet below the crest, she
crawled onto a flat shelf that jutted out from the bullet-
shaped top. She could hear voices below.

Belle's voice and a man's voice.

She turned her head to her left and looked down. Belle
sat her paint horse thirty feet below. Three men sat their
own horses, facing Belle. Two wore black hats and black
dusters. The man between them wore a black duster and a
cream Stetson.

Hank's heart lurched into yet a faster gallop. She drew
her head back sharply. Not forty feet away from her was
the leader of the Devil's Horde—the main demon himself!

If he or the other men facing Belle had lifted their
heads, they could have looked up past their hat brims and
seen Hank sprawled atop the butte above them. She drew
deep breaths, trying to slow her heart, pricking her ears
to hear above its thudding what Belle and the head devil
were saying.

"Pulled into town yesterday, you say?" the man asked. Not unexpectedly, he had a deep, menacing voice, oddly resonant.

"That's right," Belle said.

"Wells Fargo agents?"

"*The* Wells Fargo agent himself," Belle said tightly with quiet exasperation. "Wolf Stockburn."

"Stockburn?" asked one of the other men. His voice was high and raspy.

"You've heard of him," Belle said. "Wolf of the Rails, the newspapers call him."

"Are you sure it's him?" asked the man with the deep, resonant voice.

"Of course, I'm sure!" Belle said. "I've talked to the man. He talked to *me*! He asked me a bunch of questions about the gang robbing the Northern Pacific up north. You think I'd ride all the way out here if I didn't know for sure the Wolf of the Rails himself has rode into Paradise?"

"Come on, sweetheart," said the outlaw leader, Shevlin. He chuckled. "Even Wolf Stockburn is only one man. In fact, he's a notch I'd just love to have on my gun."

"I wouldn't mess with him, Hart. Not even you. He's bigger than what I thought. And he wears two big nickel-chased Peacemakers with ivory grips, and purely seems to love makin' 'em roar! Besides, a girl rode into town with him. A fiery redhead."

"Who's the girl?"

"Just some express messenger. A pretty face with a doll's mouth in a fancy skirt is all she is. But I fixed her wagon. It's not her I'm worried about."

"What'd you say happened to your face, sweetheart?"

Shevlin asked, his voice oddly intimate but still somehow menacing, at least to Hank's ears.

"Never mind about my face, dammit!"

Hank snorted into her arm. *Yeah, never mind. The redhead with the pretty face and doll's mouth gave you something to remember her by—didn't she?*

Wincing as she became aware of the burning cuts and bruises marring her own countenance, Hank had to concede, albeit only half-consciously, that her opponent had wielded a formidable left hook.

Shevlin's voice rose with anger as he said, "Belle, honey, if Stockburn did that to your—"

"I said never mind about that!" Belle scolded him. "Wolf of the Consarned Rails followed you fellas down here! Leastways, he followed Early, Dawson, and Pelt Andrews to Paradise. Like I was sayin', he killed 'em all. Shot 'em all down like ducks on a slough! Johnson said he never seen anything like it. I got Stockburn believin' they came from the Box Star and sent Stockburn up north to Miller's ranch. But soon he'll know that—"

Her voice was cut off by two rifle reports spaced about a second apart. Those shots were still echoing when one more rifle crash sounded to rocket around the bluffs with the other two echoes, all dwindling quickly.

"Three riders, boss!" The voice came from somewhere above Belle and on her right.

The devils had posted a lookout on a bluff somewhere above Hank.

She turned her head, raising it slightly to peer up over the conical crest of the butte on her right. A gasp escaped as she pulled her head back down, mashing her chin into the chalky soil of the shelf. The lookout stood on another, slightly higher butte to the west. Hank thought for sure he must have seen her. How could he not have? *How could he not see her right now?!*

She pressed her body flatter against the shelf, wanting to make herself as small as possible to blend with the shelf itself. *Please don't let him see me, please don't let him see me,* Hank prayed to the gods watching over foolish Wells Fargo messengers. If these men caught her, they would kill her slowly. Torture her in the worst male ways possible.

Pressing her body as flat as possible, grinding her chin into the chalky shelf, she heard the thuds of galloping hooves behind her. The thudding grew louder. Hank lifted her head a little and turned to stare into the gap to her left.

Three riders galloped toward the opening where Belle sat her paint with her outlaw lover, Shevlin, and the two black-hatted devils. A stone dropped in Hank's belly when she saw that four riders were men from town—Dudley Udder, the apron in the Sheyenne River Saloon; Vance Johnson, the skinny, bald-headed barber; Nils Bergman, the big blond Swede who owned the livery barn; and, last but not least, Herman Hartford, the fat butcher whose unmentionables she had turned to jelly earlier with her Winchester's butt. She noted with a vague satisfaction that the grocer had padded his saddle with a red velvet cushion and that his face betrayed discomfort.

The feeling of satisfaction was as fleeting as it was vague. Fear as cold as the Dakota winter raced back in to replace it. She was surrounded by killers above and below her. Just enough of the shadow of the bullet-shaped butte crest must have concealed her from the man above and to her right. But if the men approaching from below, the four citizens of Paradise, happened to glance up, they would see her. To them, the lower half of her body was exposed.

"What the hell are you fellas doing here?" Shevlin called to the newcomers, dryly adding, "The rest of the town behind you?"

Hank watched the four townsmen draw up behind Belle, who regarded them skeptically from over her left shoulder.

"Have you seen her?" the grocer with the battered oysters asked. His voice betrayed his discomfort.

"Seen who?" Belle asked, sounding as annoyed as she looked.

"Miss Wells Fargo," the grocer said.

Hank flared a nostril. *Cretins.*

"What're you talking about—have I seen her?" Belle said. "Not since I left town."

"Well, she followed you," the bald barber said.

"What?" both Belle and her lover, Shevlin, asked at the same time.

"We all seen her ride out of town just after you did," the tall, bland-faced bartender Dudley Udder said. A cigarette dangled from one corner of his mouth as he glanced to his left and then behind him.

Hank sucked a sharp breath through gritted teeth. If he turned his head to look up, he would see her. No way he could miss her with the lower half of her body fully exposed to the newcomers where they sat their horses ten feet behind Belle.

He did not look to his right. Why he did not, Hank did not know. He turned his head straight and regarded Belle and Shevlin and the two other kill-crazy devils.

"We tracked her out here," said Bergman. "We seen her

horse grazing off the side of the trail not a quarter mile back. She's out here, all right. She knows. She knows all about it!"

"We want our cut," said the barber, Johnson. "We came for the town's cut."

Shevlin said testily, "We told you we'd meet you in town on Sunday night. Same time, same place. Just like always. That's what we agreed to."

"That was before Stockburn and Miss Wells Fargo came to town," Udder said. "That was before Miss Wells Fargo trailed Belle out here to your lair. Now they know where you're holin' up, and they'll send others."

"Belle, honey," Shevlin said, "did you let yourself get shadowed out here?"

"No! I'm not that stupid!" The protest was loud but lacking in conviction. Belle had gotten careless.

That was how Hank had been able to trail her.

Hank resisted the urge to smile. She really didn't have anything to smile about, surrounded by killers as she was. The townsmen might not have done any killing themselves, but they'd aligned themselves with killers. That much was obvious. They were, indeed, in league with the butchers. Why that was, she had no idea, but hoped she'd live long enough to find out.

Meanwhile, she kept her head down and willed her body as small as possible, hoping that the shadow concealing her from the picket above her did not slide away to reveal her.

Chapter 36

"You men go back to town," Shevlin ordered the townsmen. "If Miss Wells Fargo is out here, we'll find her. If Stockburn rides out this way, he'll get the same thing Miss Wells Fargo's gonna get."

Hank ground her molars. Why was she the only one with a condescending nickname? Why didn't they give Wolf one?

"Don't get your bloomers in a twist," said the man sitting to Shevlin's right. "He's only one man, and the girl—well, she's just a girl. Uh, no offense, Miss Belle," he added with an oily smile to the Paradise constable. (Since her face was concealed by her hat brim and her chin was down, Hank couldn't see Belle's expression, but Hank knew Belle well enough by now to know a nostril flare was involved.) "We're damn near twenty-five men out here," the cutthroat added to the newcomers.

"We talked to the rest of the Paradise businessmen," said Bergman. "They all want their cut of that last robbery now. We got us a bad feelin' about Stockburn and Miss Wells Fargo. If two came, others will no doubt come, too. We think it's time to close up shop, divide up the plunder, and for you boys to pull your picket pins and cool your heels in Mexico for a while."

"You fellas aren't the ones callin' the shots," Shevlin said, his voice growing testy. "I say when we're done here."

"We started this thing," said the barber. "We bank-rolled this thing, found out when the largest shipments of money were being shipped on the NP. *We* say when we end it, and Nils is right. It's time to end it while we're ahead."

"And before we're behind bars," added the saloon keeper, Udder.

A tense few seconds passed. Shevlin's two partners looked at him. They grinned. Shevlin kept his gaze on the four townsmen flanking Belle. She shifted her horse to one side and turned it sideways to the townsmen, Shevlin, and the other two devils, well out of the way in case lead started flying.

Seemed like a wise move to Hank. Maybe the constable was smarter than she looked.

"Hold on, now," Belle said, shifting her nervous gaze to Shevlin. "Hold on now. Hold on now!" She held her hand up to the man, palm out. "There's no point in goin' an'—"

"Shut up, Belle," Shevlin bit out through gritted teeth. "You talk too much."

You can say that again, Hank thought. *Tell her again, Shevlin.*

Belle swallowed and lowered her hand slowly. Her face hung slack with fear.

"Like the girl said," said Bergman, fear entering his own voice now. "There's no point in—"

Shevlin cut him off with "You don't seem to understand.

We don't need the town. We don't need *you fellas*. We ain't afraid of you. We're the muscle an' guns you hired, but, you see, maybe we done decided to quit already. To pull out already. What're you gonna do if we decide you've done had all the percentage you deserve?"

The saloonkeeper's long, sullen face flushed with exasperation. "You mean to say you'd—"

"Double-cross you?" asked the devil on Shevlin's left. He grinned. It wasn't a pretty sight. It was a death's-head grin. He chuckled then turned to Shevlin, still grinning.

"We got the whole town backing us!" Johnson said, pointing a long, skinny finger at Shevlin. "You can't double-cross a whole town. You're here because of us. This was our idea. We assembled you, called you up here to do this, to get even with the railroad." He waved a hand in front of him. "We set you up out here with all the food, whiskey, and women any outlaw pack could want. You and your boys get half of every robbery, and the town gets the other half. That's more than fair! We set it up! We bankrolled it!" He thumbed himself in the chest. "*We're* in charge, doggonit!" His voice had risen quickly until he was practically screaming.

Hank thought he was going to give himself a heart stroke.

Shevlin just stared at him, a menacing smile lifting one corner of his mouth.

She could see his face because he half-faced her and had lifted his chin to regard the four townsmen sitting their horses fifteen feet back along the trail over her left shoulder. Belle was staring at Shevlin, her eyes wide as silver dollars beneath her hat brim. Even she was scared.

"You know what the final piece of advice the great

old train robber, Red Bascom, gave me on my last visit to Cold Water Wells?" Shevlin asked. "'Only share the labors of your toil as long as there's a profit in sharing. When there's no more profit in the sharin', stop sharin' an' start shootin' before the other side does the same to you.'" He grinned, slitting his eyes. "Those were his exact words, Red's."

Hank lifted her head and stared down in hang-jawed shock at what was happening . . . about to happen.

The four men from Paradise stared in shock at the three outlaws facing them.

"Our business association ends right here," the outlaw leader said casually. He slid his hand to the revolver and slowly pulled the piece from its black leather holster. Raising the gun, he clicked the hammer back.

"Right here," he said. "And right now!"

"Now, wait!" Bergman cried, raising both hands as though to shield his face.

The Colt thundered. The bullet tore through the butcher's right hand, which he slapped his own face with.

Shevlin whooped and hollered like a madman as the big Colt leaped and bucked, the three ensuing roars causing the ledge beneath Hank to vibrate. Watching the three men punched backward off their pitching horses, screaming, she recoiled from the grisly scene, jerking back against the shoulder of the slope. As she did, the ledge gave way beneath her.

"Oh, my God!" she cried as she clawed at the slope, trying to keep her place.

Didn't work.

The ledge crumbled beneath her and she was rolling down the side of the butte. Rolling . . . rolling . . . rolling.

The world spun around her. Her own cries of protest at the grim circumstance fate had dealt her assaulted her ears. She stopped rolling only to be slammed down on the floor of the V-shaped gap in a billowing cloud of chalk-colored dust and gravel.

Her head spun and her body ached. She blinked against the grit in her eyes. It took several seconds for the cobwebs to clear, for the numb disorientation to dissolve.

Hank lay on her back, breathing like a landed fish. Her ears still rang. She stared up at the turquoise sky obscured by the sifting dust and then slid her gaze to the left.

"Oh," she heard herself gasp as she found herself staring up at a hand-tooled leather stirrup and a man's broadcloth-clad leg and into the cold-eyed, hard-lined face of the killer called Shevlin. He stared almost blandly down at her, as did the men to either side of him. Shevlin blinked once and then turned to Belle, who stared down, hang-jawed, at Hank.

The leader of the Devil's Horde said, "Belle, my heart, this wouldn't happen to be Miss Wells Fargo, would it?"

Stockburn followed Belle and Hank's trail around the edge of a small slough that smelled like an overfilled latrine. Red-winged blackbirds screeched like rusty door hinges as they swayed upon the bending cattail tips. He booted the bay up and over the next low hill to the south, and stopped.

To his right, a large sign had been nailed to two stout posts driven into the ground on the trail's right side. It was an old sign. A hawthorn bush had grown up to partially obscure it. The red paint was old and faded to a dusty pink. Still, the words were legible. STOP AND GO BACK! TRESPASSERS WILL BE SHOT ON SIGHT WITHOUT WARNING!

It was signed at the bottom. *Ansel Thornburg,* OWNER OPERATOR, BITTERSWEET CREEK RANCH.

Wolf looked around at the rolling grassy country billowing around him. Cattle peppered the hillsides, and he'd seen a good twenty or thirty grazing along a creek bottom a half mile back, but he'd seen no riders. He clucked to the bay and rode on.

He dipped down into another shallow valley, still following the trails of the two shod horses he'd followed out from Paradise, and rode up to the crest of the next hill. He'd been hearing a raucous lowing for the past five minutes—the calls of a cow in distress. Probably a mother cow separated from her calf.

He'd been right. The mother cow stood at the edge of a buffalo wallow, facing her calf stuck in the mire of the muddy wallow. The white-faced calf, a little larger than a large dog, was being helped by a cowboy standing in the mud with it while two other cowboys sat horses to the right of the braying mother cow.

One of the two mounted men had tossed a lariat around the head of the calf then dallied his end of the rope around his saddle horn. He was backing his pinto pony slowly, pulling the calf toward the edge of the wallow while the cowboy in the wallow pushed the mewling young beast from behind, walking with it through the deep mud.

Just as the calf came free of the muck, the cowboy who'd been pushing it straightened and looked down at the mud on his boots and pants. Laughing, he mentioned something to his partners about the muck then turned his head toward Wolf. He turned away then snapped his head back to Wolf again, his eyes meeting those of the Wells Fargo detective. "Hey!" the cowboy said, pointing.

The other two turned sharply to follow the muddy man's pointing finger. One of them cursed then reached for the rifle jutting from the scabbard strapped to his saddle.

"Easy, now, pards," Stockburn said, raising his gloved right hand palm out in a sign of peace. "Easy, now—easy!" he called loudly enough for the three cowboys to hear.

Whether they heard or not, they weren't listening. The man with the carbine snapped the rifle to his shoulder quick as sin on a hot day in hell, cocked it, and pressed his cheek to the stock.

"Holy Hannah," Wolf grunted, ramming his heels into the bay's loins. "Those fellas mean business. Let's go, bay!"

Just as the horse lunged forward, the carbine cracked a quarter second after a slug whistled just behind Wolf's head, close enough that he thought it might have kissed the nap at the back of his black sombrero.

"Those Bittersweet Creek boys are stayin' true to their word—I'll give 'em that!" Wolf said as the rifle belched again and the men shouted behind him. He remembered the sign he'd come upon. It had been old and faded but the sentiment was obviously as fresh as when it had been newly erected.

Stockburn leaned forward and whipped the bay into more speed. He'd been of a mind to have a peaceable word with the three punchers, to explain his situation, but since they preferred the language of Winchesters, it was best to light a shuck and live to palaver another day. He had to find Hank before the Devil's Horde did. That Belle was riding out to the outlaws' lair was growing more and more likely. She'd likely sent him off on that wild-goose chase to the Miller ranch to buy her time to warn the Devil's Horde of the Wells Fargo twosome's presence.

And she was leading Hank right into one hot bailiwick!

"Paradise. Paradise—my ass!" Wolf growled as more rifles popped behind him and he turned a quick glance back to see all three punchers galloping after him, shouting.

He turned his head forward, widened his eyes in deep consternation, then leaned back in the saddle, drawing the reins up taut against his chest. "Whoa, bay! Whoa, whoa!"

The bay stopped and shook his head, rattling the bit in his teeth. It didn't seem to enjoy seeing the three men before them anymore than Wolf did. The three sat their horses on a hill about forty yards away. The man in the middle, seated on a blue roan mare, held a Henry rifle to his shoulder. Head tipped toward the rifle's stock, he aimed down the barrel at Wolf.

Stockburn felt the bead lined up on his forehead like a chunk of ice pressed against his skin. Tensely, he waited to see flames stab from the barrel.

The man holding the rifle on him was middle-aged, thick through the middle. Wolf couldn't see his face, because it was shaded by his Boss of the Plains hat and further obscured by the Henry's stock, against which he pressed his right cheek. The two riders sitting to either side of him shucked their own rifles, cocked them, and raised them, also aiming at Stockburn.

The punchers who'd been tending the calf were galloping up behind him, the thuds of their horses quickly growing louder.

Wolf winced. *Caught in a damn whipsaw. And I do not have time for this crap.*

"Hold it right there, mister," said the oldest man of the three in front of Wolf. He lowered his rifle and, holding it one-handed, galloped his mare down the hill. The other two followed suit, drawing up about twenty feet away and ten feet apart just as the punchers caught up to Stockburn from behind.

The older man's beefy face was craggy and carpeted in a scraggly, gray-brown beard. He wore a red bandanna and a Russian .44 in a soft leather holster on his right hip.

Stockburn raised his hands and said, "Pull your horns in, fellas. I'm—"

The old man wasn't listening. His face was mottled red with anger, and his small blue eyes were fiery. He glanced at a man behind Wolf and said, "Cass, throw a noose around this gentleman's head, and then he'll know as well as anyone else that you take the Bittersweet Creek folks at their word or you'll be dancing the midair two-step!"

"You got it, Clell," said Cass, riding ten feet out to Wolf's right side, jerking his lariat off his saddle horn and expertly tossing out a loop, adjusting it as he turned the loop in the air before him.

"Hold on, dammit! I'm Wolf Stockburn, railroad dick for Wells Fargo!"

"I don't care who you *say* you are, mister!" said the old-timer called Clell, keeping his Henry aimed straight out over his horse's right wither and narrowing his eyes with a churning, self-righteous animosity. "You know what happens to rustlers found on Mrs. Thornburg's land? They join the rest of same on Rustlers' Roost." He half turned, jerking his chin toward a near ridge.

"See that bluff over yonder? The one with the cotton-wood all decked out like a Christmas tree? That's Rustlers' Roost. That's where rustlers who prey on Bittersweet Creek beef go to roost—in that damn tree!"

Stockburn narrowed his eyes to scrutinize the tree indicated. The sprawling cottonwood, all alone on the butte, had been decorated, all right. But it wasn't with any Christmas-tree ornaments. From its stout branches hung a good dozen or so men. Crows rode the shoulders of a few—probably the most recent of the "ornaments."

Dead men.

The sight took Wolf off guard, giving time for Cass to drop his loop over Stockburn's head and draw it taut around his chest. Cass gave a victorious whoop, but before he could dally his end of the rope around his saddle horn, Wolf pulled his arms up out of the loop and grabbed the rope with both hands, giving a fierce grunt as he tugged on the lariat.

Hard.

Cass screamed as the tug pulled him out of his saddle. His spurs rang as his boots shot out of their stirrups and they rang again as the cursing young man hit the ground beside his startled mount.

The loud metallic rasps of rifles being cocked sounded angrily. Stockburn turned to see Clell aiming his Henry at him again as were those of the punchers to either side of him. The one to Clell's left appeared to have some

Indian blood. Long, black hair hung down his back, and his cheeks were high and broad. There was an Indian reserve in his eyes, as well, though they were blue, not brown. He was dressed like the others in a checked cotton shirt, denim jeans, and chaps, a battered black Stetson on his head.

Unlike the others, he appeared not yet twenty though he was tall and rangy. His skin was too smooth, his body lacking in full development, for him to be much over sixteen.

"Give the word, Clell," said the kid with the Indian blood, aiming down his Winchester's barrel at Stockburn. "Just . . . give . . . the word."

Wolf said, "You'd better give me a chance to reach into my coat for my bona fides. If you don't, you'll be killing a Wells Fargo detective. Best bury me deep. Don't let anyone find me."

"Don't worry, we will," the kid replied, lifting a mouth corner with a mocking sneer.

"Stand down, Pete," Clell said, glancing at the young half-breed firebrand. "The rest of you, stand down." He looked at the man on the ground, who was sitting with his bent legs spread before him, glaring up at Stockburn. He'd lost his hat in the tumble from his horse, and his sandy blond hair hung down over his pasty white forehead and one gimlet eye. "How you doin', Cass? You break anything the boss can't fix?"

Cass stared at Wolf for another couple of beats then spat to one side, and ran his sleeve across his mouth. "Nah." He glared at Wolf again. "He's fast for an old codger."

"Let's leave age out of it, Cass," Clell said, off-cocking

his Henry and resting it barrel up on a broad thigh that stretched the seams of his corduroy trousers. "That hits too close to home for this old mossyhorn who turned sixty last week." He'd spoke those words with an ironic air and a faint twinkle in his eye. He was a man of humor.

Stockburn sensed the younger men around him held him in high esteem.

The old man pulled his mare up close to Stockburn and turned it so that his horse's head faced the bay's tail. He narrowed an eye at Wolf as he said, "Mr. Stockburn, my name is Clell Sager. I'm foreman of the Bittersweet Creek outfit, and I will thank you to keep your weapons to home. I'll be watching you carefully as we meander on down the trail to the Bittersweet Creek headquarters. Leave the smoke wagons alone or I'll empty your saddle. We're gonna go talk to the boss. She's pretty much judge, jury, and executioner out here. She'll decide your fate. What she decides you'll live with. Or, as the case may be, die with. Now, do we have that straight, sir?" He spoke with the folksy-formal joviality of a frontier judge or doctor, but his eyes were as hard as diamonds.

The burn of rage blew through Stockburn like the suffocating heat of a summer wildfire. "I don't have time to pay a social call to—"

"Oh, don't misunderstand, Stockburn," Clell said, shaking his head exaggeratedly. "It's no social call. You will not be a guest. Now, you can join us over at the head-quarters or you can pay a visit to Rustlers' Roost, your so-called bona fides be damned! Your call, my friend."

Stockburn drew a deep breath. He looked from Clell to the other hard-eyed, rough-hewn faces surrounding him. They all held their Winchesters though none was aiming his weapon directly at the detective. They could mighty quick, though. They were a hard-bitten bunch of cowboys. The gaudily decorated cottonwood atop Rustlers' Roost was proof enough.

Wolf looked at Sager and gave a taut smile. "Let's visit the boss, Mr. Sager."

Chapter 37

Fifteen minutes after leaving Rustlers' Roost, Stockburn crested a low rise awash in stirrup-high green grass. He followed the two-track trail under the obligatory ranch portal and into a large bowl surrounded by low, wooded hills.

The bowl cradled the headquarters of the Bittersweet Creek Ranch, as impressive a layout as Stockburn had seen anywhere in Dakota Territory. Cows contentedly grazed on the low hills encircling the headquarters buildings. The almost glaring green of those wooded hills and the grass that velveted them was no doubt due to the creek sheathed in willows and wild berry shrubs and old box elders and elms cutting through the ranch headquarters.

Stockburn crossed the bowl with his three companions—Clell Sager, the young half-breed Sager had called Pete, and another puncher he'd called Lonny. Sager had left the other three punchers out on the range where they were doing the preliminary work leading up to the fall roundup—mainly, figuring out where all their cows had strayed over the summer.

Stockburn and the three Bittersweet Creek riders flanking

him cautiously, holding their rifles across their saddle pommels, crossed the creek via wooden bridge. They passed through the shade of the trees fluttering their dark-green leaves that flashed like newly minted pennies in the sunshine. The creek rattled musically over the rocks of its bed.

The riders came out of the trees and into the intense sunshine of the hard-packed ranch yard comprised of stout, well-tended log buildings and an elaborate system of adjoining chutes and corrals. Good bloodlines shone in the clean lines of the horses and cows that milled in the paddocks, including a broad-shouldered red Hereford bull with a white face and short pale horns curling forward.

One of the outbuildings was getting a new roof. The naked backs of two men glistened with sweat as they paused in their labors and watched the newcomers pass the Essex windmill and corrugated steel water tank, the water singing from the pipe and into the nearly full tank. The riders drew up before the large, barracklike, two-story main lodge.

Sager and the half-breed swung down from their horses.

As Stockburn dismounted the bay, Sager said, "Lonnie, tend these hosses."

"Keep mine handy," Wolf said with a piqued air. He was deeply frustrated by the lost time, and worried about Hank. "I'll be riding out of here soon."

Lonnie looked at Sager, who stopped at the top of the lodge's broad front porch and half turned to Stockburn climbing the steps behind him. "We'll see." The foreman gave Lonnie a nod and then crossed the porch to the front door.

Stockburn followed him. The half-breed, Pete, came up behind the detective but stayed a few cautious feet back, holding his carbine.

The stout front door opened before Sager could knock on it. A heavy, round-faced Indian—obviously full-blood and likely Sioux—woman in a sky-blue dress with a white collar and wearing a clean white apron, drew the door back and stared with a vague curiosity up at Sager and the stranger on his heels.

"Good afternoon, Mary," the foreman said, removing his hat and scraping his boots on the hemp mat at his feet. "I'd like a word with Melissa Ann."

The woman's expression did not change. She merely drew the door open wider and threw out her arm. Apparently understanding the gesture, Sager stepped forward, glancing at Stockburn and jerking his head as a command to follow him.

Giving his own boots a cursory scrape on the mat, Wolf removed his hat and followed the man into the house. Pete scraped his boots and followed along behind the two men as they strode down a hall, skirting the perimeter of a sunken library or parlor. It was a large, cavelike room impressively appointed with heavy masculine furniture complete with game trophies on the walls and a glass cabinet housing many rifles. Some of them appeared to be expensive sporting rifles though Stockburn was too far away for a good look.

When they reached the rear of the room, they stopped at a door abutted on one side by a grand piano over which a large grizzly rug sprawled, snarling head attached. Several piles of books and folded clothes likely recently washed but still not put away also vied for space atop the piano. From what Stockburn had seen of the house, there was an air of shabby elegance about it, with pockets of clutter and dust and cobwebs clinging to picture frames and wall corners, as though its occupants were too busy for meticulous order and tending.

Above the heavy oak mantel of the large stone hearth in the parlor hung an oil painting of a strikingly beautiful young woman. In her early twenties, she had long, thick black hair and dark-blue eyes. She wore a rich green velveteen gown with a hooded black cape fringed with red lace. Gold rings dangled from her ears, and on one hand was a large ruby ring. The painting gave Stockburn pause and he returned his gaze to it after he'd started to turn away.

Sager knocked on the door before them and said in a voice halting with deference, "Melissa Ann . . . it's Clell and Pete. Could we have a word?"

"Oh, what is it, Clell?" came the response in a weary female voice. "I'm awfully busy going over these book values of Ansel's overseas assets . . ." She let her voice trail off as Stockburn followed Sager into the room.

The half-breed boy stepped into the room and stopped beside Stockburn, canting his head toward Wolf and saying, "Found him out on the range, Ma."

Stockburn had only vaguely heard the boy, though the word *Ma* had not gone without notice somewhere in his consciousness. His eyes had locked on those of the beautiful, black-haired woman sitting at the immensely messy and badly cluttered desk abutting the wall to the right.

That she was the woman in the painting, albeit a few years older, there could be no doubt. It was as if that hauntingly beautiful vision had walked out of the painting to seat itself at the desk in this masculine office half the size of the parlor and in which the aroma of old cigar smoke lingered, mixing with the molasses odor of varnished wood, old leather, and expensive whiskey.

The heavy velvet drapes were drawn over the windows as though against distraction. A Tiffany lamp burned on the desk, its gold reflection dancing in the cobalt blue eyes of the woman seated in the brocade armchair, her body facing the desk but her head—her beautiful head with perfect lines and a soulful, intelligent aura about it—was turned toward the three men lined up in front of the open door.

Her eyes held the stranger's gaze and for a couple of seconds Stockburn thought she'd quit breathing, as he had himself. He remembered to draw in a breath when he became a little light-headed, the floor with its heavy Oriental rug starting to slide around beneath his boots.

"Thought you'd want to talk to him, Melissa Ann," Sager said, betraying that the hierarchy at the Bittersweet Creek Ranch was so recognized formal address was superfluous. "Caught him up near Rustlers' Roost."

"Oh?" Melissa Ann Thornburg raised a thick black brow and put some steel into her voice. "Why didn't you hang him? Why pester me?"

"He says he's Wells Fargo."

She raised the other brow and turned her upper body in her chair to face Stockburn. She had not removed her eyes from his since he'd first entered the room. "Does he now?"

"I've got bona fides," Stockburn said.

"Let me see them." She set down the pen she'd been holding and took a breath, drawing her mouth corners down as though in tolerance of this annoying interruption.

Wolf stepped forward, digging his wallet out of his inside coat pocket. When he looked at the woman again, he saw that she was still staring up at him, tipping her head farther back to keep meeting his eyes now that he'd moved closer to the desk. Her gaze was vaguely probing, questioning.

He supposed his own was, as well.

He opened the wallet to show his shield and identification card. She looked down at them briefly, almost cursorily, then returned her gaze to his, putting that commanding steel back into her voice—the imposing tone that likely came in handy for a woman running a ranch the size of this one and populated mainly by male underlings. "We've found men on Bittersweet Creek graze claiming to be stock detectives. They even had identification papers and badges. It turned out, after Clell found their running irons, that they were rustlers."

"Decorated the tree on Rustlers' Roost with 'em," said the boy, Pete. A faint smile flickered across his face as he glanced up at Sager, who gave his own brief, approving grin.

The woman looked up at Wolf again. "How do I know your credentials aren't forged, Mr. Stockburn?"

"You don't, ma'am. But if I don't get back on the trail I was following, one young Wells Fargo express messenger is going to get crossways with a gang I believe is holed up not far from here. Having witnessed the result of that gang's handiwork, she will suffer a most excruciating death. If that fate befalls Miss Holloway, I'm gonna be one mighty piss-burned detective . . . if you'll pardon my French." He narrowed a pointed gaze at the woman.

"I don't understand. Where do you think a gang is holed up? There's nothing south of here . . ."

"Except the old Kavanaugh Circle 7, Ma," Pete said. "On the other side of the Snake Creek Buttes." Sager turned to the half-breed boy, who added, "That place's been abandoned for years. Ever since old Patrick Kavanaugh died and his wife moved back to Ireland."

"We run our beef on that graze now," said Mrs. Thornburg. Her brow furrowed more severely as she studied Sager more closely. "Wasn't it in that area where two of our men disappeared a couple of weeks ago, Clell?"

Sager nodded. "They went out to shift the herd around. Didn't come back. We looked, didn't find a thing. No sign of 'em." He glanced at Pete. "We didn't cross the creek, though." Turning back to his boss, the foreman said, "I thought they might've just pulled out. Got tired of the work, and headed to Wahpeton. It's happened before. Some men are cut out for this country . . . some aren't."

As a sudden thought dawned on him, he snapped his fingers together. "I forgot to tell you this." He dug into a pocket of his cracked brown leather vest and stepped forward. "I found this on the range yesterday. Along with a cartridge casing." He set the first object atop an open ledger on Mrs. Thornburg's desk. Digging into a pocket again, he set another small object on the ledger so that both objects rested side by side—a five-pointed star into which TOWN CONSTABLE had been stamped, and a brass cartridge casing almost as long as a cigarette, minus the bullet that had once been seated atop it.

Mrs. Thornburg frowned down at both objects then up at Sager.

Wolf said, "That's a black powder cartridge, fifty-ninety

caliber, most likely. Fired out of a Sharps Big Fifty. Long-range rifle. Good at hunting both buffalo and men."

"Fifty-ninety, all right," Sager said. "It wears that stamp on its rim."

Stockburn picked up the tin star, scrutinized it closely, brushed his thumb across one of the five points, and then dropped it back down onto the open account book. "And this no doubt belongs . . . or belonged, rather . . . to Rowdy Lockwood, Constable of Paradise." He tossed the badge down on the book and said, "Lockwood's gone missing, too. Just like your men, Mrs. Thornburg."

"Who is this gang you're looking for?" she asked.

In a few sentences, he explained the situation.

"They must be holed up at the old Kavanaugh ranch, Ma," Pete said, having moved up to stand off Stockburn's right elbow. "I've seen tracks heading that direction, but I was too busy trying to pull calves out of thickets and wallows to pay much attention. I figured if it was rustlers, we'd chase 'em down after roundup."

Mrs. Thornburg switched her gaze back to Wolf. "Do you think they have her, Mr. Stockburn? This young express messenger?"

"I think there's a good chance, Mrs. Thornburg. She was following Belle Lockwood out from town. I have very good reason to believe Miss Lockwood has hitched her star to the Devil's Horde. In fact, I think most of the town has."

Mrs. Thornburg drew a breath and gave her head a single shake. "I wouldn't doubt it a bit. About Belle, I mean."

"Belle's reputation precedes her, I take it?"

"Her father tried to raise her well, but . . . more often than not fate is out of our hands. Wouldn't you agree?" She gazed at him pointedly.

His heart hiccupped.

No. Couldn't be. Could she? After all these years . . . ?

Wolf nodded. "It sure is, Mrs. Thornburg. Thanks for the hospitality"—he cast Sager a cold glance—"but I reckon I'll be on my way." He set his sombrero on his head and headed for the door.

"Not so fast, Stockburn!" the woman called commandingly.

Wolf stopped, turned to face her with a sigh. "Look, lady, I'm clean out of patience with—

"With help, Mr. Stockburn? If that gang is as large as you say they are, you're going to need all the help you can get." She rose from her chair, a tall woman beautifully put together and wearing a crisp white shirtwaist with a doeskin leather vest with silver conchas from which whang strings dangled. She wore a long doeskin skirt and highheeled black boots with silver-tipped toes. A dyed hemp belt with a rawhide buckle encircled her lean waist, accentuating the up thrust of her bosom.

She looked at her son and said, "Pete, summon all the men here at headquarters. Have them armed and ready to ride in ten minutes—fully outfitted and loaded for bear!"

"You got it, Ma!" Pete hurried from the room.

Sager looked at the woman. She gave him a cool nod. He glanced at Stockburn then turned and followed the boy out of the office.

Without another word to her guest, Melissa Ann Thornburg swung around, long hair and skirt swirling, and headed for a cabinet in which several Winchester rifles were racked.

"Hold on, now, Mrs. Thornburg," Wolf said. "Don't you think you'd better—?"

"Stay here in the safety of my office? Let the men take care of it? Maybe have a cup of tea to calm my nerves?" She grabbed a rifle and swung back to him, smiling beautifully and with no scarcity of challenge and defiance in her suddenly wild eyes. "If you knew me, Mr. Stockburn, you'd know that is not the woman I am!"

"Yes," Wolf said, studying her closely as she loaded her rifle. "I suppose I would. I suppose I would at that."

CHAPTER 38

Hank lay on the ground, trying to regain her wits after the shelf atop the butte had given way beneath her and sent her tumbling.

Belle booted her horse toward Hank, stopped, and stared down at her red-haired nemesis, a look of deep incredulity creasing Belle's features. She spat to one side and narrowed her eyes in fury. "What the hell are you doing out here, Miss Fancy Pants?"

"Obviously, dear Belle," said Hart Shevlin, gigging his horse forward, as well, "she followed you. You let yourself get followed out from town." He spoke those last words tightly, his eyes cold and hard as he stared down at Hank.

He was an odd-looking man. Lean but not very tall. Sort of snakelike, actually. He had longish hair the color of old dishwater after a greasy pan had been washed in it.

Beneath the brim of his dusty cream Stetson that boasted a braided rawhide band trimmed with many colored Indian beads, his flat eyes were copper brown. It was hard to pinpoint his age. The skin was pulled drum-tight across his angular face. Deep lines ran down from both corners of his mouth, and many short, fine lines radiated out from his eyes, like the spokes on a wheel. There were many small sores on his mouth, and his lips were peeling. He was deeply tanned, and clean-shaven save long sideburns the same colorless color of his hair.

He might have been handsome a few years ago, but Hank suspected hard drinking and all-around hard living had made him appear older than his years. She guessed he was somewhere in his forties, but his face was that of a much older man.

"Don't worry," Belle said, sliding her Schofield from the holster on her right hip. "I'll take care of this little problem." She cocked the piece, extending it out and down toward Hank.

"No, you won't!" Shevlin said, flinging his arm out and forward, closing his hand over the gun. As he ripped it out of Belle's hand, it thundered.

The bullet plunked into the ground just over Hank's head.

"You damn polecat!" Shevlin yelled, resting the Schofield on his thigh. "You do what I tell you to do and only what I tell you to do!" He smashed the back of his right hand against Belle's left cheek with a decisive *smack!* "Don't you sass me, you little ringtail! We depend on you to let us know what's going on in town. What the hoopleheads are up to. I told you over and over to make sure that, whatever you do, you don't let yourself get followed. And what do you do? You let yourself get followed by *a damn Wells Fargo agent*!"

Belle pressed her hand to her cheek. The flesh was turning red behind her hand. She glared at the man called Shevlin, her jaws set hard as concrete. "I told you I'd take care of her. Now, give me my gun back and let me take care of her."

"No." He glanced at the man sitting to his right and said, "I'm gonna let Lester take care of her." He grinned. "How 'bout it, Les? You think you can handle that?"

Les returned Shevlin's smile then looked down at Hank, his eyes smoldering with raw male lust. "Yeah, I think I can handle that."

He was a fat man with a curly cinnamon beard carpeting his pockmarked cheeks. A large heart-shaped wart sat just above the beard on the right side of his face, which glistened with oily sweat in the late-afternoon heat. He swung his heavy frame down from his horse, black duster winging out around his thick legs. He looked down at Hank, his mouth open, his dung-brown eyes wide as silver dollars. He doffed his hat and tossed it onto the ground.

"No!" Hank said, lunging backward, trying to crawl away from the stinky beast of a man towering over her.

"Don't fight it, honey," Shevlin advised. "That just works him up even more. He loves it when they fight. He'll keep you alive longer, and, believe me, when ole Lester gets goin' on ya, you'll pray for a fast end!"

Shevlin and the other man laughed.

The other man said, "Get after her, Lester! I think she likes you!"

Again, they laughed.

Hank thrust herself up off the ground, but she was still clumsy with dizziness. She'd just gained her feet but hadn't risen from a crouch before Lester grabbed her, tossed her back onto the ground, and threw himself on top of her. He groaned deep in his chest like some half-mad grizzly going to work on an early supper. He grabbed her chin in one hand, squeezing and thrusting her head back. Still groaning, his eyelids half-closed over his eyes, he thrust his big, shaggy, sweaty head down on Hank's chest and sniffed and snorted, biting her through her clothes.

"No!" Hank cried, heart thudding as his teeth dug into her bosoms. "*Nooo!* Make him *stop!*" As she thrashed beneath him, trying to fight him off, her hand brushed the handles of a revolver holstered on his left hip. He grabbed her hand and thrust it up above her head, still groaning as he continued molesting her.

Hank couldn't believe what was happening. She was being mauled by a stinky, shaggy-headed lunatic!

While the other two men laughed hysterically, seated on their horses above, Lester ripped a button off her blouse with his teeth and spat it onto the ground. He showed Hank his scraggly, tobacco-rimed teeth, laughing, mewling, snarling, and groaning all at the same time.

Then he buried his face in her bosom again.

"*Nooo!*" Hank screamed, and ripped her right hand free of the big man's grip. Thrusting that hand down to Lester's left hip, she fumbled the keeper thong free from over the hammer, slid the revolver from its holster, clicked the hammer back, and pulled the gun back up toward her chest.

She set the barrel against Lester's left temple and closed her eyes.

One of the men staring down at them shouted, "Watch it, Lester! Watch it—she's got your—!"

The gun roared, instantly kicking up a wild ringing inside her head.

She felt the sticky wetness of blood and viscera spraying

across her face and neck, and recoiled, knowing she'd just blown the big man's brains all over herself.

"Should have let me shoot her!" she heard Belle yell beyond the ringing in her ears. "Now look what she did!"

Hank opened her eyes. Lester lay on top of her. His head looked like a cantaloupe that had been broken open against a rock—if a cantaloupe was as red as a tomato, that was. And filled with the white of a man's brains. Hank felt the filth dripping down her lips and off her chin. Some of it had the texture of corn. She knew that that was probably the man's blown-apart brains.

Revolted, gagging, she heaved the big man off her. It took some doing, because he was nearly as heavy as a full-grown cow. Seeing Shevlin swing down from his saddle and step toward her, grim-faced, she tried raising the gun again. The Colt as well as her arm clear up to her elbow were bathed in Lester's blood and brains. She clicked back the hammer again but before she could squeeze the trigger, Shevlin kicked the gun out of her hand.

Hank stared up in horror as he squatted over her, sitting on the heels of his boots. He still had Belle's Schofield in his hand. He rammed the barrel between Hank's bloody, brain-stained lips, cocked it, and stared into her eyes. His face was strangely expressionless. The eyes were snake eyes, reflecting not an ounce of soul. His skin, too, was like the skin of a snake—something waxy and scaly about it. His mouth was a straight slash, the scarred lips tightly compressed. His colorless hair curled down behind his ears. The brim of his cream hat buffeted in the breeze.

The lead killer. The head of the Devil's Horde. Here he was at last. Every bit as savage as she'd expected he'd be.

Hank was doomed. She'd been a fool to ride out without Wolf. What had she thought would happen?

You ride into a wolf den, you become wolf bait, Hank, you simple fool!

"Kill her, Hart!" Belle cried, sitting her horse to Hank's left, Shevlin's right, staring down in red-faced anger. Her swollen eyes blazed with rage. "Kill her and be done with her, for god sakes, you simple fool!"

The other man, still seated on his horse, looked edgily from Shevlin to Belle then back again.

Shevlin gave the slightest of winces, a faint twitch of a muscle just beneath his left eye. He pulled the Schofield's barrel out of Hank's mouth, rose, swung around, and aimed the cocked revolver at Belle.

"Oh-oh," said the other devil.

"Wait, Hart!" Belle said, stark terror flashing in her eyes. Shevlin fired.

The bullet punched through the dead center of her chest. She didn't even scream, tumbling backward off her horse as though she'd been lassoed from behind and hitting the ground with a hard thud. She lay unmoving, dead.

Her paint leaped forward, whinnying shrilly, then wheeled and galloped south along the crease.

"Damn!" exclaimed the other rider.

"There," Shevlin said, tossing the Schofield into the brush. "Takes care of her. Damn, I got tiring of listening to her caterwauling."

He crouched over Hank and smiled a lunatic's smile. "As for you, darlin'—you got some fire in you! We're gonna have us a celebration tonight back at the ranch, since it's our last night an' all." He smiled up at the other devil, who grinned back at him.

Shevlin grabbed Hank's hand and pulled her to her feet. "And you, my pretty catamount, are gonna be the guest of honor!"

Was Melissa Ann Thornburg his kidnapped sister, Emily?
The thought preyed on Stockburn's mind as he and Mrs. Thornburg, her half-breed son Pete, the old foreman, Clell Sager, and seven other men galloped across Bittersweet Creek graze, heading toward a pale line of buttes lumping up against the southern horizon. They rode in a loose group, hunkered low in their saddles, the wind nipping at their hats and shirt collars.

Stockburn rode up front with Mrs. Thornburg on his right and old Sager on his left. Pete followed close behind his mother. The seven ranch hands were fanned out behind them, forming a ragged wedge bounding across the prairie.

Wolf glanced at the woman. She sat the saddle of her fine sorrel Morgan expertly, long black hair bouncing on her shoulders. She wore gloves and a black vest over her cream shirtwaist. She'd strapped a Second Frontier Model Merwin & Hulbert .44-40 caliber revolver around her waist, snugged down in a black leather holster. A Winchester saddle-ring carbine jutted from her saddle scabbard. A round, green felt hat was tugged down low over her forehead, shading her eyes from the west-angling sun that bathed the grass in a soft, lemony light edging toward salmon.

She turned her cobalt gaze to Wolf, returning his look with an obscure one of her own.

Emily?
He wanted to ask the question outright. But now wasn't the time. Also, he was a little afraid of the answer. What

if she wasn't his sister? Maybe even more haunting—and he hadn't expected to feel this way—what if she *was* Emily?

How did you relate to a sister who'd been absent from your life for so many years? Who'd likely gone through the horrors of Indian captivity? And had birthed a boy during that captivity . . . ?

It was too much to think about. Besides, deep inside, he knew that Melissa Ann Thornburg and Emily being the same person was unlikely. True, Mrs. Thornburg was around the same age Emily would be if she were alive, but there were a lot of women Emily's age and bearing her general features.

Weren't there?

The thought of finding his sister one day had been Wolf's only friend. It had added depth and dimension, not to mention purpose, to his life that otherwise had little outside of his job. Maybe that's what had kept him from marriage, from raising a family. This single-minded pursuit *had been* his marriage. It had replaced his family.

No, that probably wasn't true.

His quest for Emily had only given him a good reason to not go through the pain of getting close to someone again while knowing full well that he could easily betray them as he had betrayed Mike. A darkness inside him had made him unworthy of deep friendship and of love most of all.

What if he had found Emily finally after all these years? His old friend, the quest, would be gone. He would then be faced with Emily herself. Of having to negotiate a possible relationship with her . . .

Maybe that's what frightened him the most.

Wolf, get your damn fool head back on the task at hand, on Hank and the Devil's Horde, for crying in the preacher's wine!

Melissa Ann raised her right hand and drew back on her reins with her left. The handsome sorrel Morgan slowed, kicking up its front feet feistily, tossing its head friskily, wanting to keep running. Mrs. Thornburg had a sure hand, however. The horse stopped.

Wolf, Sager, Pete, and the others stopped their own horses around her, the mounts blowing and snorting and switching their tails at flies and the infernal, ever-present mosquitoes.

She glanced at Wolf and jerked her chin forward. "Just beyond those bluffs is the old Kavanaugh Circle 7 headquarters. If the Devil's Horde is holed up out here, we'll likely find them there. Along with your friend . . . if she's still alive."

"All right." Stockburn considered the cedar- and oak-stippled bluffs jutting ahead of him. "Let me ride ahead, get the lay of the land. If they're over there, they'll likely have lookouts posted. They'll need to be taken care of first." He looked at Mrs. Thornburg then at Sager, and slid his Yellowboy from its boot. He pointed with the rifle and said, "I'll signal you from atop that highest bluff yonder." Wolf nudged the bay ahead.

"Hold on, Mr. Stockburn," Mrs. Thornburg said.

He glanced at her. She canted her head at her son sitting to her left. "Take Pete. You'll need help."

Stockburn frowned at the boy.

Pete heeled his steel dust pony forward, his young handsome face with eyes the same blue of his mother's eyes owning little expression. "You got it, Ma."

She said something to him in what Wolf recognized as Sioux in the Lakota dialect. She spoke it perfectly in the flat vowels, hard consonants, and primitive tones he'd heard so many times on his quest for Emily. Listening to his mother, Pete turned to stare curiously at Stockburn.

Wolf wasn't sure why, but his ears warmed with self-consciousness.

Melissa Ann stopped talking and turned to him. He stared back at her, his own expression curious. But no translation was forthcoming, and the woman's expression betrayed nothing.

"All right, then," he said, drawing a deep breath. "Come on, Pete."

They booted their mounts toward the high buttes and the Devil's Horde lair.

Chapter 39

A half hour later, Stockburn lay flat against the side of a butte. He'd slid his bowie knife from the sheath on his belt. Clutching the hide-wrapped handle, his gloved index finger was pressed taut against the hilt. His heart thudded as he anticipated a death-dealing thrust.

The man he'd spied through his field glasses stood just above him on the crest of the butte. Wolf watched the man's shadow slide from his right to his left, brushing across him, as the devil milled restlessly atop the bluff, pacing a short distance from side to side, turning, keeping an eye on the country north of the old Kavanaugh Ranch.

They'd figured, correctly, that if trouble came it would come from the north, for that was the direction of Paradise. If trouble came, it would come from Paradise.

Wolf gave a savage grin. It had, all right.

He smelled the smoke of the cigarette the man was smoking. He could hear the man sighing from time to time, yawning. He was bored and tired.

Stockburn turned to gaze off to his left. Another sentinel stood atop a bluff roughly a city block away, to the east. The man leaned against a cedar twisting up from the bluff and forming a gnarled Y. Wolf could see only the man's silhouette, but the devil appeared to be facing south, the direction of the outlaw ranch. He also appeared to be cradling a rifle in his arms. He'd gotten lazy and careless.

Wolf saw another silhouette on the side of the bluff, directly below the feckless devil. The second silhouette was Pete, who also had a bowie knife. He'd assured Stockburn he knew what to do with it, that he'd been taught the ways of stalking and killing prey, human and otherwise, by a Sioux warrior. No one better at it than a Sioux warrior.

When Stockburn had spied the two sentinels through his glasses, he and Pete formed a plan. They'd each take a sentinel as quietly as possible. There appeared to be the only two lookouts. Wolf hoped that was true. They'd find out in a minute.

Stockburn stared at Pete. He couldn't tell if the boy was looking back at him. He probably was. He'd told the boy to follow his lead.

Stockburn lifted his chin to gaze up at the crest of the butte above him. The man had just turned, giving him his back, cigarette smoke webbing over his right shoulder, peppering Wolf's nose.

Here we go . . .

Wolf gained his feet and climbed. The bluff was steep, the chalky soil slippery, so he had to use the inside of his boots for the first two steps, walking like a duck. Then he was on the butte, directly behind the lookout. Hearing him, the lookout gave a startled grunt, dropped the cigarette, and started to turn.

Stockburn grabbed the man's left bicep with his own left hand, turning his quarry forward again then sliding the bowie knife up and around the man's right shoulder. Wolf kept the blade so sharp that it sliced across the man's throat, several inches deep. Like a hot knife through butter, there was hardly any resistance. He felt the blood, thick and warm, bathe his hand before he pulled the knife back.

The man dropped to his knees, the rifle falling from his hands. He clutched his neck, gasping and gurgling, as his life fluid geysered out of him to pool thickly on the pale dirt around his knees. Wolf grabbed him by the back of his duster collar, dragged him backward off the top of the butte, and tossed him like so much trash down the north side.

Stockburn turned just as Pete discarded his own prey in similar fashion.

"He'll do," Wolf muttered. "He'll do just fine." He looked around, making sure no other pickets had shown themselves. Turning his gaze south, he saw the creek. Sheathed in summer-green trees and brush, it snaked around the far side of the bluffs, roughly a quarter mile away. Beyond the creek and the trees, in a bowl among more chalky bluffs to the south, lay the old Kavanaugh Circle 7.

It was time to pay a visit.

He swung his gaze north. He couldn't see Mrs. Thornburg, Sager, and the other Bittersweet Creek hands, but he knew Melissa Ann was keeping an eye on him and her son through her spyglass. He waved his rifle, giving the agreed-upon signal, then hurried through a crease between the bluffs toward where he'd tied the bay.

He and Pete joined up first then waited for the boy's mother, Sager, and the others to ride up along an old horse and stock trail. Wolf saw their dust first, then their jostling silhouettes.

"How did he do?" the woman asked him, checking down the Morgan and glancing at her half-breed son, who sat his pony stone-faced but proud, the wind brushing his long hair back behind his shoulders.

Stockburn smiled at the lad. "Just fine." Looking back at the woman, he furrowed his brow and said, "It's going to get tougher from here. Like I said, there's a good twenty-five of them. I culled the herd a little on the way down here, but—"

"Lead on, Mr. Stockburn," she said, cutting him off.

"You've no dog in this fight, Mrs. Thornburg."

"Oh, I believe I do," she said with a very faint flash in her cobalt eyes.

Sager, sitting to her left, turned his grizzled head to regard her curiously. The other riders flanking them also looked vaguely intrigued.

Wolf studied the woman for another couple of seconds. His heart quickened. He felt a tightness in his throat but chalked it up to worry about Hank. Melissa Ann held him with her frank gaze, eyes that he tried so hard to remember . . . to recognize. They were the same color as Emily's, but beyond that the mists of time shrouded his sweet sister in the murk of memory.

"All right, then . . ." He swung the bay around, booted it forward. He and Pete led the pack along the trail marked with the fresh prints of several horses, which likely included the sign of Belle Lockwood and his partner. He looked around at the passing brush, rocks, the twisted oaks and cedars, the conical buttes, half-expecting to find

Hank lying dead, killed and cast away, her body badly ravaged.

He turned his gaze ahead, and his gut tightened. Something lay spread across the trail. He approached the bodies with dread sitting heavy inside him. He halted the bay and, as the others drew rein around and behind him, he stared down at the four dead townsmen in shock.

The barber, the butcher, the saloonkeeper, and the liveryman all lay dead in twisted, bloody piles.

Just beyond them and to the left lay the body of a young woman. Stockburn quickly swung down from the saddle and strode over to where Belle Lockwood peered skyward through half-open eyes. Blood matted the front of her shirt, directly between her breasts. She lay with her arms stretched out to each side, one leg tucked under the other one. An expression of deep befuddlement remained on her tomboy-pretty face.

"Damn," Stockburn muttered, grimacing. He raked his fingers gently over Belle's eyes, closing them.

Mrs. Thornburg swung down from her saddle, gave her reins to Sager, then dropped to a knee beside Wolf. She shook her head. "That girl was rotten from the inside out. Still . . ." Again, she shook her head as she looked down at the dead young constable. "There was something about her I couldn't help feeling tender about."

"Yeah," Wolf said, feeling sick.

Belle was likely responsible for the murder of her own father and an accessory to the murders of so many more. But, like the lady beside him, he still had a soft spot in his heart for her. She had probably deserved to die like this—a bullet to the heart and left with four of her coconspirators, food for the carrion-eaters. But that didn't make him regret her death any less.

Mrs. Thornburg turned to Wolf. "What does this mean?" She glanced at the four dead townsmen and then at Belle again.

"It means the two factions—the town and the Devil's Horde—got crossways with each other." He straightened and cast his gaze around, looking for Hank. Not seeing her anywhere, he stared off through the trees that sheathed the creek, toward the old Kavanaugh Circle 7. "And it likely means that those demons have my partner."

His voice had come low and raspy. He'd brushed his fingers across the grips of the Colt Peacemaker holstered on his right thigh as he'd spoken the words. He felt a hand on his left forearm. He turned to see Mrs. Thornburg standing beside him, looking up at him sympathetically.

"We'll get her back." She gave a resolute nod. "We'll help you get her back."

"I don't know," Wolf said. "We're outgunned."

"I've been outgunned many times in my life, Mr. Stockburn. I've made it this far. We just need a plan." She smiled.

Three big crows cackled at her from a box elder branch. They were laughing, mocking her misery. Her terror. Or maybe the cackling was just their way of salivating, savoring the ripe female carcass that would soon be their supper.

The right time of the day, too. The sun was tumbling westward to her right though there were likely still a couple of hours of summer daylight left.

Hank splashed across the stream, the rope cutting into

her bound wrists. With the other end of the rope firmly grasped in his gloved right hand, Shevlin led her, jerking her along like a trailing packhorse. Occasionally, when she slowed her pace, for she couldn't keep up with his fast trot, he gave her a hard tug, jerking her forward and nearly making her trip over her own feet and drop to her knees.

At those times he'd glance at the other man riding beside him, mutter something in a bemused voice, and the other would glance back at Hank and snicker and laugh.

He pulled her up out of the stream, up the bank, and into the woods beyond. She was soaked from the waist down. Her boots were heavy, waterlogged, and made sucking sounds as she jogged to keep up with her captor. Her soaked skirt hung heavy off her hips, dancing like a sodden curtain around her running legs. Shevlin led her around snags of thick brush and blowdown trees. Branches reached out to scratch her cheeks, pull her hair, and snatch at her blouse and skirt.

She saw something hanging from a tree ahead and on her right. She looked at it, looked away. Looked back at it again and gasped.

Two bodies hung from that oak branch. The bodies of two men dressed in range garb, including colorful neckerchiefs and leather chaps as well as high-heeled, badly worn boots with silver spurs. One was fair, the other dark with a dark mustache. Both were young. They'd both been shot several times. Blood stained their striped poplin shirts and vests. Their faces were bloated, large eyes staring out darkly from sockets embedded deep in swollen flesh the yellow color of jaundice. Of death.

Their sickly-sweet stench reached out to assault Hank's nostrils. She grimaced, shook her head, looked away from the grisly scene. The men had been dead for a couple of weeks.

Who were they? Two of the Devil's Horde themselves? Likely not. They were likely cowboys who'd gotten cross-ways with the gang. Maybe they'd stumbled onto the killers' hideout and had to be silenced.

And there they hung . . .

Hank would likely join them soon, when the gang had had their fun with her.

She shambled out of the trees and found herself enter-ing an open area with crude buildings and corrals. The distant pattering of a piano reached her ears, as well as a woman's singing.

Hank peered ahead of the jouncing figures of Shevlin and the other man. A large house lay at the far end of the ranch yard—a two-story log house with a front porch mounted on stones. Most of the house's windows except a single front one were boarded up. The building had a dilapidated, abandoned look, and the yard was shaggy with uncut grass. Men lounged on the porch, some resting hips against the porch rail or were tipped back in chairs, their boots crossed on the porch rail before them. There were a lot of them.

Some wore long, black dusters and coal-black Stetsons. They were smoking and passing around bottles. They might have been ranch hands lounging around, resting after a long hot day on the range.

Only, Hank knew they were not.

They were the Devil's Horde. She'd been dragged into their lair.

The crows followed her, cawing, winging over her in a gush of displaced air and the sinewy creaking of flapping wings. They settled on the peaked roof of the ranch house, above the porch where the devils milled, swilling liquor and listening to a woman playing a piano and singing inside the wretched place.

The woman—she sounded very young, with a high, reedy voice—was trying to sound jovial, but there was a brittleness to her voice. She was scared. Her voice cracked occasionally. Sometimes her fingers came down on a wrong key, or came down wrong on the right key, kicking up a raucous reverberation.

Hank didn't blame the girl for being afraid. The men on the porch were a nasty, mean-looking lot. Their faces were dark and angular, eyes flat and dull, betraying an animal-like savagery. All appeared armed with six-shooters. Some held rifles, always alert.

Three or four scantily clad women sat among the men. They didn't look any happier than the young woman singing and playing the piano inside the house sounded. Some appeared bruised—almost as beaten up as Hank. She could see the discolorations of cuts and bruises on their arms and legs as well as on their garishly painted faces.

Hank remembered what the barber had said about the town providing women for the killers. These girls were those women—likely doxies from one of the larger surrounding towns, brought there to keep the Devil's Horde entertained between jobs. The killers had not been kind.

And they would not be kind to Hank.

As if to prove her point, Shevlin stopped his horse near a windmill and stock tank in the middle of the ranch yard and gave the rope a savage tug forward, pulling Hank ahead so fast that she lost her footing, dropped to the ground, and rolled, groaning.

"What you got there, Hart?" one man called from the porch. His flat-featured face with deep-set eyes broke into a rare smile. "Fresh meat?"

Hart Shevlin swung his right leg over his saddle horn, dropped lithely to the ground and wheeled to face Hank—wet, muddy, and exhausted—writhing on the ground.

He strode over to her, his eyes grim though his mouth was curved up into a devilish smile. "She's from Wells Fargo." He reached down, jerked her up off the ground, and swung her over his right shoulder. Grunting, he said, "She killed Lester."

Shevlin swung around, carried Hank over to the stock tank ringing the base of the windmill, and tossed her into the water. "I'm gonna clean her up a bit then take her upstairs!"

From under the water, she heard the savage gang leader yell it to the others.

"When I'm done—if there's anything left of her—the rest of you can give her a go!"

As Hank bounced up off the stock tank's floor, thrusting her head above the water, Shevlin grabbed her by the hair and pulled her toward him. She screamed as he swept her up out of the tank and over his shoulder again, water streaming over them both.

"Make way, boys!" He called to the men on the porch. "Fresh flesh for the lair!"

He laughed as he carried Hank on his shoulder toward the house, her head and arms dangling down his back. He was blissfully unaware of the pearl-handled stiletto she clutched in her right fist. While in the stock tank, she'd sneaked the nasty but effective little pigsticker out of the hand-sewn sheath concealed by the folds of her skirt.

She lifted her head and right hand, and gave a savage scream. Raising her arm and swinging her hand above the killer's shoulders, she buried the blade hilt-deep in the devil's neck.

Chapter 40

Shevlin grunted as he stopped in his tracks. Straightening, he flung Hank off his back.

She hit the ground with another grunt and looked up to see Shevlin stumbling forward and twisting around, staring at her in mute shock, eyes wide, jaws hard.

With his right hand, he tried reaching for the knife in the back of his neck, near his left shoulder. When that didn't work, he reached for the knife with his left hand. He grabbed the pearl handle and jerked the blade out of his neck with another, louder grunt. He kept his glassy, stunned, enraged gaze on Hank.

"What the . . . ?" said one of the men on the porch in a hushed tone.

What had just occurred appeared to register on the men on the porch only gradually. By ones and twos they exclaimed softly, curiously, and rose from whatever positions of languor they'd been assuming before Hank had shoved the stiletto into their leader's neck. Boots dropped to the porch floor. Spurs chinged. Chairs creaked as men rose and moved slowly and with hushed interest toward the rail.

Wet and filthy and in nearly as much shock as Shevlin was, Hank lay on her side about eight feet from the stock tank. Her wet hair hung in red tangles over her face. Shevlin stared at her, wobbling on his feet, holding one hand over the blood that spurted out of the nasty hole in his neck.

"You," he said, removing his left hand from the gash and looking at the blood that coated it liberally. He lowered the hand to his side and staggered to one side then backward, fighting to remain upright. He raised his left hand halfheartedly toward Hank. "You . . . little . . . polecat . . ."

Realizing what had happened, the men were filing down the porch steps. They may not have seen Hank stick Shevlin with the stiletto, but they'd seen the result—the blood dribbling down their leader's back. They saw Shevlin facing Hank and moved out slowly from the porch but slowed their pace when they approached him, some hanging back, others spreading out to either side, warily—as though worried that the bad luck that had befallen their leader might befall them, as well, if they got too close.

Moving toward Hank, the Devil's Horde men began forming a ragged circle around her and Shevlin, whom they kept about eight feet away from. The three girls on the porch stared over the porch rail in wide-eyed, wary fascination. One wore only a filthy chemise with one torn shoulder strap and a few, faded, forlorn-looking feathers in her hair. Her face paint was badly smudged, making her look like a circus clown who'd gotten caught in the rain.

Inside, the other girl still sang and played the piano with too much exultation, as though trying to cheer herself up.

From atop the house, the three crows watched, black eyes glinting eagerly.

Hank shifted her gaze to Shevlin. He brushed his right hand across the walnut grips of his revolver then made another grab for the gun and unsnapped the thong from over the hammer and slid the weapon from the leather. The others watched with their own crow eyes, waiting, anticipating the bullet that would tear through Hank's flesh . . .

Or maybe they didn't want her to die so fast.

One or two furrowed their brows in consternation, shifting gazes quickly between Shevlin and Hank.

An outlaw moved toward the young woman on the ground, frowning at the outlaw leader then smiling lustily at Hank, holding out his arms, opening his hands placatingly. "Whoa, now, Hart. Whoa, now."

"She killed me," Shevlin said tightly. "That . . . little . . . *Wells Fargo whore* . . . killed me!"

"Oh, I wouldn't go that far," said another, shorter man, stepping out away from the others, also moving cautiously toward Hank. "That's just a little nick, Hart. Why, Leo'll sew you up in no time, make you good as new. Why don't you go inside? Leo, take Hart inside and sew him up before he bleeds dry!"

He returned his eager-eyed gaze to Hank and shuffled toward her, a lewd smile spreading across his hairless, moon-shaped face. He was thick through the shoulders, fat in the belly, with arms so long they resembled those of an ape.

"Get away from her!" Shevlin barked hoarsely. "I'm

gonna shoot her!" He raised his Colt and cocked it. His hand quivered slightly, and the Colt sank, as though it weighed too much for him to lift. He raised it again, gritting his teeth with the effort, and aimed down the barrel at Hank's head.

She closed her eyes and lowered her chin.

A plunking sound—like a cantaloupe hit with a rock—was heard.

A gun barked distantly. Too far away for it be Shevlin's gun.

Hank looked up, still petrified but also puzzled. Shevlin was stumbling backward again, clutching his left shoulder while staring down at it in shock. Blood oozed up between his gloved fingers. He took another step back then plopped to the ground on his butt, looking around in even more shock.

Somebody said: "What the . . . ?"

Inside the ranch house, the girl stopped singing. The piano's incessant pattering finally ceased, as well, a few dissonant chords reverberating in the air.

The rumbling grew louder. Hank could feel the ground shaking beneath her.

Another thumping sounded. One of the men surrounding Hank screamed and dropped.

"Take cover!" another man shouted. Then he, too, screamed, twisted backward, and fell.

Guns popped distantly, growing louder. Hank turned to look toward the creek. She sucked in a sharp breath of surprise when she saw a tall man in a black frock coat and a black sombrero galloping a bay horse directly toward her. His black foulard tie snaked around his neck like a noose, buffeting behind him in the wind.

The Gray Wolf held his horse's reins in his teeth as he cocked his Yellowboy repeater, slammed the butt to his shoulder, and aimed toward the men scrambling around Hank.

A good thirty yards to Stockburn's left, a woman with long black hair and a white shirtwaist and a black leather vest was galloping hell for leather toward the ranch yard, as well. On a fine sorrel Morgan, she fired a rifle as the horse kicked up gouts of sod and dirt.

To Stockburn's other side, a slender young man crouched low over the neck of a steel dust pony, his reins in his teeth, firing and levering a Winchester rifle, his long black hair trailing out in the wind behind his black Stetson. He yipped and yowled like a rampaging Indian!

Turning her head farther to her right, Hank saw more men galloping toward the ranch yard. Looking left, more were coming from that direction, too. They were like the spokes on a wheel converging on the hub of the ranch yard in which the Devil's Horde was yapping and screaming as the attackers' bullets punched into them.

"Take cover, Hank!" Stockburn's voice cut through the din of thudding hooves, screaming men, and belching rifles.

She didn't need to be told twice.

She scrambled to her feet, ran crouching toward the stock tank, launched herself off her heels, and dove over the lip of the stone trough and into the water.

Stockburn chomped down hard on his reins, the taste of leather in his mouth. Chomping down even harder, he aimed his Winchester at one of the scrambling killers and squeezed the trigger. The Yellowboy screeched and bucked against his shoulder.

The devil with an extended rifle in his hands who'd just dropped to a knee in front of the stock tank plopped straight backward as Wolf's bullet punched through his forehead. The bullet blew the back half of his skull onto the ground behind him. The man lay spread-eagled and quivering as though he'd been struck by lightning.

Wolf pulled the reins from his teeth and shouted, "Take cover, Hank!"

He shoved the ribbons back into his mouth then quickly ejected the last spent cartridge from the Yellowboy's breech and rammed a fresh one into the action.

He grimaced in dread as Hank gained her feet straight ahead of him. Crouching and looking around at the shocked killers scrambling to return fire around her, spread out in front of the ranch house, she ran toward the stock tank. Wolf prayed one of the shooters didn't shoot her either on purpose or errantly. Wolf smiled then as she propelled herself off her heels and formed a perfect arc over the side of the tank.

A white splash licked up from the tank as the redhead disappeared beneath the water.

"Attagirl!" Wolf yelled, snapping the Yellowboy to his shoulder once more.

To his right, Mrs. Thornburg flung two quick rifle shots toward the ranch yard. One round clipped the arm of one killer swinging around to return fire at the riders swarming around them, closing on them from all points of the compass and putting a big kink in their day. Several others still standing or kneeling and shooting were also wheeling in confusion, trying to settle on targets.

Giving the gang a taste of its own medicine, Stockburn and Melissa Ann Thornburg's men had surprised and overwhelmed those of the Devil's Horde. Three were just then running toward the ranch house, intending to take refuge inside.

Wolf jerked his bay to a halt near the stock tank and slid the empty Yellowboy into its scabbard then shucked both Peacemakers. Melissa Ann halted her horse beside Wolf's bay, and they shot all three of the fleeing killers.

The one who had turned to fire at them as he climbed the steps took three rounds to the chest and fell back, screaming, against the steps. The other two took bullets to their backs, which Wolf thought fitting since they'd killed so many train passengers while the passengers had been trying to flee the gang's merciless savagery.

One of those two wounded killers screamed and staggered forward across the porch, black duster flapping like the wings of a giant crow, ramming against the house's closed timber door. He flipped the latch but the door didn't open.

"Open up, you soiled doves!" he wailed to the girls who'd taken sanctuary inside the house. He tried the latch again.

Wolf blew another .45-caliber bullet into the back of the devil's head. The man slammed his forehead against the locked door and slid down the door until he lay in a bloody heap on the porch's blood-splattered floor. He left a long, wide, vertical blood streak on the halved-log, Z-frame door above him.

Wolf looked around, sliding both smoking Colts this

way and that, looking for more targets. He raised both barrels, holding fire.

The gang was down—all twenty-plus men lying in bloody heaps, limbs flung across each other. One knelt against the stock tank, facing the windmill, as though in prayer, but his head and both arms were in the water.

Inside the tank, Hank knelt near the dead man, regarding him skeptically through her swollen, discolored eyes. She looked like a half-drowned, red-haired badger.

Stockburn continued to look around the yard. Only one of the gang was moving, trying to crawl off across the yard, dragging his two badly bullet-riddled legs and cursing shrilly. Riding into the yard beside Clell Sager, Pete calmly finished the killer with a Winchester bullet through the back of the man's head. The seven Bittersweet Creek cowboys rode up on their own mounts, hooves thudding, tack squawking, aiming their smoking Winchesters at the strewn dead.

Like Stockburn, they found no one left to shoot.

It looked like the gang had been sent to their fitting rewards in Hell.

Wolf returned his gaze to his waterlogged partner. "Are you all right, young lady?"

She opened her mouth to respond but swung her head sharply to Stockburn's left, toward the ranch house. "Wolf, look out!" she screamed.

He ducked as a gun roared near the house. The bullet shrieked over his head and spanged off a rock beyond him, near the yard's edge.

"One devil's still kickin'!" Clell Sager bellowed as he and Pete flung lead at the man who'd been playing dead on the porch floor to the left of the door.

Stockburn couldn't tell if either man's bullets hit the killer. After flinging the errant round at Wolf, the man had thrown himself through a sashed window to the right of the door and disappeared into the house in a wail of breaking glass.

Inside, the hiding girls screamed. The man shouted angrily.

Stockburn cursed and swung his right leg over his saddle horn, dropping straight down to the ground. He strode quickly up the porch steps, crossed the porch, and hurled two .45 rounds into the door latch, blowing it out of the heavy panel. Kicking in the door with a single, powerful thrust of his right foot, he then stepped into the shadows rife with the smell of unwashed men, tobacco smoke, and the cheap perfume of the parlor girls.

He raised both Peacemakers straight out from his shoulders.

The killer faced him from the back of the parlor, to the left of an oak stairway rising to the house's second story. He'd been shot in the left shoulder. Blood matted his shirt. He'd lost his hat, and his sweat-matted, colorless hair stood up in spikes around his head. His face was craggy, his eyes wide and crazy with fear, anger, and pain. His chapped lips were stretched back from yellow teeth.

He held one of the girls in front of him—a slender young doxy with a black eye and wearing a sheer red dress that matched the red feathers in her hair. Tears dribbled down her pale cheeks, and her painted libs trembled.

"I'll kill her, Stockburn! Throw down them big Colts, or I'll blow her head clean off her shoulders!"

"Hello, there, Hart!" Stockburn said, grinning tightly.

"I had a feelin' you were part of that horde of kill-crazy devils. You learned from your old mentor, Red Bascom. He taught you well, Red did!"

Back in Bascom's heyday, Hart Shevlin had been one of Red's right-hand men. Stockburn hadn't seen or heard of the killer in years. Hart had likely been cooling his heels in the tall and uncut of Montana or Wyoming until he'd been called to Paradise.

"Throw down the Colts, Wolf!" Shevlin pressed the barrel of his revolver more snugly against the trembling doxy's right temple.

The girl screamed, and her knees buckled. Shevlin held her up in front of him, only half of his head exposed to Stockburn.

Wolf wanted to try the shot, but he couldn't take the chance. He might hit the girl. "All right, all right."

Shevlin was sweating and gritting his teeth. His right hand shook as he pressed the barrel to the sobbing doxy's head. "Now, Stockburn! Now!"

"I heard ya, I heard ya." Slowly, Wolf leaned forward, holding both Peacemakers out in front of him, barrels pointed toward the floor. He kept his gaze on the killer.

Shevlin frowned as he kept his eyes on Wolf's. "What in the hell you smiling abou—."

A gun roared in the shadows behind Shevlin. He dropped both arms straight down to his sides and staggered forward, head wobbling as though his neck had been snapped. The doxy screamed and dropped to her knees. The girls who'd been cowering in the parlor's shadows converged on her, crying.

Hart Shevlin stopped five feet in front of Stockburn

and raised his chin. His eyes rolled back in their sockets, showing only white. His knees buckled, and Wolf stepped to one side as the leader of the Devil's Horde dropped face-first to the floor.

"Nice shootin' girl," Wolf said into the shadows at the back of the parlor.

Hank stepped forward, lowering the smoking revolver in her right hand. "Thanks," she said, drawing a calming breath. Water dribbled from her soaked clothes and hair. "I'm just glad there was a back door."

Stockburn glanced at the doxies all huddled on the floor near the piano, comforting the little one in the red dress. He returned his gaze to Hank, scowling at her.

"I know, I know," she said, drawing her mouth corners down in shame. "Riding out after Belle was another foolish move on my part."

"Almost got yourself killed . . . again!" Stockburn walked up to her and lifted her chin until her contrite gaze met his. "You all right?"

She gave a weak smile and nodded.

He leaned forward to peck her cheek. "Crazy polecat."

"Will Mr. Winthrop hear about this?"

"He just might," Wolf said, not meaning it. He turned toward the door.

Melissa Ann Thornburg stood behind him.

Wolf walked over to her. "Your men all right, Mrs. Thornburg?"

She nodded. "Scully took a bullet to the arm. It's just a flesh wound. Mr. Sager is tending him now." She frowned curiously at Wolf. "I don't understand. Why was the town in league with these . . . these *killers*, Mr. Stockburn?"

"The good citizens of Paradise were enraged that Northern Pacific routed its rails through Fargo, farther north. They'd originally intended to lay track from Wahpeton, in the east, through Paradise. The townsfolk got their hopes up, certain prosperity was on its way!" Wolf shook his head. "When N.P. changed its mind, the good folks of Paradise were bound and determined to exact revenge as well as the wealth they thought they were unjustifiably denied."

"Even if it meant cold-blooded murder?"

"Go figure." Wolf sighed. "Thanks for the help, Mrs. Thornburg." He squeezed her arm. "I am much obliged."

"It's the least I could do." She looked up at him frankly, her dark-blue eyes glinting with affection. "For my brother." Her mouth corners quirked a tender smile. She blinked once, slowly.

Wolf's blood quickened, warmed. He'd never been so overcome with emotion. At least, not since Mike had died. But that had been sorrow and self-revulsion. He swallowed down a hard knot in his throat and heard his trembling, raspy voice say, "Emily . . . ?"

Again, she smiled. She reached up and placed her hand against his cheek. "I haven't been called that in years, Henry Kyle. I changed my name when I left the Lakota with my boy. I was no longer that child. So much had happened. I'd been known as *Sanomi* by the Sioux. Emily was gone. Dead with the rest of my family . . . or so I thought . . . until I saw you earlier today. Right away, I knew!"

Her smiled broadened. Her soft, gentle voice, pitched with familial intimacy, was music to his ears. A tear bubbled out of her left eye and ran down her cheek. "I think we have some catching up to do—you and I. Don't we?"

Watching the two from the other side of the room, Hank opened her mouth in shock then cupped her hands to it, stifling a sob.

Wolf smiled, blinked away a tear or two of his own. He took his long-lost sister's hand in his, and kissed it. "I reckon we do, sis. I reckon we do!"

He laughed, drew her to him, and gave her a big warm hug.

CHAPTER 1

Spotting trouble, Wolf Stockburn reached across his belly with his right hand and unsnapped the keeper thong from over the hammer of the .45-caliber Colt Peacemaker holstered for the cross draw on his left hip. He loosened the big popper in the oiled scabbard.

Just as casually, riding along in the Union Pacific passenger coach at maybe twenty miles an hour through the desert scrub of central Wyoming, he unsnapped the thong from over the hammer of the Colt residing in the holster tied down on his right thigh. He glanced again at the source of his alarm—a man in the aisle seat riding four rows ahead of him, facing the front of the car, on the right side of the aisle.

An old couple in their late sixties, early seventies, sat beside him, the old man against the wall idly reading a newspaper. The old woman, wearing a red scarf over her gray head, appeared to be knitting. Occasionally, Stockburn could see the tips of the needles as she tiredly toiled, sucking her dentures.

Most folks would have seen nothing out of kilter about the man in the aisle seat. He was young and dressed in a cheap suit—maybe attire he'd purchased secondhand from a mercantile. The left shoulder seam was a little frayed and both shoulders were coppered from sunlight.

The young man wore round, steel-framed spectacles and had a soot-smudge mustache. Stockburn had gotten a good look at him when the kid had boarded at the last water stop, roughly fifteen minutes ago. Right away, something had seemed a little off about the lad. Wolf wasn't sure exactly what that had been, but his seasoned rail detective's suspicions had been activated.

Maybe it was the pasty look in the kid's eyes, the moistness of his pale forehead beneath the brim of his shabby bowler hat. He'd been nervous. Downright apprehensive. Scared.

The iron horse was still new to the frontier West, so the kid's fear could be attributed to the mere fact that it was his first time riding on a big iron contraption powered by burning coal and boiling steam, and moving along two slender iron rails at an unheard-of clip—sometimes getting up to thirty, thirty-five miles an hour. Forty on a steep downgrade!

That could have been what had the kid, who was somewhere in his early twenties, streaking his drawers. On the other hand, Stockburn had spotted a telltale bulge in the cracked leather valise the kid had carried pressed up taut against his chest, like a new mother holding her baby.

Adding to Stockburn's caution, a minute ago the young man had leaned forward over the valise and reached a hand inside it. At least, Stockburn thought he had, though of course he didn't have a full-frontal view of the kid, since he was sitting behind him on the opposite side of the aisle. But he had a modest view over the kid's left shoulder, and he was sure the kid had shoved his hand into the grip.

And he'd turned his head to peer suspiciously over his left shoulder, his long, unattractive face pale, his eyes wide and moist. He'd looked like a kid who'd walked into a mercantile on a dare from his schoolyard pals to steal a pocketful of rock candy.

He'd run his gaze across the dozen or so passengers riding in the car, the train's sole passenger car for this stretch of rail, between the town of Buffalo Gap and Wild Horse. His eyes appeared so opaque with furtive anxiety that Stockburn doubted the lad would have noticed if he, Stockburn—a big man—had been standing in the aisle aiming both of his Colts at the boy. Wolf didn't think the kid even noticed him sitting in an aisle seat four rows back, staring right at him.

Stockburn's imposing size wasn't the only thing distinctive about him. He also had a distinct shock of prematurely gray hair, which he wore roached, like a horse's mane. It stood out in sharp contrast to the deep bronze of his ruggedly chiseled face. He wore a carefully trimmed mustache of the same color. He wasn't currently wearing his black sombrero. It sat to his left, atop his canvas war bag, which the barrel of his leaning .44-caliber Winchester Yellowboy repeating rifle rested against. His head was bare.

When the kid's quick survey of the coach was complete, he turned back around to face the front of the car, his shoulders a little too square, his back too straight, the back of his neck too red.

He was up to something.

Stockburn started to look away from the back of the kid's head then slid his gaze forward and across the aisle to his more immediate right, frowning curiously. A pretty young woman was staring at him, smiling. She sat two rows up from him in a seat against the other side of the car. The two plush-covered seats beside her were empty.

She was maybe nineteen or twenty, wearing a burnt-orange traveling frock with a ruffled shirtwaist and burnt-orange waistcoat, and a matching felt hat a little larger than Wolf's open hand was pinned to the top of her piled, chestnut hair. Jade stones encased in gold dangled from her small, porcelain pale ears. She was as lovely as a Victorian maiden cameo pin carved in ivory. Her deep brown eyes glittered in the bright, lens clear western light angling through the passenger coach's soot-streaked windows.

Stockburn smiled and looked away, the way you do when you first notice someone staring at you. It makes you at first uncomfortable, self-conscious, wondering if you're really the one being stared at so frankly. Certainly, you're mistaken. Wolf's gaze compelled him to look the girl's way again.

Her gaze did not waver. She remained staring at him, arousing his curiosity even further.

Did she know, or think she knew, him?

Or, possibly, she did know him but he didn't recognize her . . . ?

He smiled more broadly, holding her gaze with a frank one of his own, one that was tempered ever so slightly with an incredulous wrinkle of the skin above his long, broad nose. That made her blush as she turned timid. Cheeks coloring slightly, she looked down and then turned her head back forward.

But the smile remained on her rich, full lips, which were the color of ripe peaches . . . and probably just as cool and soft, Stockburn couldn't help imagining. They probably tasted like peaches, as well.

He chuckled ironically to himself. *Get your mind out of the gutter, you old dog,* he admonished himself. *This girl probably still wears her hair in pigtails at home, and you're old enough to be her father*—a disquieting notion despite it being more and more true of late.

Stockburn returned his attention to the back of the shabby-suited lad's head then looked around the car—a quick, furtive glance. He probably saw more in that second and a half gander than the suited lad had in his prolonged one.

Wolf counted fifteen other passengers. Three were women, all older than the chestnut-haired cameo pin gal. Two were doxies or he didn't know what doxies looked like, even off duty. A young woman, likely a farmer's wife, sat directly in front of Wolf, rocking a baby he guessed wasn't more than a few months old. She and the child were likely en route to their young husband and father who'd maybe staked a mining or homesteading claim somewhere farther west.

A couple of men dressed like cowpunchers sat nearly directly behind Stockburn, three rows back at the very rear of the car. An old gent with a gray bib beard was nodding off on the other side of the aisle to his right. The rest of the men included a preacher and several men dressed in the checked suits of drummers.

One could have been a card sharp, because he was dressed a little more nattily than the drummers, but he probably wasn't much good with the pasteboards. You could tell the good ones by the way they carried themselves— straight and proud, usually smiling like they knew a secret about you and wouldn't you just love to know what it was?

This fellow, around Stockburn's age, with some gray

in his sideburns, was turned sideways and laying out a game of cards, furling his brow and moving his lips, counseling himself, as though he were still learning the trade. Like his suit, his pinky ring had likely come from a Montgomery Ward wish book.

He wasn't a train robber. Stockburn knew his own trade and could usually pick a train robber out of a crowd. At least, seven times out of ten he could.

The two men behind him might be in with the lad near the front. He couldn't tell about the others, including the old couple. Just being an old, harmless-looking married pair didn't disqualify them from holding up a train. Stockburn had arrested Jed and Ella Parker, married fifty-three years, who'd preyed on passenger coaches for two and a half years before he had finally run them down.

They'd enlisted the help of their forty-three-year old son, Kenny. He had been soft in his thinker box, as the saying went, but he, Ma, and Pa had gotten the job done, stealing time pieces and jewelry and gold pokes as well as pocket jingle from innocent pilgrims.

The Parkers had lost their Kansas farm to a railroad and had decided to exact revenge while entrepreneuring an alternative family business. Jed and Kenny had been as polite as church deacons. Ella, on the other hand, had cursed a blue streak, jumping up and down and hissing like a devil, as Stockburn had locked the bracelets around her wrists.

If the detective business did one thing for you, it taught that you never really knew about people. Even when you thought you did.

Hell, the cameo pin gal might even be in cahoots with the lad with the lumpy valise. Maybe she'd smiled at Wolf earlier because she suspected what line of work he was in, and she'd been trying to disarm him, so to speak. He didn't think she was a train robber, but he'd been surprised before and it had nearly gotten him a bullet for his carelessness. He wasn't going to turn his back on the pretty little gal, which wouldn't be hard, as easy on the eyes as she was.

When the train slowed suddenly—so suddenly that everybody in the passenger coach became human jackknives, collapsing forward—Stockburn was not surprised. His heart didn't even start beating much faster than it had been when he'd just been riding along, staring out at the sage and prickly pear, going over the assignment he had ahead of him—running down the killers who'd massacred a crew of track layers working for a spur line near the Wind River Mountains.

Wolf could tell by the violent abruptness of the stop that the engineer had locked up the brakes. That meant there was trouble ahead. Maybe blown rails or an obstacle of some kind—a tree or a telegraph pole felled across the tracks.

The brakes kicked up a shrill shrieking that caused Stockburn to grind his teeth against it. Gravity pushed him up hard against the forward seat in which the young mother had slipped out of her own seat and fallen to the floor. The baby was red-faced, wailing, and the mother was sobbing, staring up at Wolf with holy terror in her eyes.

The train continued slowing, bucking, shuddering, squealing, throwing Wolf forward and partway over the seat before him. He felt as though a big man were pressing down hard against him from behind, one arm rammed down taut against his shoulders, the other clamped across the back of his neck. He wanted like hell to reach for one of his Colts in preparation for what he knew was coming, but at the moment gravity overwhelmed him.

"Oh, my God—what's happening?" the young mother screamed. She and the child were a nettling distraction.

Stockburn's attention was torn between them and the young lad near the front of the train. That danger was borne home a moment later as the train finally stopped, and the big bully—gravity—finally released its ironlike grip on Wolf's back and shoulders. While Wolf stepped into the aisle, moving around the seat before him to help the young mother and the baby, the lad whom he sus-pected of chicanery bounded up out of his own seat.

He too stepped into the aisle but without chivalrous intent. He raised an old Schofield revolver and tossed away the valise he'd carried it in. He fired a round into the ceiling and bellowed in a high, reedy voice, "This is a holdup! Do what you're told and you won't be sent to hell in a hail of hot lead!"

At the same time his words reverberated around the car, evoking screams from the ladies and curses from the male passengers, another man—the one sitting at the front of the coach and on the same side of the aisle as Wolf—leaped to his feet and swung around, giving a coyote yell as he pumped a round into his old-model Winchester rifle. He was a scrawny coyote of a kid with a pinched-up face and devilishly slitted eyes.

Stockburn hadn't noticed him before. He was so short the detective hadn't seen him over the other passengers. He doubted the kid was much taller than your average ten-year-old. He wore a badger coat and a bowler hat, and between his thin, stretched back lips shone one nearly black, badly crooked front tooth.

"Do what he says and shut that baby up back there!" the human coyote caterwauled at Stockburn. He couldn't see the baby nor the mother, but the baby's screams no doubt assailed the ears of everyone on the coach. They sure were assailing Stockburn's. "Shut that kid up or I'll blow its head off!"

Instantly, Stockburn's twin Colts were in his hands. He aimed one at the coyote-faced younker and one at the taller, bespectacled youth with the Schofield. "Drop those guns, you devils! Wolf Stockburn, Wells Fargo!"

Both youths flinched and shuffled backward a bit. They hadn't been expecting such brash resistance.

"S-Stockburn?" said the bespectacled younker in the shabby suit. He was aiming the Schofield at the rail detective but Wolf saw the hesitation in the kid's eyes. That same hesitation was in the coyote-faced kid's eyes. They might have leveled their sights on him, but he had the upper hand.

For now . . .

"Wells . . . Wells Fargo . . . ?" continued the bespectacled youth, incredulous, crestfallen. One of his clear blue eyes twitched behind his glasses, and his long, pale face was mottled red.

The coyote-faced youth swallowed down his apprehension, and glowered down the barrel of his cocked carbine at the big rail detective. "I don't give a good two cents who you are, Mister Stockburn, sir. If you don't drop them two purty hoglegs of your'n, we're gonna kill you and ever'body else aboard this consarned train—includin' the screamin' sprout!"

CHAPTER 2

The passengers had settled down. Most had, anyway.

A few women sobbed and the baby, still on the floor with the mother to Stockburn's left, was still wailing. The other passengers were in their seats, merely casting frightened glances between the two gunmen at the front of the coach and Stockburn standing near the feet of the mother with the crying baby, in roughly the center of the car.

He kept both silver-chased Colts aimed at the two firebrands bearing down on him with a rifle and a hogleg, respectively.

"Children," Stockburn said tightly but loudly enough to be heard above the baby's wails, "you got three seconds to live . . . lessen you lower those guns and raise your hands shoulder-high, palms out." On the scout for a deadly change in their eyes, he slid his gaze between the two would-be train robbers. Knowing they were too wet behind the ears not to telegraph when they were about to squeeze their triggers, Wolf stretched his mustached lips back from his large, white teeth and barked, "One . . . !"

Both younkers flinched. Fear passed over their features. Their hands holding their guns on Wolf shook slightly.

"Two . . . !" Stockburn barked.

Again, they flinched. Both men's faces were pale, their eyes wide. No, they hadn't expected this. They hadn't expected it at all. They'd expected to fleece the defenseless passengers as easily as sheering sheep, then they'd be on their way to the nearest town to stomp with their tails up. "Apron, set down a bottle of your best labeled stuff and send in your purtiest doxy!"

Stockburn shaped his lips to form the word *three* but did not get the word out before the coyote-faced lad slid his gaze past Stockburn toward the rear of the car, shouting, "Willie! Roy! Take him!"

A black worm flipflopped in Stockburn's belly when he saw the two men dressed as cowpunchers behind him lurch up out of their seats, cocking the hammers of their hoglegs.

Ah, hell . . .

Like any experienced predator, human or otherwise, when the chips were down and all bets placed, Wolf let his instincts take over. What he had was a bad situation, and all he could do was play the odds and hope none of the passengers took a bullet.

He squeezed the triggers of both Peacemakers, watching in satisfaction as the bespectacled youth, who'd triggered his Schofield at nearly the same time, screamed as he flew back against the coach's front wall. The coyote-faced lad screamed, as well, but merely fired his rifle into the ceiling before dropping it like a hot potato and falling back against the front wall.

Shielding his face with his arms, he screamed, "Kill him! Kill him!"

Stockburn dropped to a knee in the aisle. Wheeling

hard to his right, he faced the rear of the train as the two "cowpunchers" triggered lead through the air where his head had been a heartbeat before. All the passengers were yelling and screaming again, and the baby was wailing even louder, if that were possible.

He intended to take down the two men at the rear of the car as fast as possible, before a passenger took a bullet. He shot one of them with the second round out of his right-hand Colt. The man jerked back, acquiring a startled expression on his thinly bearded, red-pimpled face, as he triggered one more round into the air over Wolf's head before collapsing, Wolf's bullet instantly turning the bib front of the shooter's poplin shirt red.

Wolf shot at the second "puncher" with the next round out of his left-hand gun. That kid—they were all wet-behind-the-ears, snot-nosed brats, it appeared—ducked and ran for the back door, and triggered his own gun wildly. Fortunately, his bullet only hammered the cold woodstove in the middle of the car before ricocheting harmlessly through a window on the car's north side, evoking a scream from the girl with the cameo-pin face but otherwise leaving her unharmed—so far.

Straightening, Stockburn aimed both Colts at the kid running out the rear door just as the kid twisted back toward him, raising one of his own two hoglegs again. Wolf hurled two more rounds at the kid, his Peacemakers bucking and roaring fiercely, smoke and flames lapping from the barrels.

The kid yowled and cursed as, dropping to his butt on the coach's rear vestibule, he swung to his left and leaped to the ground, out of sight. A gun barked in the direction from which he'd disappeared. The bullet punched a hole through the back of the car and pinged through a window to Stockburn's right.

Cursing, Wolf ran out onto the vestibule. Swinging right, he saw the kid hunched over as though he'd taken a bullet, running toward where three other men sat three horses about fifty feet out from the rail bed. They were holding the reins of four saddled horses.

Apparently, those were the men who'd blown the rails. They were trailing the horses of the four robbers in the coach. Rather, the four *who'd been in* the coach. Three still were there though they were likely dead or headed that way.

The three outside the train didn't look any older or brighter than the four Wolf had swapped lead with. They appeared startled by the dustup they'd been hearing in the passenger car, and their horses were skitter-stepping nervously. One man was having trouble getting his mount settled down and was whipping the horse's wither with a quirt.

They were all yelling, and so was the kid who was running and limping toward them, tripping over the toes of his boots.

"What in the bloody tarnation happened?" one of the horseback riders yelled at the wounded kid coming toward him.

"Wells . . . Fargo . . . !" the younker screeched.

Another horseback rider pointed toward Wolf. "Look!"

The kid stopped and glanced warily back over his shoulder toward Stockburn standing on the rear corner of the vestibule, aiming his right-hand Colt toward the bunch while holding the other pretty hogleg straight down in his left hand. Stockburn shaped a cold grin and was about to finish the limping varmint when a girl screamed shrilly from inside the coach.

His heart leaped. He'd forgotten that he'd left that sandy-haired little devil with that dead front tooth still alive.

He lowered his right-hand Peacemaker and ran back into the car, stepping to his right so the open door wouldn't backlight him. Good thing old habits die hard or Wolf would have been the one dying hard.

A gun thundered near the front of the coach. The bullet screeched a cat's whisker's width away from Stockburn's right cheek before thumping into the front of the freight car trailing the passenger coach.

Stockburn raised his Colt but held fire.

The nasty little sandy-haired devil with the dead front tooth held the pretty cameo-pin girl before him, his left arm wrapped around her pale neck. He held his carbine in his right hand, jacked it one handed, and aimed it at Stockburn. Spitting as he bellowed, "I'm takin' the girl, big man! You come after me, she's gonna be wolf bait!"

The kid backed up, pulling the girl along with him toward the coach's front door, keeping her in front of him. She stared in wide-eyed horror at Stockburn standing at the other end of the car.

Her hat was drooping down the side of her head, clinging to her mussed hair, which had partway fallen from its bun. A red welt rose on her left cheek. The sandy-haired devil had slapped her. Her mouth was open, but she didn't say anything. She was too scared for words.

Rage burned through Stockburn.

As the kid pulled the girl out the coach's front door and then dragged her down off the vestibule, Wolf hurried forward, yelling, "Everybody stay down!" He holstered both Colts and grabbed his Winchester rifle from where it lay on the floor in front of the seat he'd been sitting in. He was glad to see that the young woman with the baby appeared relatively unharmed.

She sat crouched back against the coach's left wall, rocking the still-crying baby in her arms, singing softly to the terrified infant while tears dribbled down her cheeks.

Stockburn pumped a cartridge into the brass-breeched Winchester Yellowboy's action and strode down the central aisle. The passengers were muttering darkly among themselves while another child cried and the old lady with the old man wept, the old man patting her shoulder consolingly.

Wolf stepped out through the coach's front door, swung to his right, and dropped to a knee. The sandy-haired little devil was running toward the three men on horseback, pulling the pretty gal along behind him. The young robber Stockburn had drilled was toeing a stirrup and hopping on his opposite foot, trying unsuccessfully to gain his saddle and sobbing with the effort, demanding help from the others.

"Look out, Riley!" one of the men on horseback shouted, pointing at Wolf.

Riley stopped and swung back around. He pulled the girl violently up against him and narrowed his mean little eyes at Stockburn, showing that dead front tooth as he spat out, "I told you I'd kill her, an' I will if you don't— owww!" the kid howled.

The girl had spun to face him and stomped one of her high-heeled, black half boots down on the toe of his right boot. The kid squeezed his eyes shut and hopped up and down on his good foot before snapping his eyes open once more and then smashing the back of his right hand against the girl's left cheek.

There was the sharp *smack* of hand to flesh.

The girl screamed, spun, and fell with a violent swirl of her burnt-orange gown.

"I'll kill you for that," Riley bellowed, raising his Winchester, his face wildfire red with fury. "I'll fill you so full of holes your rich old daddy won't even recognize you, you McCrae whore!"

"Don't do it, you little son of Satan!" Wolf narrowed one eye as he aimed down the Yellowboy at the kid.

In his indignation at having been assaulted by the girl he'd been trying to kidnap, the little devil seemed to have forgotten his more formidable opponent with the Winchester.

"Raise that carbine one eyelash higher, and I'll send you back to the devil who spawned you!"

Riley snapped his gaze back to Stockburn, eyes narrowed to slits. A slow, malevolent smile spread his lips. "My father is Kreg Hennessey. Yeah, Hennessey. Get it? Understand now?" The kid bobbed his head twice as though Stockburn should recognize the name. "If you shoot me you're gonna have holy hell come down on you, mister. Like a whole herd of wild hosses!" He turned his slitted demon's eyes back to the girl, who stared up at him fearfully. "This little witch just struck me. Thinks she's so much 'cause she's a McCrae! You just struck a Hennessey, and you're about to see what happens when even an uppity McCrae strikes a—"

Stockburn squeezed the Yellowboy's trigger. He had no

choice. No way in hell the kid was not going to kill the girl. The little snake was not only cow-stupid, he was poison mean. And out of control.

The Yellowboy bucked and roared.

The bullet tore through the kid's shoulder and whipped him around to face Stockburn directly. Riley triggered his carbine wide of the girl, the bullet pluming dust beyond her. She gasped and lowered her head, clamping her hands over her ears.

Holding the rifle to one side, angled down, he held his other arm out to the other side as though for balance. The kid glanced at the blood bubbling up from his shoulder as he stumbled backward, rocks and little puffs of dust kicked up by his badly worn boots. A look of total shock swept over his face, his lower jaw sagging, his mouth forming a wide, nearly perfect O.

Still on one knee, Stockburn ejected the spent cartridge from the Yellowboy's breech, the brass casing clattering onto the vestibule floor behind him. He pumped a fresh round into the breech and lined up the sights on the kid's chest as gray smoke curled from the barrel. "Drop it," he ordered. "Or the next one's for keeps."

Riley stared back at him. The kid glanced at his shoulder once more then looked at Stockburn again. The shock on his face gradually faded, replaced by his previous expression of malevolent rage. Jaws hard, he gave a dark laugh as he said, "You're a dead man, mister!"

He cocked the carbine one-handed then took it in both hands, crouching over it, aiming the barrel at Wolf, who pumped two more .44 rounds into the kid's chest. The rounds picked the scrawny kid up and threw him two feet back through the air to land on his back.

The girl screamed.

The kid writhed like a bug on a pin, arching his back, grinding his boot heels into the dirt and gravel. He hissed like a dying viper, snapped his jaws like a trapped coyote. He lifted his head to look at Wolf, and he cursed shrilly, his oaths growing less and less violent as the blood leaked out of him to pool on the rocks and sage beneath him.

Finally, his head sagged back against the ground.

"Dead man," he rasped, chest rising and falling sharply. "Oh . . . you're a . . . dead man . . ."

His bloody chest fell still. His head rolled slowly to one side as his body relaxed against the gravel and sage.